My head was spinning. "What are you saying?"

"You are here in the Black because of me, Cooper Foley."

"Wh . . . No. It was an accident."

"An accident that I caused. I created the illusions that led to your death."

"But . . . why?"

"I brought you here to help release me from captivity."

He kept stalking me and I kept backing off.

"This is . . . this is crazy. I'm not going to help you."

"Even though I have the power to end your existence?"

"What are you going to do? Stab me with that black sword?"

"Perhaps. Or I could raise the stakes even higher."

"Higher than ending my existence?"

"That depends on what value you put on the life of your friend, Marshall Seaver."

I stopped moving. That was it. There was the threat. If I didn't help Damon, he was going to kill Marsh. Like he had killed me.

Also available from D. J. MacHale

PENDRAGON

JOURNAL OF AN ADVENTURE
THROUGH TIME AND SPACE

MORPHEUS ROAD

MORPHEUS ROAD
THE BLACK

D. J. MACHALE

Aladdin
New York London Toronto Sydney New Delhi

ALADDIN

An imprint of Simon & Schuster Children's Publishing Division
1230 Avenue of the Americas, New York, NY 10020
First Aladdin paperback edition February 2012
Copyright © 2011 by D.J. MacHale
All rights reserved, including the right of reproduction
in whole or in part in any form.
ALADDIN is a trademark of Simon & Schuster, Inc.,
and related logo is a registered trademark of Simon & Schuster, Inc.
Also available in an Aladdin hardcover edition.
For information about special discounts for bulk purchases,
please contact Simon & Schuster Special Sales at 1-866-506-1949
or business@simonandschuster.com.
The Simon & Schuster Speakers Bureau can bring authors to your live event.
For more information or to book an event contact the Simon & Schuster Speakers Bureau
at 1-866-248-3049 or visit our website at www.simonspeakers.com.
Designed by Sammy Yuen Jr.
The text of this book was set in Apollo MT.
Manufactured in the United States of America 0112 OFF
2 4 6 8 10 9 7 5 3 1
The Library of Congress has cataloged the hardcover edition as follows:
MacHale, D. J.
The black / by D. J. MacHale. — 1st Aladdin hardcover ed.
p. cm. — (Morpheus Road ; [bk. 2])
Summary: Cooper Foley, who has a knack for getting into trouble, ends up
in the middle of a border war between the worlds of the living and
the dead, trying to find out about the mysterious Morpheus Road.
ISBN 978-1-4169-6517-6 (hc)
[1. Horror stories. 2. Supernatural—Fiction. 3. Death—Fiction.] I. Title.
PZ7.M177535Bk 2011
[Fic]—dc22
2010033521
ISBN 978-1-4169-6520-6 (pbk)
ISBN 978-1-4424-1988-9 (eBook)

For Taylor

Foreword

Ready to travel farther along the Road with me?

As many of you know, I love spooky stories. That's why I was inspired to write the Morpheus Road trilogy. I can't begin to count the number of ghost stories I've read or watched . . . or written over the years. I may not be an expert on the subject, but I'm definitely ahead of the curve. After all those fright-filled experiences, I've found that there's one thing that really bugs me about many ghost stories. In order to create mystery, ghosts are often depicted as being capable of performing certain tasks, but not others. For example, how many times have we seen a story where the ghost is able to, say, write a maddeningly oblique clue in blood that the living must then decipher in order to solve a mystery? It makes for an interesting story, but it begs the question: If a ghost was able to write the mysterious clue, why didn't he just skip the subterfuge and write something like "In case you were wondering, my wife killed me for the insurance money and dumped the murder weapon in the wishing well. The treasure is under the stairs, the antidote is behind the OJ in the fridge, and I forgot to pick up the dry cleaning last Tuesday, so would you get on that for me?"

I have to admit, I've been guilty of using the same device myself. I did it in *The Light*. More than once. And that's what brings us to *The Black*. If you remember from the final chapter of *The Light*, we have switched the point of view. (SPOILER ALERT! If you haven't read *The Light*, stop right here. Seriously. Go read it. Don't worry, we'll still be here when you get back.)

Okay, is everybody up to speed? Good. Here goes. After having witnessed the haunting of Marshall Seaver, we're now going to see it from the other side . . . from the point of view of his best friend, Cooper Foley. And of course, Coop is a ghost. (There. I said it. If you didn't heed my warning and go back to read *The Light*, don't blame me for ruining the surprise.) The fun thing is that we are about to explore the *other* side of the conversation. Meaning, we've seen what it's like when a living person is being haunted, and we're now going to see what it might be like for a ghost to try to communicate with the living. It's my way of offering a possible explanation as to why ghosts don't leave detailed messages about dry cleaning.

Before we step back onto the Road, I want to offer a few quick thanks to those who helped bring my latest story to you. I've done this so many times, in so many books, that I could probably do a cut-and-paste job. I think by now everyone knows how much I appreciate their continued support, so rather than go into the usual detail I'll just offer a partial list of those I am very grateful to.

Big thanks go to my good friends at Simon & Schuster Children's Publishing, especially my wonderful editor,

Liesa . . . who has now edited four of my books, going back to *Raven Rise*. Also to Sammy Yuen Jr., who designed the terrific covers for Morpheus Road (as well as the new Pendragon covers). A nod of thanks also goes to the many talented folks who did such a terrific job designing and implementing the www.djmachalebooks.com website.

Richard Curtis has my gratitude for generously sharing his publishing acumen and for being so supportive.

As always, thanks to Eve and Keaton, my two blondies, who must put up with a guy who spends most of the day living inside his head, which can be a strange place. I love you both. I can't say for sure yet, but after reading some of the stories that Keaton has written and listening to her crazy tales and hearing her jokes, it's looking as if Eve may have another nutburger on her hands. Excellent.

The biggest thanks is reserved for the many faithful readers who have been with me for years as we journeyed through the flumes and now walk the Morpheus Road. It's been an honor to travel with you.

Okay, enough business. Let's get back up to speed.

When last we left Marshall Seaver, he had finally encountered the spirit who was responsible for haunting his thoughts . . . Damon. (Remember the cemetery that erupted with thousands of the living dead? Wasn't that a picnic?) Damon threatened to kill Marsh unless he helped him find a weapon called a poleax. What stopped Marsh from giving in was Cooper. Or Cooper's spirit. Coop had finally appeared to Marsh to let him know he was there to help him. With Cooper's support, Marsh found the courage to stand up to Damon and send him back to wherever he came from.

For now.

Marshall was then given a second golden crucible by Ennis Mobley. Ennis warned Marsh that he would need the crucible for safety and for the protection of his eternal soul.

More disturbing for Marsh was learning that the crucible had once belonged to his mother. His dead mother. That meant Damon's haunting had something to do with her.

Marsh hoped that the nightmare was over and he could return to a normal life. Too bad he didn't realize that it was only the first book of a trilogy and he was just getting started.

That's where we left off, but it's not where we're going to begin. Before we can go forward, we must travel back. Back to a happier time. Back before our guys knew anything about crucibles or spirits or ghouls named Gravedigger.

Back along the Morpheus Road.

Next stop . . . Trouble Town.

—D. J. MacHale

Prologue

This isn't what I expected death to be like.

Not that I thought about it much. Or at all. For the record, it isn't completely horrible. Being dead actually has perks. Nobody tells me what to do. I don't get hungry, though I do miss calzones. I don't even need sleep. Or deodorant . . . I think. Best of all, being a spirit means I'm no longer bound by a physical body so I'm free to travel to places and see things I could only imagine before.

There, I said it. Spirit. I'm a spirit. "Dead" refers to what I was. "Spirit" is what I am. The number one fact of life is that you can't duck death. That's normal. What *isn't* normal is what's been happening to me since I died, and that's why I'm not ready to accept this fate. Something twisted is going on and I'm having a hard time dealing because I've yet to learn all the rules of this new life. Or death. I'd just as soon mind my own business, have a little fun, kick back, and make the most of the afterlife. But that's not an option because I have landed square in the middle of Trouble Town. I'm not alone, either. This isn't just about me, it's about those I've met in this new life . . . and those I've left behind.

So much has changed, but one thing hasn't: I'm still me. I have the same thoughts and feelings I had when I was alive. That's both a comfort and a curse because as wild as it's been to glimpse eternity, I'd be lying if I said I didn't miss my family. Even my witch sister, Sydney. That's the biggest downside of being dead. You have to leave behind the ones you care about. And calzones.

Though, I can't leave everything behind completely. Not yet, anyway. People I care about are in danger and I may be the only one who can help them. For reasons I'm still trying to understand I've been targeted by a spirit who is bent on causing trouble between the worlds of the living and the dead. Based on what's happened already there's no way to know who will be left standing when the dust settles.

I've traveled a long way since the day of my death. To explain exactly what brought me to this point means going back to the other side. To the Light. It's a place on the far end of a long road that stretches two ways. I know the route back. What lies ahead is another story. A mystery. There are still choices to be made . . . choices that will affect my future and the future of everyone else who travels the road.

The Morpheus Road.

My name is Cooper Foley and this is my story.

1

"Don't be an idiot. Just go to the lake until things calm down."

My sister was telling me what to do, as usual, because she knows everything.

"I'm not going to run away," I countered. "I can handle those guys."

Sydney groaned. She did that a lot, mostly when I didn't do what she wanted, which was always. Sydney and I might have looked like each other—we shared the same dark hair and blue eyes—but that's where the similarity ended. For one, I'm better-looking. The guys who tried to get with her probably had a different opinion but I'm sticking with mine. She was only a year older than me but treated me like I was a lower form of life that shouldn't be allowed to breathe air that could go to someone more deserving. Like her.

I didn't care what she thought.

"Wow," she said sarcastically. "Such a tough guy. What if the police want you to give up their names? What'll you do then?"

I shrugged. "I already gave them names."

"What!" she screamed.

"Relax. I didn't tell them about you. Or your dim boyfriend."

Sydney glared at me with anger and confusion. Her cool was broken, which was saying something because normally she was ice.

"Why?" was all she managed to get out.

"I didn't have a choice. If I didn't give them something, I'd be sitting in juvie right now fighting off a bunch of hard cases who really *are* tough. Besides, they had it coming."

"I don't believe this." Sydney moaned as she paced my bedroom floor.

It was her fault that I was in Trouble Town to begin with and I think she felt guilty about it. Guilt was an alien emotion to Sydney so it was fun to see her squirm. She normally had it all going on . . . which was her biggest problem. Our parents expected her to be perfect and she mostly was, for a heartless vampire. But she resented the pressure and that caused tension in Foley-world. Her latest act of defiance was to announce she was getting a tattoo. Our parents went nuts and threatened to hold back her college money. For somebody headed to Stanford, that was serious. I don't think Sydney really wanted to get inked, but my parents' threat drove her straight to the low-life tattoo guy.

Her big rebellious statement backfired. The tattoo caused a nasty infection that landed her in the emergency room, where she got fixed up and smacked with a bill for a couple hundred bucks . . . money she didn't have and couldn't ask our parents to put out. She didn't want them to have the satisfaction of knowing they were absolutely right about the tattoo being a dumb idea. She was stuck until her boyfriend, Mikey, offered a way out. He knew some guys with Yankees tickets that they were willing to let Sydney scalp. Whatever profit she made, she and Mikey would split. Sydney had no idea how to scalp tickets and Mikey was an idiot, which is how I got involved. I knew how to get things done.

I liked the idea of Sydney owing me so I took the tickets, sold them for a decent profit, and bailed her out with the doctor bill. I felt good about it, too. She was still my sister. Everybody was happy . . . until the cops showed up at our door. Turned out the tickets were bogus. Counterfeit. I guess there were some angry people at Yankee Stadium who found people sitting in their expensive field-level seats . . . with legit tickets. Oops.

"I should give them Mikey's name too," I said. "That fool had to know the tickets were fake."

She shook her head. "No, he's not bright enough to do something so dumb."

"Well, those other dirtballs knew. Nobody messes with me like that. I hope they do time."

Sydney jumped to her feet. "Why?" she screamed. "Why is it always about you?"

"You made it about me when you asked me to get you out of trouble."

Sydney's eyes flared. "Go to the lake, Cooper," she said in a seething whisper. "Do the smart thing for once in your life."

She stormed out of my bedroom, throwing a parting shot for the rest of the house to hear, "Get over yourself for once and just go!"

I actually felt bad for her, not that I'd tell her so. Whatever problems I had would blow over. I always found my way out of Trouble Town. But Sydney was different. It must have killed her to know how badly she had messed up . . . and brought some lesser mortals down with her. Still, I wasn't about to do what she wanted, which was to go to our family's lake house and hide out for the summer. I didn't want to run scared. That wasn't me.

"What the heck?" came a voice at my door.

It was Marshall Seaver, my best friend.

"Can you believe it?" I said. "They want me to get out of town like some mob guy who has to lay low until the heat dies down."

Marsh knew about the tickets, but not about the tattoo and Sydney's involvement in the whole mess.

"Maybe you could just go for a week or two," he offered.

"No. They're talking the whole summer. That lake is death, Ralph. What'll I do up there? Fish? That gets old after eight seconds. The place is great if you're six or sixty. For everybody else . . . torture."

My family had a cottage on Thistledown Lake, a couple of hours north of our home in Stony Brook. I used to love spending summers there, especially when Marsh came up. We always had a blast just hanging out and being kids. But we weren't kids anymore.

"What's Sydney's problem?" he asked.

Marsh stood there in his hoodie with his blond hair falling into his eyes. We'd been tight since kindergarten. He was like my brother. But the older we got the more he seemed like my *little* brother. He wasn't an idiot. Far from it. But where he liked building model rockets and reading comic books and camping out, I was, well, I was scalping baseball tickets. I can't say which of us was better off.

"Who knows?" I said, ducking the question. "My parents aren't even making her go. She gets to be on her own for the whole summer while I'm sentenced to two months at Camp Kumbaya."

I hated not telling him the whole truth but it bothered me more that I was being forced into a corner by everybody, including my best friend. I picked up a football and threw it into a chair. Hard. It didn't make me feel any better.

"Mikey the Mauler's downstairs," Marsh said, pressing. "He threatened to hurt you. What's that all about?"

"Nothing," I said. "Forget it."

"Did he give you the fake tickets?"

"No! Let it go, all right! It's none of your business."

Marsh was asking all the right questions and I didn't want to lie to him so I jumped up and went to the bedroom window. It was wide open . . . a tempting escape hatch.

"It *is* my business!" he shouted back. "You did something stupid, and now you're going to have to take off for a couple of months to get away from the mess, and *poof!* There goes summer."

I slammed the window shut so hard it made the house rattle. "That makes it your business? Because I'm ruining your summer?"

"That's not what I meant," Marsh said, backpedaling.

"Yeah, you did," I countered. I hated it when he only saw things through his own naive perspective. "Gee, sorry, Marsh. I should have thought it through before doing anything that might spoil your fun. How inconsiderate of me."

"Don't go there," he shot back. "I know this isn't about me, but it's not just about you, either. The stuff you do has fallout."

"Fallout? I'll give you fallout. The cops threatened to throw me in juvie unless I told them where I got the fake tickets . . . so I gave up a couple of guys. And you know what? I don't care because those dirtballs set me up. But now I'm looking over my shoulder in case they find out I ratted and come after me. That's fallout. So I'm sorry if I messed up your plans to pretend like we're still twelve, but you know, things happen."

"That's cold," he said softly.

"Move on, Marsh. We're not kids anymore."

"I know that."

I should have stopped right there but I was too worked up.

"But hey, who am I to judge? Do whatever you want. I'm sure there are plenty of guys who want to hang out with you and watch cartoons. I'm not your only friend."

I hesitated, then added the killing blow, "Or am I?"

The pained look on Marsh's face said it all. I'd gone too far.

"Have a good summer," he said, and walked out of the room.

I didn't mean to hurt him but I was frustrated and Marsh was an easy target. I should have yanked him back into the room to tell him why I was so angry, but I didn't want him to know the truth about Sydney. Marsh liked Sydney. Heck, he probably loved her. To him she was perfect and I wanted to protect him from the truth. I did that a lot, especially after all he'd been through.

Marsh's mother was killed a few years before. It was a tragedy that seemed to freeze time for him. I'm no shrink but I think he didn't want to let go of the life he had when his mom was there, which is why he still thought like a kid while the rest of us continued to grow up. But he was my best friend and as years went by I did my best to shield him from anything negative that came his way. Who knows? Maybe it was partly my fault that he still acted like he was twelve.

There aren't a lot of things I regret, but not stopping him from leaving that day is definitely on top of the list. Instead of sucking it up and going after him, I picked up my football and slammed it against the wall again . . . an act of total futility. I knew I wasn't thinking right and had to get control of the situation.

"Ralph!" I yelled, calling out as I ran out of my room and down the stairs. That's what I called him. Ralph.

I already had a plan. Summer vacation had just started and Marsh had come up with all these adventures for us to go on that I had promptly trashed. I didn't want to waste time camping or sailing when we could be at the beach hooking up with any girl who drew breath. But now the beach was out and I had the perfect compromise: Marsh could spend the summer with me up at Thistledown. We'd roll the clock back and goof off like the old days. We could even hang at the lake beach and scout for local talent. Everybody would win.

Except I was too late.

"He's gone," my mother said.

"I'll catch him."

I went for the door but Mom stopped me.

"He said he thought you'd agree to go to the lake," she said. She looked stressed. I guess having one of your kids arrested will do that.

"Yeah. Maybe it's not such a bad idea."

Her tension melted. "Oh thank god."

"One condition," I said. "I want Marsh to come up."

It was a no-brainer. Mom loved Marsh.

"Are you kidding? That's a *great* idea but—"

"But what?"

"I just invited him. He wasn't enthused."

I thought about chasing after him, but decided not to. It was the second time I had made that same mistake in five minutes.

"We had an argument," I said. "I'll give him time to cool off and then make nice."

Mom frowned. "He's the last person you should be arguing with."

"Yeah, I know, Mom. I'm an idiot."

"You're not an idiot. You're just—okay, sometimes you're an idiot."

"Thanks. When are we leaving?"

"Tonight," she said quickly, headed for the stairs.

"What's the rush?"

"The sooner we get out of here the sooner I'll stop stressing about police and . . . and . . . counterfeiters. I can't believe I just said that."

"This isn't TV, Mom. Nothing's gonna happen."

"I know, because we're leaving tonight. Pack."

Mom was being dramatic but if it made her happy to be on the next stagecoach out of Dodge, I wasn't going to ruin it for her. Besides, it could work out perfectly. I'd take a few days to scope out the situation at the lake and lay some groundwork for the festivities. By then Marsh would have calmed down and would be open to my invitation . . . and apology. Neither of us carried a grudge for long. We were too good of friends for that.

I was beginning to think that after the drama of the past few days, the summer could actually end up being pretty decent.

It's amazing to know how totally wrong I was.

2

The town of Thistledown existed for exactly three months every year.

That's what it seemed like, anyway. As far as I knew, every fall the place was dismantled, packed up, and put into storage to wait for the tourists to show up again the following summer. The lake was about seven miles long and surrounded by miles of thick woods and the occasional summer cottage. The town itself was at the southernmost tip. It was three blocks long and loaded with places to buy T-shirts, ice cream, and fried food. There was a mini golf course, a drive-in movie, and a marina where tourists rented boats that they'd take onto the lake and try not to run into one another with.

We had a big cottage right on the water with a dock, a float, and a motor boat that we used to take out for hours, hunting for the best fishing spots. Since Sydney and I spent most of the summer trying to injure each other, my parents always let us invite friends up to keep us occupied. Though I had lots of company, the best times were always when Marsh was there.

The guy was amazing. He knew about everything. All you had to do was mention some random topic like seaweed and he'd know that Chinese people use it as medicine because it has a high percentage of iodine. Me? I didn't even know what iodine was. Whether we were building rafts or launching model rockets, we were always doing something different and fun. Marsh wanted to know how things worked. He was fascinated by the science. I just liked the boom.

Having Marsh around was a good thing because life among the Foleys was usually intense. Somebody was always pissed off at somebody else for not doing something they should have known better about. I got away from it as much as possible, which is what made hanging out with Marsh so great. Marsh didn't judge. We pushed each other, but in a good way. He made me think and I made him act.

I thought a lot about Marsh and the good times we'd spent together as I sat on the dock in front of our lake house. Part of it was due to my guilt over having insulted him, but that wasn't the whole story. I was becoming a different person and it wasn't just about getting older. If I was to guess when it was that things started to change, I'd say it was around the time that Marsh's mom was killed. Her death was tragic . . . and violent. She was a photographer who was on assignment somewhere in Europe and got trapped in a building that collapsed in an earthquake. It was a bad way to go . . . not that there's any *good* way to go. It destroyed Marsh. I didn't see much of him for a couple of months afterward, and in that time things got strange.

For reasons I can't explain, guys started getting in my face. Challenging me. It was usually over dumb stuff like

"Hey, who you looking at?" But it often led to a fight. I got a reputation for being a brawler, which only led to more guys challenging me. I didn't want to fight, but what could I do? I became a target for every tough guy who wanted to prove they could take me.

For the record, nobody could.

The fighting put me on the radar of some guys who weren't exactly model citizens. They were still in school but didn't go to class much. Or at all. They always had money but none of them had jobs. At least not in the regular sense. They always had something going on, most of which was illegal, like taking bets on football games and printing fake IDs. One time I went with them to rip off some copper from a construction site. There was nothing clever about it. It was flat-out stealing. I knew it was wrong but I have to admit, it gave me a rush. I didn't even make that much money out of the deal but it didn't matter. It was exciting.

It wasn't the kind of fun Marsh would approve of so I didn't tell him about it . . . or about anything else I did with those guys. Marsh eventually came out of his self-imposed exile, but things were different and we didn't hang out as much, and I guess I have myself to blame for that. It was tough being one way with my new friends and another person with Marsh. I wasn't even sure which was the real me. A couple of times Marsh got on me for skipping school, but I told him he sounded like a grandpa and he backed off.

Looking back, he was right, but I didn't realize that until my new "friends" set me up with the bogus Yankees tickets. Yes, they were the guys who gave the fake tickets to Mikey Russo, knowing full well he would come to me. I'm not even sure why they did it. Maybe it was a game to them. Maybe they didn't like me after all. Or maybe they were just dirtballs. Whatever. They sent me straight to Trouble Town . . . and I got even by giving them up to the police.

So much had happened that the idea of going fishing or exploring hidden coves didn't hold the same interest for me as it once had. I wish it did. I guess my hope was that bringing Marsh to the lake would help me recapture some of the old magic. If nothing else I wanted Marsh to know why I had insulted him. It was because I was angry.

Not at him, at myself.

I sat alone for an hour before I decided to stop feeling sorry for myself and make the best of the situation. There weren't a lot of options for fun in Thistledown. I could go for a swim. That would eat up a solid ten minutes. I could drive into town and play mini golf. There was a word for that: pathetic. I could see what was playing at the drive-in, but sitting alone at the drive-in goes beyond sorry and straight to weird. It was looking like the best option was to hang out with my parents and play Uno. Yeah. It was that bleak.

I was headed inside when I heard a distinct *thump* sound come from farther along the shore. It was so distinct that it actually made me stop, though there was nothing to see but our old boathouse. I figured the thump was our fishing boat banging around inside. It didn't dawn on me that the lake was totally flat. Still, the sound made me think of the old boat, and that sent my mind racing to other possibilities. I realized that I had one very good option for the evening and decided to take it. I ran inside to tell my parents but they weren't around. Just as well. They would probably have tried to talk me out of it. Before they could get back I grabbed my red Davis Gregory High football jacket and ran for the boathouse.

The structure was nothing more than a double-wide shed that was built half on land, half over the water. I'd like to say we had a super-hot ski boat that could tear up the lake, but what we had instead was the *Galileo*. Marsh named it after the shuttle craft of the USS *Enterprise* from *Star Trek*, though there was nothing futuristic about it. It was your basic wooden fishing boat that was held together by the many coats of paint we'd slapped on over the years. It may have looked like a clunker but it had a sweet 85-horsepower outboard that always got us where we wanted to go.

I kicked off my Pumas and stuck them behind a cooler on the shelf. People think I'm nuts but I swear I have a better feel for the boat and navigate better with bare feet. After throwing off the stern line and pushing off, I hurried to the bow and reached out before the boat hit the large double doors that led out to the lake. I unhooked the door latch and pushed one door open while pulling the boat through. Dad had me trained to keep the doors closed and locked. He was afraid that if they were left open somebody might be tempted to steal our stuff. I didn't think any scurvy lake pirates would be interested in pilfering rusty tools and a cooler, but I always humored him and locked the place up tight. After two vicious tugs on the manual starter, the engine sputtered to life and I was on my way.

The sun was already casting a deep orange glow on the calm water. It always got dark early in Thistledown because of the mountains that surrounded the lake. I hated that when I was a kid because it cut down on playtime. As I got older I didn't care much because I played different games that didn't necessarily require sunlight. Part of me wanted to turn the boat north, open it up, and motor over the glassy surface for a couple of hours with nothing to keep me company but the low rumble of the powerful outboard. It was tempting, but I had a better plan in mind. I turned south toward town and the marina at the foot of the lake. Things never seemed to change much in Thistledown. I hoped that meant the same family was still running the marina . . . and that their daughter still worked there.

Her name was Brittany and she was my summertime

girlfriend, though she probably wouldn't appreciate that I called her that. We first met when we were eleven but didn't really hit it off until two years ago. I'm not sure what took me so long to make a move. She was cute and there weren't a whole lot of other girls in Thistledown. Most came and went with their families on vacation, and very few were over age eight. I started hanging around the marina asking for boating advice I didn't want and gas I didn't need. Brittany wasn't a fool. She knew I was interested but she made me work for it. At first she was all business and I thought I was out of luck until the day she asked me to play mini golf . . . the Thistledown equivalent of a big night on the town.

We ended up having a great summer together. She taught me more about boats than I ever wanted to know and I made her laugh. When summer was over we texted every once in a while but I guess we both got caught up with our normal lives and it didn't last. But the next summer we picked up right where we left off and had an even better time. Neither of us talked about things we had going on at home. Good or bad. We had fun in the moment, which was exactly what I wanted back then . . . and wanted again.

The sales office of the marina stood on solid wooden piles above water level. As I approached in the *Galileo*, I saw Brittany's car parked in the lot. Yes! The summer was looking better by the second. I puttered past the big sternwheeler boat called the *Nellie Bell* that they used for lake tours and rented out for parties. Britt and I used to sneak onto the *Nellie Bell* after closing and sit up top for hours . . . making out and talking and making out. Like I said, it was a great summer. I tied the *Galileo* up to the empty gas dock and made my way across the labyrinth of floats until I got to the door of the sales office. With a big smile, I stepped inside.

Britt was behind the sales desk. She was as cute as ever

with her short blond hair and freckles. When she heard me come in, she looked up from her paperwork with a big smile as if to say: "Hi! What can I do for you?" It was a warm, welcoming moment . . .

. . . that didn't last. The smile dropped from her face so fast, I could swear I heard it hit the floor.

Uh-oh.

Brittany was frozen in place, her eyes boring into my head. A long few seconds passed.

I couldn't take the silence anymore and said, "Is it me or did the temperature just plummet forty degrees?"

"You're kidding, right?" she said curtly.

"Well, yeah. It didn't really get colder. Or did it?"

She shook her head, obviously annoyed, and started clearing off the counter. It was a bad beginning.

"You look great!" I exclaimed.

"Don't," she commanded without looking at me.

"Don't what?"

"Don't think we're going to pick up again."

"Oh. Got it. Uh . . . why not?"

"You can't be serious," she said, exasperated.

"What's wrong? Do you have a boyfriend back home or something? I'm sorry, I didn't know."

"You wouldn't know because you didn't call. Or write. Or text. Or Facebook. Or acknowledge in any way shape or form that we spent a lot of time together last summer."

"Oh. Right. I guess I should have poked you back, huh?"

"Ugh! Good-bye, Cooper. Have a nice summer."

She rounded the counter, headed for the door. I cut her off.

"That's impossible. I can't have a nice summer up here without you."

"My heart bleeds," she said, dripping sarcasm.

"I'm sorry, okay? I didn't text because we did that last

year and it just made me miss you more. So we both stopped and it got easier. Right? I didn't want to put either of us through that again."

She looked me square in the eye. She softened. I saw it. I had her.

"That's not only pathetic," she said. "I'm insulted that you think I'd buy it."

I didn't have her.

She went for the door again. I cut her off again.

"Okay," I said quickly. "You're right. That was lame. I'm sorry. What can I say? Things happen. Besides, you have a boyfriend."

"I *don't* have a boyfriend!"

"Really?" I said with a big smile. "So, then, we're cool."

She responded by pulling the door open and standing aside, clearing a path for me to leave. Glaring.

Beaten, I stepped through the doorway onto the dock.

"Last shot," I said. "Let me make it up to you. It's going to be a beautiful night. Let's go out on the lake, kill the lights, and count the stars. You know how much I like doing that."

"Better idea," she said. "Find somebody who cares what you like."

"Ow."

"You're a selfish guy, Cooper Foley. I don't like selfish guys."

"You're making a big mistake," I said. "It's going to be a long—"

She slammed the door in my face.

"Summer."

She turned the lights off on the walkway. Ouch. It got so dark so fast, I had to grope my way along the railing or risk falling into the water. I had been totally, unceremoniously rejected and I suppose I deserved it. I decided to make a calculated retreat, then come back the next day and the next and the next until she forgave me. It would be worth it. I liked Britt. I should have texted.

Night had come to Thistledown Lake. Though my plan was all about hooking up with Britt, I really did like being out on the lake at night. As I motored back toward the house, I saw that I wasn't the only one who had that idea. The lake was full of boats, all with their lights off. I'd never seen so many boats at one time. They all looked empty, but I knew that everyone was lying on their backs, gazing up at the sky. It was one of the great things about being in the middle of nowhere. On a clear, moonless night the sky would come alive with a billion stars. If you were lucky, you might see a shooting star. Or a meteor. Or whatever they were. Marsh had explained how it all worked to me but I hadn't been listening. I'd been too caught up in the spectacular show that was taking place right above our heads.

People would turn off their running lights to make it as dark as possible. You wouldn't normally do that on the water at night but on Thistledown, where everybody else was doing the same thing, it was totally safe.

The scene was incredible . . . and incredibly peaceful. There were more glittering stars in the sky than I remembered ever seeing before, so I decided to make the most of a bad situation and get lost in the heavens. I motored slowly through the floating boats, careful not to disturb anybody or cause a wake that would bounce them around. I had to go pretty far north before I found an empty spot in the center of the lake. It was across from a remote spot where we used to fish, called Emerald Cove. I killed the engine, then the running lights, and let the silence wrap around me as I stretched out on my back with my legs up on the driver's seat. It was a warm night so I took off my jacket and put it under my head as a pillow.

There's something about being on the lake under a brilliant canopy of stars that makes the stress wash away. I thought about a lot of things that night. I wasn't all that happy with the way things had been going. I'd made some bad choices and was lucky that nothing worse had happened to me other than being arrested for pushing fake tickets. Maybe it was a warning shot. I'd been hanging with the wrong guys and paid the price. But it wasn't too late. As I lay on my back absorbing the immense universe, I understood that there was a whole lot more out there that I could do. I may have messed up, but life was just getting started. It was a good feeling. I liked being in charge of my own destiny.

The sound of a far-off engine broke the moment.

I couldn't get annoyed. I'd just done the same thing myself. I hoped that whoever it was would find a spot and kill their engine quickly so I could get back to my private meditation.

The engine didn't stop. If anything it got louder. It sounded powerful, too. I didn't want it to ruin the night so I grabbed my iPod out of my jacket pocket. If I wasn't going to get total silence, it was better to have music. I picked a classic rock tune that Marsh had turned me on to. It was a song called "(I Know) I'm Losing You" by the Faces. I'd never heard of them, but the song rocked and had a great drum solo. I caught Marsh playing air drums to it once. Geek.

The song didn't fit the peaceful scene but it drowned out the sound of the engine. I lay back down and laughed, picturing Marsh playing drums with chopsticks. There was no way I'd let our argument stop him from coming up to the lake. To me, Marsh represented a life I wanted back. I was going to hit the reset button and be good friends again.

The guy in the boat was taking his sweet time finding a spot to settle in. I took a peek up over the side of the *Galileo* but didn't see him. In fact, I didn't see any boats at all. That was odd. Where did they all go? And so quickly? Maybe the sound I was hearing was actually the combined sound of a bunch of boats calling it a night and taking off. Fine by me. I lay back down and cranked the volume as the drum solo began. The wild pounding filled my head. My universe. I gazed up at a sea of stars. At the future. At infinity.

I had the volume up so loud that my ears rang. It was too loud. I spun the iPod control to turn it down but the volume didn't change. If anything it got louder. The wild drum solo was coming at me like a freight train. My head throbbed. It felt like the boat itself was rumbling, but that was impossible.

The last thought I had was that the sound had become so huge that it no longer sounded like drums.

It was a thought that didn't last long.

3

Black.

There's no better way to describe what I was experiencing. There was no sound. No sensation. No smell. No up or down. There was absolutely nothing but . . . black.

I wasn't scared. Or confused. Curious, maybe. Even a little excited but I wasn't frightened because whatever it was that was happening felt right. I can't say how long I was in that state. It wasn't like I was looking at my watch. Assuming I had a watch. Or an arm to put a watch on. Or eyes to see it with. I could have been drifting for a second or a century.

My feet felt the first sensation. Something was pressing against them. The pressure traveled up my legs, making me tense up. It was alien at first, until I realized what was happening. Gravity. I was standing. Feet down. Head up. You know . . . standing. Got it.

The black gradually turned to gray. I was surrounded by movement with no detail, as if I was standing in a dense, swirling fog. Colors came next. The clouds took on muted shades of purple and blue. Green came next, followed by yellow and finally red. I laughed. At least I think I laughed. I couldn't hear anything. But I was enjoying the show that seemed to exist for me alone. Whatever was happening had purpose. I knew that, though I can't say why. I sensed my own body. It was the first recognizable thing I could see. I was wearing jeans, a black T-shirt, and my Puma sneakers. When I first looked down at myself, there was no color to my clothes or my skin. It was like looking at a black-and-white picture. As the colorful clouds moved past, they filled in the blue of my jeans, the flesh color of my arms, and the white trim on my red sneakers. The same thing was happening all around me. I began to make out shapes. As each colorful puff swept by, it deposited another color to the environment like an animated paint-by-number picture.

I wasn't freaked by any of it. It was actually fascinating to see an entire world being created just for me. I recognized what looked like trees and buildings. Something more solid than a cloud moved by. A car. It had to be a car because I heard the horn. Sound had arrived. And far-off voices. Music played somewhere but I couldn't tell what it was. Trees rustled in the soft breeze. I felt the warmth of the sun and smelled something delicious. Something fried.

"Garden Poultry," I said out loud.

There's something magical about smells. It's like your nose has a direct line to the memory center of your brain. When I got that unmistakable smell of cooking french fries, I knew exactly where I was. The colorful clouds finished their job and evaporated, leaving me standing in the pocket park next to the Garden Poultry deli in Stony Brook. As reality returned, so did my focus. Up until that moment I had been floating in a peaceful sea of detached consciousness. It was a magical dream . . . that ended abruptly.

Along with my peace of mind.

How the hell did I get here? The last thing I knew I had been floating on Thistledown Lake listening to music. Why was I suddenly standing on the Ave in my hometown? I had on the same clothes as when I was in the boat, but with sneakers. Hadn't I left those in the boathouse?

My heart started pounding. A block of time had been totally erased from my memory. Did I have a brain tumor? What time was it? What *day* was it? The sun was out. Did that mean I'd been on the lake the night before? I looked at my watch. It wasn't there. Had I suddenly snapped out of a coma? Had I *been* in a coma? What if I had somehow wandered out of the hospital and found my way there, drawn by the sweet smell of Garden Poultry fries?

I dug in my pocket for my cell phone. It was gone. I felt naked without it. I took a deep breath and sat down on a park bench. *Think. Think.* My house was a few miles from the Ave. A long walk but no problem. Yes. That was the way to go. I'd head home and find Mom, and she'd tell me exactly what the deal was. Having a plan calmed me down. It was no use speculating on what might have happened. That would only work me up again. Answers weren't far away.

Once I got my head back on straight, more or less, I began the long walk home. Part of me wanted to grab some fries, but I wasn't hungry. Normally I'd pound down a box of those fries even if I'd just eaten lunch, but there was nothing normal about what I was going through. I stepped out of the park and glanced up and down Stony Brook Avenue.

I'm not a sentimental guy, but as I stood there looking at the main street of my hometown, I got a warm feeling. I had grown up in Stony Brook. I liked the town, not that I knew much about other towns, but it was a pretty cool place to live. Stony Brook Avenue was the main commercial street but there were no chain stores or fast-food restaurants. The Ave was lined with local shops, many of which had been there since long before I was born. It was a safe, familiar hometown. Fluffy white clouds drifted lazily across a deep blue sky; leafy green trees swayed gently in the warm breeze; people strolled casually along the sidewalks, shopping and generally enjoying the picture-perfect day. A few folks gave me a friendly smile and a nod as they walked past. I felt pretty lucky to be living there.

"Young Master Foley!" bellowed a chubby guy in a gray uniform who hurried up to me. "Hello, my friend! Surprised to see you here."

"Bernie?" I asked, more than a little surprised myself.

Bernie was the mailman who delivered to our house when I was a kid. He was always laughing and telling corny jokes. I hadn't seen the guy in a long time, but I recognized him instantly.

"Who else?" Bernie said with a laugh. "Hey, did you hear the one about the deaf mailman?"

"Uh . . . no."

"Don't feel bad, neither did he." Bernie burst out laughing like it was actually funny. I had to laugh too . . . not at the joke, at Bernie. The guy was a goof.

"You back on our route?" I asked.

Bernie gave me a strange look, as if he didn't understand the question. Then he burst out laughing again and clapped me on the back.

"That's a good one," he said, and continued walking. "See you around, Chicken Coop. Shame you had to get here too soon, but that's the way it goes."

"Too soon for what?"

He walked off without answering, whistling a happy tune. "Hello, Mrs. Swenor!" he called to an old lady on the other side of the street. The woman smiled and waved back. Everybody liked Bernie. I hoped we were on his route again.

I was about to head for home when I got a better idea. The trophy shop where Marsh worked was on the Ave. He would know what had happened to me. I did an about-face and walked quickly down the Ave. I wasn't worried about him being mad at me anymore. How could he still be ticked if I'd been in a coma?

I passed several people who smiled or gave me a friendly "Hello." Everybody seemed to be in a good mood. I guess none of them had recently come out of a coma, either. I returned the greetings. Why not? I may have had temporary amnesia but I remembered enough to know that I wasn't a jerk. I reached Santoro's Trophies and was about to go inside when something got my attention that was so out of place, it made me shiver.

The quaint buildings on the Ave were mostly made of brick and were all two or three stories high. Across the street from me, on the roof, I saw a guy standing with his toes right up to the edge. He wore a dark shirt and pants and was totally normal-looking in every way except that he was staring directly at me. There was no doubt. He was watching me. He didn't wave or acknowledge that I had seen him. He just . . . watched. Seeing the strange guy creeped me out, though I wasn't sure why. It wasn't like he was going to jump or anything. He wasn't doing anything wrong at all, but still, it felt off.

I pulled the door open and ducked inside.

Once in, I looked back through the glass door to see that the guy had left. He must have walked directly away from the edge because I didn't seem him moving north or south. What was up with that?

I chose to focus on my own problems and went looking for Marsh.

The door to the trophy shop was right on the Ave, but to get to the shop itself, you had to go inside and then down a flight of stairs. I ran down quickly and blew right through the front door, jingling the little bell that hung over it. The showroom was nothing more than a counter with samples of trophies and plaques everywhere. A short corridor led to the workroom where Marsh did his engraving. Beyond that was Mr. Santoro's office. I'd been there plenty of times, trying to get Marsh to blow off work so we could go do something fun, but Marsh always made me wait until he finished whatever he was working on. The guy was dedicated.

"Hello?" I called out.

Usually Mr. Santoro would rush right out as soon as he heard the bell.

"Anybody home?"

Silence. Strange. The door was unlocked but nobody was minding the store. I walked down the corridor to see if Marsh was working and concentrating so hard that he didn't want to answer. But when I entered the workroom, the engraving machine was empty.

"Mr. Santoro?"

I peeked into the guy's office. Nobody was there. Marsh worked part time so he might not have been in that day, but it was weird for the place to be empty with the door unlocked. I went back through the showroom, wondering if I should lock the door, but I was afraid Mr. Santoro might have gone to the men's room or something and I didn't want to lock him out. I didn't want to hunt him down in the bathroom either, so I gave up and left.

When I got back to the top of the stairs, I peered out through the glass door out to the Ave to see if the guy in the dark clothes had returned. He hadn't. Nothing about this day was making sense. I had to talk to somebody I knew. The sooner the better.

Directly across the street from Santoro's was a drugstore called Meade's. Score. My dad was friends with Mr. Meade. The guy would definitely give me a ride home. I blasted out of Santoro's and jogged across the street, but only got halfway before I stopped short.

Somebody was watching me from inside the toy store next to Meade's.

I saw her through the window. It was a woman who wore the same kind of dark clothes as the guy from the roof. I might not have noticed her except that she had the same body language as the guy. She stood straight and still with her hands clasped in front of her, staring me down.

I sensed movement to my right and realized I was standing in the middle of the street, blocking traffic. A car had stopped not two feet from me. The driver didn't honk or yell for me to get my oblivious butt out of the road. He just smiled and waited patiently for me to move on. I gave an apologetic wave and jumped onto the sidewalk. A quick look back to the toy store showed me that the woman was gone. I thought about running in to ask what her deal was and why she was watching me, but decided I had bigger problems to deal with so I went straight for Meade's.

There was another bell over the door that jingled when I entered. Maybe it was some kind of ordinance in Stony Brook that shops needed to have bells. Stepping into Meade's was like taking a trip back through time. It had been around for a hundred years and didn't look any different from the day it had opened. The shelves were built out of dark wood and the ceiling was a big stained-glass window. The back of the store was where they had all the drugstore stuff, but the front of the store is where I usually hung out. There was a soda fountain counter with a long marble top and stools like you'd see in old movies. It wasn't just for show, either. I'd pounded down many milk shakes and sundaes there.

Across from the counter were padded booths with tables where Marsh and I used to plot our adventures.

Meade's was a kid magnet, but not that afternoon, which was strange for a hot summer day. The only customers were two older people sitting at the counter, both sipping on straws in the same milk shake. The two of them smiled and gave me a friendly wave as I sat down on a stool.

A gray-haired lady wearing a white uniform dress with the name Donna stitched on the pocket was wiping up the stainless steel soda dispensers. She looked like a classic soda jerk, complete with a white cap that matched her dress. I thought she looked kind of old to be called a "jerk," or to be working as one, for that matter. Mostly it was kids who worked behind the counter and they never wore uniforms. It was like Mr. Meade was trying out a gimmick to make the place seem even more retro.

The lady saw me and frowned.

"Geez, so young," she said sadly as she shook her head. "Too young."

"Too young for what?" I asked. "I don't want a beer or anything."

"This your last age?" she asked.

"What are you talking about?"

The lady shook off the gloom and broke out in a big, bright smile. "No matter. It is what it is. What can I do you for, sport? Malteds are my specialty, in case you were wondering."

She seemed like a nice old lady, but I wasn't in the mood for a malted . . . whatever that was.

"I'm looking for Mr. Meade."

"Ooh, sounds like you've got important business. Sure, sweetie, I'll get him for you."

She hurried off, headed for the back of the store. It was a relief to know I was finally going to talk with somebody familiar. My eyes wandered to the mirrored wall in back of the soda fountain, where a bunch of ancient black-and-white pictures were on display. They were photos of people taken at the drugstore throughout time. I knew most of the pictures because whenever I sat at that counter, I'd stare at them and wonder who the people were and what their stories might be. It was weird to think that people came in and sat at that same counter decades before I did. As I glanced at the ancient shots, one of them jumped out at me. I'd seen it a hundred times before and never gave it a second thought . . . until then.

It was a yellowed photo of a man and a woman standing next to a car in front of the store. The car was a big gray tank that looked older than dirt. The guy was tall with an enormous gut and slicked-back hair. The woman was much shorter than him and looked old enough to be his mother. Something about her wasn't right. What was it? I leaned forward to get a closer look and instantly realized what was wrong: She looked exactly like the lady who was working behind the soda fountain. Donna. She even had on the same soda jerk uniform.

"No way," I muttered.

"You looking for me?" a guy said, sounding all gruff.

I looked behind the counter and did a double take. The guy walking toward me was the same guy with the big gut from the picture. I looked to the picture, then to him, then back to the picture. No mistake. It was him. The old lady trailed behind. It was definitely her in the picture, too. But that was impossible, unless it was a fake old-time picture like they take at carnivals.

"Uhhh," was all I could get out.

"What's your business, son?" he asked.

"I . . . I'm looking for Mr. Meade," I managed to croak.

"You found him," he said.

"No, I mean my dad's friend. What's his name, uh, Doug Meade."

The guy glanced to the old woman. She shrugged.

"What's the problem?" I asked.

"Unless you know something I don't, Dougie won't be coming this way for quite some time," the guy said. "Let's hope not, anyway."

"What? He's here, like, every day. Who are you?"

"Who am I?" he asked as if I'd insulted him. "I own the place, buster. I'm Dougie's father."

"No, you're not. He's way older than you!"

"Look," the guy said, getting angry. "Unless you want to eat something, keep moving and stop bothering my customers."

I sat there stunned, wondering if a brain tumor could cause amnesia *and* create hallucinations.

"I . . . I . . ." I couldn't form words.

The old lady patted the big guy on the shoulder. "Temper, Harry. Go on back. I think I know what this is about."

The bogus Mr. Meade gave me a sour look and skulked away.

The old woman smiled warmly and said, "Don't let him bother you. My boy's got anger issues. It's one of the things he's working on."

"Your boy?" I asked, more confused than ever.

"Yup. Harry's my son. Dougie's my grandson."

My brain locked.

The couple that had been sharing the milk shake walked past me on their way out. The guy patted me on the shoulder and said, "Don't sweat it, sonny. It'll get better. Just you wait."

His lady friend gave me a sympathetic smile, and the two left. I looked back to the old woman behind the counter and said, "I think there's something wrong with me."

She smiled. "You just got here, didn't you?"

"Well, yeah, you saw me come in."

"No, I mean you just came through to the Black."

What the heck did that mean? I thought back to when

I was passed out and everything was dark. It was black, all right, but how could she know that?

"I thought so," she said without waiting for an answer. "It's unsettling at first but things'll come clear in no time."

"There is nothing clear about what I've been seeing. I think I'm . . ."

The bell over the front door jingled and I looked to see the silhouette of a man entering the store.

"It's okay, Donna," he called out. "I'll handle this."

The guy's voice was familiar but I couldn't place him because all I saw was a shadow.

"He's a handsome one, Gene," she said, then winked at me. "Sure you don't want a malted?"

I shook my head and turned to the guy who had just come in. He walked deliberately, like an old man with sore joints.

"I figured on finding you here," he said. "Either here or that place with the french fries. Never cared for 'em myself. Too greasy."

My head was spinning. The guy knew me.

"This is much better," he said. "If I had a nickel for every ice cream I brought you here, I could buy the place out myself."

The guy sat down on the stool next to me and I got my first good look at him.

It was the best possible person I could have hoped to see . . . and the worst. He was my favorite person in the world. The old lady called him Gene. That was short for Eugene.

Eugene Foley.

My grandfather.

"Close your mouth, Cooper. You look like a trout."

Seeing my gramps made me want to throw my arms around him and hug him like I was six again. Only one thing stopped me.

My grandfather was dead.

4

I jumped off the stool and backed away from the old guy.

"No, no way," I babbled. "You can't be him."

The guy scratched his head and frowned . . . exactly the way Gramps used to when he was thinking. In fact, the guy looked exactly like my gramps, complete with his glasses the size of windowpanes, walrus mustache, and thinning gray hair.

"Don't get all lathered up," he said, which is something Gramps always used to say. "There's nothing wrong here."

"Bull! Everything is wrong here!"

"Hang on now," he said. "Let me think a second."

He scratched his head, again. And frowned, again. Either this guy was really my gramps or he was an incredible impersonator.

"Okay, I got it," he declared. "Who else knows about this?" He held up his hands like claws and bellowed in a thick Transylvanian accent, "Beware! I have come to suck your blood, for I am . . . the Grampire!"

"Grampire?" the old lady said with a chuckle.

The old man looked to her and shrugged. "He loved that when he was six."

I did. But it only helped to confuse me more.

"Stay the hell away from me!" I yelled, and ran for the door.

"Cooper!" the old man barked in a stern voice that I had heard many times before. I froze, probably out of habit.

"I know this is confusing, kiddo," he said with sympathy. "But running outta here ain't gonna help."

I wanted to believe he was my gramps. But if it was really him, it meant I had to buy into a whole lot of other things that weren't as good.

"My grandfather's dead," I said slowly to make sure he understood every word. "That means you're an imposter, or I'm insane."

The old lady sniffed and patted the old man on the arm. "Good luck with that one, Gene," she said, and left us alone to go back to work.

"I'm afraid there's a third possibility," the old man said.

"Please. Tell me."

"You won't like it."

"I'm not liking *any* of this."

He squinted. Gramps always did that when he was debating with himself. "You want it straight, or should I ease you in slowly?"

"Just tell me!" I shouted.

"You're dead, Cooper."

The words rang in my ears. I felt dizzy. How could I be dead? I was dizzy! You can't be dead and dizzy at the same time.

"You got hit by a speedboat out on Thistledown," he

added. "I'm not sure who was the bigger fool, the kid driving the speedboat or you for being out on that lake at night with the running lights off. What were you thinking?"

I had to breathe. Air. Real air. Dead people didn't breathe and I wanted to prove to myself that I wasn't dead. I ran out of the drugstore and onto the sidewalk to take in a lungful. Everything was so normal. I couldn't be dead.

Somebody clapped me on the back, making me jump.

"Hey, Chicken Coop." It was Bernie the mailman. "Feelin' any better?"

He winked at me and kept moving up the Ave. I suddenly remembered why Bernie wasn't our mailman anymore.

"Damn fool."

I whipped around to see the old man standing in the door of the drugstore with his hands in his pockets. "He got himself electrocuted by jiggering somebody's antenna to try and get free cable. His jokes aren't funny here, either."

"Here?" I asked. "What do you mean 'here'? We're in Stony Brook, right?"

He gave me a sad smile and reached out to pat me on the cheek. It was so familiar.

"Wish I could say I was happy to see you, Coop," he said. "Cripes, you're still a kid. Sometimes life just ain't fair."

"Where are we?" I implored.

"We're in Stony Brook all right, but it's *your* Stony Brook. The town as you remember it."

I glanced around, wondering why something so familiar could suddenly seem so alien.

"This must be a dream," I said. "It's all happening inside my head."

"Nope. Sorry."

I looked to the toy shop next door.

The woman in dark clothes was back, watching me. Not moving. Smiling.

I ran straight for the store, yanked open the door, and jumped inside.

"Who are you?" I screamed . . . at an empty store.

"Can I help you?" a salesgirl asked, walking toward me from the back of the store. It was a cute girl who looked high school age, definitely not somebody who was dead.

"Where did the lady go who was just here?"

She looked around. "I didn't see anybody."

"I don't know you," I said. "Do you go to Davis Gregory?"

"I did," she replied. "Didn't make it to graduation, though."

"Transfer?"

"Drunk driver."

I took a step back as if her words pushed me. "You got hit by a drunk driver?"

"No," she said, looking sheepish. "Homecoming party. Some guys brought beer. I only had a couple but I never should have tried to drive home. It was totally my fault. Thank god nobody else died. You looking for a toy?"

She reached to a counter and picked up a small, threadbare brown teddy bear with one eye missing. It was my teddy bear. I hadn't seen it since I was seven.

"I'll bet you miss him," the girl said with a smile.

I stumbled backward and pushed my way out of the store to where my Gramps, or whoever he was, waited.

"It's okay, Coop," he said. "You'll be fine."

"Fine!" I screamed. "You're telling me I'm dead. How is that fine?"

Gramps chuckled. "I said the exact same thing when I got here. I was running all over the place, trying to figure out why everybody I saw was somebody dead." He waved his hands in the air, rolled his eyes dramatically, and yelled, "Get me outta here! I don't belong here!" He laughed. "Yeah, that was me. I was in denial. It's natural."

I didn't know what to say. I didn't want to believe him

but didn't have any other explanation. He put his arm around my shoulders. I didn't fight. He was my gramps.

"Try to relax, kiddo. It gets better once you realize it's just part of life. Everybody comes through here eventually."

"Where is 'here'?"

"C'mon," he said. "I'll buy you an ice cream."

A few minutes later we were back in Meade's, sitting in a booth like we had done hundreds of times before. Donna, the soda jerk, served us two impossibly perfect banana splits. I wasn't hungry. How could I be? I was dead. It didn't stop Gramps, though. He chowed. Once he scooped out the last of his sundae and let out a healthy belch, he was ready to talk.

"They call this place the Black. Not sure why. Maybe because of what we go through to get here. Kind of ironic, don't you think?"

"What do you mean?"

"Everybody talks about going toward the light when they're dying. Truth is it's just the opposite. Back there, where the living exist, *that's* the Light. Must be somebody's idea of a joke."

"But this is Stony Brook," I said.

"To *you* it is. Everybody sees it differently. That's the point. When you're here, it's pretty much like how you remember it from the Light. Only difference is, the people still living back there aren't here. Not yet, anyway. That's the biggest downside. Leaving folks behind. I've been waiting on your grandma for . . . How long's it been since I took the dirt nap?"

"Dirt nap?"

"Don't be dense, boy. When did I die?"

"About five years ago."

He whistled. "Never would have guessed that. Time doesn't mean much here. Doesn't mean *anything*."

"So you see this place like Stony Brook too?"

"When I'm with you. I can see things the way you see them, and you can see through my point of view. My vision." He leaned in and gave me a mischievous smile. "Think you're ready to give it a try?"

"I don't know what to think anymore," I said.

Gramps slid out of the booth and called out, "Put this on my tab, Donna."

"Will do!" the old lady called back. "You got a fine grandson there, Gene. You should be proud."

"He's all right," Gramps said. "A little full of himself but what can you do."

Donna laughed. "So he's just like you."

"That's enough out of you, young lady," Gramps said playfully.

She winked, "Have fun, you two."

"This is just wrong," I said, numb.

"Sorry, Coop. It's as right as can be," he said, holding out his hand, beckoning me to join him. "C'mon."

I slid out of the booth but didn't take his hand. "Where are we going?"

"Home."

We were suddenly enveloped in a swirling mass of colored fog. It was exactly like the experience I had when I first found myself standing in the pocket park. The drugstore washed away and was quickly replaced by green trees. The temperature changed and it was suddenly chilly. When the fog dissipated, I saw that we were surrounded by tall trees that were alive with the colors of fall. It was the height of the changing season and the leaves were brilliant shades of red, yellow, and gold. We had not only left Stony Brook Avenue, we had left summer.

Gramps and I were standing in the exact same position as when we were in the drugstore, only we were in a field of grass. I didn't know if we had moved, or if everything else had moved around us.

Gramps took a deep breath, filling his lungs with brisk fall air.

"Perfect," he declared. "My favorite time of year."

"Where are we?" I asked.

"C'mon now! Hasn't been that long, has it?"

There was something familiar about the surroundings. We were standing at the edge of thick woods. I made a slow turn until I saw a white clapboard farmhouse sitting on a rise not thirty yards from us.

In spite of how impossible it all seemed, I had to smile. "It's your house," I said with a gasp.

"That's better," he said. "C'mon, let's have a sit."

The two of us walked across his yard together like we had done so many times before. It made me remember all the time I'd spent with him, helping him with his garden or putting in brick walkways or raking leaves. When I was little, Gramps and I were pals. Seeing that house took away any shred of doubt I had. He was really Gramps.

"This is my vision of the Black," he explained. "My house. In fall. Everything's perfect, 'cept for your grandma not being here."

Gramps lived in a rural area north of Stony Brook. It wasn't far from civilization, but going there always felt like we had entered another world. On the far side of Gramps's house was a property that was almost as big as his, with another farmhouse and a large barn. A split rail fence separated the two yards.

Someone was standing on the other side of the fence, watching us. It was a girl who could have been my age. She had short black hair and wore a plain, flowered dress and an old blue sweater. She stood there staring at us, but it wasn't unnerving like with the silent creeps in black on the Ave.

When she realized that I had noticed her, she turned and hurried toward her house.

"Who's that?" I asked. "I don't remember her living next to you."

Gramps didn't even look her way. "She lived in that house long before your grandma and I lived here together."

"Seriously?" I asked. "She's from a different time?"

"Yup."

"I don't get it. Is this your vision or hers?"

"Depends on who you're talking to. Things tend to overlap, but that's what makes it so interesting. You never know who you might run across or where they might take you."

"So what's her story?"

"Don't know," Gramps said abruptly. "She doesn't talk much . . . or at all."

I got the impression that he didn't want to talk about the girl next door. She stood watching us from her porch, peeking out from around a corner as if she didn't want us to know she was there. I gave her a friendly wave and she ducked back like I had whipped a rock at her head.

Gramps led me up onto his porch, where he sat in his favorite white wicker rocking chair. I took my regular place on the wicker couch with the flowered cushions. It felt like I was eight again. Eight and dead.

"You want some iced tea?" Gramps asked.

"I want to go home. I can't be dead. I'm still in high school."

"I know, Coop. I wish you didn't have to know about any of this yet. But unfortunately, age has got nothing to do with it."

"But it's wrong. I shouldn't be here."

"Lots of folks feel that way at first."

"I don't care about other folks. I can't accept this."

Gramps scratched his head again. "Look, Coop, everybody travels the same road. You step on it when you're born into the Light and you follow it all the way through here until you reach the place where you'll spend eternity. We're all on the way there. No use trying to fight it."

"Whoa, wait. This isn't the end of the line?"

"The Black? Nah, this is only a stop along the road. Everybody comes here first. What you do while you're here determines how long you stay, and where you go."

"How's that?"

"Nobody's perfect, Coop. We all had different lives. Different personalities. The way I understand it, being here in the Black gives you the chance to look back on your life and who you were and make whatever changes it takes that'll help you to move on. It's a chance to be the person you want to be. Or should be."

"And then what?" I asked.

Gramps shrugged. "Damned if I know. There ain't any instruction manuals. People come, people go. We all just kind of share information. But what I'm thinking is that once we make things right, we get to go on to the big reward."

"Heaven?"

"I guess. I don't know. Nobody calls it that. I can't imagine that floating around in white robes with wings and playing a harp is any kind of reward. If that's the case, I'd just as soon stay here and rock on the porch. But there's definitely something further down the road. I've seen lots of people move on."

I looked out over Gramps's yard. Every detail was familiar and perfect, right down to the wishing well in front.

"You sure this isn't heaven?" I asked.

"To me it is, but it's only temporary."

"So we're supposed to go back to the Light and fix something we messed up? Like taking care of unfinished business?"

"No! Uh-uh." he said quickly. "That's the last thing we're

supposed to do. What's done is done. It's a big no-no to mess with things in the Light."

"Then, what are we supposed to change?"

"Ourselves. Like I said. You may have died but you're still you. What you get here is the chance to become the best person you can be. Personally, I don't know why I've been here as long as I have. Far as I can tell, I'm pretty near perfect."

He gave me a sly smile. "Then again, maybe that's why I'm still here. Humility isn't one of my strengths. I'm thinking you might suffer the same problem."

"So, what do I do?"

"For one, keep your nose clean. You may think you're all that and a bag of chips, but you've been acting like a fool with all your brawling and nonsense. And what you did with them fake tickets had 'dumb' written all over it."

"How did you know about all that? I thought you aren't supposed to interfere with the Light."

"Observing isn't the same as interfering. Fact is, what we are has a lot to do with the people we left back in the Light. We can learn from them and maybe see things about ourselves we couldn't see before."

"We can see into the Light?"

"Of course. It's one of the things that keeps me from missing your grandma too bad. And the family. And you. But you're here now, I'm sorry to say."

"Can I do it?" I asked.

"Look into the Light? Absolutely."

"How?"

"It's as simple as using your imagination. In fact, that's exactly how it works. Close your eyes and think about something you might want to see."

"That's it?"

"Give it a try."

Nothing I had seen since I woke up from that blackout-coma made much sense and this was no different. I had nothing to lose so I closed my eyes and thought about home. The first thing that popped into my head was Marsh. I'm not sure why. Maybe it was because I was thinking about him playing the drums just before—well, just before things went black.

"Take a look," Gramps said.

I opened my eyes to see that the multicolored fog had appeared as a small cloud that hovered in front of my face.

"Look inside," he said, gesturing toward the cloud.

I wasn't exactly sure what he meant, but I leaned forward and put my face into the swirling cloud. It was like pushing my way through a curtain. I was still on Gramps's porch, but another image appeared in front of me. It was mostly transparent so I could still see the yard, but I could definitely make out that I was seeing something else.

It was Marsh's bedroom.

The door flew open and Marsh hurried in. He stood at the foot of his bed with his fists clenched. I rarely saw Marsh get angry, but when he did, watch out.

"Marsh?" I called tentatively.

Marsh didn't react.

"He can't hear you," I heard Gramps say.

Marsh's whole body was tense. He whipped his head around as if looking for something. His eyes settled on a shelf next to his bed that was full of stuff his mom had sent him from her travels. It was mostly junk like small statues and bamboo flutes, but it all meant something to Marsh because it reminded him of his mom. He stormed over to the shelf and picked up a golden ball that was about the size of a plum. I'd never seen it before. It looked ancient, with odd characters carved all over it. Without hesitation, he spun around, cocked his arm, and threw it across the room.

"Whoa!" I shouted in surprise. Of course he didn't hear me.

The ball nailed a framed picture on the far wall and smashed to bits. I thought I saw it spew something red and wet all over the wall but I can't say for sure because as soon as the ball exploded, the ground moved as if the destruction of the ball had caused an earthquake. I saw Marsh grab on to his desk for balance.

Stranger still, I felt it too.

"Gramps?" I called out in confusion.

The image of Marsh's bedroom jumbled to nothing. The shaking was so severe it knocked me off my feet. As soon as I fell to my knees, the shaking stopped. The bizarre event lasted only a few seconds.

"What the heck was that?" I gasped.

I opened my eyes to see that I wasn't kneeling on the wooden floor of Gramps's porch anymore. I wasn't in Marsh's bedroom, either. I was on my hands and knees in brown, hard-packed sand. I lifted my hands to see they were covered with fine grit.

"What happened?" I asked Gramps as I got to my feet.

Gramps wasn't there. Or maybe I was the one who wasn't there. Wind kicked up more sand, stinging my eyes. I looked around to try and understand. What I saw made me want to drop to my knees again.

I was standing in front of an old-style stone building that looked like something out of ancient Greece. Only, the building didn't look all that ancient, and neither did the guy standing in the doorway.

"Hello," he called to me in a deep, booming voice. "I have been looking forward to meeting you."

5

Up until then, everything I had seen was familiar.

Weird, but familiar. Now I had landed in alien territory. I was standing in what looked like a village square straight out of ancient Rome. The buildings were made of stone, surrounding a fountain in the middle of the dusty street. The fountain was a huge stone sculpture of a muscular, godlike warrior with a massive sword battling scrawny soldiers half his size. The smaller statues in the fountain had water coming out of their mouths that didn't flow so much as trickle, landing at their feet with a steady *drip . . . drip . . . drip* like they were bleeding. The sound was small, but it filled the ancient-looking square.

The village was tucked into a narrow valley. Steep, rocky hills rose high up on either side, covered by what I'm guessing were olive trees. At one end of the square was a tall building with a dome that could have been a church or a temple or a library or I really didn't know what. As old as the buildings looked, they weren't falling-down ancient. Still, it looked as though I had been transported to a vision in the Black from another era. Question was, whose vision was it?

I didn't have to wait long for the answer.

"I am so pleased that you have arrived!" the guy called to me from the building. He was short and stocky and looked to have come from a different time. Different from mine, that is. He wore a light brown loose-fitting wrapped thing that drooped down below his knees. On his feet were sandals with leather straps that wrapped around his lower legs. His hair was short and black with bangs that cut straight across his forehead. He hurried down the steps and shuffled toward me quickly with a broad, welcoming smile.

"I trust you have not been waiting long," he said.

"Where is this?" I asked.

"We are in my vision of the Black, of course. You would call it Macedonia."

"Who are you?"

The guy bowed formally but didn't take his eyes off me. "I am Damon of Epirus. Welcome to my humble village."

His dark eyes bugged out of his round face in a way that would have been comical if not for the fact that he kept staring at me as if expecting me to make a wrong move. Now that he was closer, I saw that his face was badly scarred. Dozens of thin white streaks crisscrossed his cheeks and nose. The guy had been messed up. I didn't think you could survive something like that.

Maybe he didn't.

"So . . . you're dead?" I asked.

He shrugged and chuckled. "Aren't we all?"

"Right. Dumb question. Why am I here?"

He took my arm in a friendly way and we strolled toward the large building.

"I brought you here, Cooper Foley."

"Whoa, you know me?"

"I do. I know all about you. You are resourceful. And loyal. You never back away from a fight. In fact, you enjoy the occasional battle. Perhaps most important, you are a survivor."

"Yeah, well, not exactly. I'm here, right?"

"Indeed!" he exclaimed jovially. "Very good!"

"How do you know so much about me?"

"I have been observing you for quite some time now."

"How? I just got here."

"My observations of you have been in the Light."

The little guy was starting to creep me out. He seemed harmless, but spying on me from the afterlife was just wrong.

"Why?" I asked.

"To help you. There are many roads to take through the Black. Select your course wisely and your future can be a glorious one."

"What are you, my guardian angel?"

That made him chuckle. "Hardly."

"But you know the right roads to take?"

"I do," was his simple, confident answer.

"Wait, how long have you been here?"

He shrugged and scoffed. "Time has little meaning."

"Yeah, I heard that, but seriously. When did you die? People don't dress like that anymore, unless you drowned bobbing for apples at a Halloween party."

Damon shot me a quick, vicious glare. He didn't appreciate my sense of humor. The guy may have looked like a Hobbit, but he had a temper. The look disappeared as quickly as it arrived, and he smiled. "By your calendar I entered the Black in the year 323 BCE."

"Seriously? You've been here, like . . . a couple thousand years?"

"That surprises you?"

"Well, yeah. I thought the point of being here is to become the person you're supposed to be and move on. What makes you think you can help me if you haven't figured out how to move on yourself?"

Damon lunged at me and grabbed my shirt. It was so sudden, I didn't have a chance to react. His eyes turned dark again. He was a few inches shorter than me and pulled me down so that our noses nearly touched. The guy was small, but strong.

"Use care," he said with a seething whisper. "Many graves hold the bones of those who have shown me disrespect."

I was so stunned by his sudden snap that I didn't pull away. But I didn't back down, either.

"Yeah, well, I'm already dead. What are you gonna do? Kill me again?"

His eyes flared. I'd seen that look before. We were about to fight. That was okay by me. Spirit or no, I'd kick his ass. But rather than attack, his lips twisted into a hideous smile. He laughed, sending out a spray of spittle.

My brain froze when I saw that his two front teeth came to sharp points. It was such a freakish look that it made me catch my breath.

"There are fates worse than death," he said with a giddy chuckle.

He shoved me and I stumbled to the ground, hitting my shoulder against the base of another statue. It hurt. I may have been a spirit, but I still felt pain.

"No matter," he declared cheerily as if it was all a big joke between friends. "You will learn."

His sudden mood swings had me totally off balance, in more ways than one.

He added, "We would all be best served if you understood the consequences you face."

"Consequences of what?" I asked.

"For underestimating me. I am not a typical spirit of the Black."

Damon gestured toward the big building. On cue, two other guys rushed out. They were big, dangerous-looking dudes with long, wild hair. Their raggedy clothes were covered with brown stains that could have been dirt . . . or dried blood. The two hurried up to Damon, keeping their heads bowed obediently. Whoever Damon of Epirus was, he was the boss.

One guy carried leather body armor that he helped Damon put on over his robe.

"That's how it's going to be?" I said, getting to my feet. "We're gonna fight?"

"Of course not," he said. "You and I are friends."

I didn't argue with him. What was the point?

The second grubby-looking guy held out a long, dark sword. It was solid black, from the thick blade all the way to the heavy handle. The surface was smooth, like it was carved from stone and polished to a brilliant luster. Damon took the weapon and held it out horizontally to admire it. The sun glinted off the glossy blade, making him laugh like a happy kid with a new toy.

The guy was insane.

I had to fight the urge to turn and run.

Damon looked at me over the blade. "You are afraid."

I shrugged.

"Good," he said. "You should be."

"That's it? You want to prove how bad you are? Fine. Nice job. Put the sword down."

He glared at me with his wild, buggy eyes and smiled. I wondered how much it would hurt to be impaled by a sword . . . or bitten by those sharp fangs. What had I done to deserve this? Where was Gramps?

Five more guys marched out of the large building. All but one looked like the guys who had brought the sword and the armor to Damon. The fifth guy had on leather armor like Damon's, but where Damon's gear was new and unscratched, the armor on this guy was beaten up as if he'd been through more than one fight. He too had a sword, only this one was traditional with a metal blade.

The guy in armor was surrounded by the others, who escorted him like a prisoner. He kept glancing around nervously as if he didn't want to be there any more than I did. They marched toward us and stopped a few yards away.

Damon let out a small, muffled chuckle. "Isn't this exciting?" he asked me softly.

I didn't know how to answer that, so I didn't.

Damon turned to face the group. When the prisoner saw him, he stiffened in surprise.

"Damon," the guy said with a gasp of horror.

"Philip, my old friend!" Damon called out gregariously. "Why the surprise? Surely you knew this moment would come."

"I—I was loyal to you in life, Damon," the guy stammered nervously.

"Indeed," Damon said. "You waited until journeying further along the road until betraying me."

"This must stop!" the guy named Philip begged. "You are challenging the very nature of life."

"I suppose I am," Damon declared casually. "Does that frighten you?"

"Yes," the guy shot back. "This is a war that cannot be won."

"Perhaps not by you," Damon replied. "But I will give you the chance to prove me wrong. I see you have not given up your weapon."

Philip raised his silver sword. "My sword has served you well."

"Then, let us see if it will do the same for you," Damon declared, lifting his black sword.

When Philip saw the black blade, his knees went weak and he swayed as if about to pass out.

"I cannot hope to compete," Philip said, barely above a whisper.

"Then, perhaps you can take it from me," Damon declared.

The guys who were guarding Philip backed off. I took a few steps back too. I didn't want to get caught in the middle. It didn't seem like a fair fight. The prisoner named Philip was obviously an experienced soldier, where Damon was more of a pretender with a scary-looking sword. The real question was, what happened when you lost a sword fight in the Black?

"I do not want to battle you, Damon," Philip said.

"I know," Damon replied, and attacked without warning.

Philip quickly raised his sword to defend himself, and the fight was on. Damon took it right to Philip. He hammered away at the larger guy, driving him back across the courtyard. Philip was good. He blocked every one of Damon's violent attacks. The sound of clashing metal echoed off the buildings, along with the grunts from Damon that proved he was giving it his all.

There was nothing skillful about the way Damon fought. Philip, on the other hand, was quick and agile. He deftly swung his sword back and forth as if he knew exactly where the next blow would come from. Damon soon built up a sweat. Philip was barely challenged by the smaller man. He conserved his energy, letting Damon wear himself out. Philip's confidence grew. He anticipated Damon's attacks and was ready to block them before Damon even swung. Where Philip was barely out of breath, Damon was grunting and breathing hard. There was no way he would last much longer.

I couldn't take my eyes off the two warriors, though I was afraid to see what would happen when one of those swords finally hit skin and bone. Did spirits bleed?

Damon grew exhausted and his attack slowed. The black sword seemed to grow heavier each time he swung it.

Philip saw this and went on the offense, attacking Damon with short, quick swings. There was no wasted effort. Philip had fought the perfect fight. He let Damon burn himself out and would soon find an opening to strike back and end it.

It took everything I had not to yell out, "Kick his ass, Phil!"

Damon didn't seem nervous at all about how the fight was going. He taunted Philip as if he were in complete command.

"Pity," Damon said, breathless. "Such a skilled fighter."

Each time Philip swung, Damon laughed. Or squealed with delight. It was eerie. What kind of tactic was he using?

Philip didn't talk back. He was too busy wearing Damon down.

I looked to Damon's pals. They didn't seem concerned at all that their boss was being taken to school.

Damon lunged at Philip, but the more skilled fighter easily knocked away the blow. The force of the block threw Damon off balance. He stumbled forward, turning his back on Philip, and the superior fighter took advantage of his mistake. Philip expertly reached around Damon and grabbed his throat in a choke hold. At the same time he jammed Damon against a wall, pinning his sword arm.

"Release the weapon, Damon," Philip commanded.

Damon's answer was to open his mouth and viciously bite down on Philip's forearm with his vampire-like fangs.

Philip let out a scream of agony and released his grip to try and push Damon away, but Damon kept his mouth clamped on Philip's bare arm like an attack dog. The whole time, he was laughing. The guy was enjoying himself. It was disgusting.

Philip finally yanked his arm free and kicked Damon away. Damon stumbled, tripped, and fell. With a deft flick of his silver sword, Philip knocked Damon's black sword out of his hand, leaving him wide open for an attack. Damon lay flat on his back, breathing hard. Philip stood over him, holding the tip of his sword to Damon's chest.

I expected to see blood on Damon's lips, but there was none. Philip held his own sword with his damaged arm . . . that wasn't damaged. There was no wound. Philip may have felt pain from the bite, but there was no lasting injury.

Damon's pals didn't move to help their boss, which made no sense. Maybe they wanted him to lose as much as I did.

"No! Please!" Damon screamed, suddenly in a panic.

In seconds he had gone from supremely confidant to begging for mercy.

"I will spare you," Philip said. "If you give up your quest."

"Truly?" Damon cried. "You will release me?"

"You have my word," Philip said.

Damon's pathetic cry turned to a laugh. He actually laughed.

I didn't see the joke, but then again, I'm not crazy.

Damon laughed so hard that his face turned red and tears rolled down his cheeks.

Philip looked pained.

"I beg you, Damon," he said, his voice cracking with tension. "In the name of all those who fought and died for you, end this."

I didn't understand what was happening. Philip had won the fight. All he had to do was lean forward and drive his sword into Damon's chest and that would be it. End of story. Philip was acting as if Damon was still in control.

"Oh, Philip," Damon said, catching his breath. "Did you seriously believe this was an actual battle?"

Before Philip could answer, Damon lurched forward, driving the tip of Philip's sword straight into his own chest. He let out a howl of agony as the blade tore through him, his mouth opening wide in an anguished grimace to reveal his hideous pointed teeth.

"Oh man!" I screamed, and turned away.

Damon continued to wail with pain. I'd never seen anybody stabbed; I kept my eyes on the ground. Damon had committed suicide. Could a spirit commit suicide? I looked back to see Philip release the sword and take a few steps back from the skewered Damon. The sword had passed straight through Damon's upper chest and poked out his back. It was horrifying. Damon was breathing hard, his buggy eyes wild and darting every which way.

I thought he was finished . . . until he reached up to the sword, grasped the handle, and pulled it out.

I cringed. The sound of steel going through flesh was something I'd never heard before and didn't care to hear ever again. Damon held the sword out in front of him, still breathing hard. He examined the weapon, and laughed.

Nobody seemed all that surprised, except for me. There was no blood on the sword. Damon felt the pain, but there was no injury.

If I had any doubts before, they were now completely gone. We really were spirits.

My eye caught movement by the large building at the end of the square. Standing on the steps was another one of those people wearing dark clothing. It was a guy with gray hair and a mustache who didn't belong in ancient Macedonia any more than I did. He stood stock-still on the top step of the ancient structure, silently watching.

Damon stood and casually brushed dirt off his leather

armor as if getting dirty was the worst thing that had happened to him. He then scooped up his black sword and stalked toward Philip.

Philip fell to his knees, whimpering.

"You knew it would end this way," Damon said, looming over him.

"Please, Damon," Philip whimpered. "You must end this."

Damon smiled, revealing his sharp teeth. "Why, Philip, that is precisely what I intend to do."

With a move so sudden it made me jump back, Damon lifted his black sword and drove it into Philip's chest. Philip cried out in agony, but his pain didn't last long because the warrior instantly exploded in a small black cloud.

"Whoa!" I screamed, and dropped to one knee.

Dark vapor that was once a spirit named Philip rose up and blew away with the wind, leaving nothing but a memory. Damon raised his black sword into the air, a sign of victory.

His men cheered.

I looked to see the reaction of the gray-haired guy who was watching from the temple, but he was gone.

Damon turned to me with a look that I can best describe as crazed. He bared his sharp teeth and pointed the black sword toward me.

I didn't want any part of him, or that weapon, and backed off. With three quick steps Damon was on me. My back hit a building. I was trapped with the point of the sword digging into my neck.

"And there is your answer, Cooper Foley," he said with a casual calm that gave no hint of the violence that had just taken place. "If I choose to, I will kill you again."

6

Damon stared me down, daring me to make a move.

All he had to do was shove that black sword another inch and I'd be . . . what? Dust? Vapor? The only sound was Damon's heavy breathing and the steady *drip . . . drip . . . drip* from the fountain.

"I . . . I don't understand any of this," I managed to say.

Damon snickered. He pulled the sword away and backed off but I still didn't move. I had to be careful. The guy was a psycho.

"What happened to him?" I asked.

"I ended his existence," Damon replied casually. He pointed the black sword at me threateningly and added, "Do not tempt me to end yours."

"It's that sword," I said. "How could it do that? We're spirits. You bit him—which was disturbing, by the way—but there was no blood."

Damon licked his lips, which turned my stomach.

"That sword is different," I added.

"Do you wish to continue stating the obvious, or shall we move on?" he asked.

I was beginning to hate this guy.

He motioned to one of his goons and the guy came running up. Damon handed him the black sword and the guy backed away while bowing his head. Another guy ran up and helped Damon take off his armor. They were terrified of him. I wondered why one of them didn't just grab the black sword and take a whack at Damon themselves.

"Why the armor if he had no chance of hurting you?" I asked.

"I am a warrior," he answered proudly. "A soldier. In life I commanded an army of thousands. I am most comfortable when dressed appropriately for battle."

The guy didn't look anything like a warrior, or fight like one, but I wasn't going to point that out. He must have been the guy who gave orders and stayed back where it was safe. Though he wasn't a physical threat, he was smart, which made him even more dangerous. Once the armor was off, all six guys hurried away and disappeared back into the stone building, leaving Damon and me alone.

He said, "You observed, correctly, that I have existed in the Black for quite some time. There is a reason."

"Can't imagine what that might be," I said. "You seem like such a great guy."

Damon gave me a nasty look. I decided not to jab him anymore.

"Unlike most other souls who simply pass through, I am trapped. A victim of those I once trusted."

He glanced up to the fountain and the giant statue of the stone warrior.

"Friend of yours?" I asked.

"No," he said coldly. "This is the vision of where I was betrayed in the Light, along with several of my loyal soldiers who chose to die rather than abandon me. We are all trapped here in the Black, unable to move further along the road."

"Okay. Why?"

"Our path is blocked. But now, finally, I have found the means to remove the obstruction."

"Good for you," I said. "How are you going to do that?"

"I'm not," Damon said with a smirk. "*You* are."

"Uh . . . what?" I muttered.

Damon stepped aside to reveal a swirling cloud of color like the one Gramps brought me through when we were on the Ave. Or my vision of the Ave. Or whatever it was. He gestured for me to enter.

"No, thanks," I said. "I'll hang here with the statue."

"To understand you must observe."

"Observe what?"

His answer was to gesture to the cloud again.

It didn't seem like I had a choice. Not if I wanted to understand what was happening. So like I did with Gramps, I took a breath and stepped into the swirl.

It wasn't the same experience as before. No sooner did I lean into the cloud than the world changed. I was no longer standing on the sandy soil of the ancient square but had been transported to another place. Another time. It was totally disorienting because the surroundings were so different from where I'd been . . . yet at the same time it was all very familiar.

I was standing in the living room of my best friend, Marshall Seaver.

Damon stood next to me. Seeing this ancient character in Marshall's living room was like a surreal dream. I glanced around to see nothing but a lot of normal—right down to a TV show about sharks on Marsh's wide-screen.

"It's my vision of the Black," I declared. "So what?"

"It is not your vision," he replied. "We have entered the Light."

"We're here?" I asked, astonished, looking around. "We're really here? I mean, this is all . . . real?"

Damon yawned.

It didn't seem right. According to Gramps we could only observe the Light, not hang out there. I took a few tentative steps and saw something that proved Damon was telling the truth.

Lying on the couch, asleep, was Marsh.

"Hey, Ralph!" I leaned on the back of the couch but my hands passed right through as if it was a projection.

"Whoa!" I declared, and jumped back.

I looked to Damon, who shrugged, bored.

I swept my hand through the couch, testing to see if it was really there. It wasn't. Or I wasn't. It took a few seconds for me to understand: The couch was solid . . . I wasn't. I was a spirit in the Light. It wasn't the same as when I watched Marsh break that golden ball. This time I was actually in Marsh's living room. His *real* living room.

"Ralph!" I called out again. "Hey, Ralph! Wake up!"

"He cannot hear you," Damon stated flatly.

I wanted to scream in frustration. I may have been there in the same room with Marsh, but I was a ghost. A freakin' ghost. I wandered around to try and understand what it meant to be a spirit in the Light. I reached down to grab the remote from the coffee table and my hand traveled through it.

"Damn," I said with dismay.

"Did you not believe me?" Damon asked.

"Give me a break. This is all new to me. Why don't we just, like, fall through the floor?"

"You could," he responded. "Would you like to?"

"No, I'll pass on that." I turned to watch Marsh sleeping.

He had no idea that there were two invisible spirits keeping him company.

"Wait," I said, turning to Damon. "You said you were trapped in the Black."

"I am prevented from moving further along the road. However, I am quite capable of visiting the Light in spirit form."

"So, then, what's the point?"

Damon walked toward the couch. "You need to understand that I am not an ordinary spirit. As you have astutely pointed out, I have been in the Black for quite some time. Longer than any other since the dawn of man."

"Do you get a prize for that?"

"You meant that as a sarcastic comment, but there is some truth to it. I have used my time wisely and developed certain . . . skills. I know more about the ways of the road than any other entity."

He knelt down next to Marsh. I would have pulled him away if I thought he might try and take a bite out of him, but I knew that was impossible. We were spirits. We had no effect on the living.

Damon leaned in close to Marsh and whispered, *"Morpheus."*

Marsh's eyes sprang open.

He had heard Damon. What I thought was impossible, wasn't.

"Get away from him!" I shouted, and rushed forward to protect my friend.

Damon stood up and I tackled him. Hard. The two of us stumbled into the swirling fog and found ourselves back at the fountain. Things were solid again. We were back in the Black. I jumped to my feet and squared off against the guy.

"How did you do that?" I demanded.

Damon laughed. "That is the least of my skills."

"What do you want from me?"

"I seek a weapon. A particular weapon. A poleax. It was mine in life and I want it returned."

"So what? What's that got to do with me?"

"The poleax remained in the Light when I was banished to the Black. Now, after so many centuries, it is finally within my grasp. I need your friend to find it and return it to me."

"Marsh? Why Marsh?"

"Because he alone has the ability to locate it."

"No way. He doesn't know about any ancient weapon."

"He knows more than you realize. He will find the poleax . . . and you will help him."

"Uhhh, no. I won't."

"Yes, you will. You both will, or I will return to the Light. A small whisper in the ear of a sleeping boy does not come close to demonstrating the extent of my abilities. Your presence here is proof of that."

I was getting too much information, too fast, and none of it was making sense.

"My presence? What does that mean?"

Damon stalked toward me. I wanted to hold my ground but the little guy scared the hell out of me and I had to back away.

"The lake was beautiful that night, was it not? So peaceful with a sky full of shimmering stars and a lake teaming with dozens of stargazers. It all seemed so inviting. So safe. But what happened to the other boaters? How could they have disappeared so quickly . . . unless they were never there?"

"W-what? What does that mean?"

"I have observed the Light for centuries. I have seen every behavior known to mankind and learned how it evolved. From strength to cowardice. Brilliance to treachery.

I can reach into the depths of a man's soul to draw out his greatest fear or grandest desire, and make it appear before him. It is quite simple, really. A play of light, the bending of a shadow, and the illusions appear real. This is what I have achieved in the time I have spent here."

"That's . . . that's not right. Spirits aren't supposed to monkey with the living."

"And what would be my punishment? Eternal captivity? That has already been my fate for too long."

"I don't believe you."

"No? Why was that young boy in the speedboat traveling so quickly the night of your death? It was so foolish. Unless there was something that compelled him to act recklessly. Perhaps he was drawn into a race with another boat? A boat that was not actually there."

My head was spinning. "What are you saying?"

"You are here in the Black because of me, Cooper Foley."

"Wh . . . No. It was an accident."

"An accident that I caused. I created the illusions that led to your death."

"But . . . why?"

"I brought you here to help release me from captivity."

He kept stalking me and I kept backing off.

"This is . . . this is crazy. I'm not going to help you."

"Even though I have the power to end your existence?"

"What are you going to do? Stab me with that black sword?"

"Perhaps. Or I could raise the stakes even higher."

"Higher than ending my existence?"

"That depends on what value you put on the life of your friend, Marshall Seaver."

I stopped moving. That was it. There was the threat. If I didn't help Damon, he was going to kill Marsh. Like he had killed me. That wasn't going to fly. I was ready to take this guy apart, and I would have if I hadn't caught movement to my right. I thought it might be one of his pals coming to jump me, and I spun toward the ancient building.

Three people in black were on the steps, watching us. They stood shoulder to shoulder, all looking like normal people except that they were totally out of place in that ancient square.

And they didn't look happy.

I didn't care.

I spun back to Damon, ready to take him out.

Damon's eyes flared as he bared his teeth and hissed like an animal about to be attacked. I wanted to knock those pointed teeth out of his head, but as I moved on him, I felt a hand on my shoulder. An instant later I was yanked backward, hard, off my feet into another swirling mass of color and fog.

7

I hit the ground and bounced right back to my feet, ready to take on whoever it was that had grabbed me from behind and yanked me into another dimension. I expected it to be one of Damon's soldiers, but when I looked around, I saw that I was alone.

It took a few seconds for me to calm down and register my surroundings. I was standing next to a split rail fence. On the other side of the fence was a long stretch of patchy brown grass that led to my grandfather's house. Yes! I was back at Gramps's place!

But I wasn't. The yard didn't look the same as when I'd been there before. The colorful fall leaves were gone. The trees were bare gray skeletons that swayed in a frosty breeze, and the sky was a dark, cloudy ceiling that threatened to drop snow. It was like I had skipped through fall and landed in late November.

"Gramps!" I called out. My shout echoed across the empty property.

It was definitely Gramps's house but instead of gleaming bright white, it looked kind of puke yellow. I couldn't tell if it was because there was no sun or Gramps had somehow painted it since I'd been there last, which wasn't likely. I doubted that spirits bothered with home improvement projects.

I saw somebody dart from behind a tree and run behind Gramps's house. It was only a quick glimpse, but I could have sworn it was a little kid.

"Hey! Wait!" I screamed.

I was about to vault over the fence and go after the kid, when I heard the slam of a screen door. Not from Gramps's house, from the house next door. I turned to see that I was much closer to the next-door neighbor's house than I was to Gramps's place. I figured that whoever it was that had yanked me out of Damon's vision had gone inside, so I ran to the bottom of the porch stairs.

"Hey!" I yelled. "Who's in there?"

It didn't make sense that Damon and his centuries-old Macedonian soldiers would suddenly be holed up in a Connecticut farmhouse, though I wished they were. I was fired up and wanted a piece of somebody.

"Who are you?" I called. "Why did you bring me here?"

I saw movement through the window. Somebody was watching me from inside. I walked closer, expecting to see one of those strange people in black who were always lurking around.

Instead, I saw the face of a young girl.

"I see you!" I shouted. "Come out here!"

The girl crouched down, thinking she couldn't be seen.

"Either you come out or I'm coming in."

She left the window and appeared a few seconds later

inside the screen door. It was the same girl who was watching us when Gramps first brought me to his house. She wasn't a threat, or so I hoped.

"Somebody pulled me into this vision," I called. "Was it my grandfather?"

The girl didn't respond.

"Or that kid next door. Do you know who that is?"

She stared at me, blank, as if she didn't know who I was talking about. Or *what* I was talking about. Did she even know English?

"Are Damon's soldiers around?" I asked, glancing around the yard.

Still no response.

"Wait . . . was it you?"

She gave me a subtle nod.

"You pulled me back here? Why? *How?*" I said as I climbed the first stair.

She quickly backed off and started to close the door.

"No, wait! I'm not mad. I just don't get it."

She didn't close the door all the way and peered out through the crack. I stood on the bottom stair, not moving any higher for fear she'd slam the door and be gone for good.

"I'm Cooper Foley. My grandfather is the guy who lives next door. I mean, who used to live next door. Or . . . I don't know what I mean. What's your name?"

The girl looked like a frightened kitten with big brown eyes that watched my every move, waiting for me to do something that would prompt her to slam the door.

"I'm pretty confused," I said. "My gramps says you've been around for a while, so you must know how things work here. Right?"

She gave me a slight shrug.

"Okay, cool, I'll take that as a yes. Maybe you can tell

me why things look different. I mean, you saw me with Gramps, right?"

She nodded.

"So what happened? I mean, all the leaves were on the trees and now it's, like, almost winter. And my grandfather's house is a different color. That's . . . weird. Or maybe I'm the weird one. What do you think? Am I weird? I *feel* weird."

The girl smiled. I saw it. It wasn't a big smile but it was there. I was getting through to her.

"I wish you'd come out," I said. "I'm not going to hurt you."

She pushed the screen door open tentatively and I backed away so as not to intimidate her. She stepped outside but kept her back against the wall, ready to jump inside at the first hint of danger.

I'm guessing she was around my age. Her hair was dark and cut very short. The flowered dress went below her knees and she wore gray socks and brown shoes that looked like something a guy would wear . . . a guy from another time. She had on an old blue sweater that was open in front and at least two sizes too big for her. Seeing her up close like this, wearing such old-fashioned clothes, made me understand what was happening.

"Wait, you didn't live here when my grandfather did. In the Light, I mean."

She didn't react.

"I'm guessing you lived here a long time before that. Is this what the place looked like when you were alive? I mean, is this your vision in the Black?"

She nodded.

"Yeah!" I exclaimed, and punched the air in victory.

The girl frowned and inched away from me.

"Sorry, sorry. Didn't mean to go off like that. I'm totally normal. Usually."

She stopped moving, though she looked ready to bolt at the next sign of lunacy.

"I'm scaring you and I don't mean to," I said. "I'm just as scared as you are. No, I take that back, you look pretty scared. I hope it's not about me because I'm not a scary guy. At least I don't think I am."

She gave me another small smile. That was progress.

"Can you talk?" I asked. "I mean, are you able to speak? I'd love to know your name."

I was afraid that she was actually mute and our whole conversation would have to be about yes and no.

Finally, in a voice that was so soft I could barely hear it above the wind, she whispered, "Maggie."

"Maggie!" I exclaimed, making her jump again. Bad move. "Whoa, sorry. Maggie. Great name. Good to meet you. Sort of. This isn't the kind of place that it's good to meet anybody, right? I mean, we'd all just as soon not be here."

I was talking too fast. She looked confused.

"Sorry, my mouth's outpacing my brain. So . . . who are you? If you lived in the Light a long time before my gramps, then you've been here in the Black for a while. Why is it taking you so long to move on?"

She scowled and ran back into the house.

"No, wait!"

Too late. I had just asked her the all-time worst question possible. You don't meet somebody and immediately ask about what's wrong with them. Idiot.

"Maggie! Wait, I'm sorry! I'm a dope. Really. Everybody thinks so. I won't ask you any more stupid questions. I promise."

She peeked back out the door with those big, frightened eyes. It looked like she was on the verge of tears and I felt horrible about it. She looked so vulnerable and, yes, I'll say it, pretty.

"I'm sorry. This is all new to me. I'm very confused and I was hoping you could help me out a little. Can I come up and sit on the porch?"

She hesitated a second, then nodded.

"Great. Thanks."

There was an old wicker couch like Gramps's near the door. I climbed the stairs onto the porch and walked to the far end, where I sat down, trying to look as nonthreatening as possible.

The screen door squeaked open slowly and Maggie poked her head out.

"I won't move," I said, crossing my heart with my finger. "Promise."

She slipped out the door and slid down onto the far end of the couch, crushing her folded hands between her knees. The girl was fragile, but she wasn't weak. I knew that much from what she had done for me.

"I'd like to know why you pulled me out of that fight," I said. "Has Damon been bothering you too?"

She shook her head.

"Do you know Damon?"

She shook her head again. This seemed strange, but maybe not. From what I knew of the Black, billions of spirits passed through. There was no way that everybody could know everybody.

"But you pulled me out of that fight," I said. "How come?"

She glanced over to my grandfather's house. That was the connection.

"So after I saw you before, when I was with Gramps, you started to watch me?" I asked.

She shrugged and I saw her face flush red with embarrassment. It was as simple as that. She saw me and was curious. It wasn't the first time that had happened to me with a girl. Just sayin'.

"Well, thank you," I said.

She smiled. She had a sweet smile.

"But I could have taken that weasel," I added.

She frowned. She didn't agree and that was okay. The important thing was that I had made a friend, or at least I thought I had. As long as I didn't say the wrong thing and send her running off like a scared rabbit again, we'd be cool.

"I'm only beginning to learn about how things work in the Black," I said. "But I'm already in Trouble Town. That guy? Damon? He's not like the rest of the spirits here. At least that's what he tells me. He threatened to hurt my best friend who's still living in the Light."

Maggie looked at me and her expression turned dark.

I paused, debating about whether or not to keep going. I took the chance and said, "He'd do it, too. I'm here because Damon killed me."

Maggie winced, like the news physically hurt her.

"He went into the Light and somehow manipulated things that led to my getting killed. Nice guy, huh?"

"Why?" Maggie asked.

"Because he wants me to help him find something that belonged to him in life. Something called a poleax. It's still in the Light and he wants my friend Marsh and me to get it for him."

"Why does he want this . . . poleax?"

I laughed. I couldn't help it.

"Why is that funny?" she asked, hurt.

"It isn't. I'm just glad you're talking."

She blushed.

I continued, "He says he's stuck here in the Black and that weapon will somehow help him get out. Does that make sense to you?"

Maggie shook her head.

"Great," I said with frustration. "If you don't know how things work around here, then I don't stand a chance."

"So you don't want to help Damon?" she asked.

"No!" I shouted, a bit too loud, because it made her jump. "The guy killed me! I'd rather wring his neck. But what can I do? I don't want him hurting Marsh."

"Then you *will* help him?"

"I don't know," I said with exasperation. "I don't know anything. What I'd like to do is warn Marsh that he's in trouble, but I can't even do that."

She looked to the ground, lost in thought. I saw her lips twitch, like a nervous tick. This was a troubled girl and I wasn't making things any easier for her.

"Maybe you can," she finally said.

I sat bolt upright.

"Seriously? How? Damon said he was the only one who knew how to influence things in the Light."

"Some are better than others," she said. "But we all have the gift."

My heart started beating faster. "You're saying I can talk to Marsh? I can warn him about Damon?"

"Maybe," was her maddening answer.

"Have you ever done it? I mean, communicate with people in the Light?"

Maggie scowled, as if she wasn't sure if she should answer.

"Have you?" I asked again.

She nodded, reluctantly.

"That's great! Will you help me warn Marsh? Whoa, wait. We're talking about voices from beyond the grave. That'll freak him out."

"It won't be a voice," she said. "He may only sense a presence."

"No," I countered. "It's possible to do more than that. Damon whispered in his ear and Marsh heard it."

"Then Damon is as different as he says. I can't do that kind of thing."

"What *can* you do?"

Maggie looked me square in the eye and for the first time I sensed that there was more to her than a meek, frightened girl. I couldn't imagine what had been so wrong about her life that she had been kept in the Black for so long. I wanted to know all about her, but I had to take care of Marsh first.

She answered, "He can be made to understand that he isn't alone."

"O-kay," I said, skeptically. "I guess that's a start. Would you do it for me?"

Maggie took a deep breath and gave me a small smile. "I'll try."

"Awesome. Thank you. How does it work? What do we do?"

She stood up and turned her back to me. "Think of your friend," she said over her shoulder.

I closed my eyes and pictured Marsh. I saw his blond hair and brown eyes. In my head he wore a hoodie sweatshirt and jeans. He was building a model rocket at his kitchen table. His cat, Winston, was on the table next to him, watching.

"Got him," I said. "Now what?"

I opened my eyes to see that in front of Maggie, the colorful fog had appeared.

She turned back to me and winked. "Now we pay him a visit."

I liked Maggie.

She took a step into the fog . . . and disappeared. I leaped after her, jumped into the swirl of color, and landed in Marsh's bedroom.

Maggie was already there, standing at the foot of his bed, looking down on a sleeping Marsh. It was daytime.

Sunlight streamed in through his bedroom window. When I had been in the Light with Damon it was night. How long ago was that? A few minutes? A couple of hours? A hundred years? I kept hearing that time had no meaning in the Black, and that looked to be true, at least in how it corresponded with the Light. Passage of time in the two dimensions wasn't necessarily relative.

"It's going to take a while to get used to this," I said, stunned.

"Is that him?"

"That's the guy," I said. "Yo! Ralph. Rise and shine!"

He didn't move.

Maggie rounded the bed and knelt down next to Marsh's head. She looked at my sleeping friend with a sad smile. Did she feel sorry for him? Did she think he was vulnerable and cute? Did she miss being in the Light?

Seeing Marsh gave me mixed feelings. It was good to see my friend, but the last time we were together we'd had a blowout fight that was mostly my fault. I'll always regret that because I'll never get the chance to tell him how sorry I was. More than that, I didn't want to be dead. I wanted my old life back. I had to force those thoughts away. Why sweat over something that could never be?

Maggie barely moved. She kept looking at Marsh, concentrating. After a few seconds she closed her eyes and started breathing deeper. It seemed like she was going into some kind of trance.

"What are you doing?" I asked.

My answer came in the form of rippling color. All around her the air began to move and shimmer. It wasn't dramatic like when we moved from place to place. It was barely perceptible but it was there and Maggie was causing it. The aberration, or whatever it was, grew around her until it enveloped Marsh too. Finally, Maggie leaned down, pursed her lips, and without opening her eyes she gently blew air at Marsh's face.

Marsh's hair moved.

It was subtle, but it moved, and it woke him up. He smiled as if he was having a great dream as he brushed the hair out of his eyes.

"You did it!" I exclaimed.

My spontaneous outburst broke the spell . . . or whatever it was. Maggie stood and backed away into the swirling fog that appeared behind her. I jumped right after her and a second later we were back on her porch in the Black. She sat down on the couch as if the effort had taken a lot out of her. I felt like an idiot for disrupting the whole thing, but was way more excited about having made contact with Marsh.

"How did you do that?" I asked.

"The stronger your connection is with the person in the Light, the less difficult it is. It's about focusing your thoughts and energy."

"Who taught you that?" I asked.

Maggie shrugged. "I've made friends across many visions."

"Well, it was awesome! We could like . . . like . . . write stuff on one of his sketch pads to tell him what's going on. Or maybe even whisper stuff to him. This is great."

"It's not like that," Maggie said. "I'm barely able to move a little air."

Instantaneous deflation. How was I supposed to warn Marsh that he was in trouble if all I could do was get Maggie to blow a little breath across his forehead? I fell down onto the couch, defeated.

Maggie said, "If you could talk to him, what would you say?"

"He should know I'm looking out for him and that if things start getting scary, he isn't alone."

"What about his family?" she asked.

"It's only him and his father. His dad is a good guy but he isn't around a lot. Marsh is going to need more coverage than that."

"Do you have a family?"

"Yeah. So?"

"You could try to send your friend to them."

That made me laugh. "Yeah, right. My dysfunctional family wouldn't be any help."

"But it might help him understand that you are part of what is happening to him. That would be a beginning."

"I don't know, maybe. But it's not like a breath of air can do that."

Maggie jumped up and went into her house. I thought maybe I had scared her off again but a couple of seconds later she came back with a piece of paper and a big old-fashioned number two pencil.

"Draw something that will connect Marsh to you," she commanded. "To your family."

"Uh . . . what?"

"Draw something that will send him to your family looking for answers. Something simple."

I didn't know what she was planning to do but didn't have any better ideas. What could I draw that would make Marsh think of my family? The answer wasn't obvious . . . until I thought of it. I took the pencil and drew a symbol. It was a cluster of three swirls.

Maggie examined it closely and gave me a questioning look.

"It's a tattoo my sister just got," I said.

"Your sister has a tattoo?" she asked, incredulous.

"Yeah, she's a piece of work."

"I didn't know girls got tattoos."

"Maybe not in your time. When did you, uh . . . Man, I can't believe I'm asking this but . . . when did you die?"

Maggie's expression turned dark. She folded her arms across her chest and she sat back on the couch. I saw her glance over my shoulder at something. It was quick, as if she did it unconsciously. I looked to where she had glanced to see a barn that was about thirty yards from her house. My first thought was that maybe she had died in there. My *second* thought was that I had yet again asked an incredibly insensitive question.

"I'm sorry," I said. "I promised not to ask any more dumb questions. It's just that the tattoo thing made me remember we came from different times and I wasn't being nosy or anything. I was just interested in when you died—*lived*. I meant lived. That's all. I'll shut up now."

Wow. Could I have been any clumsier? She stared at the ground for a few seconds, then jumped to her feet and started for her door.

"Maggie, don't leave!" I called.

She stopped short, but not because of me.

Someone was standing on Gramps's property, watching us. I stood up to see another one of those odd people wearing dark clothes with their hands folded in front of them. It was a woman who looked like somebody my mom would hang out with. There was nothing strange about her at all, except that she came out of nowhere and was quietly observing us.

I saw another person inside the house, watching us from behind pulled curtains. It looked like it might have been a young kid, but I couldn't tell for sure, and as soon as we made eye contact, the curtains dropped.

"Come inside," Maggie said, and went for the door.

I followed her inside and she quickly closed the door behind me.

"Who are those people?" I asked. "They're all over the place."

"I call them Watchers," she said, and walked farther into the house.

The place looked like it had been decorated by some-body's grandmother. The furniture was heavy and dark. The lamps had flowered shades that matched the curtains. It was totally old-fashioned but that made sense. Maggie had probably lived there when that stuff was in style. I wasn't about to ask her when that was. No way. Lesson learned.

A fire crackled in the fireplace, making the place warm and inviting. Maggie went right to it and sat down on a rug. Though she was my age, seeing her plop down so easily made her seem more like a little girl. I took a chance and sat next to her.

"Who are the Watchers?" I asked.

Maggie stared into the fire, her mind a million miles away.

"Spirits," she finally said. "But not like us. They never speak to anyone and you never know when they might appear."

"What's their deal?" I asked.

Maggie kept her eyes on the flames. "They are the ones who decide when we are ready to move on."

"You mean like judges? They're out there keeping score?"

She nodded.

"Wow. So they could be your best friend or . . . not."

"I hide when I see them," she said absently.

I didn't ask her why. If the Watchers hadn't sent her on, then they obviously didn't like what they saw. I couldn't imagine why. Maggie was the sweetest, most innocent . . . *ghost* I'd ever met. Sheesh.

"Would they help me?" I asked. "What if I told them about what Damon was doing?"

She shook her head. "When spirits try to speak with them, they vanish."

"So we're on our own here."

Maggie was still clutching the sketch of Sydney's tattoo. I reached forward and gently took it from her.

"Then, would *you* help me?"

Her eyes were glistening, on the verge of tears. I couldn't imagine what was going through her head and didn't dare ask.

"We aren't supposed to interfere with the Light," she said. "I may have already done too much."

My heart sank. She was right. At least based on what Gramps told me. It was looking as if all those stories about people being haunted or getting contacted from the great beyond might actually be true. I'd seen proof. But were those spirits guilty of interfering with the Light? Did the Watchers, or whatever they were called, make those spirits pay by keeping them from moving on to their next existence? What exactly was the penalty for messing with the Light?

"Damon's been causing a lot of trouble in the Light," I said. "If that's so wrong, maybe we'd be doing a good thing by trying to stop him."

She gently took back the sketch of the tattoo. "Maybe," she said, and took my hand. "Or maybe it doesn't matter because it's already too late for me."

Before I had a chance to ask her what she meant by that ominous comment, she pulled me to my feet. The swirling fog returned and by the time we were upright, we were standing in Marsh's kitchen. In the Light. I still wasn't used to jumping between dimensions and it took me a few seconds to stop my head from spinning.

It was a sunny morning with light streaming in through the window over the sink. It might have only been a few minutes since we had been there before. Or not. I'd spent a lot of time in that kitchen, mostly raiding the Seavers' pantry for snacks. Marsh sat on a stool at the island in the middle of the room eating breakfast. Raw Pop-Tarts and chocolate milk. His mom used to hate it when he ate like that. He never told her I was the one who introduced him to that particular breakfast of champions. Seeing him made me laugh, and my heart ache.

I wondered where his father was, then remembered he was planning a business trip to Las Vegas. Mr. Seaver never had to worry about leaving Marsh on his own. Marsh was too responsible of a guy to get into any trouble.

"He's alone," I said to Maggie.

"I see that."

"No, I mean he's all alone. His father is out of town. There's nobody around to help him if things go south. We've got to make this work."

She held up the sketch and examined it, as if memorizing the design.

"What are you going to do?" I asked.

"I don't know yet."

She glanced around the kitchen, then stood behind Marsh, gazing over his shoulder.

"Ovaltine," she said, thinking out loud.

On the counter in front of Marsh was an open container of the chocolate drink mix.

"Are you sure he can't sense that we're here?" I asked.

"Some people can, but your friend doesn't seem to be one of them."

I got right up next to him and screamed, *"Raaaaaalph!"*

The only person who jumped was Maggie.

"Sorry," I said.

"If you want him to feel our presence, we have to use our spirit to manipulate the Light."

"Like when you blew on his hair?" I asked.

Suddenly Marsh's cat, Winston, jumped up onto the counter.

"Whoa!" I shouted in surprise and backed off. Some ghost I was.

Marsh was startled too . . .

. . . but Maggie stayed focused and reacted instantly. She leaned forward and the same swirling haze I saw when she blew on Marsh's forehead appeared in front of her. She let out a quick, sharp breath aimed at Winston, and Winston reacted. The cat jumped to the side . . . and knocked over the can of Ovaltine, spreading chocolate powder all over the white counter.

"Whoa!" Marsh cried. "Winston!" he yelled angrily, but the cat was already long gone, probably terrified and confused after her brief encounter with the spirit world.

"That was great!" I shouted. "How did you do that?"

"We can create movement in the air, like a ripple of energy. That's about all I can do."

"Damon could do a lot more than that," I pointed out.

"I'm not Damon," she shot back. Blunt.

I was right about Maggie. She wasn't as meek as she seemed.

As Marsh got up and went to the sink to get stuff to clean up the mess, Maggie moved in. She leaned directly over the pile of spilled powder with her nose just above the mess. Her eyes were closed and her forehead was creased in concentration. Whatever she was trying to do with the powder it would have to be fast because Marsh had gotten the trash can and a sponge, ready to wipe it up.

"Hurry," I said.

"Shh!" Maggie chastised.

Marsh stopped moving. It was like he had sensed something. Was it Maggie's "Shh"? He put the garbage pail down and left the kitchen. I went with him. I didn't want him taking off before Maggie did whatever it was she was trying to do.

"Ralph," I called to him. "Ralph. Don't go anywhere. C'mon, man. Don't leave."

He didn't hear a word. I followed him into the living room, where he checked the thermostat. That was classic Marsh. He figured there had to be a scientific explanation for what had happened. The idea that two spirits were lurking around and moving energy fields around would never have entered his mind.

Which raised a question: Did he even know I was dead? Seemed to me like he was going about life, business as usual. He'd be one of the first people my family told about my dying but he didn't look upset or anything. And that raised still another question: Did my family even know I was dead? I'd been all alone out on that lake. Was it possible that nobody even knew what had happened?

I didn't have time to stress about it because Marsh was headed back to the kitchen.

"Excellent, dude, keep moving!" I coaxed, hoping that somehow my words would seep into his brain.

He pushed through the swinging door and went back for the sink. I, on the other hand, focused on Maggie. A colorful rippling cloud had formed between her face and the chocolate powder on the counter. I stood beside her without saying a word for fear of breaking the spell, or whatever it was. Maggie's eyes were scrunched tight and her head seemed to shake from concentration.

Marsh grabbed the cleaning supplies and moved to the counter to start wiping up the mess, when he stopped short. We stood on either side of Maggie, though Marsh had no idea that he wasn't alone. His eyes grew wide and when I looked to the counter, I saw why.

The powder was moving. It was subtle at first, as if a faint breeze was brushing it around, but even a faint breeze would have made no sense to Marsh. The windows were closed. The heater fan wasn't on. He was seeing something impossible.

The breeze grew stronger, blowing the fine powder across the counter. Most of it spread out across the white tiles but some of it remained where it had spilled. The more powder that blew away, the more was revealed of the pattern that Maggie was creating.

It was the triple swirl. Sydney's tattoo.

Bang! Bang! Bang!

Marsh jumped. I did too. I might be a ghost but I could still be surprised. Somebody was at the front door. Maggie kept concentrating, working to complete the triple swirl. Marsh looked terrified, which made no sense. How could he be more scared about somebody at the door than by an impossible phenomenon happening in his kitchen?

Ding-dong.

The doorbell. Marsh took one last glance at the chocolate pattern, then ran back for the sink. From underneath he pulled out a small fire extinguisher. What was up with that? There wasn't any fire. He held the metal cylinder in one hand as if to use it as a weapon. Why was he so frightened about somebody at the door? He ran out of the kitchen and I was about to follow him when another swirling cloud of color appeared on the far side of the island from us.

"Maggie?" I called.

From out of the cloud came a shadow . . . a big shadow. It moved from the cloud of color and pushed across the counter like an oncoming storm that totally messed up the message Maggie had painstakingly created.

And it didn't stop. The dark shadow hit me, hard, knocking me off my feet and onto my back.

When I landed, I looked up to see I was staring directly into Damon's angry eyes.

8

"Is that your response?" he barked, spraying spit into my eyes. "Do you truly believe you can protect him from me?"

I was pinned on my back with Damon's knee on my chest. He may not have been much of a fighter, but he was heavy. And strong.

"He's my friend," was all I could say.

"He is beyond your help," he spat through his sharp teeth.

He jumped off me and bounced to his feet while brushing himself off.

I tentatively stood up and looked around to see that he had knocked me out of the Light and straight back to his vision in the Black. We were on a rocky ledge, high above the village where I had first met him. Below us was the square with the statue and the fountain. *Far* below us.

"While you struggle to move dust, I have the power to alter the course of human lives," he snarled. "No pathetic warning from you can prevent me from doing whatever I wish in the Light."

"Then what do you need *me* for?"

He glared at me through coal black eyes. I can't say for sure what crazy looks like, but I'd guess this guy came close.

"Do not challenge me," he said, pointing his finger at my head.

I forced a cocky smile and said, "If you think you can scare me, you aren't as smart as you think you are."

As he stared at me, his upper body started to shudder. At first I thought he was about to erupt with anger, but quickly realized he was actually stifling a laugh.

"Then, let's see," he said, and launched himself at me.

It happened so fast, I had no time to react. With two quick steps he hit me square in the chest, wrapped his arms around me, and drove us both toward the edge. I tried to dig my heels in but it was too late. We both went over.

I screamed.

His black eyes were locked on mine as we plummeted to the ground.

"I know exactly what frightens you," he said above the howl of rushing wind.

He laughed, I think. I couldn't be sure because I was out of my mind. I twisted away from him and looked down to see the ground rushing closer. I may have been dead but I didn't want to know what it would feel like to fall twenty stories and land on jagged rocks. All I could do was close my eyes and brace for impact.

A moment later I landed. It was rude, but not the violent, bone-jarring slam I expected. I hit solid ground and lay there, wondering what had happened. I wasn't in pain. I wasn't even outside. I opened my eyes to see I was staring at a man-made floor. I had been transported from the ancient village of Damon's Black to a modern building.

"It's good to be a ghost," I said to myself.

Lifting my chin, I came face-to-face with a cat. A regular old cat. It sat with its tail curled around its paws, staring at me. Or through me. The thing didn't budge so I wasn't sure if it knew I was there. Once my brain stopped jangling, I focused and realized it wasn't just any old cat. It was Marsh's.

"Winston?" I called out tentatively.

The cat didn't react.

"Winny?" came a guy's voice. "C'mere."

I spun to see Marsh walking slowly toward me. Or toward the cat. I was back in the Light. After a quick glance around I realized I had fallen into a hallway at Davis Gregory, our school. Damon was gone. Somewhere between here and there, he had bailed.

It was summer vacation so the school was empty and dark.

I watched as Marshall continued to try and catch up, and Winston kept evading him.

"Stay there . . . that's good . . . don't move . . . good kitty," Marsh cajoled, walking slowly, trying not to scare the cat off.

"Ralph! Do you see me?" I shouted, jumping to my feet.

Why was he at school during summer vacation? Alone? With his cat? How much time had passed since the Ovaltine incident? Just as important, why was *I* there? What was it that Damon said? *"I know exactly what frightens you."*

That couldn't be good.

Winston jumped to her feet and scampered off.

Marsh ran after her. I hurried right along with him. "Ralph, dude, listen. Try to hear me. You're in Trouble Town. You gotta get help."

Of course, he didn't hear a thing. I was a ghost. A useless freakin' ghost.

Winston ran for the door leading to the guys' locker room. What was that cat doing at school? It didn't make sense. There was nothing right about this.

"Ralph! C'mon, man!" I screamed. It was a waste of energy. I never felt more helpless in my life. Or in my death.

The locker room door was open slightly and Winston ran in. Marsh wasn't far behind. I was set to follow them both inside, when somebody grabbed my hand, stopping me.

I think I yelped in surprise as I turned to see that the person who grabbed me . . . was Maggie.

"Hold my hand," she commanded.

She closed her eyes and concentrated, the same way she had in Marsh's kitchen. I felt a tingle, as if a slight electric current was moving through us both. Before I could question what was happening, the door to the locker room closed and the door next to it, a door that led outside, blew open.

Marsh stopped. He was almost as shocked as I was.

Almost.

"Was that you?" I asked Maggie.

She nodded. Marsh hesitated, looking at the door as if he were debating about whether or not to go outside.

"Get outta here, Ralph!" I shouted. "Go home."

He didn't listen. He didn't hear. He turned away from his chance to escape and followed the cat inside the locker room.

"How did you do that?" I asked Maggie.

"You have a connection with Marsh," she explained. "That helped."

I wanted to know everything about what she had done, but there wasn't time.

"Something bad is gonna happen," I said. "I know it. Can we warn him?"

Maggie shrugged. There was nothing else to do but

follow Marsh and hope that I was wrong. We ran into the locker room but Marsh wasn't there.

"Ralph?" I called. No answer, of course. I looked to Maggie and shrugged.

Maggie wasn't looking at me. She was focused on something behind me, and whatever it was, wasn't good. Her eyes went wide as she backed away.

"Who is that?" she asked, her voice cracking with fear.

I whipped around quickly to see something that probably would have scared me to death . . . if I wasn't already dead.

Standing inside the locker room door was a tall character dressed all in black with a wide-brimmed black hat and a skeletal face.

Gravedigger.

"No way," was all I managed to say.

Gravedigger was a graphic novel character that Marsh had created. It was a skeletal horror-story demon that had somehow jumped out of his imagination and was now standing in front of us. For real. His face was pasty white with skin that barely covered the contours of his skull. His eyes were sunken sockets. On his shoulder was a gleaming silver pick, like you use to dig out rocks. The character was about as frightening as anything I'd ever seen drawn on paper, and here he was standing in the locker room in the flesh, or whatever it was that apparitions were made of.

Gravedigger floated forward, his feet a few inches off the floor. As he moved past us, his head slowly turned in our direction and he broke into a wide, hideous grin.

"What is that?" Maggie asked with a nervous hitch in her voice.

"It's a character Marsh created," I said, barely whispering. "It isn't real. At least I don't think it is."

Gravedigger floated past the rows of lockers and continued on into the large shower room.

"It looked pretty real to me," Maggie countered. "But it must be a spirit because it saw us."

I grabbed Maggie's hand and we ran through the locker room after Gravedigger. We jumped into the shower room to see that a door was open on the far side. I'd taken hundreds of showers there and had no idea a door existed, but it was the *least* weird thing I'd seen so I didn't stop to question. I pulled Maggie through the tiled shower, through the door, and into a large room that was just as surprising and impossible to me as the secret door was.

It was a long-abandoned gym. Desks were piled everywhere, along with outdated gymnastics apparatus and dusty cardboard boxes. I would have been fascinated by the discovery if not for the drama that was playing out there.

Marsh was on the far side of the gym, facing back toward the shower. Toward Gravedigger. The dark specter was directly in front of us, blocking Marsh's path back to the shower.

Marsh looked frozen with fear, his eyes like headlights.

"He sees it," I said. "He sees Gravedigger."

"That's impossible. The living can't see spirits."

"It's not a spirit," I said. "It's gotta be something Damon conjured to scare Marsh."

"Why?"

"To prove that he can."

I couldn't imagine what was going through Marsh's head. Coming face-to-face with a creation from your imagination had to be mind-numbing.

"Try to tell him!" I screamed at Maggie.

"Tell him what?" she asked, backing away from me. I had scared her again.

"Tell him it's just an illusion."

"I can't," she whimpered.

It was too late anyway. Marsh wanted no part of Grave-digger. The vision blocked his escape route so he tried to jump over a pile of furniture. He didn't make it and knocked over a tall stack of chairs that tumbled down all around him.

I went for Gravedigger. His back was to me and I drove into him from behind, trying to tackle him. But the instant I hit him, he disappeared. Or maybe he was never there.

"Cooper!" Maggie called, pointing up to the ceiling.

Four thick climbing ropes that hung from the ceiling had suddenly come alive. Like angry snakes they snapped and whipped through the air until one of them caught the top edge of a stack of tall window frames that was lean-ing against the overhead running track. The rope tightened, pulling the windows over.

I looked at the floor to see that Marsh was directly under the path of the falling windows. He was on his back, staring up at the looming danger, not moving. Either he was in shock or his mind wouldn't accept what was happening.

"Ralph!" I screamed. "Get out of there!"

I ran to the heavy stack of windows and tried to push them back. Waste of time. I moved right through the solid glass panes. I was a spirit. Worse than that, it meant the windows weren't an illusion.

"Help him!" I screamed to Maggie.

There was nothing she could do. The stack of windows had reached center and was on the way down . . . directly over Marsh. I focused on my friend, willing him to snap out of it and move.

He didn't.

The windows were picking up speed.

In desperation I got down on my knees, leaned in close to him, and whispered. "Move."

Marsh sprang off the floor. With his arms out in front of him, he launched himself over a stack of chairs and got out from under the falling windows the instant before they hit the floor. The glass exploded into a shower of sharp projectiles. Marsh got pelted, but he was okay. I looked around quickly to see if anything else was about to tumble on him, but the room had lost its energy.

Gravedigger was gone. Winston was gone. The ropes hung lifelessly.

Damon had completed his demonstration. He had done exactly what he wanted to do. He proved that he could hurt Marsh, and scare me.

Maggie ran to Marsh. I thought she was going to see if he was okay, but that was ridiculous. There was nothing she could do. At least that's what I thought. She knelt down in front of him and stared at the floor. The ripple of color appeared around her head, just as I'd seen back in Marsh's kitchen. Maggie's eyes were closed, her concentration intense.

"Hold my hand," she commanded.

I knelt next to her and grabbed her hand, hoping to provide any small bit of psychic energy. I heard the faint crackling of glass and looked up, afraid that something else might be flying in to hurt Marsh.

"It's okay," Maggie assured me.

I looked to the floor to see thousands of shimmering bits of shattered glass spread across the floor between us and Marsh.

Marsh must have heard the crackling sound too because he slowly looked up. His eyes were huge and his breathing hard. He glanced around the old gym, looking for signs of danger. Or for Gravedigger.

"Concentrate," Maggie commanded.

"On what?"

"On Marsh."

I focused on my friend. What was he thinking? Did he have any idea why this craziness was swirling around him?

I heard more crackling and looked to see that the glass on the floor was moving. Like thousands of tiny ants, the shimmering bits shifted and jumped. As she had in Marsh's kitchen, Maggie saw an opportunity and went for it. I realized what she was doing so I closed my eyes and visualized the triple swirl design of my sister's tattoo.

It's me, Ralph, I thought, willing my thoughts to reach him. *I'm here for you. I'm right here.*

I heard the faint crackling sound of the glass pieces moving over one another but didn't dare open my eyes. I kept the vision of the tattoo in my head while repeating over and over, "It's me, Ralph. It's me."

"Look," Maggie said.

I opened my eyes to see that the tiny pieces of glass had formed the triple swirl.

"Amazing," I said in awe.

Marsh saw it too and stared with wide eyes. Where I saw a miracle, he saw the impossible. He backed away as if the symbol was about to go nuclear. He scrambled to his feet, nearly tripped over a desk, and sprinted out of the gym.

"Hopefully that'll send him to Sydney," I said.

"And then what?"

"I don't know."

"Damon scares me," Maggie said. "Maybe you should do what he wants."

"Can't."

"Why not?"

"Because he killed me. That kind of pisses me off."

"Is that it? You want to get even?"

"Yeah, I do."

"Even if that means he'll keep haunting your friend?"

I was about to answer quickly, but the reality of the situation hit me hard. Of course I didn't want Damon haunting Marsh, but at what price? Giving in and helping the guy who murdered me?

"Death shouldn't be this complicated," I said with frustration.

Maggie shrugged. "So, what are you going to do?"

"I wish I knew," was all I could answer.

9

I had to take control.

Up until then, each time I had moved through the Black or the Light it was with another spirit. They had called the shots and I went along for the ride, whether I wanted to or not. It was time to start getting around on my own.

"You can go wherever you want," Maggie explained. "And you can enter anybody's vision, so long as they allow it. Close your eyes and think of the spirit, or a place you want to be."

"Just like that?" I asked.

She shrugged as if it were the simplest thing possible. I closed my eyes, got a mental image of where I wanted to be, took Maggie's hand, and stepped through the colorful fog that appeared before us.

When we stepped out, I saw that Gramps was sitting in the wicker rocker on his porch, right where I had left him.

"Hey! Where you been?" he called.

Maggie let go of my hand and ran toward her own house, acting as frightened as when I had first met her.

"Hey, where are you going?"

She didn't answer. Or stop.

"He doesn't bite!" I called.

Maggie sprinted past the fence and directly into her house, slamming the door behind her.

"Bye," I said, though she couldn't have heard it. "Thanks."

I climbed up the stairs onto the porch, expecting Gramps to make some wisecrack about her running away, but he stared straight ahead, acting like it didn't happen.

"That was strange," I said.

Gramps shrugged.

"You don't know anything about her?" I asked.

He gave a quick, uncomfortable look to Maggie's house.

"I know you should avoid her," he answered.

"What? Why?"

"Everybody's here for different reasons, Coop, but they're all working on the same thing. They're trying to better themselves so they can move on. I suggest you worry more about yourself and not get your head turned by some pretty thing who has a bundle of her own problems."

"She was trying to help me."

"Was she? Or was she helping herself?"

"Who cares? Maybe we're helping each other."

"Maybe. What did she do for you?"

I told Gramps about Damon. About his quest for a weapon that was still in the Light and how he needed Marsh and me to find it for him. I told him about Damon's ability to create visions and the black sword that could end a spirit's existence. And finally, I told him how Damon had threatened to kill Marsh if I didn't help him and how I believed he was serious because he had already killed someone. Me.

Gramps listened to my story without interrupting or asking for details. When I was done, I expected him to say something clever, or make fun of me or tell me it all sounded like some big joke. Instead, he stared off into the distance, looking troubled.

"A spirit from the Black caused your death," he said softly, shaking his head. "Now I've heard it all."

"Help me out here, Gramps. What am I supposed to do?"

He scratched his head, frowning. "As outlandish as your story sounds, some of it is all too familiar."

"Familiar? It's normal to be murdered by a centuries-old psychopath?"

"No," he replied. "But like I said, the spirits here are all looking for a way to move on. We don't all come from the same time or place. Doesn't matter if your time in the Light was spent in ancient China or Dickens's London or puttin' on a Cheesehead and rooting for the Packers, we're all in the same boat."

"That's why we can understand one another's languages?" I asked.

"I s'pose. I don't know all the mechanics. But I do know that as much as everybody here is all about trying to punch their ticket out, we're still the same people we were in life. If you were a foul ball in the Light, you're still one here. If you were an honest Joe, you will be here too. That's the whole point. We're all trying to make up for whatever wrongs we did in life, which is why some are here longer than others. And why some spirits aren't above using others to get what they want, like this Damon character."

"Yeah, tell me about it," I said with a snicker. "But this is more than just some dirtball trying to make up for being a creep in life. He can mess with the living. I'm proof of that. The guy killed me. Does that happen a lot?"

"No. At least not that I know of. That's why you can't have anything more to do with him."

"Fine by me, but it's not like I have a choice."

"You always have a choice," Gramps said, dead seriously. "That's what the Black is all about."

"Then what about Marsh?"

"Forget him," Gramps answered coldly.

That didn't sound like Gramps. I didn't know how to react.

"You can't mean that," I finally said.

"I absolutely mean it," he said quickly. "Come here."

Gramps rocked to his feet and walked to the end of the porch, where he pointed to Maggie's house.

"See them jokers?" he asked.

Two people in black were standing by the split rail fence, looking our way.

"Maggie calls them Watchers," I said.

"I don't know what they're called but they are definitely watching. Everything. Everybody. Those spirits hold your future in their hands. Mine too. And the future of that Damon character and every other soul in the Black. You don't want to do anything to make them question you."

"But how can protecting a friend be wrong?"

"Because it's meddling with the Light!" Gramps shouted so sharply, it made me jump. Gramps had never raised his voice to me, even when I was being a jerk.

"What happens back there isn't our concern," he added. "Not anymore. You can go back and watch things if you're feeling lonely, but that's it. Let me say that again, Cooper. *That's it!* We all had our time there and now it's done. If you try to influence things, they'll see what you're doing and you'll be stuck in the Black for a good long time. Or worse."

"There's something worse?"

Gramps took a tired breath and walked back to the rocker. He seemed like a very old man. Older than I remembered him to be. He sat down but I leaned on the rail. I was too wired to sit.

"We're all on the Morpheus Road, Cooper. We all make the journey. It begins in the Light, with life, then moves straight on through the Black. What you do here determines your next stop."

"Yeah, you said that. Next stop is heaven, or whatever the next best place is."

"That's one route," Gramps said gravely. "There's another. There's no time limit on getting through the Black, so long as you keep moving along the right way. Or try to, anyway. Not all spirits try. Or care."

"What happens to them?"

"There's another destination. If you call one way heaven, I guess you'd call the other way hell. It's as good a name as any. I've heard it called something else."

"What's that?"

Gramps fixed his eyes on me and said, "The Blood."

It didn't sound like a place you'd want to visit.

"It's the last stop for the lost souls. The irredeemable. Those spirits watching us? They're the judges. They don't interfere, they don't offer advice or guidance. They just watch . . . and decide. The future of every last soul in the Black is in their hands. It's always been that way. Do not give them reason to decide you're better suited for the Blood."

"So, what are you saying? I'm supposed to let Damon hurt Marsh?"

"If that's what he wants to do, yes," Gramps snapped. "That's his business, not yours."

"But that's just wrong."

He leaned forward and looked me square in the eyes. "Look, Cooper, I believe everything you told me. There's been trouble brewing here since before you arrived. Most everybody's felt it. It's like things are a bit . . . off, though nobody has any idea what it might be. I never heard of this Damon character but from what you say it sounds like he's been interfering with the Light in ways nobody else can. Maybe he's the one that's causing the tension."

"So why hasn't he been sent to the Blood?"

"No idea. He told you something was keeping him here in the Black? Maybe that's true and he can't go anywhere . . . good or bad."

"So how does he have so much power in the Light? I mean, Maggie moved some little things around but he was able to—"

Gramps jumped to his feet. "She *what*?"

Uh-oh. His face got so red, I'd say he was in danger of a heart attack . . . if he hadn't already had one that killed him.

"It was no big deal," I said quickly. "I just wanted to let Marsh know he wasn't alone."

"But he *is* alone! Haven't you been listening? You can't do anything to help him."

"You're wrong, Gramps. I think I can."

"But you shouldn't! If you start monkeying with the living and those Watchers catch wind of it, the fix you're in now will seem like a picnic."

"So what's my other choice? Help Damon? What happens then? I've seen what he can do, Gramps. If getting that poleax thing is going to give him even more power, blowing some air around in the Light is going to seem like a joke compared to what he might do. You think those Watchers will cut me slack for not warning Marsh, while I helped a devil wreak havoc? That doesn't make sense."

"You've got another choice," Gramps said calmly.

"Tell me. Please."

"Don't do anything."

"And what happens when Damon comes after me?"

"He can't if you don't want him to. We have control over

our visions. You can decide who comes into yours and who doesn't. If you don't want Damon to bother you, he won't. He can't. It's just that simple. Keep your head down, mind your own business, and you'll be safe."

"But Marsh won't be," I argued.

"Forget Marsh!" Gramps yelled. "I'm sorry, Cooper. I liked that kid too, but there's nothing you can do. And that's not your fault. I lived to a ripe old age because I didn't go sticking my nose into business that didn't concern me. I always took care of number one, and that's what you should do too."

I thought hard about what Gramps had said. The idea that I could block out Damon and not deal with him was definitely tempting.

"I hear you, Gramps," I said. "And I know you're trying to help me, but maybe your decision to only look out for number one wasn't so smart."

He shot me a surprised look. "And how's that?"

"Maybe it's the reason you're still stuck in the Black."

I couldn't believe I actually said that to my grandfather, but it was how I felt. Gramps stiffened, ready to argue. He opened his mouth to fire something back at me, but nothing came out.

"I'm sorry," I said.

"I love you, Cooper. I hate that you're going through this. Heck, I hate that you're here at all. But it is what it is. You're a smart kid. I know you'll do the right thing."

"I'm not as smart as you think."

"Go home, Cooper. Think about what I said."

"Home? What home?"

"To your vision in the Black. You can go to your house in Stony Brook. I'll come check up on you from time to time, and I'm here if you need me."

I nodded and turned to head off the porch.

I saw that Maggie had come out of her house and was

standing on her porch, watching us. Gramps joined me and put a hand on my shoulder.

"You have to understand," he said. "Everybody here is out for themselves. Not just that Damon fella. Everybody needs fixing and the kind of person they are determines what they're willing to do to get out of here."

I looked to Maggie. "Even her?"

"Yes, even her," Gramps said. "Maybe more so than most. You'd be smart to avoid that one."

"Why? She's just a scared girl."

"True," Gramps said with a sigh. "But that scared little girl has been here for quite some time."

"Do you know why?"

"I do," Gramps answered, and fell silent.

I waited for him to continue, but he didn't.

"Well, are you going to tell me?" I asked impatiently.

"Not if you're giving me a choice."

"I'm not. Why has she been here so long?"

Gramps hesitated and then said, "They say she killed her parents, Coop."

I felt as if the porch had moved under my feet. That's how jarring the news was. I looked to Maggie, who must have sensed that something was wrong because she hurried back into her house.

Gramps added, "You'd think she'd have gone straight to the Blood, but she's been here for at least as long as I have."

"I . . . I'm going to go," I said.

I gave Gramps a quick hug and stepped off the porch.

"I miss you, Coop. Don't be a stranger."

The colorful mist appeared in front of me and I stepped into it. But I didn't go to my home in the Black. I couldn't imagine going there. What would I do in an empty house? Being there without my parents would be wrong, no matter how familiar it was. I couldn't even imagine being there without Sydney the Sinister. No, I needed to be somewhere sane. I needed to go to my *real* home.

I stepped out of the cloud and walked into my backyard in the Light . . . just in time to hear a familiar sound.

"Let him go!"

It was Sydney. Inside the house. Yelling. As usual. I was home.

But this sounded more serious.

"You want to mess with me?" I heard a guy shout from inside. Angrily.

This was definitely more serious than usual. A second later the back door flew open and Marsh came flying out. He stumbled down the stairs and landed in the grass. Behind him was Mikey Russo, Sydney's idiot boyfriend.

This was bad news. Did Marsh confront Mikey about the fake tickets? I ran up and got in Mikey's face.

"Stop right there," I warned.

He walked right through me. Literally. Like I wasn't there. Or a ghost.

Sydney burst out of the door.

"Mikey, stop!" she yelled.

He ignored her and stalked down the stairs toward Marsh. I'd seen guys worked up like this before. He was going to hurt my friend. Marsh lay on the ground, looking up, helpless. I hoped that he'd at least jump up and throw a punch, but there was no chance of that. I forced myself to watch. Marsh deserved that much.

But Mikey stopped. His body tensed as he looked past Marsh into our backyard. Something had caught his eye.

I looked to see three huge dogs standing on the edge of the property. I couldn't even say what breed. Rottweilers? Dobermans? Whatever they were they were breathing hard with open mouths showing very large teeth. They were on edge, ready to pounce.

Mikey looked at them, then back to Marsh, who cautiously stood up. Mikey took one step toward Marsh . . . and the dogs charged.

"Hey, hey, no!" Mikey mumbled as he backed away from Marsh. "Sydney!"

Sydney stood at the top of the stairs looking confused.

"What is your problem?" she called to him.

She couldn't see the dogs. Marsh couldn't either, or he would have been running away too. Mikey took two steps, tripped, and fell onto his butt, holding his hands up to protect himself from the oncoming monsters.

"Stop! Help! Help me!" he screamed in terror.

Marsh called out, "What's going on?"

The dogs attacked. At least, one of them did. The biggest of the pack went for Mikey, grabbing at his arms and legs, growling viciously.

The other two went for Marsh, but not to attack. The giant dogs stood on either side of him, as if to protect him. But from who? Or what? Mikey? No way Mikey was going to bother Marsh again. He was too busy being munched. He scrambled to his feet and ran for the front of the house with the dogs nipping at his legs.

"Get it away!" he cried.

Marsh and Sydney exchanged quick, confused looks and took off after him. The two other dogs trotted along on either side of Marsh like demonic escorts. Marsh had no idea they were there. I followed close behind.

When we all got to the front of the house, I watched as Mikey fought to get into his car while kicking at the dog. It didn't look as if the animal was doing any damage, but it must have been terrifying just the same. These dogs were demons on four legs. Mikey finally got inside, slammed the door shut, gunned the engine, and screamed off with the dog chasing behind. The two other dogs left Marsh and sprinted after their pal. I could hear their vicious barking as they ran behind the car. They followed it for maybe half a block, then disappeared. Vanished. Poof.

Marsh and Sydney had no idea what had just happened.

But I had a good idea. What I didn't know was why.

"Then there's that," Sydney declared, numb.

"I don't get it," Marsh said. "He just started going nuts. Should we call somebody?"

"Like who?"

"I don't know. His parents?"

"And say what?" Sydney replied with her usual sarcasm. "Hi, Mrs. Russo. Mikey just had a mental breakdown and he's driving around like a lunatic. Have a nice day."

Sydney was annoying, but smart.

Marsh said, "I'm calling your parents."

"Don't bother," my sister replied. "I spoke with them this morning. Cooper isn't back yet."

Huh? They were talking about me. Sydney even looked a little shaken, and that was saying something because she didn't shake easily.

"He's been gone two nights?" Marsh declared anxiously. "That's not right. *Now* are they worried?"

Sydney nodded. "They called the police."

That proved it. Nobody knew I was dead. At least that explained why they weren't very upset.

"Such a tragedy," came a voice from behind me.

I turned to see Damon sitting on the steps of my house with his feet casually up on the banister.

"No one is aware of your untimely demise. Pity."

The sight of the guy made me want to jump at him, fists first.

"It was you," I declared. "You sent those dogs to attack Mikey."

Damon snickered. "Such a typical brute, that one. His

sense of superiority is based solely on his ability to physically dominate. It's so . . . unimaginative. Did you enjoy his humiliation as much as I did?"

"Enjoy? That was for fun? Man, you are sick."

"Marshall Seaver is mine," he stated flatly. "It would not have served me for that ruffian to have injured him."

"No," I said. "You want to do that yourself."

"That depends on you," Damon said with a shrug. "Will you help me? Or does your friend mean so little to you?"

The only thing that stopped me from attacking the guy again was seeing Sydney run past him and into the house. I was torn between the reality of a familiar life and the horror of a supernatural villain being part of it. I needed time to think, and to understand. Before I did something stupid, I took a step back and became enveloped in the colorful fog.

My destination was in the Light. Thistledown Lake. Emerald Cove, to be exact. I stood on the shore looking out at the quiet lake. There was something I needed to do but wasn't sure if I was capable. Damon said that if I wanted to, I could fall through the floor. I was a spirit, after all. I needed to know if that meant I could also move over something that wasn't solid. I closed my eyes . . . took a step onto the water . . . and didn't get wet. I don't want to say that I walked on water, it was more like I hovered over the surface. I wanted to move forward and that's what happened. I drifted across the lake, headed toward the center. The experience was both strange and strangely cool.

As I floated over the water, I heard the cracking of a branch in the woods behind me and glanced back to see a man, an old guy, picking through debris that had washed ashore. He was a real river rat with a beard and long stringy gray hair. His jeans were dirty and he wore a torn flannel shirt even though it was a hot summer day. The guy was scavenging, and he had scored. He knelt down and picked up a bright red jacket that was all wet and dirty. Good for him. I was about to turn my attention back to my journey when he opened up the jacket and I saw it for what it actually was. Printed in big white letters across the back were the words DAVIS GREGORY on top of a big football.

My jacket. Nobody knew what had happened to me. As far as I knew, nobody was even looking. The only clue to my fate had been discovered by this old guy and he didn't even know what he'd found.

I was in the right place.

I drifted out until I reached the spot. I felt it more than remembered it. I hovered over the water, then dropped down until I was below the surface. I was a ghost. I couldn't drown. Hovering in water was no different from floating in air, only a little colder. I still felt sensation. The lake was deep. The bottom had to be more than sixty feet down. I didn't want to go there, but I had to.

Through the murky silt, I saw the shattered bow of the *Galileo*. Undisturbed. Undiscovered. I forced myself to stay there. I had to see the one thing I dreaded most. I scanned around, searching the debris field, until I saw something that no person should ever have to see.

A hand was sticking up out of the mud. My hand. I was buried under mud, sixty feet below the surface of a frigid lake . . . and nobody knew I had even gone out in the boat.

10

Rest in peace? What a joke.

The afterlife was turning out to be a busy place. I needed time to get my head around all that was happening and figure out my next move, and I couldn't think of a better place to do it than in my own vision. In the Black. Why not? That's how things were supposed to work. So I left the scene of my demise in the Light and imagined being at my house in the Black.

I arrived to see there was nothing out of the ordinary about the afterlife version of my house, except that I was the only one there. It was both totally familiar and freakishly alien because no matter how normal it all looked, Mom or Dad or Sydney would not be showing up.

As I stood in my driveway debating about whether or not to go inside, I found that I wasn't alone after all.

"Chicken Coop!" Bernie the mailman yelled as he

hurried up the sidewalk. "Nice to see you back at the old homestead."

"Are you delivering mail?" I asked.

"Nah, but I still make the rounds." He leaned into me and whispered conspiratorially, "It keeps me in the know, if you get my drift."

"Not really."

"There isn't a whole lot that goes on around here that I'm not aware of. For one thing, I know you've been spending time with the Salinger girl."

It took me a second to realize who he was talking about.

"You mean Maggie?" I asked.

"Right. Maggie. Not a good idea to be hanging around with that one."

"Why not?"

Bernie's eyes went wide. "You know why she's still here, don't ya?"

"Yeah, I heard."

"It's tragic. That girl is on an express train headed straight for the Blood. I'm not sure why she even stopped here in the first place."

"Maybe you don't know the whole story."

"I know enough. What she did? You can't fix something like that."

Bernie was starting to piss me off. Who was he to judge?

"What are *you* here to fix, Bernie?"

The question surprised him and he got all self-conscious. "Uh, well, you know. Nobody's perfect."

"Thanks, I'll remember that."

He backed away and added, "Take care of your own business, Coop, and you'll be fine."

"Couldn't have said it better myself."

Bernie tipped his mailman baseball cap, winked, and

then turned on his heel and continued on with his route to nowhere.

His gossip about Maggie was obnoxious, but it made me wonder if Gramps might be right. Was everybody in the Black out for themselves at any cost? That seemed to go against the purpose of being there. If people were supposed to try and elevate themselves so that they could move on to some higher plane of existence, being all selfish and self-centered seemed like the exact wrong thing to do. I wondered if that was why so many people ended up staying in the Black for so long . . . like Damon.

And Gramps.

I had been so jammed up with everybody else's drama, I hadn't thought about what my own purpose was supposed to be in the Black. What did I have to do to fix the person I was? Sure, the past few years I hadn't exactly been a model citizen, so I guess there was a price to pay for that. But what was it? I was on the Morpheus Road just like everybody else. My actions in the Black would either get me to a better existence or dump me into the Blood. Part of me wanted to do exactly what Gramps suggested. I could block out Damon and throw Marsh under the bus and hang out in the perfect vision of my home and stand just as good a chance as anybody else for moving on to the big ol' reward in the sky.

As long as I could handle the guilt.

I stood in front of the perfect image of my perfect house, wishing I knew the right answer. I wanted to talk to somebody who was just as conflicted as I was, and the only person I knew of who fit that profile was Maggie. I'd been warned to stay away from her by two people who'd both said the same thing: She was bad news and would only cause me trouble. Maybe that was why I wanted to talk to her. I usually did the exact opposite of what people said was good for me, which meant I was probably going to be a resident of the Black for a good long time.

I closed my eyes and pictured Maggie in front of her house in early winter. Her vision. When I opened my eyes, the rippling colors had appeared in front of me. I took one step away from my house . . .

. . . and a second step into her yard. So simple. I stood on a dirt and gravel driveway that was between her house and the large gray barn.

"Maggie?" I called out.

No answer. I was about to head toward her house but the barn grabbed my attention. Something about the old building bothered Maggie. She looked right at it when I asked her when she had died. I couldn't help but wonder why. There was no way I'd just come out and say, "So? What's up with the barn?" I was bold but not that bold. I thought maybe the barn itself might provide some answers. So I turned away from the house and approached the old structure.

The building looked big enough to hold a couple of cars and maybe a workshop. There were two big swinging doors in front that were latched together. They each had to be ten feet high, and together, twice as wide. The wood was gray and weathered but as I got closer I could see that it had been painted white at one time. Most of the paint had worn off, probably from years of weather and sun, but when I stood directly in front of the door, I saw that there were patches of paint that looked to have bubbled up and peeled away. It was like there were random places where the paint hadn't grabbed hold of the wood. Or somehow had lost its hold.

I wasn't sure if I actually felt it, or if I was remembering the dark look that Maggie got when she stared at it, but something seemed wrong about the place. I feared that whatever I would find inside wouldn't be good. It made me want to open the door all the more.

A heavy padlock hung open on the latch. There was nothing to stop me from swinging open the tall double doors and letting the light of day expose whatever it was that was hidden inside. I reached forward and unhooked the rusty latch, then used it to pull open the right door. The hinges groaned as it slowly swung open a few inches, and I was instantly hit with a smell that was so strong it made me cough. It wasn't a bad smell, but it definitely proved that the barn hadn't been opened in a very long time. It was like I had released a dank cloud that had been bottled up inside. I was afraid that if I thought about it too long I'd chicken out and take off, so I grabbed the latch and was about to yank the door wide open, when I saw movement to my right.

Somebody was watching me from around the corner.

"Maggie?" I called, and left the door to run and see who it was. I sprinted for the corner of the barn and rounded it to see . . . nobody. Whoever it was, was probably behind the barn.

"Is that you, Maggie?"

"No," came Maggie's answer.

I turned back quickly to see her behind me, closing the barn doors. There was no way she could have run all the way around so fast.

I was hit with a wave of guilt. Seeing her standing there with those big sad eyes made me realize that I had crossed a line I shouldn't have.

"I—I'm sorry," I stammered. "I shouldn't be here. I know. But I was afraid to ask you about, you know, things and I thought I could just find out for myself and . . . I'm sorry."

Maggie slammed the doors closed and hurried back toward her house.

"C'mon, talk to me," I said while running after her. "I'm just trying to understand."

I felt like I had to make things right or she'd block me from her vision and I'd never see her again. I couldn't let that happen, so I took a chance and grabbed her arm to stop her.

"Please, talk to me," I begged.

Maggie whipped around and pulled away from me with strength that surprised me.

"Don't touch me!" she screamed.

I was thrown by her violent reaction because I had barely touched her. She was in tears and I wasn't sure if it was because I was snooping around where I didn't belong or because I had grabbed her. I backed away with my hands up.

"Okay. Sorry."

She stood there breathing hard and crying, but she didn't leave. I had nothing to lose so I decided to stop treating her like a frightened deer.

"I know about your parents," I said.

Her surprised look crushed me. Whatever pain she was feeling, I'd just added to it. But there was no turning back.

"I mean, I don't know how it happened but you're still here. In the Black. That's a good thing, right? I mean, as opposed to . . . you know."

"I don't know why I'm here," she cried. "They're going to come for me, I know that. And you know what? I want them to. I want this to be over."

Her words came out between tortured sobs. It felt like she was letting stuff out that had been building up for a long time. It suddenly made sense why she was so afraid. She was waiting for the ax to fall on her.

She squinted at me through puffy red eyes and said, "Sometimes I wonder if this is really the Blood because I can't imagine anything worse."

She sat down in the gravel driveway, her head bowed, her hair falling down in front of her eyes. I wasn't sure what to do, seeing as I was the one who set her off in the first place. I sat down, but not too close to her.

"This isn't the Blood," I said calmly. "And if you're still here, it means you don't have to end up there."

Maggie didn't move. She didn't argue either.

"I won't judge you, Maggie," I continued. "I'm sorry I tried to look in the barn. That was just me being curious and it was wrong. But you helped me and I'd like to try and help you too."

"You can't," she whispered without raising her head. "I don't belong here. There's nothing I can do to change the person I am, or what I did."

I wanted details but there was no chance I was going to ask for them.

"You helped me," I said. "That's a good thing, right?"

She snickered. "I reached out to your friend in the Light. That alone could send me to the Blood. But you know something? I don't care. I did it because it was the right thing to do."

"I agree."

"And I did it again."

"Wait. You *would* or you *did*?"

"I did. I went to the Light and showed your friend the symbol again. The three swirls. He was in the shower. I made it appear in the steam on the glass wall."

The idea that Maggie was in the shower with Marsh was a little wrong, but there were bigger issues to deal with so I didn't go there.

"How did he react?"

"He's scared," she said with certainty. "And not just from what I did. There's more going on with him. I'm afraid I only made things worse."

"But you didn't! Marsh is with Sydney now. He's not alone anymore, thanks to you."

Maggie looked up and actually smiled. "He is?"

"Yes, but if contacting Marsh could send you to the Blood, you shouldn't do it anymore."

"I don't care," she said quickly. "Maybe it'll get me there faster and end this nightmare."

"What if the Blood is an even worse nightmare?"

She pushed her hair out of her eyes and sat up straight, back in control. "Then, it is. I don't care. We're supposed to be here so we can become better people and make up for the things we did in life, but how can ignoring somebody who's in trouble make you a better person?"

"My grandfather says that everybody in the Black is only out for themselves and would do anything to move on to a better existence."

"I don't believe that," she said. "If turning your back on somebody who needs help is the Watchers' idea of what makes you a better person, I'm not so sure I want to know what that better existence is. I mean, if you can't live with yourself, what's the point?"

Her words rocked me. "Yeah, what *is* the point?" I repeated to myself.

I wanted to lean over and give her a hug of thanks, but didn't dare. With those few words, she made everything completely clear to me. "You're right," I said. "And I'm somebody who needs help, if you're still willing."

"What else can I do?"

"For one, I don't want you messing around in the Light anymore. You shouldn't be getting in trouble for battles I should be fighting."

"But you don't know how to contact Marsh," she said.

"Teach me," I said quickly. "That's how you can help. How did you move the chocolate powder and the glass?"

"It's hard. The most we can do is create a ripple of energy that nudges something or pushes it into a shape."

"But you moved all that glass. That's not so light."

"I'd never done anything like that before. I think it worked because of you."

"Me? I didn't do anything."

"But you did, just by being there."

"Because I have a connection with Marsh?"

"Yes. I've been in the Black a long time and had the chance to move through many visions and learn from spirits that existed in more times than you can imagine. It seems to me that the Light and the Black and whatever else is out there all exist in the same place. It's all just one big universe of lives that sometimes touch one another. From what I can tell, those who meant something to one another in life share a powerful bond. It's that connection that helps create the energy. It was your connection to Marsh that helped me move those things."

"So, then, I might be able to contact Marsh on my own," I said, thinking out loud.

"Maybe. It's all about focus and concentration and visualizing what you want to have happen."

"So I just think it? Like moving around in the Black or into the Light?"

"More or less. But don't expect big results."

My mind raced to a couple of possibilities, but I needed to know more.

"My gramps said that we can block spirits from entering our vision. How do I do that?"

"You want to keep Damon away?"

"Well, yeah. Duh."

"Then, it's done. If you don't want him in your vision, he can't go there."

"Simple as that?"

"Yes, but only in the Black. You can't keep him away from you in the Light. The Light is neutral."

"Got it. The Light is Switzerland."

She frowned. She didn't get that. I stood up and helped her to her feet.

"I think you're right," I said. "If we're here to become better people, then we have to follow our conscience. If that's wrong, then maybe I belong in the Blood myself."

Maggie's eyes focused on something behind me. I turned to see two Watchers standing in front of Gramps's house.

"Did you hear that?" I yelled to them. "I'm gonna do what I think is right! If you don't like that—"

The Watchers vanished.

I laughed. "Guess that wasn't such a good start."

Maggie chuckled. Her face lit up when she laughed. I hated it that she was so troubled, no matter what she might have done in a previous life.

"Good luck, Cooper. I hope your friend will be okay. And you too."

I wanted to kiss her, but didn't think that would be cool. "I'll let you know."

I took a step back and turned to face the colorful fog. I knew exactly where I wanted to go, and with two steps I was there.

I found myself standing on the grass between the lake and our cottage on Thistledown Lake, in the Light. Sydney was on the float in the lake, working on her tan. She had on a red bikini top and jean shorts. I knew why she had on the shorts, too. She was hiding the tattoo.

Marsh was lying on a blue towel, asleep. On his chest was a Batman graphic novel. He had no idea that the spirit of his dead friend was standing there, watching him snore. Heck, he didn't even know his friend was dead. Nobody did. They probably all thought I'd taken off to be alone for a while. I'd done it before. That had to be why they weren't searching for the body that was lying in sixty feet of water. Somehow, some way, I had to let them know. If I was going to protect Marsh from Damon, he had to know that I was dead.

I knelt down next to my sleeping friend and barked out, "Ralph!"

He didn't react, no big surprise. The graphic novel was open on his chest. I thought that I could do something with the pages. Maybe move them around until it opened to a page that would get Marsh's attention. I leaned over and stared at the book, focusing my thoughts on the page, willing it to move.

I felt the odd tingle move through me. It was the strangest thing I'd ever felt and I had to believe that it was the kind of energy ripple that Maggie had created. If there were any two people who had a connection that would make this work, it was Marsh and me. The air in front of the book went blurry. I blinked. It wasn't my imagination. It was really happening. Slowly, ever so slowly, the page lifted and gently flapped over as if blown by a slight gust of wind.

"Yes!" I shouted, and jumped to my feet.

I had actually done it! Marsh's eyes opened lazily and he laughed. He must have felt the air move. Psyche! But when I knelt down and looked at the book, my excitement ended. As dramatic as it was to have turned the page, it meant nothing. It wasn't like there was a page in the book that said, "Hey, Marsh. Cooper's dead and his body is lying on the bottom of the lake, and you're being haunted by a Macedonian madman."

I sat down, trying to figure out a plan B, when I noticed that a breeze had kicked up. A real one. There was a field of dandelions next to our house and the gentle wind had blown in a storm of gray seeds that floated in the air like a fuzzy cloud. I stared at the floating seeds as they danced on the breeze, thinking how they were so light. And moveable. Was it possible that I could direct them somewhere? If I did, what would I do with them? Spell out "Coop is a ghost!" in the sky? Not likely. I had to come up with something simple like the triple swirl tattoo. Marsh was a smart guy. He could put two and two together and get twenty-two. But what could I possibly tell him that would put him on the trail to the truth?

The night I died I had gone out on the lake to look at the stars. Marsh and I had done that a hundred times ourselves, without the gruesome speedboat death part, that is. What kind of clue could I give him that would get him thinking that way?

I was interrupted by a splash of water, and a scream. While I was focused on floating dandelion seeds, Sydney had come in from the float and tossed a bucketful of lake water onto Marsh's head. Witch.

Marsh sat up fast, sputtering water and wiping his eyes. "What was that for?"

"You were creeping me out, lying there laughing like that," Sydney said. "I thought you were having a freak seizure."

"That's idiotic," Marsh shot back, more stunned than angry.

"Idiotic? Me?" Sydney laughed and picked up Marsh's book. "You're lying here reading comic books and laughing like a lunatic and *I'm* the idiot?"

I said, "It's not a comic book. It's a graphic novel."

Of course she didn't hear me.

"It's a graphic novel," Marsh said.

"Thank you," I added for nobody's benefit but my own.

Marsh tried to grab it back but Sydney held it away. "Seriously?" she said, scoffing. "Batman? Isn't that for kids? Pow! Bam! Crunch!"

"If you looked closer, you'd see it's a much edgier, multi-faceted version of the legend of the Bat than the comedic version you're referring to."

I said, "You're not helping yourself here, dude."

Sydney turned cold and stared Marsh down. I'd seen that look before. It could burn through lead. Marsh didn't stand a chance.

"I'd laugh if I thought you were kidding," she said with disdain. After dropping the graphic novel onto the towel, she turned away, clutching whatever thick important textbook she was reading, and marched for the house.

Sydney was an expert at making people feel small. It made me wonder if Marsh needed protection from Damon *and* my sister. He stood there looking lost, then lifted his chin and closed his eyes. I wasn't sure what he was doing at first, until I registered the dandelion spores again. The storm of seeds was pretty thick as it floated past him, some getting caught in his hair. Seeing them gave me an idea.

I dropped to my knees in front of the dark blue towel and focused my thoughts. My idea was to use the dandelion spores to create a pattern, like Maggie did with the chocolate and the glass. It was more complex than the triple swirl, but I knew that if I could pull it off, it would put Marsh square on my trail. I closed my eyes and created a mental image in my mind. Five images, actually. The ones I knew best. It was Marsh who'd taught me about them. He was the expert. I made fun of him at the time. Now I hoped the knowledge he shared with me would pay off.

I felt the same tingle of energy move through me. I didn't dare open my eyes for fear of breaking the tenuous connection. I stayed focused, seeing the patterns in my head. The five patterns.

The tingle left as abruptly as it had come. I tentatively cracked open one eye, looked down at the blue towel, and saw them. Right there, in front of me, the five patterns I had imagined, created by dandelion spores.

Hercules. Draco. Cassiopeia. Ursa Major. Ursa Minor.

Five constellations in the summer sky.

"I rock," I said, and glanced at Marsh.

He saw the patterns, and looked pale. He was too smart to think that he had just witnessed a random accident. He had already seen enough impossible visions to begin questioning what was going on. My hope was that this would get his mind working the problem over, the way I knew it could.

Between the two of us, only one of us wasn't freaked. Marsh grabbed his Batman book and ran for the house, terrified. I felt bad about it, but I knew Marsh. The wheels were now turning. The triple swirl led him to Sydney . . . Now he was on a path that would lead to me. I was sure of it.

I sat down and laughed. I'd done it.

I had made contact.

11

I had finally taken some control.

It was a small victory, but it gave me hope. Ever since my death I'd felt like a cork floating down a wild river, bouncing off every rock along the way. When I created the constellation patterns on the towel, it made me realize that I could start calling my own shots . . . or at least dodge some of the rocks.

The question then became, what would I do with the ability to communicate with Marsh? Gramps wanted me to stick my head in the sand and let Damon do whatever he wanted, but what kind of friend would let that happen? I didn't think being a jerk who let his friend hang out to dry was working toward becoming the best person I could be. I always had Marsh's back in Trouble Town and I wasn't going to let a little thing like dying change that. If it meant spending extra time in the Black as punishment, fine by me.

It wouldn't be such a horrible place if not for the fact that I was being harassed by a centuries-old creep with an attitude. That part sucked. I wanted to get even with Damon for what he had done to me but there was an eternity for that. I could wait.

Helping Marsh wouldn't be easy, though. He was a sci-fi geek who had dissected Starfleet schematics since he was six, but he didn't believe in ghosts. Before he could learn and accept the truth, he first had to know that I was dead. So did my family. It wasn't a happy thought. My death was going to be rough on everybody. Even Sydney would shed a tear. I hoped. They had to know sooner or later. Sooner would be better and not just because of Damon. I didn't like the idea of my body lying in mud under the lake. It wasn't like I needed it anymore, but still. Other than the time I had a vicious appendicitis attack, that body did okay by me. It deserved better than that. I figured that since I was missing, the best place to see how the search was going was to visit the sheriff's office in Thistledown, so I went there.

Sheriff Vrtiak was a total Barney whose crime-fighting skills pretty much began and ended with giving speeding tickets to tourists. The guy caught me once partying on the mini golf course after closing but I convinced him that it would be a mistake to arrest me because if word got out that the golf course was a great place to hang out after hours then he'd have to set up a permanent patrol and tell the owners to put up a security fence and alarms and spotlights, which wouldn't make him a popular guy and would hurt his chances for re-election, and I promised that if he let me slide I'd never go back there again. Even to play golf. He didn't buy a word of it but he didn't want to have to deal with me so he let me go with a warning. I wasn't sure if he was a good guy or just lazy. From then on I partied at the drive-in movie next door.

The Thistledown Police Department consisted of him and a secretary named Connie who was older than cracked paint. I was hoping that when I got to the office I'd see a flurry of activity with maps on the walls and calls coming in from volunteers who were poised to search the countryside, and news crews swarming to find out what had happened to the most popular guy at Davis Gregory.

Instead, I saw Connie, alone, talking on the phone with her feet up on the desk. Connie was a grandma who always wore brightly colored stretch pants and flowered blouses. She had blond hair thanks to modern technology and a single ponytail that came out of the side of her head. She was a cartoon of somebody from the eighties you'd see on TV Land.

"Yeah. That kid's trouble," she said to whoever she was talking to. "I knew that since he was old enough to light firecrackers. Good thing he's only here in summer."

If I didn't know better, I'd have sworn she was talking about me.

She listened, then said, "He's been gone a couple of days. Everybody thinks he took off to run away from the mess he got himself into down in Stony Brook."

Whoa. She *was* talking about me!

"Who's on the phone?" I asked, but of course she couldn't hear me.

"His parents aren't so worried. They know he'll turn up. What? Nah, there's no search going on. What's the point?"

I wanted to yank her sideways ponytail. That would give her the point.

Sheriff Vrtiak ambled in from his office and tossed something down on Connie's desk. She didn't even sit up and *pretend* like she was working, that's how lame the place was.

"Make some copies of that for me, would ya?" Vrtiak asked. "If he doesn't turn up, we'll start sending 'em out tomorrow."

Connie didn't acknowledge his request and Vrtiak shuffled back into his office. What a couple of tools. I looked at the paper and was surprised to see it was a picture of me. It was my school shot from the previous year. I hated that picture. I'd worn a tie, thinking nobody did that anymore and I'd be all cutting edge, but it turned out all the geeks wore ties and I just ended up looking like some doofus who was trying too hard. And this was the picture everybody was going to use to try and track me down? No way they'd find me! Then again, my body was underwater and I probably didn't look much like any picture that was ever taken of me. Yeesh.

Connie carried on with her phone call as if Vrtiak hadn't been there. "Tell you the truth, I hope he stays lost. I never liked that cocky kid."

I'd heard enough. She was going to pay for that. I searched around the office for something I could move around to spook her. The only thing that looked light enough for me to move was my own picture. Perfect. I leaned over the desk and focused on my image. All I wanted to do was push it closer to her, though I wouldn't have minded if it burst into flames or something. That would have been cool. I closed my eyes and concentrated, willing the picture to move. To rise up. To flip over. To do anything. I peeked out through squinted eyes, expecting to see the ripple of color in the air.

It wasn't there. I doubled down and held my breath, but the picture didn't budge. After a minute of wasted effort, I gave up. Maggie was right. The only reason I was able to do something with the dandelion seeds was because of my connection with Marsh. I had no connection with Connie . . . other than the string of firecrackers I'd dropped into her mailbox.

Yeah, it was me.

I had to relax and tell myself that it didn't matter. Marsh

was the only person I wanted to contact anyway. If I was going to steer the living into finding out what happened with me, it was going to have to be through Marsh.

I was spinning my wheels at the sheriff's office so I went back to the Black. To Maggie's house. I told myself that I wanted to learn more about how things worked with the spirits, but that was only partly true. I really wanted to get to know her better. I'd only known her a short time but nothing I saw made me believe that she could have killed her parents. Not that I'm an expert on homicidal behavior, but it didn't add up. She didn't seem like she could hurt anybody. And then there was the question of why she wasn't sent to the Blood. You'd think that killing your parents earned you an express ticket.

The Blood. What exactly was that? I never really believed in the concept of hell. The idea that guys with pitchforks and pointy tails ran around poking people into caves filled with fire didn't fly with me. I once burned my finger on a sparkler and it hurt for a week. How could anybody live in fire for eternity? Especially since we still have feeling after death. It just didn't make sense.

The concept that there was a place where the hard cases were sent to keep them away from the rest of us normal folks didn't seem so far-fetched. But what was it like? I wanted to know, if only because I might have been setting myself up for a trip there by interfering with Marsh's life. Or maybe it would be better if I didn't know.

When I got to Maggie's farmhouse and knocked on the door, there was no answer. For a second I feared that the ax had finally fallen and the Watchers had carted her off to the Blood. But that didn't make sense. Would a spirit's vision still be around even if they had moved on? Or down. Or wherever the Blood was.

I started walking off the porch, when I caught sight of

a young kid running from behind Maggie's house toward the off-limits barn. I only caught a glimpse, but it looked as though it was a little girl. Was it the same kid I saw run to Gramps's house?

"Hey!" I shouted. "Hang on!"

I took off after her, closing the distance from the house to the barn quickly. I rounded the barn but when I reached the back side, she was gone. Again. My first thought was that I had seen a ghost. That made me laugh. Of *course* I had seen a ghost. It would have been a lot scarier if it *wasn't* a ghost.

I didn't want Maggie to catch me snooping around the barn again so I jogged toward Gramps's house, or whoever's house it was. I had never heard about the people who owned the house before Gramps did. I wondered if the mysterious little girl lived there.

That raised another question. I'd seen Maggie and her house from Gramps's vision, but Gramps wasn't in Maggie's vision. How did that work? Did Maggie prevent Gramps from entering her vision? If so, did that mean the house next door was Gramps's house, or the house of whoever lived there when Maggie was alive? The Black was a complicated place.

I walked out to the road, which was a dirt lane back in those days, to look at the name on the mailbox. The name BRADY was painted there in precise letters. It was definitely not Gramps's house. He was a Foley. I decided it was a mystery that could wait for another time because I had more important things to deal with.

I turned my thoughts to our cottage on Thistledown Lake and stepped back into the Light. It was nighttime. I was on the porch, looking out toward the lake, where two people stood on the deck. One was Marsh. The other was . . . me.

What?

Marsh was talking to me. It had to be me. It looked just like me. I stood with my back to the house wearing my red Davis Gregory football jacket. How was that possible? My body was at the bottom of the lake and that old river rat had my football jacket.

Marsh walked up to the guy and grabbed his shoulder saying, "Stop with the riddles. What journey are you talking about?"

When he pulled the guy around, it all became clear.

It was Gravedigger. It looked like my body in every way except it had Gravedigger's skeletal face. Marsh's creation was back to harass him, which meant only one thing.

"Damon!" I screamed, looking around for the ancient spirit. He had to be there, pulling strings, bending the light to make Marsh see this horrifying sight. But why? What was he trying to do to Marsh? Scare him? Or something worse?

Marsh spun around to head back for the house but Gravedigger disappeared and reappeared in front of him, blocking his way . . . only he was back to his normal look with the long black clothes, black hat, and silver pick. Marsh panicked, spun, and ran for the water.

"Ralph!" I screamed, running off the porch.

Marsh kept going, hitting the lake and swimming furiously toward the wooden float that was out beyond our dock. There was no way I could do anything to stop him, but I hoped there was something I could do about Gravedigger. I charged at the ghoul and dove for him, intending to tackle him and drive his bony white face into the ground. I leaped, laying myself flat out, and wrapped my arms around him, only to come up with air. The ghoul had disappeared, just as he had in the school gym. Forgot about that.

Marsh reached the float, pulled himself up, and looked

toward shore to see what Gravedigger was doing. He didn't see the ghoul.

I did. Gravedigger materialized on the float behind him.

"Turn around!" I couldn't help shouting.

I can't say that Marsh heard me, but he did turn around, just in time. Gravedigger took the pick off his shoulder and started swinging it at Marsh. Was the pick real? Or an illusion? Damon dealt in both. He could do a lot more physically in the Light than blowing around dandelion seeds. That much was proved in the school gym when the ropes pulled over the windows. Either way, Marsh needed help and I couldn't give it to him.

Unless, I thought, I could get somebody else to help. It killed me to leave but I left the shore and sprinted into the house. I started for my parents room on the first floor, ready to do whatever I could to wake them up.

I never made it to their room because a better idea came to me. Marsh had been in love with Sydney since he was in kindergarten. I can't say much for his taste, but if he had a thing for Sydney, I hoped there might be some kind of cosmic connection between all of us that would give me a better chance of getting her attention. It was as good a plan as any.

Sydney was in her room, asleep on her back. For a change I didn't bother shouting out "Wake up!" Instead I tried the same thing that Maggie had done to wake up Marsh. I fell down onto my knees right next to her head and concentrated my thoughts to try and create some kind of energy. A second later the swirling color appeared. I leaned in close to Sydney and blew on her forehead.

Her hair rustled!

Sydney opened her eyes and brushed the hair back. I'd done it! I jumped to my feet and ran to the window.

"Look!" I shouted. "Marsh is in trouble!"

Right. Wasted effort. Idiot. Sydney sat up, looking confused. I had to do something that would get her attention to the window. It was the kind of window that opened out on hinges so I closed my eyes and visualized it opening.

And it did. With a soft *creek* sound, the window pushed out.

"Yes!" After what happened, or didn't happen at the sheriff's office, the only explanation for my success had to be because of my connection with Marsh and Sydney.

I spun to see she was sitting up straight, staring at the window, her eyes wide and awake.

"So get your butt out of bed and get over here, you lazy—!" I screamed.

She didn't budge. I couldn't tell if she was scared, or confused, or thinking she was dreaming. Whatever the reason, she was hesitating and I had to get her past it. I heard a splash outside and looked to see that Marsh had jumped off the float into the water. I had to do something more to get Sydney to look out the window. I saw a bunch of papers on her dresser that looked like study notes. Sydney was always studying. I wished she would try studying the window a little closer.

I ran to the dresser and focused on the smallest, lightest sheet. It looked like something that was ripped out of a spiral binder, complete with frayed edges where it was torn from the rings. I wasn't sure if I should clear my head of the horror of what was happening outside, or use it to help me create the energy to move the paper. Truth was, there was no way I could clear my head. I was way too charged up and it proved to be a good thing because unlike the failed attempt at the sheriff's office, the paper twitched. I'd moved it! That amped me up even more so I knelt down and did the same thing I did to wake up Sydney. I blew on the page . . . and it lifted into the air.

I didn't even look to see if Sydney was watching. I didn't want to break the spell, or the magic, or whatever it was that was allowing me to float this piece of paper. I waved my arms, trying to stir up energy to direct the floating page into Sydney's line of sight. The page skipped and danced like a feather on the wind, headed for the open window. Perfect. Then the page darted up, floated back, and sailed out of the window into the night. I immediately spun around to see if Sydney saw it.

She was sitting bolt upright, her back flat against the wall, her eyes wide. She definitely saw it. But instead of going to investigate, the sight had frozen her in fear.

"Ahhh!" I screamed in frustration.

Looking outside, I saw that Marsh was flailing in the water. His head went under as if something were pulling him down. It had to be Gravedigger. Or Damon. I was so emotionally charged up that my next move was the simplest yet. I focused on the window, and a second later, it slammed shut.

I spun to see Sydney's reaction. Her eyes were even wider than before, but she didn't budge. Instead of tempting her to look, I was paralyzing her with fear. Marsh didn't have much time left so I made one last desperate attempt to get her attention. I lifted my hand and pushed the air, hoping it would open the window. Slowly, the window swung open.

That did it. The last movement of the window was the invitation Sydney needed. She crawled out of bed and cautiously made her way to investigate.

"C'mon, c'mon!" I cajoled. "Pick up the pace, Agnes!"

Sydney had her eyes on the window but when she reached it she saw something else. Something beyond. Her eyes focused and her back went straight. She had seen Marsh struggling in the water.

"Go help him!" I shouted.

I don't think she heard me, but she got the point. The strange movement of the window was temporarily forgotten as she took off running for the door.

"Finally!" I said to myself.

I didn't even follow her. What was the point? There wasn't anything I could do to help. It was up to Sydney now. I watched through the window as she sprinted out of the house and covered the distance to the lake with three long strides. It was an alien feeling, but in that moment I loved my sister. She ran to the end of the dock and made a perfect lifeguard jump, feet first, keeping her head above water and her eyes on the flailing victim. Sydney had taken the same junior lifeguard course that I had. She would bring Marsh in.

A horrible thought hit me: Gravedigger could just as easily drag her under as Marsh. Had I just sent my sister to her death?

"You have surprised me," came a voice from the other side of the room.

I spun to see Damon standing next to the bed. I was so fired up that I went for him without thinking, ready to take him apart. As soon as I took a step, he reached to his belt and wrapped his fingers around the handle of the sword that dangled there.

The black sword.

I backed off. "You're a real brave guy when you've got that weapon."

"I do not need a weapon to control you," he said dismissively.

"Then, put it down and let's see how brave you really are."

"So typical," Damon said. "You equate power with the ability to use physical force. So many others have made that mistake with me. I have a name for them . . . victims."

"That's tough talk, but you're still not dropping the sword."

He laughed. "Do you honestly believe a schoolboy challenge to my virility would compel me to give up an advantage? Are you that simple?"

His smug confidence made me want to hit him even more, but not as long as he had that sword.

I looked over my shoulder to see that Sydney had gotten to Marsh and the two of them were swimming for shore. There was no sign of Gravedigger. The two crawled onto the grass and collapsed. Sydney had saved him. She wasn't a total Agnes.

"How did I surprise you?" I asked Damon, without looking at him.

"You chose to protect your friend though you knew it was against the ways of the Black. I am impressed by your selfless loyalty, foolish as it may be."

"You say that like I should care."

Damon chuckled. "So brash, in spite of the impossible position you find yourself in."

"Really? I don't see it that way. I think you need us. If you didn't, you'd either leave us alone or kill us. All this stuff with Gravedigger is just for show. I'm thinking *you're* the one in the impossible situation, scar-boy."

Damon's eyes went wide and his hand went to his face. It was as if I had thrown the worst possible insult at him, and maybe I had. He was a ruthless, arrogant manipulator yet he was vain about the scars on his face. I had to remember that.

"Perhaps you are right," he said. "You both may be more trouble than you are worth and I should simply snuff you out."

"But you won't, will you?"

"So sure of yourself," he said with a cocky sneer.

I shrugged. "Yeah, pretty much."

"You are correct," he said. "I do need your help and the help of your friend. Make no mistake, I will continue to haunt him until I get what I want."

"Or you kill him," I spat.

Damon chuckled. "Oh no, his death won't stop me. I have seen thousands die and will see thousands more. A single life means nothing. However, I know how precious life means to you, so perhaps we should take another route. I can offer you something in return for your cooperation."

"There's nothing you can offer me. I'm dead."

"Exactly," he said slyly.

"Uh . . . what?"

"I need the poleax to free me from this prison."

"You told me. You want to move on to the final reward."

"That isn't what I said," Damon countered.

"Yes, it is. You told me you wanted to get out of the Black."

"Indeed, but the Morpheus Road runs both ways. Tell me, as you stand here right now, what is your greatest desire?"

"You mean besides getting rid of you?"

He didn't react.

I looked out the window to where Marsh and Sydney were sitting on the grass. Seeing them made me understand what Damon was getting at.

"Of course it is," he said knowingly. "It is the same wish of every spirit who travels the road. The possibility of a greater reward is tempting, but the known, the familiar, is so much more . . . desirable."

"You don't know what I'm thinking," I argued.

"I know *exactly* what you're thinking," he countered. "For I wish the same thing. It is all I have ever wished. I want to rip open the veil between the Light and the Black to reclaim what was so ingloriously wrestled from me and live once again."

"But that's impossible."

"Don't be so sure."

I turned to face the little guy. "You can't be serious," I said soberly.

"But I am. I want to travel back along the road. Help me and I'll take you with me."

"But . . . you can't."

"Yes, I can!" he bellowed. "With the poleax, I can create a physical pathway back into the Light. I can live again, and so can you."

I stood there, stunned, unable to form a coherent thought.

Damon smiled and said, "Now, do you still wish to be rid of me?"

12

"You can't raise people from the dead," I exclaimed.

"Maybe *you* cannot," Damon said with a superior sneer.

I didn't want to be in that room anymore, especially not with Damon. It was a personal space that belonged to me, and my family. He was an unwelcome intruder. I glanced outside to see Marsh and Sydney on the grass talking. Safe. For the time being, anyway.

"I'm going to the Black," I told Damon.

Damon sat down on Sydney's bed as if he owned it, leaning back on her pillows. He gave me a knowing smile. Things had played out exactly as he'd expected them to. I felt like a fish caught on a hook.

"Are you allowing me into your vision?" he asked.

"No," I said quickly, and stepped out of the Light.

Returning to my vision would have given me time to

think about Damon's offer. Was he telling the truth? Could he actually give me my life back? It seemed too good to be true. But going along with him would be like making a deal with the devil. Was it worth the price? In the few seconds it took me to move to the Black, I decided that I needed to know more. So instead of returning to my vision of Stony Brook, I went directly to the courtyard in ancient Macedonia where I had first met Damon.

He was standing next to the fountain, waiting for me. He knew I was coming, which pissed me off. I don't like being predictable.

Unlike the last time I was there, the place was busy with people. They were mostly men who looked to be peasant laborers doing grunt work like sweeping up the stone walkways and lugging around baskets of fruit and nuts. A handful of Damon's ragged warrior dudes were scattered around, keeping watch over the workers.

"I knew my offer would interest you," he said with a cocky smirk.

"Well, yeah. You said you can raise the dead. I'd say that's interesting."

"Please understand, I do not have that ability as yet. For that, I need the poleax."

"I don't get that," I said. "A weapon is about killing, not raising the dead."

"Correct. A weapon extinguishes life, but not spirit. Certainly you are able to grasp that concept, now that you have journeyed this far along the road."

"I guess. A person's spirit moves on after death. You can't kill a spirit."

Damon chuckled and pulled his black sword from its scabbard. I thought back to how it had vaporized the soldier named Philip, and I backed off a step.

Damon giggled like a child.

"A most remarkable weapon," he said. "So many have fallen to its bite."

Damon returned the black sword to its scabbard and then strolled over to one of his scruffy warrior buddies and took his sword. It had a thick silver blade and leather handle.

Damon held it up and said, "The simple weapon of a soldier, like so many others that belong to warriors who pass through the Black."

He walked to one of the peasants who was on his hands and knees, scrubbing the stone walkway.

He looked to me and said, "As you say, you cannot kill a spirit."

He drew the sword back . . .

"Whoa, no!" I screamed.

. . . and stabbed the defenseless worker in the side.

The guy screamed in pain and doubled over. Damon pulled the sword back and held it out to me. There was no blood. The poor guy rolled back to his knees, wiped the sweat from his forehead, and went back to work scrubbing the stone walkway, unhurt.

Damon tossed the silver sword down at the feet of his warrior buddy as if it were a worthless prop.

"You cannot kill a spirit," he said, and pulled his black sword out again. "But I can."

He raised the sword high, and with one quick move he slashed it down across the peasant's back. This time the poor guy raised his arm to protect himself. He knew what was coming. The blade hit his arm and traveled right through his body, creating a gash of black ash. The look of fear was frozen on the worker's face, but only for a second, for as soon as the sword's arc was complete, the peasant turned into a cloud of cinder that drifted away and disappeared.

I stood there in shock, realizing that I had just seen a person's spirit snuffed out.

"His journey along the Morpheus Road has ended," Damon announced casually while sliding his sword back into its scabbard.

A million thoughts flew through my head, not the least of which was the horror of seeing the end come to somebody's life. For good.

"How?" was all I managed to get out.

"This sword is imbued with the spirit of all those who have fallen to its blade. Its strength does not come from steel but from the lives of its victims, and believe me there were many."

"And that gives it the power to kill a spirit?" I asked, numb.

"And in so doing, adding to its strength," he explained.

"So you destroyed a guy's spirit, forever, just to show me you can?"

"You need to understand that I am not making idle boasts. The stakes are too high."

"You're a murderer!" I shouted.

He shrugged. "War has casualties."

"There's no war going on!"

Damon gave me a sly smile and said, "Not yet."

I walked away from the scene, sick to my stomach.

Damon followed. "Understand, Foley, this weapon is a trifle compared to the power of the poleax. Countless thousands have fallen to that blade, at my hand."

"So you're a *mass* murderer," I muttered.

"I am a *soldier!*" he bellowed.

"I don't get this. Why aren't you in the Blood? How come you're still here?"

Damon looked around to see two Watchers standing on the opposite side of the fountain. They didn't seem bothered by the execution that had happened right under their noses. Damon faced them and yelled, "He wishes to know why I have not been sent to the Blood!"

The Watchers didn't react.

I walked around Damon, headed toward the two. "What is your deal?" I yelled to the dark figures. "How come this guy gets a free pass?"

They watched me without expression. It was making me nuts. What good were these guys if they weren't doing their job?

"Here is your answer, Foley."

Damon pulled his black sword and pushed past me, headed for the Watchers . . .

And the Watchers disappeared.

Damon turned back to me with a satisfied smile on his scarred face.

"Fear is a powerful weapon," he boasted. "No spirit is safe from me."

"They're not afraid of you. It's that sword. You can't go anywhere without it."

Damon returned the black blade to his scabbard and said, "A small price to pay."

"And the poleax is even more powerful?" I asked.

"It is."

"So, what does that have to do with raising the dead?"

"You have seen a small demonstration of what I can do in the Light. Over the centuries I have learned to manipulate the energy that courses around us, on all levels of existence. But it is illusion. Shadow play. With the spiritual energy contained in the poleax, I will be able to make those illusions real . . . to not only take shape, but substance. And yes, to create life."

"Like *Frankenstein*."

"Are you referring to the cinematic depiction, or the work of literature?"

"You know *Frankenstein*?" I asked with surprise.

"Of course. I much preferred the original tome. The Shelley girl and I have had many discussions concerning the nature of life versus death."

"Who?"

"Mary Shelley. The author of the story you refer to. She moved on quite some time ago. Lovely girl. But I suppose you would not know about her. You strike me as someone who would prefer watching a motion picture over reading a book."

He gave me a superior smile and added, "Did you not believe me when I said I was a student of humanity?"

I was stunned. Damon may have been an ancient warrior, but he'd witnessed much of the history of man. Millions of spirits had come through the Black since he had first arrived. This guy had access to the knowledge that had been accumulated by hundreds of generations. It made him even more dangerous than I first thought, and made me wonder if he just might have the ability to do the things he said he could.

"*Frankenstein* was fiction," I said. "This is real. You want the power to create life. You want to be god."

"'God' is only a word. People have worshipped hundreds of deities throughout time. I have no desire to be worshipped."

"So if you have so much knowledge and power, what do you need Marsh and me for?"

"Because I have enemies."

"Gee, really? Never would have guessed."

He ignored the sarcasm. "My ability to function is limited because of restrictions placed on me before my death. Six crucibles were created, golden orbs filled with the blood of an enemy. Their existence prevents me from finding the poleax."

"You mean, like a curse?"

"Call it what you will."

"Marsh broke a golden ball," I said, remembering back to when I first peered into the Light. "Is that what you're talking about?"

"That was the first crucible," Damon answered. "There are others."

"So, these things are like, what? Kryptonite?"

Damon chuckled. "Must you see everything through the prism of a cultural reference?"

"Just tell me, are they dangerous?"

"To you, no. To me they are blockades. At least one of these crucibles is protecting the poleax in the Light. It prevents me from seeing it, which is why I cannot locate it."

"How does that work? They have some kind of power?"

"More than you can imagine. Your efforts have been crude but you have seen what is possible when the connection between spirits is strong. With Marshall Seaver your connection is friendship. Imagine how strong a connection can be when it is based on hatred and fear."

"So there's so much hatred between you and this enemy that his blood holds power over you? Nice. Who is this guy?"

Damon glanced at the imposing warrior statue in the fountain.

"Him?" I asked. "He must have been important, having a statue and all."

Damon looked up at the statue with disdain. "It is his blood that prevents me from retrieving what is mine. Your friend broke one crucible. Another is here in the Black. I need you to find it and destroy it."

"Why can't you find it yourself?"

"Because I cannot see it!" Damon answered, frustrated. "Have you not been listening?"

"Well, if you can't find it, how do you expect *me* to?"

Damon pulled his black sword and lunged at me so quickly, I didn't have time to defend myself. He grabbed my arm and held the tip of the blade against my throat. I froze. All it would have taken was a slight push and I'd be smoke.

"I do not often bargain, Foley. If you continue to challenge me with questions, I will move on and find someone else to help me. I have been patient this long. I can continue to wait."

I held eye contact with him. I didn't want to show weakness, or fear.

"Just trying to understand," I said.

The madness left his eyes and he pushed me away. I didn't know if he had jumped me for effect or I had dodged a bullet to oblivion. Either way, this guy's emotions were all over the place.

"You have the freedom to move anywhere in the Black. I do not. There is a small group of spirits, traitors, who possess one of the crucibles. They were once trusted soldiers, until they chose to betray me. The only thing that prevents me from destroying them is the crucible they hold. It has kept them safe for centuries."

"You don't know where they are?" I asked.

"The crucible keeps me blinded," he said. "Until it is broken and the blood spilled, I cannot find the traitors."

"And what happens when that crucible is broken?" I asked.

"Another obstacle will be removed and I will be one step closer to the poleax. The traitors know of my weapon's location in the Light. I am sure of it. Once I find them, rest assured, they will guide your friend to its resting place. It will be a pleasure to see that they do."

"But why Marsh? Just because he broke a crucible?"

Damon gave that question some thought. I couldn't tell

if it was because he didn't know the answer or didn't want to tell me the truth.

"He was marked by the blood," he finally said, choosing his words carefully. "He alone can break the other crucibles that protect the poleax."

I couldn't comprehend all the ancient curse stuff, but at least I understood what he wanted me to do.

"It comes down to this," Damon said. "I can send you back to your family and friends and the life you so cherished. But to do that, I need the poleax. Find the crucible, destroy it, and when the poleax is mine, life will be yours once again."

"I'll think about it," I said, and then I closed my eyes and got out of there.

Seconds later I arrived at my home. Or my vision of my home. There was no way I would make any decisions under pressure. I needed time to let it all sink in.

The last time I was at my home in the Black, I was alone. Not this time. Sitting on the steps leading up to my porch was an old man with straggly gray hair. He was totally out of place, but somehow familiar.

"Something I can do for you, chief?" I called out.

The guy looked at the ground and kicked some leaves around.

"Tried to do the right thing," he mumbled. "Look where it got me. I'm dead, ain't I? Dead . . . dead . . . dead."

"Yeah, sorry. Welcome to the club."

"You too?"

"As a doornail, whatever that means."

The guy lifted his chin and looked at me. Tears ran from his eyes and down the gray beard stubble on his cheeks. He was a mess. You'd think that after you die you'd get cleaned up a little in the afterlife.

"You Cooper Foley? The guy who got killed in the boat?"

"Whoa," I exclaimed. "How did you know?"

"There isn't much that happens in Thistledown that gets by me."

I remembered who the guy was. He was poking around the lake and found my Davis Gregory jacket. He was the only guy who knew I was dead. At least he was when he was alive. Which he wasn't anymore. Not if he was talking to me in the Black.

"What's your name?" I asked.

"George," he answered. "George Ogilvy. They call me George O. I died because I tried to tell your friend the truth about what happened to you . . . and about the horror that demon'll bring to anybody who gets in his way."

13

"You saw Damon?" I asked. "He talked to you?"

"Don't know nothing about no Damon," he said. "The guy haunting me was a skeleton man."

"Gravedigger," I said. "He isn't real. It's a character my friend created."

"That ain't no character. He's as real as you or I, and since you and I are dead, maybe he's *more* real than us."

The old guy wiped away tears. He seemed disoriented, though I wasn't sure if that was because of his brush with Gravedigger or because he hadn't expected to find himself dead.

"What happened?" I asked.

"I find things around the lake. Things nobody wants no more. Some people pay good money for other people's junk. I was sleeping in the woods to get an early start on combing the north shore when I heard the two boats colliding.

Horrible sound. Won't never forget it. When I found your jacket, I put two and two together and figured you were history."

"How did you know it was my jacket?" I asked.

"Had your name in it."

Oh.

"Your parents own the yellow cottage a couple miles from town. You got that pretty sister."

"You really don't miss anything, do you?"

"When you spend your life collecting junk, you get to know who's throwing it out. I seen you every summer since you were kids, and I seen your friend. What's his name?"

"Marsh."

George's lip started to quiver and he began to cry again. I felt bad for the old guy. Not only was he dead but his last days hadn't been good ones.

"All I wanted was to tell your friend what happened," he said, his voice cracking. "That's all. Nobody should be left to rot under the water like that."

"Yeah, thanks for that image."

"But then . . . I started seeing things. Terrible things. A snake came outta my drain while I was brushing my teeth. It sunk its fangs right into my arm, but then it just up and vanished, like it was never there. Then all the tools at my house, they all turned to rubber. I know it sounds crazy but I'd pick up a hammer and it'd fall limp in my hand. But it only looked that way. I tried hammering with it and I smashed up my finger. Now, I'm a lone wolf, but I needed to see some normal folks. You know, to prove all was right with the world. So I went into town. The place was lousy with tourists, but none of them had faces. Men, women, even kids, they all looked like mannequins in a store window, just floating around all silent-like. I near went outta my mind. I realized pretty quick that none of it was real, it was just tricks that ghost was playing on me. I tried telling normal folks—you know, the ones with faces—what was going on but nobody believed me. Can't say I blame them. They all think I'm loony anyway."

"I believe you, George."

"I finally couldn't take it no more and holed up in my house. I boarded up the bedroom to keep that skeleton and his crazy tricks out. Lotta good it did. He came through the wall like it was made of air."

"All because he didn't want you to tell Marsh what happened to me?"

"Not just that. He haunted my dreams, showing me horrible things. People at war, all kinds of killing and cruelty. He told me we were all on some road and the more people who knew about it, the more would be in trouble. He said it was all your friend's fault."

"Marsh? No way."

"Ah, I didn't believe him. I think he only told me that so I'd go after the kid and scare him even more. I think I know why, too."

"Okay, why?"

"'Cause that ghost can't really do nothing. Sure, he can show you things that scare the living wits out of ya, but it ain't real. He's got it in for that boy and I think my gettin' in the act would of made it all seem more real. But I wouldn't do it. No, sir. I'm a good man."

I could have told him that not everything Damon did was an illusion, but I didn't want to mess up his mind any more than it already was.

George took a deep breath and looked around as if trying to figure out exactly where he was. "Yeah, a real good man," he said sadly. "Look where it got me."

The poor old guy had been in the wrong place at the wrong time and had paid the price.

"So you never told Marsh what happened to me?" I asked.

"I tried. Couple of times, but I was so scared. The best I could do was give him a key to my house. I got a piece of your boat there. I used it with a bunch of other wood to close off my bedroom. Lotta good that did."

My heart raced. "You have a piece of my boat in your bedroom? How do you know what it is?"

"It's got a name on it . . . *Galileo*. Must be a piece of the stern."

"It is. Did you tell Marsh what to look for at your house?"

"Didn't get the chance. The bogey came after me. It chased me into the road and, well, the truck that hit me wasn't an illusion."

"I'm sorry, man." I said, wincing.

"Why? Wasn't your fault."

"And it definitely wasn't yours. If it makes you feel any better, you did the right thing and that means you probably won't be here for long."

"Yeah? That's good. I think. Where exactly *is* here?"

How was I going to explain that to him? At that moment, Bernie the mailman came walking along the sidewalk, whistling some silly song.

"Bernie!" I called out. "Just the guy I'm looking for."

"What can I do you for, Chicken Coop?"

I pulled the mailman into my yard.

"This is George. George O. He just got here from the Light and needs the download on how things work."

Bernie lit up with a big smile. "Well, he's come to the right guy."

"George," I said, "Bernie's like you. He knows where all the skeletons are buried. Ooh, bad choice of words. He knows everything about everybody. He'll help you understand what's going on."

"You a mailman?" George asked with a frown. "You ain't one of them crazy ones, are ya? I've seen enough crazy to last me a lifetime."

Bernie laughed. "Well, you're on to another life now so keep an open mind."

George didn't look too happy. I sat down next to him on the stairs.

"You're a good man, George," I said. "What you did is gonna help Marsh after all."

George sighed. "I gotta tell ya, that bogey scares me. Not because of the things he did but because of what he showed me. If we're on this road he talked about, it ain't just your friend I'm worried about. We're all in for a load of trouble."

There was nothing I could say to that.

"I'll take it from here, Cooper," Bernie said with compassion.

"Good luck, George," I said, and stepped out of the Black . . .

. . . to arrive at our lake cottage in the Light. My goal was to get Marsh to George O.'s house so he could find the piece of the *Galileo* and figure out exactly what happened to me. That was the goal, anyway. I had no clue how to do it.

Marsh wasn't there. Both my parents' cars and Sydney's silver Beetle were gone too. Was it possible they'd gone back to Stony Brook? It wasn't likely, not before they figured out what had happened to me.

I closed my eyes and stepped away from the house, arriving in downtown Thistledown. I hoped that maybe Marsh was poking around. It was as good a place as any to look for him.

I walked along the street, invisible to everyone. It was cool and sad at the same time. I saw people I knew and some I wished I'd never met. I kept wanting to say something, but knew they couldn't see or hear me. The longer I was there, the more it made my heart ache. I didn't want to be a ghost. I wanted my life back. I wanted to hang out with Britt and party at the drive-in. I wanted to argue with my sister again. I wanted to play Uno with my parents. I wanted to be me.

Damon had offered me the chance to do all that. All I had to do was help him find his mystical weapon. But what would happen once he got it? If he got his life back, he wouldn't be returning to ancient Macedonia. He'd be part of the twenty-first century. How much damage could he really do? I mean, he'd just be some freak in a Halloween costume. He had no army. Or country. Or power. If he started causing trouble, he'd be locked up. He had more power as a spirit than he would as a living human.

Would bringing him back to life really be all that bad?

I didn't get the chance to come up with an answer because I caught sight of Sydney's silver Beetle pulling out of the parking lot of the mini golf course. Score. I had no idea where she was going so I did the only thing I could think of . . . I ran after the car and hopped onto the back bumper. Why not? What would happen if I fell off? Being a ghost had some advantages.

Looking in through the back window I saw that Marsh was with her. Double score. My plan was to stick with them until I could figure out some way to help guide them to the truth about what happened to me. Once that was done, I'd worry about how to get Damon off Marsh's back.

Sydney drove to a remote part of town where I'd never been before. She turned onto a country lane that was no more than two ruts of dirt. For a second I thought she and Marsh were looking for a place to make out, but that was about as unlikely as anything I'd seen since I'd been dead.

As I rode along, it struck me that I wasn't the least bit tired. Or hungry. Time really had no meaning to me anymore. Too bad. That was another thing I missed about being alive. Sleeping. And dreaming. And lying in bed until noon.

When we arrived at our destination, everything became clear. The rutted road opened up to a clearing where a ramshackle trailer home was parked in the center of what could best be described as a junkyard. I had no doubt that this was George O.'s house. The old man had done it. He gave Marsh a clue and Marsh had run with it. Nice going, Ralph.

He and Sydney got out of the car and surveyed the mess.

Marsh, always the philosopher, said, "Some people would look at this and see junk. Others see history."

Sydney snapped back with, "But most wouldn't be caught dead here. I'm not sure what category we're in."

I missed those guys.

While they looked around, I went inside because I had the advantage of knowing what to look for. The trailer was a sad place that was full of tools and trash. I tried not to imagine George O. living in that squalor and focused on looking for the room he had boarded up to keep Gravedigger out. It didn't take long. There were only three rooms.

The walls of his bedroom were covered with planks that he'd nailed up. I imagined him lying in his bed, terrified, thinking he was safely boarded up inside, and seeing Gravedigger float through the wall. He was lucky not to have died of a heart attack right there.

I checked out each and every board until I found the one I was looking for. Where the others were weathered gray, this was painted blue. It really stood out from the others, especially since the word "Galileo" was painted on it in black. I didn't think you could miss it.

I was wrong.

Marsh and Sydney got to the bedroom soon after. They opened the door and were both surprised when a length of board fell down at their feet. They had no idea what they were looking for and I didn't know how to help them. While they searched the room, I focused on the blue board, trying to get it to rattle, or wiggle, or do anything that would draw their attention. It didn't budge. I looked around, hoping to see something I might be able to levitate and float in front of the board to get their attention, but nothing was light enough for me to move.

"Look at the board!" I shouted in frustration.

They didn't. They checked drawers and even looked under the bed, but they didn't examine the boards that were nailed to the wall.

"Let's check the kitchen," Marsh said, and that was it. The two left the room without seeing the clue George O. had meant for them to find. I was frantic. I couldn't think of anything to get them to come back. I was about to run after them when I heard a voice that stopped me cold.

"Why is it so important to you that they learn of your fate?"

I turned quickly to see Damon examining the blue board.

I tried not to show him how surprised I was. "Closure, I guess."

It was only a small lie. What I really wanted was for Marsh to know that I was a ghost and doing my best to protect him from Damon.

"Well, then," he said. "Let me offer you a sign of good faith."

Damon turned to the wall that was opposite the blue board and closed his eyes. Suddenly light appeared through the cracks between the boards nailed in front of the window as if a high intensity spotlight had been turned on outside. A focused beam of light flashed out of the bedroom door and along the length of the trailer, toward Marsh and Sydney. Damon was doing just what I wanted to do, but couldn't.

Marsh and Sydney saw the strange light and did exactly what you'd expect . . . they followed it back to the bedroom. Marsh entered first, his eyes focused on the light that was moving across the floor, headed for the wall with the blue board.

He said, "Whatever's doing that, it wants us in here."

Marsh was getting with the program. He had accepted the possibility that supernatural forces were at work.

"I want to leave, Marsh," Sydney said nervously.

Damon made the light travel across the floor, up the wall, and come to rest on the blue board and the word "Galileo."

Sydney and Marsh stared at the board curiously.

"Is that it?" Sydney asked.

"C'mon," I coaxed them both. "Look closer."

They didn't. Both were too freaked out by what was happening to play detective.

Sydney, as usual, was growing impatient. "Yeah, and?" she said sarcastically.

Damon had even less patience. He opened his eyes and glared at the wall. Instantly the board shuddered as if it had been hit from the outside. Marsh and Sydney both jumped.

It was exactly what Marsh needed. He braced himself and stepped forward, staring at the board.

"Go, Ralph." I coaxed. "Look closer."

Marsh squinted at the bright spot of light on the letters, and gasped.

"Oh my god."

"What? What?" Sydney asked.

"Galileo."

Damon had done it. It would only be a matter of time before Marsh put it all together. I was certain of that. I only wished that I didn't have Damon to thank for it.

A second later both of us were back on the street of Damon's village in the Black. It wasn't even disorienting. I was getting used to jumping around between dimensions.

Damon stood with his foot up on the fountain and a satisfied smile on his scarred face.

"I guess I should thank you," I said. "Then again, you killed me, so it was the least you could have done."

"Now it is your turn," Damon said, all business. "Find the crucible in the Black and destroy it."

"Then I get my life back?"

"No, your friend must then locate the poleax in the Light. Once I have the weapon, I will leave your friend in peace and restore your former life. Is that too high a price to pay for getting yourself out of, what do you call it, Trouble Town?"

It pissed me off that he knew so much about me.

"And what happens to you?" I asked.

Damon looked around the ancient courtyard. "I wish I could say that I would also be returning to my former life, but that opportunity is long past. My goal is to leave this prison and right the wrongs that put me here."

"What does that mean?"

Damon leaned in close and gave me a cold stare. The scars on his face pulsed red. It turned my stomach.

"Those who are responsible for my being here will regret their treachery," he said. "You called me the devil, but did you consider there might actually be something worse?"

The idea that multiple levels of evil existed and Damon wasn't even the worst was a horrifying concept.

"So this is all about getting revenge?"

"Call it what you like."

"Okay, what if I agreed? I don't even know where to start looking for the crucible."

Damon reached into a small leather pouch that was fixed to his waist and pulled something out.

"This once belonged to my most trusted ally. A soldier named Adeipho. We were like brothers . . . until he betrayed me. And scarred me. I have carried this with me since that day. Use it to locate his vision."

He opened his hand. In his palm was a gnarly, brown piece of fungus that looked like an old mushroom.

"I took this from him the moment before he ended my life," Damon explained. "We were in battle and he did not part with it easily."

"What is it? A mushroom?"

"No. An ear."

"Ow!" I blurted out in disgust and backed off a step. "That's just . . . wrong."

"It is a piece of him, a connection that will allow you to locate him."

"It's a piece of him, all right. Geez, you gotta be kidding me."

"You asked how you can find the crucible and I am giving you that knowledge."

I looked at the mummified ear and forced myself not to gag. "So this is all about you getting even with some guys who betrayed you? That's it?"

"Surely you can understand that," he answered.

I looked up from the shriveled ear and held Damon's gaze.

"I want my life back," I said with finality.

"Destroying the crucible will be your first step back along the road," he replied.

I reached out and picked up the ear with two fingers. It felt like a dried apricot. My stomach flipped.

Damon chuckled and said, "I knew you would agree."

"Yeah, well, I always find my way out of Trouble Town."

Damon smiled, revealing his two daggerlike teeth. Seeing them made me realize exactly what had happened.

I had just made a pact with the devil.

14

I had agreed to help a murderer. *My* murderer.

What choice did I have? If I listened to Gramps and did nothing, Damon would kill Marsh and find some other way to get his precious weapon. He'd already waited a few thousand years. What would a few thousand more be? Time meant nothing in the Black. And who was I to judge him for wanting revenge on the guys who betrayed him and cut him up? It sounded like they were just as nasty as he was. Maybe worse. Maybe I'd be doing the universe a favor by unleashing Damon's revenge on them. And how bad would it really be if Damon returned to the Light, alive? What was he going to do? Organize another Macedonian army? A couple of navy SEALS would eat him for lunch. Damon might be less of a threat as a human than as a spirit. The way I looked at it, I was helping to put an end to his treachery for good. I had a lot of reasons to justify the decision I'd made, but one counted above all others:

I didn't want to be dead anymore.

If I had a chance to go back and pick up life where I'd left off, I was going to take it. To do that, I had to help Damon. So with a shriveled ear in my pocket—disgusting—I left Damon's vision in the Black and made one stop before beginning my search to find the owner of the ear. I wanted to tell Gramps what I was planning to do. He was the closest thing to a parent I had and I didn't think it would be right to make such a bold move without him knowing.

Needless to say, he wasn't happy.

"Coop, you can't," he cried. "You just can't."

Gramps was in his yard picking tomatoes. I used to love raiding his garden armed with a salt shaker. It made me wish I was six again. And not dead.

"I don't have a choice, Gramps," I said.

"Yeah, you do. What'll happen if things don't work out like you think? I told you before, there's trouble brewing."

"And what if the guy bringing that trouble is Adeipho? You should see what he did to Damon. He's not a good guy."

"Listen to yourself, Cooper. You've got this all twisted around so it'll work out the way you want it to because you think Damon can give you your life back."

"And to help Marsh," I added.

"You can't help Marsh!" Gramps yelled, his face as red as one of his tomatoes. "And you can't get your life back. That's not the way things work."

"You haven't seen what this guy can do," I argued.

"You're right," he said, taking a breath and forcing himself to calm down. "We'll play it your way. Let's say he gets this pole-thing and it really gives him the power over life and death. That don't make it right. Nobody should have that kind of power."

"What if I told you I could bring you with me?"

Gramps started to answer quickly, then turned away from me and went back to work in his garden.

"It's possible, Gramps. You said you missed Grandma. What if you could go back to your house in the Light? Where it's real. Real trees. Real tomatoes. It's still there, you know. Just like you remember it."

Gramps snapped me a look that was so full of emotion, it actually made me take a step backward. "Don't you think I know that?" he exclaimed, his voice cracking. "I spend more time there watching over your grandma than I do here, where I should be, working on my own life. I probably could have been sprung from here ages ago if I did what I was supposed to do instead of living in the past. That life is over, Cooper. No matter how bad you want it back."

"I'm not talking about the past. I'm talking about moving forward. Help me get this done, Gramps. Maybe this is what you're supposed to be doing to make yourself the best person you can be."

Gramps shook his head. "No. I can't believe that. Even if this Damon fella was wronged a long time ago, that don't justify the things he's doing. Haunting folks. Threatening you. Hell, he *killed* you, Cooper! He may be justified in wanting revenge, but that ain't the kind of thing that gets you out of here. At least not to the place you want to go."

"So how are you going to do it, Gramps? What are you going to do to get out of here?"

Gramps got down on his knees and plucked a few of the plumper tomatoes from the lower parts of the plants. I wasn't sure if he was going to answer me. It was a bold thing to be asking your grandfather to justify his existence.

"I don't know," he finally said. "Some things I did when I was alive I'm not proud of and I wish I knew what

I could do here to make up for 'em. Who knows? Maybe it ain't possible and I'll be living in this illusion for the rest of time."

"And maybe I'm giving you a chance to get out," I said. "Maybe it's my chance too."

Gramps looked up at me, his eyes filled with tears. I'd never seen him cry before.

"Or maybe you're writing your own ticket into the Blood," he said. "I'm sorry, Cooper. If you came here looking for help, you came to the wrong place."

"No, he didn't," came a familiar voice.

We both turned to see Maggie standing at the end of the long row of tomato plants.

"I'll help you," she said.

Gramps turned cold. "Leave him alone!" he yelled.

I'd never heard Gramps talk to anybody that way, let alone a young girl.

"It's okay, she's cool," I said.

He glared at me and barked, "She shouldn't be poking in other people's business, and neither should you. Go on in the house now. Let me finish up here."

"I'm not six anymore, Gramps."

"Then, stop acting like the world revolves around you." He looked past me to Maggie and yelled, "And you! Leave him be!"

Maggie gave me a sad smile and started back toward her house. I backed away from Gramps, wishing I hadn't come to talk with him. I didn't want it to be this way between us. We were always pals.

"I love you, Gramps," I said.

"Don't go with that girl," he warned. "You've already made too many mistakes."

"I'll let you know what happens," I said, and headed after Maggie.

"Cooper!" Gramps called. "This isn't a game. You're risking your eternal soul."

That almost made me stop. It definitely made me think, but I'd made up my mind. If my soul was at risk, then I wanted to be the one calling the shots.

"Maggie!" I called, and ran to catch her.

"Maybe you should listen to him," she said, and kept walking.

I fell in step beside her. "I'm done listening. I want to start doing something."

"And what's that?"

"I'm going to help Damon."

"Are you sure that's right?"

"No, but I think it's my only choice. There are spirits in the Black who are even worse than him. He wants to bring them back to life so he can kill them again, I guess. I don't know. I don't care. That's his business."

"He can bring spirits back to life?" she asked.

"So he says. But first he needs me to find them in the Black. They've got this golden ball filled with blood that he needs smashed."

"Why?"

"It's a curse of some kind. There's a bunch of them. Marsh smashed one. That's what put him on Damon's radar."

"How did Marsh get it?"

"I don't know. I didn't ask him that."

"Maybe you should."

I jumped in front of Maggie, forcing her to stop walking. We had moved from Gramps's vision of the Black into Maggie's. The colorful fall leaves were gone, leaving gray skeletal-looking trees. The sky had transformed from blue to hazy gray and the temperature fell dramatically.

"There's more to this," I said. "If I help Damon, he'll give me my life back too."

"And that's what you want? Your life back?"

"Absolutely! Wouldn't you?"

Her answer was a silent, blank stare. I felt as if I'd asked the wrong question. Again. Awkward.

I dug into my pocket to take out the—gulp—mummified ear.

"This is the ear of the spirit who has the ball o' blood. Damon said it would help me find him."

I expected Maggie to be all grossed out. Instead she grabbed the ear and examined it, bending it back and forth to test its resiliency. My stomach turned.

"Who is he?" she asked.

"His name's Adeipho. He's the guy who cut Damon up and killed him. Damon wants to return the favor but can't do it until this crucible thing is destroyed."

She handed me back the ear and asked, "You know how to use this to find him?"

"No. Do you?"

"The Black is like a sea that we're all swimming in. You already know how to move between visions." She held up the ear and said, "This is something that's important to Adeipho."

"It used to be, anyway."

"It will allow you to seek his vision."

I glanced over her shoulder to see a Watcher standing on Maggie's porch. It reminded me that I was doing something that was probably about as far away from legal as you could get. I was meddling with spirits that could lead to a major interference with the Light. I wondered what penalty I would have to pay when I died a second time. I shook the thought. I never worried about the future and this was no time to start.

"So, what do I do?" I asked. "Hold the ear, click my heels together three times, and say, 'There's no place like Adeipho'?"

"I don't understand what that means."

"How does it work?" I asked.

"It's as simple as entering the vision of a spirit you know. I'll show you."

"No! I'm going alone. You've already got enough problems and—"

Too late. She grabbed my hand and pulled me forward. I took one step in her vision . . . and a second step in an entirely different place.

"—I've got enough on my conscience as it is. Whoa."

Since Adeipho was one of Damon's soldiers, I figured his vision of the Black would be pretty much like Damon's. I expected to land in some ancient village with stone buildings and more grubby guys wearing skirts. Instead I was greeted by a loud, obnoxious sound that was coming from directly behind us.

We both jumped and barely missed getting hit by a speeding car. I stood there holding Maggie, trying to get my mind around what had just happened.

"I thought you said Adeipho killed Damon," Maggie cried.

"That's what Damon said."

"Then he wasn't telling you the whole truth, because this isn't the vision of somebody from his time."

We weren't in ancient Macedonia, or any other ancient place. Maggie and I found ourselves on a modern city street.

The roar of a motorcycle got our attention. We spun around to see a rider flash out from between two buildings, turn toward us, and accelerate. He wore dark clothes but instead of a helmet, he had on a white Halloween clown mask with a built-in hideous grin.

"I don't understand," Maggie cried.

The biker turned toward us, reached to a saddlebag, and pulled out a sword.

A black sword.

Like a knight on horseback, he raised it high to attack.

15

I grabbed Maggie's hand and pulled her up onto the side-walk.

The motorcycle didn't stop. It bounced up over the curb but the jolt knocked the guy off balance. He had to fight to control the bike, which gave us time to run. I pulled Maggie along, sprinting down the sidewalk.

"Go back to your vision!" I yelled at her.

"I can't," she called back. "I already tried."

I tried too. I visualized my house in Stony Brook and expected to step into a swirl of color and land back in my front yard. No go. We were still on the sidewalk, running from the clown on his motorcycle, who had regained his balance and was charging after us.

"What happened?" Maggie asked, frightened. "Where are we?"

I had no idea. All I understood was that there was

no magical way out so we had to save ourselves the old-fashioned way.

"Here!" I shouted, and pulled her into a narrow alley between buildings.

We were in a neighborhood of brick buildings. None were more than four or five stories high with shops on the ground floors and apartments above. We sprinted along a narrow alley that I hoped emptied out onto the next street.

I glanced back over my shoulder to see the guy on the motorcycle scream past the opening, going too fast to make the turn. His tires squealed on the pavement as he jammed on the brakes. In a few seconds he'd loop around and shoot in behind us.

"We should talk to him," Maggie said, breathless.

"Not if he's swinging that black sword," I replied.

"Spirits can't be hurt, Cooper," she said.

"Trust me, that sword hurts."

I heard the motorcycle accelerate, the sound of the engine echoing through the stone canyon. He had entered the alley and was coming up fast. We were ten yards from daylight. We'd make it. But what then?

We sprinted out of the alley into an empty parking lot. I looked around, desperate to find a place to hide.

"Across the street," I said. "Into one of those stores."

Maggie started running before I did. There was a small grocery on the far side of the street. I wanted to speed through, get out the back door, and then lose ourselves in whatever city we were in so we could figure out how to get back to our own visions.

Maggie hit the sidewalk first and was about to run into the street when she stopped short and screamed. Another guy on a motorcycle cut her off. She had to dive backward out of his way and landed hard on her butt. I pulled her to her feet as a third motorcycle came at us and screeched to a stop, blocking us from crossing the street.

I pulled Maggie to the right, ready to run along the sidewalk, but we were faced down by a fourth motorcycle that was speeding toward us, cutting off that route. I turned right again to see the first guy blasting out of the alley, headed our way. There was nowhere to go. All four motorcycles closed on us and circled, keeping us trapped between them. Maggie and I held on to each other, helpless.

Nobody made a move to attack. It was like they were playing with us. They all rode Harley-style muscle bikes that made the pavement rumble. No two of them were dressed alike. The first guy who came at us with the sword wore dark clothes with a black cape that flew out behind him like some twisted superhero . . . and he was the most normal-looking one. Another guy looked to be wearing the same kind of leather armor that Damon's pals wore. A third guy had on what I can best describe as a clown suit. He had green and white striped pants and a loud red jacket. The last guy had on a business suit, complete with a perfectly tied tie. All four wore the same white grinning masks.

And they all had black swords tucked into saddlebags.

"Why can't we leave the vision?" Maggie whimpered.

She was asking the wrong guy.

Holding her around the waist, I made a slow move as if to walk out of the carousel of circling bikes, but the cape guy nudged me back with a quick turn of his front tire. The roar of four bikes made it impossible to talk, not that I would have known what to say. It was looking like my attempt to help Damon was already a miserable failure.

The guy with the dark suit steered his bike toward us from behind, nudging us to walk toward the building on the far side of the parking lot we had just run through. The others moved to either side of us so that there was only one way we could go. Maggie and I exchanged looks and started walking toward the building, being escorted by the motorcycle clowns. There was no other option. I glanced to the alleyway we had just come through and calculated the possibility of making a run for it. It wasn't wide enough for more than one bike, but one bike would have been enough to run us down and skewer us. I figured it was best to go along and see what these guys were all about.

As we walked closer to the building, a garage door began to rise directly in front of us. Whoever these guys were, they didn't want to wipe us out right away. Then again, maybe they wanted to do it in private. Which made me think: *Where is everybody?* Looking around, I realized that for a city neighborhood, it was strangely deserted. It made me wonder whose vision of the Black this really was. It definitely wasn't that of a soldier from ancient Macedonia.

I expected to see a Watcher or two observing the show, but there wasn't a single one around.

"I don't want to go in there," Maggie whimpered. She was shaking with fear.

Every step brought us closer to the dark opening that led to an ominous-looking cave. If not for the swords, I may have taken a chance and jumped one of the riders, but I wanted to be around to fight another day.

"I'll get us out of this, I swear," I whispered to Maggie as we stepped through the dark portal.

What we found was a big garage that stretched up a few stories. Parked along one side were a dozen more bikes like the ones that were pushing us inside. I wondered if this was actually some bizarre biker gang and we'd stumbled onto their turf. The roar from the four bikes grew deafening. The throaty engine noise bounced every which way inside the large space. We were pushed to the center of the room, where the four bikers surrounded us again and, thankfully, killed their engines. It was like we had been inside a jet engine that suddenly became a library.

Maggie and I stood still, waiting for one of them to make a move. The guy with the cape swung his leg over his bike and strode toward us. He had long, curly black hair that framed the creepy mask. The others stayed on their bikes, watching silently. The cape guy stopped in front of us. He had left his sword back in the saddlebag of his bike. If things went south, I was ready to dive for the weapon and start swinging.

I couldn't take the silence anymore so I asked, "You guys in the circus?"

"Who are you?" the guy asked with a deep voice that was muffled by his mask. The mask may have been smiling, but he didn't sound happy.

"My name's Cooper Foley. This is Maggie, uh . . ."

"Salinger," she said, barely above a whisper.

"Salinger," I repeated. "Maggie Salinger. Who are you?"

I heard the squeal of a motor and turned to see the garage door slowly lowering. Maggie squeezed my hand. As ominous as that was, it wasn't the worst development. More people were arriving. They walked in slowly from other parts of the building, silently gathering to view the newcomers. Some arrived on small BMX-style bicycles but most were on foot. They moved in silently like they were filing into church. Each wore an odd costume. A few had old-time soldier uniforms. Some I recognized as being from the United States. Others I didn't know. I saw a Union soldier and a sailor. The rest meant nothing to me, though they all looked as if they came from different eras. The guys on bikes wore army fatigues. A few women wore floor-length gowns with big skirts and wigs, as if they were headed for an old-time ball. I saw a guy in a white lab coat, a frail man in a wheelchair wearing a judge's robe, a Viking-looking dude wearing animals skins, and another guy wearing a tuxedo. As bizarre as the scene was, it was made more so by the fact that everybody wore similar clown masks like they were all headed for Mardi Gras.

I didn't see how these freaks could be Damon's enemies because nobody looked as if they had come from ancient Macedonia. Still, if these were the guys Damon wanted to take his revenge on, they had to be dangerous. Maybe more so than Damon. At least I knew what Damon was all about: ancient warrior, pissed off about being killed, wanted revenge. Got it. These guys were a whole different ball game.

The people formed a circle beyond the ring of motorcycles. We were the center of attention at a masked ball from hell.

Maggie whispered, "I think I'm going out of my mind."

The guy with the black cape said, "I will ask again, who are you?"

"I told you," I said. "Cooper Foley and—"

"Why are you here?"

Good question. I wished I had a good answer. It didn't seem wise to tell the truth so I did the next best thing.

"I don't know," I said, trying to sound like a confused kid. "Maggie and I were moving from her vision to mine and we somehow ended up here. Where are we? Whose vision is this?"

I looked from the guy in black to the others who surrounded us, hoping to see a sympathetic face. I don't know why I bothered. All their faces were covered in clown masks as they stared at us in silence.

The guy in black stepped away, headed for his motorcycle. With one quick move he pulled his sword from its sheath.

"Whoa!" I said nervously. "Let's not go there. We came

by mistake. No harm, no foul. We'll just leave and pretend this never happened."

The guy stalked forward, holding the sword's point toward me.

"You say you are here by accident," he said. "Yet you know what this weapon is capable of, which makes me believe your being here was no mistake."

Oops.

"I don't know what you're talking about," I said, trying to sound all innocent and confused. "You're coming at us with a sword. Why wouldn't I be scared?"

"Because you are already a spirit," he answered.

Oh. Right. That.

"Look," I said, thinking fast. "I don't know who you are or where we are but what exactly do you think we can do to you? There's only two of us and you've got a whole bunch of, well, I don't know *what* the hell you guys are but there are a lot of you. You don't have anything to be afraid of."

"That is the first truth you have told," he said. "We do not fear you."

I was relieved by his comment, until he lifted his sword. We were seconds away from being cinder.

"Cooper!" Maggie cried, and held her hands up to cover her head.

I didn't bother. I knew it wouldn't do any good. But I did close my eyes, waiting for the worst . . .

That didn't come.

I cautiously opened my eyes to see that someone had stopped the guy from killing us. The sword was still held high but another guy had arrived and was holding the big guy's arm from striking.

"Put it down!" the new guy said, barely above a whisper.

The big guy lowered the sword, though he wasn't happy about it.

At first I thought our savior was a woman because he was slighter and much shorter than the clown with the sword, and had long, curly brown hair. But the voice could have gone either way and he was dressed like a dude in jeans, a khaki shirt, and a dark jacket. He wore leather gloves too, and his face was hidden behind one of those creepy masks. So I couldn't tell if it was a man or a woman, and frankly, I didn't care. The guy moved with confidence and authority, which made me think that he was in charge.

"There's no need for that," he said in the same low whisper to the guy with the sword.

The big clown backed off but it was killing him. He really wanted to whack us.

"Thank you," the new guy whispered.

Why was he whispering? Maybe it was his way of showing authority. I knew some teachers like that. The louder things got in class, the softer they'd talk. It made us all strain to hear, and kept the power with him.

Or maybe this guy just had a sore throat.

He turned away from the clown and looked me over as if sizing me up.

I took a chance and said, "C'mon, chief. Do we really look like a threat?"

"Your very presence is a threat," he whispered.

I didn't know what that meant so it was hard to argue, but I had to try. If there was one thing I was good at it was talking my way out of Trouble Town.

"The second we landed here we tried to leave but we couldn't. Why is that? Why can't we move back to our own visions?"

The guy didn't answer. He stepped closer and grabbed my chin, moving my head back and forth slightly like he wanted to analyze my features. He wasn't rough about it, but that didn't make it any less strange. He didn't do it to Maggie, either. Just me.

"What's with the masks?" I asked.

"It would be better if you didn't speak," was his quick answer.

"Sure. Whatever you say. You want quiet? I'll be quiet."

"Stop," he commanded. "You will go outside and walk west until you are able to leave this vision. Do not return here. Either of you. Ever. Your coming here was a mistake and I know you aren't foolish enough to make the same mistake twice. That would be tragic. Do you understand?"

"Absolutely. We're gone," I said and held up a double okay sign. I did it out of habit. It's what I did when I wanted to let somebody know that everything was cool.

His reaction surprised me. He chuckled. Why was that funny?

He looked to Maggie and said, "Do you understand?"

Maggie nodded quickly. As much as this guy seemed to be the leader of this twisted gang, I wasn't afraid of him. And not just because he was letting us go. He had definitely threatened us, but I didn't believe for a second that he would order our destruction. Then again, if it had been up to the guy with the sword, Maggie and I would be no more.

The sword guy looked to the boss and said, "I fear we will regret this."

"Go," the boss-man commanded, ignoring the biker.

"You got it. Thanks."

"Thank you," Maggie said.

The crowd of costumed freaks parted to reveal a door on the far side of the garage. I took Maggie's hand and walked quickly for it.

"What just happened?" she whispered.

"Let's get out of here first."

We stepped out of the door to find ourselves on the same street where we had first arrived.

"Which way is west?" I asked her.

"I don't know. Let's just go that way," she said, pointing down the street.

It was as good a guess as any. Still holding hands we walked quickly away from the garage.

"They're following us," Maggie whispered.

I glanced back to see that the menagerie of people had followed us through the door and were gathered in the street, slowly trailing behind. Even the guys on their bicycles were there, riding with the walkers.

"I guess they want to make sure we leave," I said.

"But we can't move between visions," Maggie said.

"That guy seemed to think we'd be able to once we get far enough away."

We walked for a few blocks, passing street after empty street. There were no cars, no people, no sign of life anywhere. It was as if the entire city was deserted.

"Look!" Maggie exclaimed, pointing ahead.

Two blocks ahead of us a swirling wall appeared. Dark shadows—some small, some immense—drifted like whales in the vast sea of color. The impossible boundary stretched into the sky and continued off to either side of us for as far as I could see.

"What is it?" Maggie asked.

"Maybe it's the end of the vision."

Standing on a street corner, a few feet in front of the colorful wall, was a Watcher.

"I never thought I'd be happy to see one of those guys," I said.

"What do we do?" Maggie asked.

"Keep walking."

When we got to within twenty yards of the Watcher,

the group of oddballs who had been following us stopped. They stood shoulder to shoulder, spread across the width of the street, frozen in place.

"They're not taking any chances," Maggie said.

I took Maggie's hand and walked the last few feet until we reached the swirling wall. The Watcher didn't move, but kept his eyes on us. I reached out to the wall to see if it was solid. My hand passed through.

"Ready?" I asked.

Maggie nodded. We stepped into the wall . . . and walked through into my front yard in the Black.

"Well," I said. "That was interesting."

"I don't ever want to go back there," Maggie said.

"You don't have to. But I do."

Maggie's eyes widened and she was about to argue, but her words were cut off by the loud roar of motorcycle engines.

"No way," I said with a gasp.

A motorcycle appeared on the street and turned onto the walkway that led to my house. Maggie and I both tried to run but were turned back by the clown with the cape who was riding up from behind my house, digging up the grass. Along with the warrior. And the guy in the business suit.

All four motorcycle clowns had followed us into my vision.

16

The guy in black leaped off his bike, grabbed his sword, and strode for us, ready to fight.

Maggie screamed and cowered behind me. I held my hand up, not that it would have protected us from that sword.

"Whoa, whoa, stop! We did what you wanted!"

"How did you find us?" the guy bellowed, holding the sword up high, ready to strike. "What brought you to that vision?"

"I told you, it was a mistake!"

"Liar!" he shouted. The guy was out of his mind. I guess he didn't like being told what to do by the whispering dude who held him back from vaporizing us.

He added, "I know you are in league with Damon!"

There it was. Damon. When we landed on that city street it was no mistake. We were in the exact right spot and now we were in a very *bad* spot. The guy held the sword up high.

His arm trembled. He was fired up, ready to swing and end it all right there. I'd been in situations where some macho guy had lost control and just started throwing punches. I had to get him thinking again. It didn't matter about what, so long as he got his brain back in gear.

"Who are you?" I asked. "Why are you wearing masks? Are you hiding? Why couldn't we leave that vision? Are you guys all part of the same vision? How does that work?"

He hesitated. It was working. He lowered his sword and yanked off his mask to reveal a fairly normal-looking guy, with a mop of curly black hair, thick features, and a sharp nose. His skin was ruddy red, like he'd been in the sun too long. Or maybe his blood pressure was making him red-faced. Do spirits have a blood pressure? He stared right through me with cold eyes. He wanted to end Maggie and me right then and there, but I had to hope the orders from the boss back in the garage kept him from doing it.

"Ree has given you a gift," he said through clenched teeth. "I would not have done the same. I believe you were sent by Damon. If not, then so be it. This will end here."

Ree? That was his boss's name?

He stepped closer to me and put the tip of the sword blade against my chin. I didn't even dare to swallow.

He added, "But if you are a scout for Damon, I have no doubt you will ignore this warning and we will meet again. When that time comes, Ree will not have the same compassion."

He turned his head and looked past me to his gang.

As soon as he turned, Maggie gasped. She saw the same thing I did.

The side of his head was covered by a tangle of black hair but there was no mistake. Pulling off his mask had revealed his left ear. Or where his left ear used to be. There was nothing there but a scarred circle of flesh. The guy who wanted to end my existence was Adeipho, Damon's nemesis. Knowing what he did to Damon, I was surprised that he held himself back from destroying us. This was a sadistic killer.

"Chicken Coop!" yelled Bernie as he peeked around a hedge into my yard. "What's going on? You throwing a Halloween party?"

Adeipho lowered his sword and backed away, but he kept his eyes on me.

"Tell Damon I would like nothing more than to meet and finish him. Again."

I said. "If you hate this guy so much, why don't you just find him and have it out?"

"If only I could," he replied. "Perhaps in another life."

"Another life? How many more lives are there?"

He ignored the question and got back on his bike. All four spirits fired up their engines, the roar destroying the peace of the neighborhood. Adeipho pulled his mask back down and hit the throttle. The spirit posse took off from my yard and roared down the street, the rumble of their engines fading quickly as they left my vision.

"Friends of yours, Coop?" Bernie asked, confused.

"Nah, they were selling Girl Scout cookies."

Bernie gave me a puzzled look, then smiled. "I'm glad you're here, Cooper. Things were getting a little dull."

He tipped his hat and continued on down the street, whistling his tune. As I watched him go, I noticed a Watcher across the street.

"Hey!" I shouted. "You! Why do you let them get away with that? What is it you do, anyway?"

His answer was to disappear.

"Those guys are starting to tick me off," I muttered.

Maggie was sitting on the grass, hugging herself. Shaking with fear.

"It was him," she said. "Did you see? His ear was gone."

"Yeah, I would have given it back to him but that would have proven we were exactly who he thought we were. And grossed me out."

"I don't understand anything that just happened," she said, her voice breaking. "Whose vision were we in? Why weren't we able to leave?"

"Here's one for you, how was Adeipho able to enter my vision? I definitely didn't want him here, so why wasn't he blocked?"

"And that man in the garage," she added. "He wasn't an ancient warrior."

"I don't think any of them were. Then again, how could you tell when they were all wearing costumes?"

Maggie dropped her head and cried. I was never good with figuring out what to do when girls cried because it was usually for some random reason that I had no clue how to deal with. But in this case, she had some pretty good reasons. I knelt down next to her but didn't say anything. Mostly because I didn't know what to say. After a long minute she looked up at me. Seeing her big sad eyes tore my heart out. This girl had been through a lot, and here I was putting her through even more.

"Thanks for helping me," I said softly. "But you should go home now. This isn't your problem."

"Maybe I want it to be my problem," she said.

"Uh . . . why?"

She sniffed and said, "Something is going to happen. I've felt it for a while. There have been more Watchers than usual but spirits haven't been moving on. It's like things have come to a standstill. Not being able to move out of visions is even more proof. I have to believe it has something to do with Damon. Or Adeipho. Or both of them. They seem to have power over the Watchers. That could be part of the problem we're feeling."

"Yeah, and who do you root for? One's a killer and the other one is, well, a killer. And I'm trying to help one of them. Does that make me a bad guy?"

"I don't know, but it puts you in the middle of it."

"Yeah, tell me about it."

"Cooper, I want to be there with you."

"What? Why?"

Tears filled her eyes again. "Because I don't want to be alone anymore."

The girl was an emotional wreck. I wanted to hug her and tell her it was all going to be okay but I had no idea if that was true.

"I don't know if what I'm doing is right," I said. "I mean, Damon said he'd give me my life back. That's not exactly . . . usual. I don't want you to suffer for that."

"But I don't want my life back."

"You don't want to go to the Blood, either."

"I want to move on. It doesn't matter which way. My vision is a very lonely place."

I hadn't thought about it before, but unlike the other visions in the Black I'd seen, Maggie's was the only one that didn't have a lot of other people in it. No wonder she kept bouncing around between different people's visions. I had no idea what had happened with her parents and I didn't care. All I saw was a girl who was trying to help me out in spite of how badly she was hurting. We'd only known each other for a short time but I liked Maggie and didn't want to see her so tortured.

"I have an idea," I said. I stood up and pulled her to her feet. "Let's go on an adventure."

"Another one?"

"I mean a good one. Our visions are supposed to be all about our lives the way we remember them, right? Maybe it's time to remember some good things."

"Shouldn't we be worrying about Damon and Adeipho?"

I took her hand and said, "If time means nothing, let's worry about it another time."

You'd think I'd want to kick back and rest after all that had happened. Just the opposite. I was as full of energy as if I had just woken up after a good night's sleep. It was one of the very cool perks of being a spirit and I wanted to take advantage of it.

"Where are we going?" she asked.

"To a better place," was my answer.

I closed my eyes and imagined a spot that had some great memories for me. The whirl of color appeared before us. We walked through it and came out the other side in the exact place I had imagined.

"Awesome," I said with a gasp, a little surprised that it had actually worked.

We found ourselves in my vision of the Playland amusement park near Stony Brook. Maggie's eyes lit up when she saw that we were on a busy midway surrounded by rides, games, and music.

"Where are we?" she asked, sounding a little overwhelmed.

"It's called Playland, so . . . let's play."

For the first time since I'd met her, Maggie gave me a beautiful, happy smile. In that one moment, her worries were forgotten . . . which is exactly why we were there.

"What should we do?" she asked, all giddy.

"Monster Mouse," I answered without a second thought.

We took off running and went on all of my favorite rides. The Monster Mouse roller coaster, the Screaming Eagle coaster, Round-Up, Tilt-A-Whirl, Scrambler . . . basically, every ride in the park. There were no lines, which was good and creepy at the same time but it made sense because the only people enjoying the park were spirits who had been there before. Or were visiting the vision of spirits they knew. I tried not to think about how everybody there was dead. I wanted to focus on enjoying the beautiful day. The sky was blue and sunny. The air was warm. We didn't have to pay for any of the rides. Or the games. Or the cotton candy. It was perfect.

And the best was still to come.

After jumping off the bumper cars, I said, "I'll bet you've never seen a park like this before."

Maggie laughed. "I'll take that bet."

"I'm talking about in the Light," I said.

"So am I."

Maggie gave me a mischievous smile and held out her hand. I didn't know what to expect but if she trusted me, I had to trust her. I took it and we both stepped through another colorful fog . . .

To find ourselves back in Playland. The same Playland, in another time. Maggie's time. Playland was built in the early 1900s and from the look of the place, we weren't far removed from opening day. If Maggie was happy before, she had skipped right into ecstatic now.

"This is how *I* remember it!" she exclaimed.

She pulled me forward to our first stop, which was a powerful carousel called the Derby Chase. It was like a merry-go-round on steroids. It spun so fast I had to hold on tight and lean hard for fear of being flung off.

"This is freakin' awesome!" I yelled to her. "I had no idea they had thrill rides in the old days!"

"Fun wasn't invented last week," she replied.

Seeing the park as it was so long ago was almost as fun as riding the rides. I knew that a lot of the attractions from my time were old, but I didn't know they'd been around since the park opened. There was the Whip and Ye Old Mill and the best ride in the park . . . The Dragon Coaster. It was a classic wooden roller coaster that was every bit as exciting as the newer rides. That was only half the fun. We also went on plenty of rides that were long gone by the time my era came around. There was a fun house with a three-story wooden slide, and a huge polished disk built into the floor that you had to try and stay on as long as you could as it spun . . . before you were flung off into bumpers. There was also a spooky walk-through castle called the Magic Carpet where things jumped out at you when you stepped on a floor trigger. It ended with a bumpy ride down a steep conveyor belt slide. It was awesome. The park layout was the exact same as the present, with a wide garden of flowers and grass running through the midway. Most of the games were the same too. There isn't much you can do to improve on a booth where you have to knock down bottles with a baseball or toss rubber hoops onto bottle necks.

The biggest difference was the people. Men walked around in straw hats and wore ties and shiny shoes as if a day at the amusement park was something you had to dress up for. The women all wore dresses with long sleeves. There wasn't a single pair of sneakers or jeans in the park. The music that played over the speaker system in my time was classic rock. I don't know what you'd call the music they played in Maggie's time, but it sounded like something you'd hear in the circus. It didn't come through speakers, either. A band with guys in striped jackets performed live in the center of the midway.

"Put this on," Maggie said.

It was a yellow straw hat with a red and blue striped band.

"No way. I'll look like a dork!" I protested.

Maggie chuckled. "I don't know what a dork is, but

everybody here must be one because all the men are wearing them."

I saw what she meant. I was the only guy not wearing a hat. She didn't wait for me to change my mind and popped it onto my head. She then grabbed a bow tie off of a teddy bear that was sitting in a booth, waiting to be won. It didn't exactly go with my dark shirt, but that didn't stop her. She giggled as she tied it around my neck.

"One more thing," I said.

All the guys working the game booths wore red and white striped jackets, like the band. The guy in the teddy bear booth was taking a break and I saw an extra jacket tucked below the counter. Before you could say "Step right up!" I nabbed the jacket and the two of us took off, giggling. It was a little small for me, but at least I felt as though I blended in.

Maggie wasn't as convinced. She took a look at me and burst out laughing.

"You look like a clown," she exclaimed.

"Hey, it's not my fault the people in your time dressed like cartoons."

She took my arm and off we went, exploring her vision. Her reality.

"The carousel!" she exclaimed, and we rode the exact same ride that was still around in my day. It probably even played the same tinny calliope music. I don't think our day could have been better and the best part of all was that I got the chance to see something rare.

I saw Maggie having fun.

After a few hours the shadows started getting longer as the sun went down, and the colorful lights that covered pretty much every square inch of every building came to life. It was cool to see how some things didn't change, no matter what era you were in.

Maggie and I decided to ride the Ferris wheel one last time before heading back to our own visions. We boarded the ride, getting a bird's-eye view of the old-fashioned park. I didn't want the day to end. Maggie didn't say it, but I knew she felt the same way. In fact, we didn't say much of anything. After spending so much time laughing and playing like little kids, we both sat back and simply enjoyed the view.

As far as I was concerned, the Ferris wheel ride could have gone on forever.

Until our adventure, my impression of Maggie was that she was a tortured soul who wore the guilt of her past like a weight around her neck. When she took that weight off, she transformed into a playful, silly girl who was daring and confident. I wished I could have known her under other circumstances.

The wheel stopped when we were at the very top. As if on cue, a fireworks show began. Playland was on the shore of Long Island Sound so the colorful explosions doubled with their reflection in the water.

"They had fireworks back then too?" I asked.

Maggie chuckled. "I'm not a dinosaur. I think the Chinese came up with them a few thousand years ago."

"Oh. Right. Cool."

She slid next to me and slipped her arm through mine. I didn't mind.

"Could this be any more perfect?" I asked.

"Yes," she answered.

"How?"

Maggie looked at me and said, "Can I kiss you?"

"Whoa. Awkward."

Maggie stiffened. "I'm sorry. I just thought—"

I pulled her closer. "Don't be. I just meant that you didn't have to ask."

She gave me a coy smile.

"No problem," I added. "You're probably a little out of practice."

"More than you know," she said. "I, uh, I've never been kissed."

"Uh, never? As in . . . *never*?"

Her answer was to lean forward and kiss me gently on the lips. I didn't mind that, either. Kissing Maggie was like being touched by a butterfly. A really beautiful butterfly.

We pulled apart, her eyes right on mine.

"*Now* this couldn't get any better," I said.

Maggie smiled, but I saw sadness there.

"What's the matter?" I asked. "Not what you thought it would be?"

"No, it was perfect. I just wanted to do that before you decided not to like me anymore."

"What? Why would that happen?"

The Ferris wheel started moving and Maggie slid away from me. I could feel her tension.

"I've never done this before," she said. "I thought I never would."

"Kiss a guy?"

"No. I want to tell you about what happened to me in the Light."

The Ferris wheel stopped. We had hit bottom and the operator opened the bar for us to get out. I didn't move. I wasn't so sure I wanted to leave. No, I wasn't so sure I wanted to hear what Maggie had to say. She got out, turned back, and held out her hand to me.

"Please let me show you?" she asked.

I took off my hat, jacket, and tie and put them on the seat next to me.

"Let's go," she coaxed.

I took her hand and stepped out of the ride car into the wall of swirling color . . .

To arrive at Maggie's vision of her life in the Black. We'd left the color and excitement of a carnival to enter a world where the sky was gray. The trees were gray, and the barn was gray.

We stood in her yard, directly in front of the barn.

Maggie said, "I want you to look inside."

17

I wanted to know the truth . . . but I didn't.

Sure I was curious. Who wouldn't be? But I felt like I was entering dangerous, dark territory. I liked this girl who was compassionate enough to want to help me solve an impossible mess. I hated that she was so sad, but I respected her for wanting to take charge of her own destiny. After our trip to Playland I was also happy to see that she liked having fun as much as I did. Marsh would like her. But she was sad for a reason and I wasn't so sure I wanted to know the details. Which was worse? Imagining what had happened? Or learning a difficult truth that might change my opinion of her?

"You don't have to show me," I said. "It's none of my business."

"I've been holding it inside for so long, I don't think I can move on unless I admit to somebody what really happened. Somebody who will believe me."

"People didn't believe you?"

"They believed what they wanted to believe."

That gave me hope. Maybe Maggie had been wrongly accused of having killed her parents. Yikes. *Killed her parents*. Strong words.

"Please," she said.

I couldn't refuse. She had done so much for me, and if she needed me to know the truth, then I wanted to know. I took a step toward the barn and stopped at the big double doors.

"You coming?" I asked.

Maggie shook her head. She was willing to reveal what had happened, but not relive it.

The heavy padlock hung open on the metal latch, just as I saw it before. I flipped the latch open, grabbed the door, and slowly pulled. I felt as if I was opening a tomb. What was I going to find inside? A couple of bodies? A gruesome scene of carnage? A murder weapon? I was hit with the same smell as before. It was a musty, sharp odor that I recognized but couldn't place. I was relieved to know it wasn't the smell of rotting flesh. When I swung the door open so that light could pour in from outside, I was faced with a scene that made total sense . . . and was absolutely horrific.

The interior of the barn had been burned. It was a black hole. Nothing was recognizable. There were lumps of ash that could have been anything but were now piles of charcoal and soot. It must have been an inferno because I didn't see a single spot that hadn't burned. The walls, floor, and ceiling looked as if they'd been painted black, that's how complete the burn had been. It made sense why the paint on the outside of the barn was bubbled . . . It had melted and pulled away from the wood under the intense heat of the fire that destroyed the place.

I didn't need to go inside to learn any more. I stepped

back and closed the door, feeling like I was dropping the lid on a coffin.

"I hated my father," Maggie said. "And he hated me. He must have, based on the way he treated me. I was their only child and he thought of me as nothing more than a nuisance that wasn't worth the food they had to waste on me."

Maggie seemed uncomfortable being that close to the place and walked away. I followed her to the fence that separated her property from the land that would become my grandfather's.

She continued, "When I was little, I thought it was because he had wanted a boy. Somebody who could help him with his work. He made furniture. The barn was his workshop. I didn't have the strength to lift the heavy pieces of wood or empty the scrap bins. He'd hit me out of frustration when I couldn't lift a chair or didn't move as fast as he expected me to."

"What did your mother do?" I asked.

"She was afraid of him too. He treated her as badly as me, but at least in his eyes, she had purpose. She cooked and cleaned, where all I did was eat his food and burn valuable wood to heat the house. But there was nothing she could do. We had no money and no other family. She was trapped. We both were. She'd defend me, but that only turned his rage on her. The fights they had were horrible."

"Did he get drunk?" I asked. "Some guys get violent when they're wasted."

"No," she said quickly. "I almost wish that were the case. At least it would explain his anger. He was just a miserable person and took it out on the people closest to him. There's one thing I will always be grateful to my mother for. She told me that no matter how much he belittled me and criticized and blamed me for everything wrong with his life, it wasn't my fault. It took a while for me to understand, but

I did. I knew I had value. I liked to write. I was good with numbers as well. My mother did the accounting work for my father's business but she wasn't very good at it. It turned out that I was much better with the figures and by the time I was ten, I was doing the books myself. But we never told my father. He never would have accepted it. So it was our secret. My father had no idea that I was the one making sure that his bills were paid and the proper money collected."

"Why didn't you tell him?"

"I wanted him to think my mother was doing it. I wanted him to believe she had value because she would be with him for the rest of her life and I planned on leaving as soon as I got the chance."

"I guess the chance never came," I said.

Maggie fell silent. The memories were tough.

"The chance *did* come," she finally said. "My mother had been stealing money from my father's business. A small amount at a time. For years. So small that he didn't notice. I realized it once I started doing the accounting. But I never let on. It turned out she was more clever than I thought. And brave. Do you know why she did it?"

I shook my head.

"To send me away to school. She had saved enough so that I could attend a boarding school upstate. When I found out her plans, it was like a new life had begun for me. I would be out of the house and finally get the chance to do something positive. My mother was a wonderful, caring person."

She swallowed hard as her tears returned.

"It happened the night before I was going to leave," she said, her voice cracking. "My father was working in the barn late to finish a project. He often did that, and then slept on an old couch. I loved those nights because it meant he wouldn't be in the house to fight with my mother. All the arrangements had been made. I can't tell you how excited I was. I was set to leave the next day. Early. I could have slept through the night and left without him knowing a thing until I was gone. But I didn't want to leave without telling him I was going. That seemed, I don't know, cowardly. Or maybe I hoped he would show some small sign of affection and admit that he would miss me. Whatever the reason, I decided to go to the barn and say good-bye."

My heart was thumping so hard, I felt like my head would explode. I wanted her to stop the story right there but I couldn't ask her to do that.

"I don't know what reaction I expected from him," she went on. "Probably a snarl and a 'good riddance.' I should have known better. When I told him that I was going, all he wanted to know was where the money was coming from. I hadn't even thought of what to say to that question. I stammered and didn't answer, but he answered for me. It turned out he wasn't as oblivious as we thought. He knew the books weren't adding up but assumed it was due to waste or improper bookkeeping. As soon as he heard that I was leaving for school, he realized the truth . . . and he hit me."

She took a deep breath but didn't stop talking.

"Normally he'd hit me with an open hand. Not that night. He balled his fist and swung with his full weight. He caught me on the side of the head and sent me sprawling to the floor. I was so dazed I don't know if he hit me again, but judging from my bruised ribs the next day, I'd say he chose to kick me a few times for good measure."

I gritted my teeth, my anger rising as I imagined this poor little girl being beaten by an enraged bully.

"When he was finished, he ordered me to go back into the house and pull out the ledgers. He said I wasn't going anywhere the next day and I had to account for every penny that was missing. I had no argument. He was right. We had stolen from him."

"But it was justified!" I shouted.

"Not in his eyes. I was so angry and hurt, I couldn't even think to argue, not that it would have done any good. The dizziness was so bad, I had to crawl out of the barn on my knees. I stood up outside and tried to clear my head. All I could think was that he would come into the house like an angry bull and it wouldn't just be about me. My mother was responsible for the books. He would be just as angry with her. I couldn't imagine what he might do to her."

She stopped long enough to wipe away some tears.

"So I did something childish. I closed the barn door and locked the padlock. In that moment I thought it would keep him locked in, caged up . . . and away from us."

I had a sick feeling that I knew where this was going.

"So he was trapped inside the barn?" I asked.

Maggie burst out crying. She couldn't hold it back anymore. "But he wasn't! I started back for the house and my head cleared enough to realize how futile it would be to try and lock him up. It would only make him angrier. So I went back and unlocked the lock. At least I thought I did. I was so upset and my head was spinning. I thought I had unlocked it!"

Her voice grew low. "But I hadn't."

"I think I know what happened next," I said.

"It's worse than you can imagine!" she shouted. "I went to the house knowing that at any moment he'd come barging in. I didn't even tell my mother what was going to happen. What was the point? It would only cause her to worry, knowing that the horror was coming. That's what I told myself, anyway. It was a totally selfish choice. I was far more upset that my plans were ruined than about anything my father would do to us. I often wonder what would have happened if I had told her. Would things have worked out differently? I went straight to my room and I don't know how but I fell asleep. Sometime later that night I woke up to see light dancing on the ceiling. I remember thinking it was a happy dream about pretty Christmas lights. As I fully woke up, I realized that the light was real and it was coming from outside. My bedroom was on the third floor. I ran to the window and looked down to see flames licking out from the top windows of the barn. I had to stare for a few moments before I realized what was happening."

"What did you do?"

Maggie's eyes dropped to the ground. "Nothing. I told myself that he had gotten out. After all, the door was unlocked. He would have escaped at the first sign of trouble. That's what I believed to be true, but I would be lying if I said I didn't hope I was wrong."

"When did you realize he was trapped?" I asked.

Maggie turned around and sat down on the ground, sobbing. I couldn't imagine the guilt she was feeling, even if her father was a vicious creep.

Through labored gasps she said, "I knew when I saw my mother run up to the barn to try and save him."

"Oh man," I gasped.

"It was a nightmare. She ran from the house to the barn. I saw her fumble with the lock. That's when I knew I hadn't opened it after all. I shouted to her that it was unlocked, but she couldn't hear over the roar of the fire. She eventually got the lock off and threw the door open—"

Maggie buried her head in her hands but continued. "It was like an oven. There was nothing but flame, but she went in anyway. After all he'd done to her, to us, she still tried to save him. I finally left the window and ran downstairs. It felt so far away. Three floors. I ran to the barn, screaming for my mother, hoping to see her staggering out of the door with my father. Or without him. All I wanted was for my mother to be safe."

Her voice trailed off. She didn't have to tell me what had happened. Or didn't happen. I didn't know what to say. That it wasn't her fault? That she didn't mean for it to happen? That it was a mistake? That it was her father's fault she didn't open the lock because he had knocked her silly? Nothing I could say would have made it any better.

Maggie took a minute to get herself together and then finished the story.

"They decided the fire started with a lantern that had fallen over. My father often worked by lantern light instead of paying for electricity. But he used so many different paints and solvents that a small fire could be disastrous. He knew that, but didn't care. He must have fallen asleep on the couch and didn't realize what was happening until it was too late. They found him at the foot of a ladder. He was trying to climb to the windows on top. My mother never got close to him. They found her just inside the door. I don't believe she suffered for long. It's amazing that the structure didn't burn. Just the inside. From out here it looks like a normal barn. I guess it's kind of like people. You never know what's on the inside."

"So you were left on your own?" I asked. "Did you have any other family?"

"None that I knew of. People pretended to be concerned about me, but I knew the truth. They thought I deliberately tried to kill my father. But nobody could prove it, or bothered to. My father was not a popular man. If not for my mother having died, they probably would have considered me a hero. But she did die. So they called me a murderer. Not to my face, though. I went to live with a woman from our church. She was nice enough, but I always felt as if she was watching me in case I tried to hurt her. I never did go to school. Instead I worked at a local mill as a felt cutter."

"You worked at the National Felt Company? I know that place."

"It was an empty existence. The work was mindless and I couldn't make friends. Nobody wanted to be seen with a killer. But I had an escape. Whenever I got the chance, I rode my bike up the river road to a spot where the water widened. It was my own private swimming hole that was away from everything and everybody. The suspicious stares. The whispering. I loved going to that spot in the river. To be alone and to float in the cool water. Far away from fire."

"I think I know that spot you're talking about."

She gave a sad chuckle and said, "It's where I died. They say you should never go swimming alone and they were right. I slipped on a wet rock and fell, hitting my head. It was just a dumb accident. It wouldn't even have been a bad injury . . . if I hadn't landed in the water. I don't know who found me. I didn't go back to see my funeral. There might not have been one. They don't bury murderers on church grounds. I ended up here. This is my vision of the Black. The most horrible memory I could imagine. I'm forced to live with it until I move on. So you can see why I'm not afraid of going to the Blood. Nothing that could happen to me could be worse than what I live with here, constantly reminded of the worst mistake a person could make."

"But it *was* a mistake," I said. "You can't be punished for all eternity because of a mistake."

"No?" she asked. "Tell them."

I looked to the barn, where two Watchers stood. I thought about screaming at them to come and listen to Maggie's side of the story, but realized it would have been a waste. They would just disappear.

"Thank you," she said. "For listening, and at least pretending that I'm not evil."

"I'm not pretending. And thank you too."

"For what?" she asked.

"For telling me the truth. And for the kiss."

She smiled sadly.

"There's one thing that's clear to me now," I said. "I get why you're here and not in the Blood. You may have wanted to hurt your father, and it sounds like he deserved it, but you changed your mind. You meant to open the lock and that means you aren't a murderer. You're here to work that out and I believe you will."

"Thank you, Cooper."

I added, "But that means I can't let you help me anymore."

"But . . . why?"

I stood up. "This is my problem and I could be going about it all the wrong way, but that's my choice. I won't let you risk your own future anymore, now that I know you really have one."

Maggie got up to face me. The tears were gone. "You can't tell me what choices to make. It's my life. My *after*life."

"I know. You'll do what you've got to do. It just won't be with me."

I leaned forward and gave her a kiss.

"When this is done, I want to take you to Playland again."

She scowled at me. My charm wasn't working.

"Cooper, you can't—"

"See you soon," I said, and stepped backward into my own cloud of color . . .

To arrive on the lawn of my family's cottage on Thistledown Lake. In the Light. It was a sunny day. Nobody was around. My plan was to find Marsh or Sydney or anybody in my family to see if they'd finally figured out what had happened to me.

The search didn't take long. I heard a horrified scream come from our boathouse farther down the shore. I knew that scream. It was Sydney.

Damon was true to his word.

He was not going to leave them alone until he got what he wanted.

18

I followed the sound of Sydney's scream, sprinting along the shore toward the boathouse.

"Damon!" I shouted.

When I got closer, I heard muffled voices coming from inside. Scared voices. And splashing. No, more like thrashing. There was more than one person inside and they were in trouble. Was it Marsh in there with Sydney? When I got to the door, I saw that the padlock was locked. I had a quick flash of Maggie's barn. Bad image.

I was about to act like a spirit and walk through the wall when I saw something seeping out between the boards of the hut. I took a step back and scanned the wall to see liquid drooling from every crack and seam. Red liquid. The building was bleeding.

More panicked voices and splashing came from inside. I'd heard enough. I walked up to the wall, stepped through . . .

and entered a world of red. It was totally disorienting. It was like the boathouse had been filled up with blood, but that was impossible. It had to have been one of Damon's illusions. The blood was so dense that I couldn't see Sydney and whoever else was with her, but I sensed movement everywhere. And panic. I saw an arm flash by, and a cooler. It may have been an illusion, but for them it was real. If the illusion drove them down into the real water, they could drown. I had to try and get them out of there.

I floated through the red . . . whatever . . . until I was outside again. Like I did when I searched the lake for the remains of my boat, I floated around the outside of the boathouse until I was in front of the double boat doors. They were closed tight and locked. Blood flowed from every crack as if it were under pressure. I expected the whole place to explode like a ripe tomato with a cherry bomb inside. The blood may have been an illusion, but the closed doors weren't. There was only one way out of that death trap. Sydney had to swim down to the lake bottom and move under the double doors. But with such a turbulent mess inside, there was no way she would know which direction to swim in.

Unless I showed her.

I dropped down into the water and moved under the doors into the dark red of the illusion. I felt another body flailing around. Was it Marsh? I never should have trusted Damon. I reached out in desperation, hoping to grab on to an arm or a leg and tug them in the right direction, but my hand passed through them as smoothly as it passed through the blood. I needed to do something to get their attention. What was there? Sound? I didn't know how I could make any kind of sound, let alone something that could be heard underwater.

I moved back out under the boat door, thinking I would

have more luck finding something outside than in the illusion where there was zero visibility. I broke the surface of the lake and looked around to see . . . nothing. I was losing my mind. Sydney was running out of time and I was helpless. My experience with being a spirit was limited. I didn't have the tools or the knowledge to save them. Damon, on the other hand, had centuries of practice. How could I compete with that?

I thought back to some of the things he had done to influence the living. There was no way I could create an illusion. I wasn't in that league. I couldn't do much physically either, like blow open the doors. I didn't have that kind of power. Not like Damon. Then I remembered the trailer. George O.'s house. Light. Could I somehow bend light in some way so that they would see it? Maggie told me that the stronger the connection between the spirit and the living, the better chance there was of using that energy to make things happen. My sister was near death. I had to believe the possibility was there.

I dropped below the surface and moved close to the boat doors, but didn't go inside. I wanted Sydney to come to me. I wanted to create a beacon that would cut through the murky water and give them a target to lead them out of the illusion. I sat on the lake bottom, looked up, and saw the blurry sun through the few feet of water between me and the surface. I felt like an idiot, but I tried to push negative thoughts out of my head. If I didn't believe it could happen, there was zero chance it would. I kept my eyes on the sun, trying to suck its rays down to me.

Nothing happened. I don't know what I expected. A laser beam of light that would streak out of the sky? It felt hopeless. Sydney was going to drown in an illusion. Maybe Marsh too. I was already planning on how I would get my revenge and make Damon suffer for what he had done.

That's when I saw a figure swimming toward me. It was Marsh! He had hold of Sydney's shirt and the two of them were kicking in my direction. I didn't know if they had just gotten lucky and picked the right direction, or it was something I had done. There weren't any laser beams of light flying around. What had happened? Maybe they could see me! I motioned for them to follow, and saw my hand. It had a faint glow. I looked at my other hand, and that too had a slight glow. Looking down, I saw that my entire body was pulsing with light. It was like I had gone nuclear. I think I can best describe it as saying I was giving off energy. I felt as if I had willed my body to absorb sunlight and give it back out.

I quickly turned and moved along the lake bottom to lead them out from under the boathouse. The water was growing brighter like a murky cloud of muck was being washed away by a rogue current. Sydney pulled away from Marsh and swam harder. Her lungs must have been screaming. Marsh grabbed her arm and pointed up. He knew they had cleared the boathouse doors and were in open water. Sydney followed and the two of them swam for the surface.

I went up too and broke out of the water at the same moment that Marsh and Sydney did. Both gasped for air. Alive. Once out of the water, the glow from my body was gone. No problem. I didn't need to be neon anymore.

Sydney turned back to the boathouse. "My god," she said through deep breaths.

Both Marsh and I looked to see that the illusion was over. Blood no longer oozed from the cracks. All was normal.

"C'mon," Marsh said, and swam for shore. Sydney swam right behind him.

I couldn't be sure if they'd seen my glowing self or not, but I had to believe that they had. Once again I had gone against the rules and influenced events in the Light. I didn't care. I was going to do whatever it took to protect my family and friend.

As I watched them crawl out of the water and up onto the grass, I saw that someone else was onshore. Damon stood laughing as if my friend's near-drowning was a show put on for his amusement.

I flew toward shore. Literally. Faster than I had moved before. I willed myself to be there, and in less than a second I sped past Marsh and Sydney and slammed into Damon, hitting him and driving him off his feet. We both landed, hard, but not on the grass near the cottage.

We hit the dusty ground of Damon's vision in the Black. We were back in the ancient town square. I sat on his chest and wailed on him, throwing punches at his face. It didn't matter that I couldn't really hurt him. My anger had taken over and I wanted him to suffer for what he had done. All he could do was throw his hands up to protect himself.

Before I ran out of gas I felt strong hands grab me from behind and pull me off. Two of Damon's soldier buddies had come to his rescue and it took both of them to hold me back. That's how fired up I was.

"You lied!" I screamed at him. "You tried to kill them!"

Damon rolled onto his side and touched his face. I hoped he was in pain and I had added another scar to his collection. He was surprisingly calm for somebody who had just gotten the snot beaten out of him. He then looked at me and smiled, revealing his two pointed teeth.

It turned my stomach.

"You're an animal," was all I could say.

"I did not lie," he said. "I told you I would leave him alone if you helped me and you have not."

"So you tried to kill him? And my sister? What is wrong with you? How is killing them going to help you get your weapon?"

Damon stood up and casually brushed the dirt from his tunic as if nothing worse had just happened to him than getting a little messy.

"Assistance," he declared.

The soldier ran up to him and while Damon stood there with his arms out, the soldier brushed all the remaining dirt from his robe like he was a regal king and they were his slaves.

"I would not have let them die," Damon said matter-of-factly. "At least not the boy. The girl means nothing to me."

I pulled away from one of the soldiers to try and get another shot at him. Damon didn't even flinch. The soldier was bigger than me and quickly grabbed my arm again, locking it behind my back.

"What is the point?" I screamed in anger.

"I want him to be afraid . . . to wonder when the next horrifying image might appear. It is quite the art, you know. It is not only about what I show him but what he fears I *might* show him."

"You're just crucl," I spat.

"Cruel, and effective. When someone has been reduced to a primal state of fear and paranoia, they will do anything to make it end. To return to normal. When I believe he has reached that level of desperation, I will offer him salvation. He will be more than willing to find the poleax."

Damon strolled casually to the fountain, reached down, and scooped some water to wash his face.

"Besides," he continued, "even if he is stronger than I believe, haunting him has the added benefit of forcing you to do what I want. Though I have to admit, you have not performed as I expected."

"I found Adeipho," I said.

Damon looked genuinely surprised. "You went to his vision of Ehalon?"

"I don't know about any Ehalon. I went to a city. It looked like New York."

"I do not understand. You used the ear to find Adeipho and it took you to a modern city?" he asked.

"Didn't I just say that?"

He seemed genuinely surprised. It wasn't an act. Damon paced, staring at the ground, trying to understand the implication of what I was saying.

"You are certain it was him?" he asked.

"How many guys do you know with one ear and a killer sword?" I asked. "Besides, he knew you. He wants another shot at you, by the way. What did you do to piss him off like that?"

"Interesting," Damon said, thinking out loud. "That cannot be his vision. Not a modern city."

"Maybe it was the vision of one of his friends. He has plenty. They're all freaks."

"Traitors," Damon spat. "Every last one of them. None would have a modern city as their vision."

"Well, somebody does," I said. "Maybe it was the guy in charge."

Damon threw me a quick, surprised look. Again, it wasn't an act. "Adeipho does not take orders from anyone."

"Well, yeah, he does. If that guy hadn't stepped in, Adeipho would have done me with the sword."

"Who was this person?"

"Adeipho said his name is Ree."

Damon's face went blank. Then he smiled, and laughed. "Ree! Of course!"

"Who is he?" I asked.

"Someone you must deal with in order to find the crucible," Damon replied. "I should have realized. Ree is protecting it, along with Adeipho and the other traitors. We are so close."

"No, we're not," I said. "They were all over me the second I showed up. Adeipho wasn't the only one who had a black sword. Those guys are serious. When we escaped, they followed me into my own vision and attacked me."

"You must have allowed it."

"I didn't allow anything! There's something going on that doesn't fit the rules. If I go back, I'm done, so I'm not going back."

Damon ran at me, got right in my face, and growled, "You *will* go back. You will find the crucible and you will destroy it."

"I won't lie. I'm afraid of you, Damon. But those freaks? They've got it all over you. No way I'm going back."

"Then your friend will suffer for your cowardice."

"You're going to make him suffer no matter what I do. I get that now. Sorry, chief, you're on your own."

Damon stepped back from me, strode to the fountain, and grabbed his black sword from one of his warrior pals. He came right back at me and held it up, ready to swing.

"Go ahead!" I shouted. "What's the difference? Here or there. Either way I get whacked."

Damon raised the sword higher.

"Forget it," I said. "I'm done."

I braced myself, ready to be blasted into ash. Instead, Damon relaxed, lowered the sword, and put his hands on his hips.

"Oh I have chosen so well," he said with a playful smile while wagging his finger at me.

He looked around at his soldiers as if for verification. They all smiled and nodded. Of course they would have done that if he had said the moon was made of cheese. Once again, Damon had me off balance.

"I can't say much for your intellect, Foley, but you are a bold one, no doubt about that."

He nodded and the soldier let me go.

"Man, you are warped," I said while rubbing my aching arm.

He chuckled as if it were a compliment. "Crossing swords with Adeipho is dangerous, I will not deny that, but the reward is so great. Are you forgetting that if you succeed, your life would be returned?"

"But it's impossible. Going back there is suicide," I said flatly. "Find somebody else for your scavenger hunt."

Damon nodded thoughtfully. "What if I could turn the odds in your favor?" he asked. "What if I could make the impossible . . . possible. Would that change your mind?"

"There's no way you can do that," I said.

Damon tossed his black sword down at my feet. The deadly weapon landed in the dust, inches from me. It wasn't a threat. He was giving it to me.

"As you have seen," he said, "you do not have to be an expert swordsman for it to be effective."

Giving up that sword was the last thing I expected him to do. No, the last thing I expected was for him to give it up . . . to me.

"You're not serious," I said.

"I am," he replied. "The question is, how serious are you? Are you willing to fight for your life?"

I knelt down to pick up the sword. Damon's warriors made a move to stop me but Damon held up his hands, freezing them. He wasn't kidding. He wanted me to have it. I grabbed the handle and lifted it from the dirt, surprised to find that it wasn't heavy. Instead of a cumbersome weapon, it was more like a graphite tennis racquet. It didn't even seem strong enough to physically damage anything, but physical damage wasn't what this sword was about. The thing was deadly.

And it was mine.

I looked to Damon and he held his hands out as if in surrender.

"I know what you are thinking," he said. "It would be so easy. One thrust and I would be gone. But along with me would go your one and only chance of retrieving your past life. What is more important to you? Destroying me and insuring that your friend will no longer be haunted? Or the promise of returning to your previous life? Those are your choices, Foley. Which is more important? Your friend's life? Or yours?"

I hated this guy.

But he was wrong. There was a third choice. If I got my life back, it would mean that Damon had succeeded and he would have no reason to haunt Marsh. I could have it all. The ticket was in my hands. I held the power to destroy a spirit. Forever. Would I have the guts to use it?

I wanted the chance to find out.

"If you're lying to me," I said. "I'll use this on you."

Damon smiled. He didn't feel threatened in the least.

"I knew you would make the smart decision," he said.

He was right about me. I was ready to fight. And the sad truth was that I was no better than he was. I would do anything to get what I wanted.

And I wanted to live again.

19

I left Damon's vision and returned to my own.

I needed time to plan my next move before stepping right back into the fire. Having the sword gave me confidence.

My goal was clear. I had to find that golden crucible and either break it or bring it back to Damon. What wasn't as clear was how to do it. First I had to find it, which was going to be tough enough. But I also had to try and avoid Adeipho and whoever else was protecting it. It didn't seem likely that I could enter Adeipho's vision, find the crucible, steal it, and then blast out of there without tangling with at least one of them.

One way or another, I was in for a fight.

Maybe I was kidding myself, but I believed I could do it. There weren't many things I've failed at. I guess you could say I'd lived a charmed life, even factoring in my untimely death on Thistledown Lake. That was a total fluke. If I'd known that Damon was out to get me, I'd never have let my guard down. That wasn't going to happen again.

I hated doing anything to help that guy, but when I balanced it out, I decided it was worth it. Was he lying about giving me my life back? Maybe. But if he wasn't, I'd be kicking myself for all eternity. What I was risking was my own life. Or spirit. I could be destroyed. Forever. But the hope of getting my life back made it worthwhile. If I was going down, I was going down swinging.

I decided not to tell Gramps or Maggie about what I was going to do. Gramps would have tried to stop me and Maggie would have wanted to come.

I stood in front of my home in the Black and looked at the house I grew up in. Or my vision of it. For a brief moment I wondered if I would ever see it again. I quickly pushed that doubt away. Doubt was bad. I wanted no part of it. Never did. Didn't want to start. I was going to see that house again but for real. In the Light.

I grasped the handle of the sword that was tied to my belt with a leather strap. With my other hand I touched the shriveled ear through the material of my jeans and visualized Adeipho. The colored swirl of smoke appeared in front of me. I took a step forward . . .

And found myself back on the same city street where Maggie and I landed before. It was Adeipho's vision after all, whether I understood it or not.

I had to make myself invisible. There was no way I could talk my way out of that particular Trouble Town again, especially since I had a black sword. That pretty much proved I was with Damon. The longer I could maneuver without being seen, the better chance I had of success, so I sprinted to the nearest building and jumped into a doorway. I held my breath, waiting for the jokers on motorcycles to appear again. I scanned the street. It was empty. No motorcycles. No clowns on bicycles. No Mardi Gras masks. No Watchers. Nobody. It gave me the creeps to be in a city that was so completely deserted, though I didn't mind being alone if the only choice of company was Adeipho's spirit posse.

I moved out of my hiding spot and worked my way along the sidewalk, close to the buildings. My plan was to go back to the garage where Adeipho had trapped me and Maggie. It was as good a place as any to start searching for the crucible. As I crept along, I kept glancing up at the windows that loomed above me. Eyes could have been any-where. Or everywhere. For all I knew they were all watch-ing me, holding back their laughter, waiting for me to drop into their laps. The street was completely silent, which only added to the eeriness. There were no traffic sounds or laughter or music or anything else that gave a city life. The loudest thing I heard was the crunching of my Pumas on the sidewalk.

I made it to the garage without any trouble. The big door was closed so I had to find another way in. I was in front of a small florist. The flowers inside looked fresh but there was nobody there to buy them. Or sell them. Farther on was a door. After that was the big garage door, which was closed. I decided to go through the small door, thinking it might connect to the garage somewhere inside. I gripped the doorknob and twisted. It was unlocked. Adeipho didn't worry about people breaking into buildings in his vision. Fool. The creaking of the door tore through the silence. Anybody within earshot could have heard it. I slipped inside quickly and closed the door as quietly as possible. I was in, but where was I? I could have gone straight along a corridor or up the flight of stairs that was just inside the door. I chose the stairs, thinking it was better to take the high ground and be able to look down on the garage floor.

With one hand on the sword I took the stairs two at a time, keeping my eyes on the floor above. I reached a landing, turned left, and stepped up into a second-floor corridor. A quick glance to the left showed I was alone. A look to my right showed me . . . I wasn't.

Standing twenty feet away was a guy in a clown mask and a business suit. He was shorter than me with black hair to his shoulders. He stood with his legs apart and his fists clenched, ready to fight.

I said, "I don't want any trouble—"

Apparently the clown did. Before I could say another word, he charged. I was so surprised I didn't have time to pull the sword. He tackled me, driving his clown face square into my chest. I flew backward and hit the floor on my back with the guy on top of me, punching wildly from his knees. It was like fighting a wild cat. He had no idea how to fight and was making up for it with effort. He wasn't a very big clown so I easily knocked him off my chest. He hit the wall, shoulder first, and squealed in pain.

But that didn't stop him. He bounced off the wall and tackled me again as I tried to get to my feet. I was in an awkward position so I stumbled and went down again, this time falling onto the landing. He threw himself at me, grabbing at my shirt to try and push me down the stairs but he didn't have the strength. I'm a solid 180 and this guy couldn't have weighed more than 120. I shot both hands up through his and drove them out, breaking his grip, and then lashed out with one short jab to his solar plexus. The punch stunned him, driving him backward.

I scrambled to my feet. Knowing how this guy fought, I had to be ready. He came at me with his arms flailing totally out of control. I turned sideways and raised my fists, easily blocking his wild punches. He was no threat. I waited for an opening and drove the heel of my palm right into his clown chin. The guy's head snapped to his left and I followed up with another quick shot to his exposed cheek.

The clown reeled back, stumbled, hit the far wall, and fell to the floor. Before he hit I pulled out the black sword, the weapon that could end his existence. He knew it, too. Instead of attacking again he tried to crawl away but I stood over him, holding the point of the sword to his neck.

"Do you know what this can do to you?" I asked.

The guy was fired up and breathing hard. I could see his wild eyes through his mask but couldn't tell if he was angry or scared.

"Tell me where the crucible is," I commanded.

The guy didn't budge, his eyes locked on mine.

I repeated, "Tell me where the crucible is."

He didn't react. Maybe he didn't know where it was. Or *what* it was. If the threat of annihilation didn't scare him into talking, what else could I do?

"Do you understand what I'm saying?" I asked.

He gave me a slight nod.

"Then understand this, if you don't tell me, your existence is going to end right here in this crummy hallway."

The guy didn't react. He wasn't going to talk, and I was stuck. What was I supposed to do? I couldn't torture him into telling me anything. Even if I wanted to, I wouldn't know how. If I let him go, he'd run for help and I'd be done. It seemed as if the only thing I could do was make good on my threat. All I had to do was lean forward. The tip of the sword would enter his neck and he'd be smoke. It would be so easy.

"Take off your mask," I ordered.

He slowly lifted his hand and pulled the mask away from his face, and I saw that the guy wasn't a guy. I found myself holding the tip of the executioner's sword into the neck of a frightened young girl. A girl! I was expecting some gnarly old soldier from ancient times, not a pretty girl who wasn't any older than me. I pulled the sword away and took a step back, desperately trying to calculate my next move. The only thing I knew for sure was that there was no way I could destroy her.

"I'll give you one more chance—," I said.

But she wasn't giving *me* another chance. The second I took my eyes off her to slip the sword into its sheath, she leaped up and was on me again. She knocked me off balance and drove me toward the wall. This time we hit a door. The force blew the door open and we tumbled onto a narrow balcony that ringed the garage. The girl wasn't done. She kept driving her legs forward and I couldn't stop her. She was small, but powerful. Two steps later we hit a wooden railing and crashed through that too. We were in freefall. The balcony was only on the second floor so we didn't fall far. We hit a stack of rubber tires, which I guess was good luck but it still hurt. The tires tumbled over and so did we, landing in a tangled heap on the cement floor.

I'd only known this girl for two minutes but knew she wasn't going to let a little thing like falling off a landing stop her from coming after me again. I rolled away from her, scrambled to my feet, and stood up, ready for her next attack.

The attack never came. When I looked up, I was faced with a dozen people in masks. It was the same group of soldiers, clowns, and warriors from my first visit. Before any of them could move on me, I yanked the sword out of the sheath and held it up menacingly.

Nobody moved. They all knew the power I held. I took a quick look behind me to make sure the way was clear and slowly backed toward a door on the far side of the garage. It was the only move I had. If I couldn't make this girl tell me where the crucible was, there was no way I could intimidate a whole group into talking. My mission was done before it had gotten started. I needed to be gone before somebody else with a sword showed up. Somebody who knew how to use it. Like Adeipho. As I walked backward, the group moved with me but kept their distance.

I imagined being back in my own vision and looked around to see if the swirling colors had appeared. They hadn't.

"Nobody follow me and we'll all be okay," I said.

I didn't think they'd listen but I had to give it a try. I made it to the door and glanced inside to see an empty office with a door to the outside. I backed through the door and then instantly scrambled for the outside door. I didn't even look back to see if they were coming after me because I knew they were.

I yanked the door open and found myself in an alley-way. I was out! I turned and sprinted for the street. What-ever was preventing me from leaving this vision was still in play. I had to get back to the spot where we were able to leave the last time. The edge of the vision.

Good plan.

Didn't work.

When I blasted out of the alley into the street and turned west, my way was blocked by a gang of guys on BMX bikes who flashed onto the street a block ahead. The alarm had been sounded. I looked back into the alley to see that the circus was following. My only escape route was to run the other way, deeper into the city.

I turned and ran. The one advantage I had was that I knew where I was going. I had to play offense and hope they couldn't react fast enough. I may have been dead, but I was still fast. I ran cross-country, so my legs knew what to do. I ran through back alleys, climbed over chain-link fences, detoured through parking garages . . . making as many turns as possible to throw off my pursuers. It was a foxhunt, and I was the fox. Each time I felt as if I'd gotten away, I'd turn a corner to face more guys in clown masks sprinting toward me, or a handful of bikers running me down. It was like they knew ahead of time which way I'd be going. I started to think that there were eyes in every window after all, and they were directing the pursuit.

I tried going back to my own vision a few times but nothing happened. It was clear that to get out of there I was going to have to find the far edge, just as Maggie and I had done before.

I don't know how many blocks I traveled but it felt like miles and I was getting winded. Something had to give. I cautiously took a look out from a doorway to see a handful of guys on BMX-style bikes turning onto the street behind me and realized I had my chance. The large group of riders had split up to hunt for me and only five guys were headed my way. In seconds they would fly right past me. The setup was perfect. I leaned back, pressing myself against the wall so they wouldn't see me when they rode past. I held my breath and waited. Two seconds later the first bike flew by. Followed by two more. Then a fourth. That's when I made my move. I jumped out and went for the trailing bike. The guy was looking straight ahead and didn't see me coming. I tackled him high, knocking him off the bike. We both hit the pavement, hard, but I used him to cushion my own fall. It probably hurt but my adrenaline was spiked too high to notice. Before the guy had a chance to recover and understand what had happened, I was on my feet and going for his bike.

The others kept going. They had no idea what was happening behind them. I picked up the bike and started running to get up enough speed to ride, when I was grabbed from behind by the guy I'd dumped. I whipped my elbow into his ribs and heard him grunt as the wind flew out of his lungs. He doubled over and I took off.

I had wheels. A quick look around told me that I wasn't being followed and didn't have to be as evasive. I poured on the speed, hoping to find the far edge of the vision and get the hell out of there. As I rode, I kept looking for the colorful wall that would mark the boundary of the vision, but didn't see a thing. After riding for block after deserted block, I reached a park and found the first clue as to what this vision was about.

I rode beneath a tall gray archway that looked familiar. I realized I had been there before. I knew where I was! The arch sat in Washington Square Park at the beginning of Fifth Avenue in New York City. Marsh and I had gone there for a showing of some Eastern European horror movie at NYU, which surrounded the park. The movie sucked but it was a great day because Marsh and I were on our own in the city. It wasn't as much fun being there this time. I stopped beneath the arch to catch my breath. Knowing where I was had answered one question but raised a few more. How could this be Adeipho's vision? He was a warrior from ancient times, not a New Yorker.

Nothing was out of the ordinary except that the normally busy park was deserted. A few yards from the arch was a street lined with parked cars. Something seemed off and not just because of the lack of people. I couldn't put my finger on exactly what it was, but there was something odd about the cars. It wasn't until I focused on a license plate that it became clear. The expiration date on the tag read: DEC 78. I walked my bike along the sidewalk to see the same thing on the other license plates. Every last one of the cars was old, but it wasn't like they were junkers. Some actually looked new. It was the style that was old. There was an electric blue number called a Plymouth Duster, a Volvo that looked more like a giant shoe box than a car, and a big yellow land yacht with a black vinyl top called a Ford Galaxie 500. It was like being in a car museum.

I walked the bike farther along until I came to a corner pizza place. In the window was a New York Yankees World Series Championship poster. The Yankees were always winning the World Series, nothing strange there, but this poster looked fresh and new like it was hung that morning, and the players were Reggie Jackson, Ron Guidry, and Willie Randolph . . . guys I only saw play on Old-Timers' Day. It was a championship poster from 1977, but it was new, which meant only one thing: This was a vision of New York City in the seventies. That made it all the more unlikely that the vision was Adeipho's. So, then, whose was it?

The sound of a motorcycle engine broke the silence. I knew what that meant. Looking back to the park, I saw the guy in the clown suit riding my way. I started running uptown but stopped when I saw the guy in the business suit on his motorcycle headed right for me . . . and unlike the BMX riders these guys had black swords.

I turned east and pedaled fast. I made a left turn then a quick right to discover . . . I was kidding myself. A line of guys on bikes had blocked the street from sidewalk to sidewalk. They had known all along where I was and which way I was headed. For all I knew they had herded me into that exact spot.

Halfway between me and the line of bikes was an entrance to a subway station marked ASTOR PLACE. It was my last option. Without another thought I turned the bike toward the entrance and rode down the stairs, rattling my teeth. It was like riding a mountain bike, with no shocks on the front fork. I hit the bottom, jumped off the bike, swung it over the old-fashioned turnstile, and remounted on the far side.

My goal was to ride along the platform to the far exit, ditch the bike, and run back up to the street before they realized what I was doing. I made it exactly halfway when I realized that I hadn't fooled anybody. In front of me, several freaks in clown masks ran up from the tunnel that traveled beneath the tracks to the opposite platform. I slammed on the brakes, skidded to a stop, and stood on the pedals to shoot back the way I had come.

The guys who had been chasing me were already flooding over the turnstile. I was trapped. The only place to go was down onto the tracks and across to the opposite platform. Before I could jump, I saw that it was too late. A bunch of guys in masks were already there.

The chase was over. I had to make a stand.

I went for my sword. A couple of the freaks realized what I was doing and jumped at me. I threw the bike at the first one, which slowed him down long enough for me to take on his pal. The second guy came at me quickly, wanting to finish me off before I could pull out the sword. He was fast. I was faster. As he threw himself at me, I crouched, and he went over my back. I flipped him head-over-butt down onto the platform. I'm not proud of having gotten into so many fights over the past few years, but I was grateful to have the experience. Before he could recover, I jammed my foot onto his throat, just below the hideous clown smile. I hated clowns. I sensed the others starting to close in so I pulled the sword out and held the point to the guy's chest.

"Stop!" I screamed.

Nobody moved. Nobody spoke. They all knew the power the sword possessed. That *I* possessed.

"You're all going to back off and let me go or this guy is done," I said, trying to sound like a badass.

There was no reaction.

"I swear!" I said. "I'll do this guy and then cut my own path through you."

Still, nobody moved.

"Clear out!" I shouted.

They didn't.

I calculated my escape. I'd thrust the sword through the guy under my foot and vaporize him. Hopefully that would be enough to prove to these goons that I was serious, and they'd let me by. If not, I could start swinging and take down as many as possible. Unless they were suicidal they'd back off. That plan took about three seconds to formulate . . .

And three more seconds for me to realize that I couldn't do it. I wasn't a killer. They had called my bluff. Or maybe it was a test to see how far I'd go. Either way, the chase was over and I was trapped in Trouble Town. I took my foot off the guy's neck, stepped back, and tossed the sword down next to him. The guy sprang to his feet and picked it up.

I held my arms out in surrender.

The crowd finally parted. For a second I thought they were clearing a path for me to leave. Maybe all they wanted was the sword. I took a tentative step forward and saw that the path wasn't for me. They had cleared the way for somebody to walk through from behind.

He no longer had on his circus mask, though I would have recognized him even if he had. It was Adeipho. He strode through the cleared path with his eyes fixed on mine. One hand was on the butt of his own black sword.

I wanted him to know that I wasn't a coward so I stood defiantly, though I did wonder if it was going to hurt. I remembered the scars he had slashed on Damon's face, and my stomach turned.

Adeipho reached the leading edge of his people and stopped, glaring at me.

"Make it fast," I said.

"You did not destroy his spirit," he declared, pointing to the guy I had stepped on. "Nor the spirit of my daughter."

His daughter? Who was his daughter?

The girl in the business suit who I had fought in the hallway stepped up next to Adeipho. She looked pissed. And she looked like Adeipho. His daughter. Swell. I hoped I hadn't hurt her. I could kiss any hope of mercy good-bye if he thought I had messed with his kid.

He added, "Why?"

"Yeah, well, I thought about it."

"And you chose not to destroy her," he said.

I shrugged. "I'm not a killer."

"Yet you are in league with a murderer."

"He doesn't have anything good to say about you, either."

"Then, why?" Adeipho asked again.

"To protect my friend in the Light," I answered.

That finally got a reaction from the crowd of clowns. They looked to one another and grumbled angrily. I had hit a chord. Adeipho raised his hand and they fell silent.

Adeipho said, "You have joined with him to protect a living being?"

I shrugged. "I know, it's against the rules. But he's my friend."

A bright light flashed across the platform. I turned quickly to see that a subway train was headed into the station. It was moving slowly, its wheels barely making a sound on the tracks. Nobody seemed surprised. Whatever the deal was with the train, it was normal. For them, that is. I, on the other hand, had no idea what was going on.

There was only one car. It rolled slowly to where we were standing and with a slight squeal of brakes came to a stop. The car was dark so I couldn't tell if anybody was inside. I couldn't help but think that this was planned. The entire time I was blasting through the city to get away from these jokers, they could have been herding me to this spot. Like in all foxhunts, the fox didn't stand a chance.

The subway door slid open to reveal the guy who bailed me out before, still wearing the masquerade mask. His name was Ree. Strange name, but it would be my favorite name in the world if he was going to bail me out again.

He stepped out of the subway car, moving with confidence. He strode toward me and stopped a few feet away with his hands on his hips while giving his head a slight shake.

"You came back," he said, sounding disappointed. He still whispered the way he did when we met last.

"Surprise!" I exclaimed.

"No surprise," he said with a snicker. "What am I supposed to do with you?"

"Well, you could tell your boys here to let me go back to my vision. That would be nice."

"I did that once."

"Yeah. And that was really cool. You know I could have vaporized a whole bunch of spirits with that sword, right? But I didn't. Tell him, Adeipho. That should count for something."

Adeipho looked to Ree and said, "I have not told him my name. Do we need any more proof that he is in league with Damon?"

Oops.

Ree chuckled and looked to the ground. I was amusing him. I hoped that was a good thing.

"I suppose it's comforting to know that some things never change," he said.

"What do you mean?"

When he answered, he no longer whispered. His voice

was clear and strong . . . and it was the voice of a woman. Ree wasn't a he. "I mean you've always been able to talk your way out of—what do you call it? Trouble Town."

I'd seen and heard some incredible things since I'd arrived in the Black. I'd learned about the nature of life and death and the afterlife. I'd been reunited with my gramps. I learned that there were forces at play that could change the way life worked. But none of that surprised me as much as what this woman had just said.

"Do I know you?" I managed to croak.

Ree reached up, grabbed her mask, and pulled it off.

My knees buckled.

Ree was not only a she, but I knew her.

She smiled and said, "But I'm afraid you can't talk your way out of this one, Coop."

It had been nearly two years since I'd last seen her, but there was no mistake. I shouldn't have been surprised. It made total sense that she was in the Black. She was dead, having been killed in an earthquake far from home.

Ree was Terri Seaver.

Marsh's mom.

20

My brain locked.

I must have been standing there with my mouth open because Mrs. Seaver laughed and said, "Well, this is a first."

Now that she was no longer whispering, she sounded more like herself.

"Lots of firsts going on," I managed to croak. My mouth was so dry I could barely move my lips. "Which one are you talking about?"

"I've never seen you at a loss for words."

"Yeah, well, that makes us even. I've never seen you dead."

She chuckled. "There you go! That's the Coop I know."

"Really? I don't know who the hell I am anymore."

It was a surreal moment. Dozens of freaks in clown masks stood staring at me and Marsh's mom. Marsh's *dead* mom.

"I wish I could say I'm happy to see you, Cooper," she said, turning serious. "But there's nothing good about your being here."

"Tell me about it."

"How did you die?" she asked.

The question caught me by surprise.

"Sounds strange to hear it like that," I said.

"Get used to it. What happened?"

"Speedboat accident. Thistledown Lake. I guess Damon had something to do with it."

"Damon," she repeated under her breath like his name left a bad taste in her mouth. "I'm sorry. Now tell me why you're here . . . and don't BS me."

How was I supposed to answer? I hadn't dropped in for a friendly visit. I was there to help Damon. My killer. It seemed like the right idea at the time, but I wasn't so sure anymore. Seeing Mrs. Seaver changed things. What had been semi-clear before had now been thrown into total chaos. I didn't know who to believe or trust. I wasn't even sure if the woman standing in front of me was actually Mrs. Seaver. Damon was able to create some incredibly real illusions. Who's to say he wasn't still playing me?

"How do I know you are who you say you are?" I asked.

"Who else would I be?" she asked, throwing her hands out for emphasis.

That was a total Mrs. Seaver quick comeback. She wasn't like any of the other moms I knew. Most were kind of stiff while she liked to toss the football around with Marsh and me. I was sad when she died, though I wasn't so sure I was happy to see her again, assuming it was really her.

"You tell me," I said. "I've seen too many things that don't make sense. You're just the latest."

"Ask me something nobody else could know."

It didn't take me long to come up with something. "Okay,

what did you give me for my birthday the year before you, uh, died?"

She dropped her eyes, thinking. If she didn't know the answer, I was done. Standing next to Adeipho was the guy who'd picked up Damon's black sword. He held it in front of his body with the point down. I was ready to leap at him and grab it. It might have been suicide, but if I did it fast enough, maybe I could surprise them all and have one chance to fight my way out.

"*Eternity*," Mrs. Seaver said. "The photo I took of the tribal elder from Kenya with his great-granddaughter. You liked it, though I think you would have preferred Madden NFL."

I relaxed.

"Okay?" she asked.

I nodded.

"Now tell me the truth, Cooper Foley. Why are you here?"

Adeipho answered for me. "He said he is trying to protect a friend in the Light."

Mrs. Seaver shot me a worried look.

"Yeah," I said. "It's Marsh. Damon is haunting him. But that can't be news to you."

From her surprised reaction it seemed like she didn't know anything about it. But that made no sense. She was Marsh's mom. She must have been watching him in the Light.

"Come with me," she said, and turned to go back into the subway car.

"Ree!" Adeipho called out. "This is not wise."

Mrs. Seaver whipped around and glared at him. Adeipho froze. Mrs. Seaver had become a tough guy. "We knew this time would come," she said to him. "We all did. The more we learn, the better prepared we will be."

"I will come with you," Adeipho said.

"No," she barked. "I've known this boy since he was an infant. I trust him."

Adeipho wanted to argue but couldn't find the words. Mrs. Seaver softened and said, "He could have destroyed your daughter."

Adeipho glanced at the girl, who still looked pissed. He relaxed and took a step back.

"Thank you," Mrs. Seaver said. She then looked at me and her eyes went cold. "You. With me."

"Yes, ma'am," I said, and obediently followed her into the train.

The doors closed behind us and the interior lights came on. It was an ordinary subway car except for the furniture. There were chairs and a desk and on the far end, a bed.

"This is my home," she explained. "I don't like staying in one place."

The subway began rolling, but slowly. I looked outside at the crowd of clown-masked freaks who watched us slide away. It wasn't until we started moving that I realized I had left Damon's sword with them. I was totally defenseless, not only from these jokers, but from Damon.

"Uh, Mrs. Seaver, we're going uptown on the downtown track."

"Call me Ree. That's how I'm known here. Short for Terri, I guess."

"I can't call you Ree. You're Mrs. Seaver."

"Not anymore."

That sounded ominous.

"Okay. So, then, *Ree*, we're still on the wrong track."

"There aren't any other trains. This is my vision. I keep things simple."

"Shouldn't your vision be Stony Brook?"

She sat down in a worn easy chair, looking tired. We were

alone on the train, though somebody had to be driving.

"That would be too hard," she explained. "Too many memories. I went to NYU in the late seventies. It's where I first studied photography."

"You get to choose what part of your life you want to relive in the Black?" I asked. "I didn't know that."

"Not exactly. Spirits end up reliving a period in their lives that was important to them, good or bad. It's pretty much the whole point of being here. This is a time that started me on the path that led to my passion in life, so here I am. Other spirits find themselves in more difficult times. I think it's even possible to visit both. It all depends on what each spirit needs to work on. The rules aren't hard and fast, but even then, this vision isn't . . . normal."

"What does that mean?" I asked.

"You'll see."

I hated surprises. "Where are we going?"

"To a place with answers. That's what you want, isn't it?"

I nodded. Sure I wanted answers, among other things.

"Do you have any idea how much trouble you're in?" she asked.

"What I think and what I'm seeing are two different things. But, yeah, I'm knee-deep in it. I haven't exactly been resting in peace."

She took a deep breath and asked, "What's going on with Marsh?"

"How can you not know? Haven't you gone to the Light to check up on him?"

She looked pained. "No."

"But . . . why not?"

Mrs. Seaver—Ree—looked anxious. That wasn't like her.

"Like I said, this vision isn't normal. You must know that."

"I know I can't leave whenever I want. When I was here before, we had to move to some border before we could leave. I haven't seen any Watchers here either, except at the edge of the vision."

"And you won't. This is a unique place in the Black . . . a kind of island. I guess you could say we're exiles here. We control how spirits come and go. Or at least how they go. We can't always stop them from coming. We're isolated by choice but it's a price we're willing to pay. Part of that price is that we can't see into the Light. Or visit. It would be too much of a temptation. I haven't seen Marsh or my husband, Michael, or anyone else I knew. Including you. You've grown up, Coop. I can only imagine what Marsh looks like now."

"What do you mean 'temptation'?"

"That's what I'm going to show you."

"Who are you people? I mean, no offense, but it looks like you're hanging out with a bunch of rejects from a cheesy sci-fi movie."

She smiled. "We're the Guardians of the Rift."

I had to let that sink in for a second. "Guardians of the Rift. What's 'the Rift'?"

Ree stood up and walked toward me. "You'll see, but first I want to know what's going on with Marsh. You said Damon was haunting him, but that's impossible."

"Well, sorry. Damon's been watching us both for a while."

"Both of you?"

"Yeah. That's why he killed me. To get to Marsh. Lucky me."

"But he can't get to Marsh."

"Yeah, he can. It all started when Marsh broke the crucible."

Ree looked like she was about to pass out. If she hadn't reached up to grab the overhead bar, I think she would have gone over.

"He broke a crucible?" she said, barely above a whisper. "How did he get it?"

"I don't know, but he did. I saw him break it myself. He was pissed off about something and threw it against a wall. The thing exploded with blood and then the ground started shaking. Damon said it had some kind of spell over him and breaking it somehow made it weaker. Does any of this make sense to you?"

Ree fell back into her chair. When she looked to me, I saw tears in her eyes.

"Unfortunately, yes."

I held back from telling her about how I knew about the other crucibles and that I was hunting for one in the Black. I didn't mention the poleax either. I wanted to know more before admitting to anything.

"How do you know?" I asked. "I thought you couldn't go to the Light."

"I discovered the crucibles when I was alive."

It was my turn to grab on to the overhead bar for support.

"So that's how Marsh got it?" I exclaimed. "From you?"

"It's why I'm here," she said. "I foolishly set something in motion that I'm desperately trying to stop before it goes too far."

"What is it?" I asked. "What's happening?"

Ree wiped the sweat from her forehead with her sleeve. "The destruction of the Morpheus Road."

The subway car lurched and stopped. Ree stood up, wiped her eyes, and once again looked like her confident self.

"You need to see this," she said as the doors slid open.

She strode out of the train and I was right after her. The signs on the pillars of this station read 42ND STREET. As we climbed the stairs, we started passing people. They looked like more of Adeipho's soldiers. Or Ree's Guardians. Or whatever the heck these freaks were. None of them wore masks, which was a relief, but they were still a strange mix of types. There were men and women. Some were dressed in ancient rags. Others wore modern suits. I saw nurses and soldiers and even a UPS guy. There was nothing that tied these people together, other than the fact that they were in Ree's vision. Someone was stationed at every intersection, which made me think they were guards or sentries. Ree gave a quick nod to a few, but that was it. None of them seemed to care that she was there. They were too busy staring at me. I was an outsider. An intruder. Trouble.

We climbed out of a stairwell into a wide, well-lit corridor with a newsstand and a coffee shop that looked familiar. I'd been there before. In the Light, anyway. It was strange to see the place so deserted because normally it was loaded with thousands of people. I followed Ree around a corner and we stopped before entering the vast expanse of Grand Central Terminal. It was a massive indoor train station that could probably house a 747. I'd been there with my parents, and with Marsh when we took the train into the city. Dad passed through every day on his way to work. It was a magical place. A crossroads. It was designed to inspire, from the massive glass windows that let in soft daylight, to the soaring ceiling that was covered in twinkle lights that were arranged like giant constellations.

Besides the fact that almost nobody was there, the place was different from how I remembered it. There were huge lighted billboards covering most every wall, advertising everything from watches to whiskey. One entire wall of the concourse held a giant lighted mural that was a stunning photo of a snowy countryside. It was an advertisement for Kodak film. It was definitely Grand Central Terminal, but not the one I remembered.

"This is 1978, remember?" Ree said, reading my mind. Her voice echoed through the monstrous, empty space.

Oh. Right. All of those billboards must have been there back in her day. They were colorful but kind of tacky-looking, which is probably why they were eventually taken down to reveal the historic station. In spite of the ugly advertisements, there was plenty about the place that I recognized. The portals to the tracks lined the wall to our left. The wall opposite the tracks held the ticket booths, over which were the big train schedules. In the center of the huge room sat the information booth. I remembered there being a big round brass ball that held a clock on top of it. The brass ball was there, but the clock wasn't. From where we were standing I couldn't tell what had taken its place. What I did see were four of Ree's Guardians standing around the booth as if protecting it.

"What's over there?" I asked.

"It's what I want you to see," she replied.

Our footsteps echoed through the empty cavern as we approached the guarded information booth.

"I'm sorry you were dragged into this, Coop," she said. "Both of you. It must be because of your relationship with Marsh and his relationship to me. But like it or not, you're in it now."

"Yeah, whatever *it* is."

"I'll tell you what it *isn't*. It isn't about protecting Marsh, or saving yourself. It's far bigger than that."

We arrived at the information booth.

"Beneath this structure is the Rift," she explained.

"I thought there was a lower level to the station," I said.

"In the Light, sure. In my vision too, but the Rift leads to an entirely different place."

I looked at the information booth to see . . . nothing out of the ordinary.

"Gotta say, I'm not sure why this needs guarding. What exactly makes this a rift?"

"This isn't Grand Central Terminal," she said, sounding a little irritated. "This just happens to be my vision. It's something tangible for the Guardians to exist in. The Rift is real. It exists and it would be here no matter what the vision was."

"So what exactly is the Rift?"

"It's a tear in the fabric of existence," she explained. "There's only one and we're here to make sure there will never be another."

"A tear in the . . . ? You're making my head hurt."

"I know. I'm sorry. But you need to understand what it is, how it came to be, and why it's critical that we protect it."

It all seemed so incredible until I focused on the brass ball that used to hold the clock. It was a beach-ball-size casing that stood on a fancy pedestal. Circling the base was the word "Information." There were four large openings in the globe where there used to be four clock faces. The brass structure was empty, except for one small item. Suspended in the center of the globe was a small golden ball about the size of a plum that was covered with strange hieroglyphic-type carved symbols.

I had found the crucible.

"Tell me," I said, staring at the golden orb.

. . . and Ree told me the truth about her death, her afterlife, and why Damon wanted me to destroy the crucible.

Terri "Ree" Seaver's Tale

I've heard that curiosity killed the cat.

But I never bought into that because to me, curiosity makes things happen. The thirst for knowledge is what drives the evolution of societies and the advancement of everything from technology to art to the basic understanding of the human condition. I was drawn to photography out of curiosity. I found that by capturing images I could peel back the superficial layers of a subject to reveal an inner truth. A photograph freezes and captures a moment that can be studied in a way that is impossible in the fleeting moments of real time. A photograph is a window into another world. An honest world.

I say this not to justify the things I did, but to try and explain what led me into making the choices I made. I was not driven by greed or glory. That doesn't mean I was not responsible for what happened. I knew what I was doing was wrong, but I told myself that there would be no harm. I was simply searching for knowledge. What I found was that curiosity may not have killed the cat, but that's small consolation because there are some things worse than death.

"I found it!" Ennis yelled. "It is here, just as I thought!"

Ennis Mobley had burst through the door of my hotel room clutching an ancient book with yellowing pages and a brown cracked binding. He was acting like Marsh on Christmas morning, thrilled with the anticipation of unwrapping newfound treasures. He opened the book on the bed and fell to his knees to leaf through the antique volume.

"I told you, Terri," he said, teasing. "You should never doubt me. I am far too thorough."

"And tenacious," I added.

Ennis and I had worked together for years. Whenever I traveled on a photo assignment, he handled the logistics, which freed me up to concentrate on taking pictures. We had been everywhere together, from the Blue Mountains of New South Wales to Prince Edward Island to the Great Wall of China. Ennis was Jamaican and though he tried to temper his accent, the lilting island patois usually snuck through. Especially when he was excited.

"It is here, near the town of Messopotamo," he announced triumphantly.

Ennis was a student of history, particularly of Greek history, which is why he was thrilled when I asked him to come along on this assignment. It was a two-week gig to photograph villages along the western coast of Greece for a travel magazine. It sounds exotic but it wasn't particularly exciting work. There are just so many ways that you can shoot a small harbor to make it look quaint and inviting. But the towns themselves were lovely and the weather was perfect. It was the kind of trip I would have loved to take with Michael and Marsh, but work and school prevented that.

"How did you find this book?" I asked.

Ennis smiled. "As you say, I am tenacious."

I gave him a look that said, "Just give me a straight answer."

"It was in the town library," he answered.

The book showed a drawing of a stone building that looked like an ancient temple with a large dome and arched doorways. The text of the book and the inscription beneath the drawing were in Greek, which meant it looked like gibberish to somebody who had barely passed high school French.

"The building dates back to Roman times," Ennis explained. "The English translation is 'Temple of the Morning Light,' though over the centuries it was also used as a school and a hospital."

"So it's a temple, not a tomb."

"Originally, yes. But its history is clear. It is what I have been looking for."

Whenever we were headed to a new destination, Ennis would first scour the Internet to research the history of the place to try and uncover obscure nuggets of information that might slip past the casual traveler. His feeling was that these jobs were special opportunities to visit far-flung locales that he wouldn't normally get to. It's one of the things I loved about Ennis. He was as curious as I was.

"So you were right," I said. "It's here. Satisfied?"

Ennis gave me a surprised look. "Well, no. I want to see it for myself."

"I was afraid you'd say that. We don't have time."

"But we do!" he exclaimed. "Our flight does not leave Athens until Monday morning and you have already completed your assignment. How many quaint harbors must you photograph?"

He had me there.

"That gives us two full days," he went on. "It is only twenty kilometers to Messopotamo. A short drive. Though I believe we should make the journey as the ancients did."

"And how's that?"

"We should drive to Ammoudia and travel by boat up the River Acheron."

I took a deep breath and said, "The River Styx."

Ennis smiled. "You know more of this myth than you let on."

I shrugged. "It's a great story . . . a river that leads to a portal where you can speak with the dead. I'll bet tour boats leave every half hour."

"Pilgrims no longer believe in the Oracle of the Dead, but the ruins of the Necromanteio are a popular tourist destination," Ennis explained.

"Sure. Who wouldn't want to spend valuable vacation time consorting with the dead?"

Ennis frowned. "From what I have read it was all a hoax."

"Gee, you think?"

"I have no desire to see the Necromanteio. I wish to find the temple."

I stared straight into Ennis's eyes, trying to read him. "Why are you so interested?"

"How can I not be?" he answered innocently. "To find a tomb that is thought only to exist in myth and prove that it is real? Those opportunities do not happen often."

"I don't believe in myths," I said bluntly.

"Nor do I," he argued. "My facts are based on history, not fables. And my interest did not begin when you called me about making this trip, Terri. I learned of this story years ago and have done extensive research. It has proven to be a fascinating hobby."

"Sure. For Indiana Jones."

"I do not seek adventure. Solving a centuries-old puzzle would be reward enough."

"I don't know," I said doubtfully. "You'd think if it was really there, somebody would have found it by now."

"You assume they would *want* to find it. The story states quite plainly that what is buried should remain buried."

"Sounds like good advice," I said.

"It does if you believe in myths." He smiled mischievously and added, "But you do not."

I still wasn't convinced.

"Look at it this way," he said. "At the very least it will be an interesting side trip and you will take photographs that will be more unique than the cliché travel shots you have been making. The temple alone is worth photographing, is it not? But if there is some small truth to the story, you may be the first to bring an image to the world that has never before been seen. I know you, Terri. Surely that intrigues you."

I looked at the sketch in the book that lay open on the bed. I had to admit, it was a unique structure. I wondered what it would look like at sunset with the low, warm light . . . and what secrets it might be hiding within.

"What was the guy's name again?" I asked.

"The English translation is 'Damon of Epirus.' Though he has been referred to as Damon the Butcher."

"I'm guessing that wasn't because he made hamburgers."

"No," Ennis said somberly. "At least not from animals."

Three hours later I found myself on a small boat being powered by a rumbling old smoke-belching engine traveling up the River Acheron, headed for a tiny town that supposedly housed the portal into the next life. As always, Ennis had made all the arrangements. He knew I'd agree to go and hired the boat long before he showed me the book with the drawing of the Temple of the Morning Light.

Ennis stood at the bow, scanning the shore of the narrow river, soaking up the view and the hot afternoon sun. The water was a deep green-blue and the banks were tangled with grass. There wasn't a building in sight. It was like we had gone back in time.

Ennis never wore a hat, no matter how hot it was. He had on a short-sleeved striped shirt and long khaki pants and looked about as fresh and cool as if he were hanging out on our porch in Stony Brook sipping lemonade. A backpack was slung casually over his shoulder that I hoped held a thermos with the aforementioned lemonade.

Unlike Ennis, I was sweating like we were slogging up the Amazon. I wore the same wide-brimmed khaki hat that I always took on such adventures. My light skin didn't take kindly to the burning sun. Marsh called it my bwana hat because he said it made me look like I was going on safari. He wasn't far from right. I never shot a gun in my life, but I was always on the hunt . . . for images. I wore shorts, my hikers, and a lightweight T-shirt. I wanted to travel light so I was armed with only my Nikon digital SLR with a single 10-to-120-millimeter zoom lens.

At the helm of the boat was an elderly captain with skin as dark as my boots. He didn't speak English, which wasn't a big deal because Ennis knew enough Greek to get us where we were going. As he piloted our course up the quiet river, I got the feeling that he had traveled this route many times before, ferrying tourists to the Necromanteio. I wondered what he would have thought if he knew our destination was someplace entirely different.

Ennis joined me by the rail and said, "Imagine how many pilgrims traveled this very same route in the hopes of speaking with their departed ancestors."

"But it was all a sham."

"That is the popular belief. People would stay at the Necromanteio for days while sorcerers prepared them to get a glimpse through the gate into the afterlife. But that preparation meant taking large doses of hallucinogenic herbs. After a few days of that, the visitors believed anything they saw."

"So they thought they were looking into the next life because they were stoned out of their minds?"

"Apparently. A pulley system was discovered that would levitate the sorcerers, who would pretend to be spirits."

"How very *Scooby-Doo*."

"But the pilgrims believed and I wonder if there might have been some truth to it."

"Seriously? A doorway to the afterlife? You'd think something like that would make the evening news."

Ennis chuckled. "I do not think it is so simple but I accept that some places hold spiritual significance. I do believe that there is life after death and perhaps it is easier to connect with spirits in some places than others."

"That's pretty—I don't know, what's the word? Cosmic?"

"Perhaps the word you are looking for is 'nutty,'" he said.

"I was being nice."

He smiled and shrugged. "I simply believe in possibilities."

"What's so important about this tomb? The guy was a soldier, right?"

"Damon was a general in Alexander the Great's army," Ennis explained. "The accounts I've read claim that Damon was responsible for slaughtering thousands, most after the battle was complete and victory assured."

"So he was a murderer."

"Of epic proportions. He was not satisfied with simply vanquishing an enemy. He wanted to wipe them out and often did so by his own hand."

"Seriously? He personally killed these people?" I asked.

"From what I've read he never took part in the battles himself. He was strictly the tactician and quite brilliant at it. Then, once the fighting was complete, he would line up the prisoners and behead them himself."

"That's barbaric," I said.

"And not the worst of it. I have read accounts where he would practice ancient pagan rituals to increase his power."

"Do I want to know what those were?"

"No."

"Tell me anyway."

"He would lick the blood of his victims from the sword that killed them and sometimes go so far as to eat the heart of an opposing general."

"He'd eat their . . . ?" I exclaimed. "Oh my god."

"Only of the generals. Those who had the most power."

"Well, of course, that makes it all okay," I said. "What a monster."

"Some said he was simply sadistic. Others felt he was justified and it was all in the heat of the struggle. I've even read some accounts that said he was trying to outshine the deeds of Alexander. Slaughtering their common enemies was his way of proving his worth."

"And eating their hearts," I said with disgust. "So he really was a butcher."

"And he made enemies among his own people. He had a loyal band of followers but the grander army realized he was dangerous."

"And crazy."

"When Alexander died at the young age of thirty-three,

many feared Damon would attempt to control the army. So he was assassinated, along with many of his loyalists."

"Yay. Good guys win. Cannibals lose. So why do you want to find his tomb so badly?"

"Curiosity. From the accounts I've read it was not an ordinary death. Or burial. This was the dawn of modern civilization. Mystical beliefs and practices were common. Many feared that Damon's evil would not end with his death."

"What did they think he would do?" I asked, scoffing. "Rise up from the grave and take his revenge?"

"Well, yes."

"Oh."

"It is why he was buried here, in a place imbued with mystical power. He was not simply laid to rest. He was imprisoned."

"Uh . . . what?"

"I do not fully understand the implications, the translations are not specific, but from what I can gather he was brought here so that the sorcerers could bury him in a tomb near the Necromanteio and use their knowledge of the afterlife to create a seal that his spirit could not break."

"What kind of seal?"

"That is what I would like to see. I have never come across a story even remotely like this one. The idea that a living being was so feared that priests were asked to imprison his spirit is unprecedented. Most scholars do not believe the story to be true or that a tomb even exists. But I have pieced together bits of information from many sources and believe I have located the spot that could very well be Damon's tomb."

"Underneath the Temple of the Morning Light."

"Yes."

"But the temple isn't that old," I said. "When did Alexander die? Like, 300 BCE?"

"In 323," Ennis corrected. "That is one reason why I believe the location was forgotten and discounted. Many structures have been built there through the centuries."

"Wouldn't other people have found it already?"

"Perhaps they have and didn't know what it was. Maybe they didn't care to find it . . . or feared to. Terri, I believe we have the opportunity to prove the existence of a site that has great historic significance while revealing physical proof of a centuries-old mystical practice that very few scholars are aware of."

"You think there's something physical about this tomb that shows what the old priests did to keep Damon dead?"

"I don't know, but I would like to find out. Wouldn't you like to be the first one to photograph it?"

"Here!" the boat captain called out. It was probably the only word of English he knew.

We both looked ahead to see that our boat was nearing a small wooden dock. We had arrived at the town of Messopotamo, home to the Oracle of the Dead.

Terri "Ree" Seaver's Tale
(Continued)

A few tourist-looking types were milling around near the dock. I saw plenty of point-and-shoot cameras in hand, ready to capture an image of the gateway to the afterlife that would probably be used as a screen saver. There were a few scruffy-looking men who acted as guides, herding their charges and directing them up a winding path that led to the ruins. I didn't hear a word of English being spoken, only Greek and French and some Italian. Seemed as though vacationing tourists from the good old United States would rather hang out at the beach than visit the doorway to Hades. Go figure.

"Let's hang back for a moment," Ennis said. "They don't need to know where we are going."

We stood by the dock and watched as the eager tourists made their way along the path.

"Do *you* know where we're going?" I asked.

"I believe the temple is near the edge of the town. It should not be hard to find."

Once the stragglers were about fifty yards from us, Ennis winked at me and started following the trail.

I turned back to our boat captain and said, "Don't you go anywhere."

He smiled and waved. I had no idea if he knew what I said. All I could hope was that Ennis had made sure that the captain wouldn't take off and leave us near the edge of eternity.

Ennis moved quickly and I was grateful that it was long past noon and the sun was already on the way down, taking the edge off the blistering-hot day. We climbed a sandy path that wove through scrubby grass and soon came upon the village of Messopotamo. It was a small, welcoming little hamlet that didn't look anything like an infamous town that hosted the Oracle of the Dead. From where we stood I could see the long line of tourists heading across the main street toward a rocky hill that was covered with olive trees.

"I believe the entrance to the Necromanteio is cut into that hill," Ennis explained.

"Probably," I said. "Unless they're all going up there to pick olives."

Ennis dropped his pack and pulled out the ancient book. He opened it to a page he had marked and showed me a crude drawing of the village. It could have been made hundreds of years before, but the street layout seemed to be the same.

"This is the location of the temple," he explained.

He pointed to a spot on the map that was nothing more than a square shape with a half-circle dome.

"Let's walk," Ennis declared, and we continued on.

We didn't say a word as we made our way through the village. Part of me enjoyed the adventure. The idea of possibly making a historic discovery was exciting, but the realist in me had doubts. Ennis may have been tenacious, but he wasn't a trained archeologist. What did he expect us to do? Start an excavation? No, the truth was he had stumbled upon a story that intrigued him and, as he so often did, he became obsessed and wanted to know all there was to know about it. My getting an assignment nearby was a happy coincidence. I had every reason to believe that we would find this temple and that would be it. His curiosity would be satisfied and the mystery of the secret tomb of Damon the Butcher would remain a mystery.

Once again, I wished that Michael and Marsh could have been there. They both would have loved going on such an exotic quest, even if it was a total wild goose chase.

"There," Ennis declared, and stopped dead.

The sight of the temple made me rethink my skepticism. The stone structure was roughly the size of a four-story house. The walls were made of light brown stone, like most of the local buildings, but what made it stand out was the large dome that topped it off. The stonework was incredibly intricate. Beautiful, even. It was part structural, part decorative mosaic. From where we stood the building looked to be abandoned. It had seen better days and I had no doubt that those days were a few hundred years before. Large chunks of wall were missing, showing small but obvious wounds. Part of the dome had collapsed, which made me wonder if it was smart to go inside.

"It really is here," Ennis whispered in awe.

"You're surprised?" I asked.

"Well . . . yes. But pleasantly so."

I reached for my camera. "I don't know what we might find inside, but as far as I'm concerned we got here at the exact right time."

We had arrived at the time of day photographers call

"the golden hour," though it's really more like the golden twenty minutes. It refers to the two times of day when the sun is low on the horizon and throws warm light at the perfect flattering angle for photos. As we stood on the outskirts of that town, I couldn't imagine a better situation to capture the temple. Without another word I started shooting. I must have taken forty shots, but I knew which one was the keeper the moment I triggered the shutter. It was the last one I took. I got down in the dirt, flat on my back, and shot through my feet. The super-low angle made the structure seem even more imposing. Once I fired off that shot, I knew there was no reason to shoot another.

Ennis had watched patiently without interrupting.

"Perfect," I said, which was my usual way of saying I was done.

"We should go inside quickly," Ennis said. "We don't have much daylight left."

That was the thing about the afternoon golden hour. Once it was gone, it was night. I didn't like the idea of going into that empty, crumbling temple after dark. When Ennis made his move toward the building, I was hit with a wave of foreboding. He realized I wasn't following and turned back to me.

"What's the trouble?"

"It's my old New England upbringing. Back in the day, when they burned witches at the stake, do you know what they did with the ashes?"

He shook his head.

"Churchyards were sacred ground so they dug the graves just outside the wall that surrounded the cemetery."

"Why did you think of that just now?" Ennis asked.

"This building," I said. "It feels as if it was built just beyond the border of the town. Is that normal?"

Ennis always had a quick answer for everything. This

time the words didn't come to him and he stood there with his mouth open.

I shrugged and gave him a sweet smile.

"Let's look inside," he said, and walked toward the building.

There was a single wooden door that I hoped would be locked. Ennis gave it a shove and it swung in on rusty hinges.

"Crack security," I commented.

Ennis stepped inside without hesitation. I took a quick look around at the setting sun and made a silent wish that I wasn't making a huge mistake.

It wasn't pitch-dark inside, but it was close. Waning daylight filtered in through window openings that hadn't held glass in forever. There was one main room that stretched all the way up to the overhead dome. The floor was littered with bits of stone and dust that had fallen over the years. A few broken chairs were lying around, but that was it. It was an empty, abandoned shell.

Ennis stood in the center, slowly turning, taking it all in.

"If this were in the States, it would be locked tight with warning signs to keep people out," I observed.

"Americans are quick to sue at the slightest opportunity," Ennis said.

"It's true. If somebody at home broke into an abandoned building that looked like it might collapse if a soft breeze picked up, and they twisted their ankle, they'd sue the owner, like it was the owner's fault they were dumb enough to go inside."

Ennis didn't get my sarcasm. He was too enthralled with the temple. I, on the other hand, was more concerned about getting hit with a stone falling from the ceiling.

"Satisfied?" I asked.

"I want to see if there is a way to go below," he said as he walked to the far end of the room.

"Whoa, wait," I said, hurrying after him. "We shouldn't be poking around here."

Ennis ignored me and disappeared through an archway that led to a dark corridor.

"It's going to be night soon," I called as I stepped through the arch after him. "How are we supposed to see in the—"

I was hit in the eyes by the beam of a flashlight that Ennis had pulled out of his backpack.

"Let me explore a bit, Terri."

"But we're trespassing," I said firmly. "And it's dangerous."

"This structure has stood for centuries," he argued. "I would be surprised if it chose this particular afternoon to collapse."

He turned and continued along the corridor, shining the beam on the narrow stone walls. The idea that we would suddenly come upon some ancient tomb seemed remote so I decided to humor him for a while and followed. The corridor led to a small, empty room.

"Dead end," I declared.

Ennis walked boldly to the far side of the room to what I thought was a boarded-up window.

"This does not open to the outside," he explained. "The building is too deep."

He put his fingers against the rotten boards, testing to see how solid they were.

"Don't!" I exclaimed.

Too late. The boards fell off the frame as if they were held on by nothing more than spit.

"Now we're trespassing *and* vandalizing," I scolded.

"Just a quick look," he said. He sat on the bottom edge of the wooden frame, lifted his legs, and swung himself around into the darkness.

I ran to the opening and peered in to see Ennis flashing the light around the small enclosure.

"This looks to have been a vault of some sort, perhaps to keep valuable artifacts."

"Or maybe it's a broom closet," I offered.

Ennis put his hands on the walls, pressing hard, examining for I-didn't-know-what.

"What are you doing?" I asked.

"Looking for weakness," he explained. "They did not have safe-deposit boxes when this was built. There could be a thin layer of mortar hiding something interesting.

His search of the wall didn't turn up anything so he started digging at the floor with his boot.

I said, "Even if you're right and there's a subterranean vault below this building, we're not going to find it by kicking around some dirt."

He ignored me.

"And what if we found something?" I said. "I'm sure the Greek government would have something to say if they knew we were digging up their turf looking for national treasures."

"Look at this place," Ennis said. "Do you think anybody cares?"

"They would if we found something," I shot back.

He kept digging at the dirt floor with the heel of his boot. If I'd actually thought he was going to find something, I would have insisted that he stop. But poking around an old building with a flashlight didn't exactly seem like the procedure for a successful archeological dig so I decided to let him play for another few minutes. It would soon be dark. I hoped the boat captain with the leathery skin had night vision.

I was about to pull the plug on the adventure when Ennis's boot hit something that sounded hollow. He looked up at me with wide eyes.

"Wood," he exclaimed.

"So?"

He threw the flashlight to me, then dropped down on his knees and started digging with his hands.

"It means there is something below us," he answered with growing excitement. "They do not make foundations out of wood."

"Ennis, please, you're going to land us both in jail."

"We are exploring," he said. "That is not a crime."

It took a few seconds for him to clear away a section of dirt to reveal wooden planks a few inches below the surface. Ennis was moving fast. He grabbed his backpack and pulled out a crowbar.

"Ennis!"

He had come far more prepared than he had let on. Ignoring my protests, he jammed the hooked end between two of the planks and pulled. With a high-pitched screech, he tore the wooden plank out of the floor to reveal another dark hole.

"There is more below," he exclaimed, and worked to pull up a few more planks.

My heart was in my throat.

"Stop. Just stop!" I shouted, but not too loudly for fear that someone passing by would hear us and call the police.

Ennis pulled up two more planks. For a change, he was sweating. He grabbed his flashlight and shone it into the hole.

"Stairs," he declared. "We can drop below right here."

"No, we can't," I insisted. "We must be breaking a dozen laws. I don't want to spend the rest of my life in a Greek prison."

Ennis stopped working, took a breath to calm himself, and looked to me.

"Terri," he said patiently. "You always talk of people who are afraid to step out of their comfort zone and take chances. Now you sound like the very kind of person you disdain. "

"Comfort zone? This isn't even *close* to my comfort zone."

"All we are doing is exploring an old structure. If the authorities have a problem with that, we will tell them that we are overzealous tourists, which is exactly what we are. This is an opportunity. We may find nothing but another empty room, but what if there is more? How can we not take that chance? You of all people should understand that."

"I do, but I'm also a mother with a son."

"And what will Marshall say when you tell him you turned your back on such a simple adventure? You have always taught him to look beyond the obvious. Is that not exactly what we are doing here?"

Common sense told me to get the hell out of there. What was a suburban mom from Connecticut doing in an abandoned temple on the edge of nowhere? I knew I should turn and walk away.

But I wasn't just an SUV-driving soccer mom. I was someone who chose to travel the world in search of images that told stories and spoke to people. My family was my life, but I had a passion for discovery. I can't say that I would have planned the adventure we found ourselves in, but looking into that dark hole gave me a thrill, I admit it. What was down there? What could I bring back to the world? As much as the safe decision would have been to leave, I found it impossible to turn back.

"Be careful," I said.

Ennis went back to work. In no time he had pulled up enough of the old floor to create an opening large enough for us to drop through.

He peered below and said, "There are stairs but this is no trapdoor. This room was intentionally sealed off."

"Is that good news or bad news?"

He slid his feet below the floor and stood on the top of

the stone steps. Ennis was breathing hard. He was as excited as I was.

"There may be nothing of interest down there," he said. "But then again . . ."

"Let's stop talking and find out," I said.

Ennis smiled, knowing that I was on board. With the flashlight beam ahead of him, he carefully navigated his way down the stairs. I watched as he slowly dropped below the floor into the dark void.

"It is safe," he declared. "A simple flight of stone stairs. Keep your hand on the wall for security."

I climbed through the window into the small room and followed Ennis through the hole and down into the dark.

"Go slow," I cautioned.

Ennis was careful to keep the light beam on the stairs so we could both navigate. The worn stone steps were flush to the foundation of the temple. There was no handrail. I didn't want to think of what would happen if we stumbled and fell. I kept one hand on the wall and the other on my camera to keep it from swinging. As old as the temple was, it felt as if we were descending through time. While the stonework of the building above was precise and clean, the foundation below looked crude and haphazard.

"This seems to have been constructed in a much earlier era than the temple," Ennis commented. "These are two distinct structures."

The long flight of stairs took us down to a deep basement, where it had to be thirty degrees cooler than outside. We stood together on the dirt floor, examining the space with the flashlight beam. The ceiling was mostly made of stone, except for the opening we came through that had been sealed with wood. The basement, or whatever it was, was empty. And small. It might have taken up a quarter of the footprint of the temple.

"Nothing to write home about," I declared.

Ennis scanned the walls until he came upon a stone archway.

"Maybe in there," he declared, and walked toward it cautiously.

"Wait. That can't be part of the basement. The temple ends at the wall."

Ennis's eyes lit up. "Then let us see where it leads."

I followed him to the archway and curled my fingers around his belt at the small of his back. I didn't want him getting too far ahead of me. Once through the portal, we entered a narrow passageway that had walls made of the same stone as the foundation. Unless my sense of direction was totally off, we were no longer beneath the temple. He moved forward cautiously, but deliberately. I didn't try to stop him or talk him out of going farther. My curiosity had been teased. We were in it, for better or worse.

The walls were constructed with layer after layer of carefully placed stones that came together in a point overhead, the force of gravity working on each side to keep it from crumbling. Whoever had made this tunnel knew what they were doing. It was crude, but solid.

"Impressive," Ennis noted.

"People must know this exists," I said. "I mean it's not like it was hard to find."

"I agree," Ennis said. "I wonder if there is some reason that it was sealed off."

"Please," I scolded. "I'm nervous enough."

We followed the tunnel for several more twisting yards. I was about to suggest that we turn back when Ennis stopped suddenly.

"What?" I asked.

"There's light," he said, pointing ahead.

Looking beyond him, I saw narrow shafts of light filtering

through from above. Daylight was almost gone so the light was faint, but there was no mistaking the fact that this tunnel was constructed to allow in light from outside. Dozens of small beams of light crisscrossed one another, lighting up small sections of the wall. There was just enough illumination that Ennis was able to turn off his much brighter flashlight.

"We should wait a few seconds to let our eyes adjust," Ennis suggested.

As the two of us stood shoulder to shoulder in that ancient, narrow tunnel, the true nature of this structure slowly revealed itself.

I felt Ennis grow tense.

"We are in a place for the dead," he said with a gasp.

"It's a catacomb," I declared. "I think we found the back entrance to the Necromanteio."

Though we were hundreds of yards from the official entrance to the ruins of the Oracle of the Dead, I had no doubt that we were standing in a far-flung offshoot of the labyrinth of tunnels that made up the mythological gateway to the afterlife. We walked farther and saw cutouts in the walls that were occupied by the mummified remains of ancient Greeks. Some were wrapped in rotting cloth. Others were in stone shells. Still other cutouts held multiple remains with dozens of skulls piled on one another like bricks in a wall. Some still had the shreds of leathery skin clinging to the bone.

"I don't think this is part of the regular tour," I said.

I had actually photographed the catacombs under Paris, so I wasn't totally repulsed. But that was a well-known spot that always had visitors and charged an admission. This place didn't look as if it had been visited by anybody who was still breathing in a very long time.

Ennis took a few tentative steps forward, examining the gruesome remains.

"How old could these be?" he asked.

"No way to tell, at least not by me."

Ennis started moving faster, giving each morbid cubby a quick look before moving on.

I said, "Do you think one of these is your boy Damon?"

"No," he answered with authority. "His final resting place was more of a prison. He would not be with the general population."

"Of course not," I said. "Wouldn't want to put a dead cannibal in with the riffraff."

Ennis scowled at me as if I was being disrespectful of the dead. Maybe he was right.

We reached a junction where the tunnel forked into two different routes.

"We should stop here," I offered. "The last thing we want to do is get lost."

Ennis didn't listen and kept moving, choosing the right fork.

"I am going by your theory," he explained. "This should take us farther away from the town."

"Ennis, we're not going to search this whole place. These tunnels could go on for miles."

"If he is here, we won't have to go far. My research said the temple was erected over his burial spot."

"So how will you know if you've found him? These guys pretty much all look the same to me . . . bony and bald."

"I am not looking for skeletal remains. I am looking for a tomb. Or a vault. Or something like—"

Ennis froze and I nearly ran into him from behind.

"Something like that," he declared.

We had hit a dead end. The only illumination came from the last faint rays of light that seeped in from the tunnel behind us. It was too dim to make out detail, but I could see that the tunnel opened into a room and there was something large and solid on the far side.

I instinctively went for my camera.

Ennis lifted his flashlight. When he turned on the beam, I could see that his hand was shaking. He began to raise the light toward the mysterious object, when I grabbed it.

"If that's it, we take some pictures and then we're out of here. If not, we're out of here anyway. Understand?"

Ennis nodded.

"How will you know if it's Damon's tomb?" I asked.

When he spoke, Ennis's voice cracked. He was more nervous than I was. "Supposedly there were six locks. Or seals. The translations I found weren't any more specific than that. Whatever ritual they used to imprison Damon's spirit, it took six locks to do it."

"So if there are six locks, it's Damon?" I asked.

Ennis gave a nervous chuckle. "I don't know. I suppose."

I let go of his hand and let him raise the flashlight toward the object. The beam revealed the unmistakable lines of a sarcophagus. It sat on a pedestal so that the top was a few inches higher than eye level. It was carved out of gray stone and looked to be large enough to hold a coffin, though I didn't think they used coffins back in ancient Greece.

Ennis didn't move. I, on the other hand, wanted to know what we had found so I skirted around him and approached the stone box.

"One thing's for sure," I said. "Whoever's inside there is special. Everybody else in this horror show was pretty much stacked up and left out for anybody to see. Look at the lid. It must weigh a ton. He could have been one of the Oracles of the Dead. Or a priest. Or one of those sorcerers you talked about."

"Or Damon of Epirus," Ennis said, barely above a whisper.

He had gotten his legs moving and joined me at the sarcophagus. I took his flashlight and shone it on the intricate carvings that covered the outside of the large box.

"I have no idea what any of this means," I said. "I don't see six locks either. Or anything that could look like six seals or six of anything."

"What about that?" Ennis asked.

He pointed to the top of the sarcophagus where a stone box sat that was roughly the size of a shoe box. It too was covered with carvings and Greek lettering.

"I suppose those symbols would explain what it was," I offered. "Can you read them?"

Ennis shook his head.

I grabbed my camera. "I'll take some shots and we can bring them to somebody who can translate." I gave Ennis a playful shove and said, "Looks like you made a big discovery after all, Indy."

I switched on my camera and took a few steps back while pulling off the lens cover. I hated using the built-in flash. It was ugly light. But this was about getting a clear image, not about art. The whine of the flash powering to life cut through the quiet of the tomb.

"Take a couple of steps back," I said to Ennis. "I want to get every detail."

Ennis didn't move. He kept staring at the sarcophagus.

"It's not going anywhere," I said playfully. "Let me shoot this."

Still, he didn't move.

"Ennis?"

Instead of backing off, Ennis reached out and grabbed the box on top of the tomb.

"Whoa, what are you doing?"

It was like he was in a trance. He pulled it toward him, the stone of the smaller box scraping across the top of the sarcophagus.

"Don't! That probably hasn't been moved for centuries—"

What happened next seemed to unfold in slow motion.

It's incredible to think how life can change so quickly and so completely, with no warning. Ennis dropped his flashlight and pulled the small stone box off the sarcophagus. It was heavy and he had to tilt it as he brought it down. The cover on the box wasn't secured and it slipped off instantly. I brought my camera up and started shooting. The room was so dark that I only saw brief moments of detail as each flash fired. When the lid came off, it crashed to the floor and shattered. For one brief instant I saw what was inside. It looked to be six golden balls, each about the size of a plum. Six balls. They could have had etchings on them but it all happened too quickly to tell for sure.

As Ennis struggled to right the box, one of the balls fell out.

The light from my strobe kicked a glint off the golden ball as it fell to the ground. I lowered my camera and reached out to catch it. Like a diving shortstop, I lunged and grabbed the small ball an inch from the ground. A moment later, a second ball fell from the box. I wasn't as quick with that one. I reached out with my free hand but I was a second too late. The ball hit the rocky floor and shattered. Tiny golden shards flew everywhere, along with what looked like red liquid. It splattered all over the rocky floor, and my hands. It felt sticky. Like syrup. Or . . .

"Blood," I said with a gasp.

The ground shook. I stumbled and fell to one knee.

"My god, it's an earthquake," I exclaimed.

"Back! Now!" Ennis yelled.

Too late. The rumbling came from everywhere and nowhere. It sounded as if we were being descended on by a dozen freight trains. I tried to stand but fell down again. Oddly, light filled the room.

"The ceiling!" Ennis shouted.

The force of the earthquake was collapsing the tunnel.

Heavy stones fell all around us. Ennis grabbed my hand to pull me to my feet, but a stone the size of a bowling ball hit him in the arm and knocked him to his knees.

The tomb was shaking so hard it was impossible for me to stand. The sarcophagus shuddered and fell off the pedestal, directly over Ennis. If that thing hit him, he'd be crushed. I scrambled on my hands and knees and launched forward, knocking him out of the way. The sarcophagus hit the floor and the heavy lid flipped off. Even with the world crashing down around us, I wanted to see what was inside. I wanted to see Damon of Epirus.

But when the box fell on its side, no mummy fell out. Instead, what came tumbling out was some sort of tool. Or weapon. It was solid black and looked to be about the size of a long sword. It came to a sharp point, but beneath the tip were two more cutting edges. One was a picklike device like you would use to dig through rock, and the other side was a sharp chopping cleaver. I only caught a brief glimpse of it, but it was all I needed to form an opinion.

It looked like the tool of a devil.

The weapon clattered to the ground amid the falling stones.

"Look!" Ennis exclaimed.

The pedestal that held the stone box had disappeared down into a dark hole. The earthquake had torn open the ground. Or had the hole always been there and the pedestal had been protecting it? Through the horrible rumbling I heard another sound. Screams. Or were they tortured howls?

Whatever they were, they were coming from the hole.

I was losing my mind. I knew we had to get out of there, but I still wanted proof of what we had seen, and that proof was in my camera. I looked around to see it lying between the lid of the sarcophagus and the howling hole.

A quick glance up showed that the cave-in had actually

given us our escape route. The pile of rock and rubble beneath it could be climbed to what little daylight was left.

"Go that way!" I shouted to Ennis. "Climb!"

He saw the pile, nodded, and scrambled for it. The earthquake was still rumbling. It felt like the longest earthquake in history, though it all could have happened in a few seconds. Ennis crossed in front of me, headed for the caved-in roof. I was ready to follow but was afraid if both of us climbed the pile of dirt it would collapse and we'd be stuck. I knew it wouldn't take long for him to climb out, just enough time for me to grab my camera.

I crawled for the camera and reached for the strap. I remember thinking that Ennis had been absolutely right. I had taken some shots that had never been seen before. In that moment I actually wondered what the future would bring to two people who had gone in search of adventure . . . and found it.

I reached for the camera, grabbed the strap, and turned back to the pile of rubble—when the floor collapsed. I was being pulled into the hole, slipping down along with an avalanche of rocks and dirt. I let go of the camera but not the golden ball that I had saved from breaking. I can't say why I thought it was important, but I protected that thing like it was a precious, fragile egg.

"Ennis!" I screamed.

Ennis was halfway up the debris pile. He turned back, saw what was happening, and leaped back for the floor. He had taken care of me more times than I could remember. I always felt safe with him around, even when we were off on some ridiculous adventure. This was no different. I knew that Ennis would save me.

"I have you!" Ennis screamed as he reached out for me.

I couldn't tell if I was falling into the hole, or being pulled.

I reached for Ennis's hand . . . and grabbed air.

The last sight I remember was the surprised look on Ennis's face when he realized that he was too late. For the first time ever, he wasn't able to take care of me. The next thing I knew, I was falling.

And then everything went black.

Terri "Ree" Seaver's Tale
(Continued)

There was no sensation.

I couldn't tell if I was falling or floating or dying. Time had no meaning. My body had no meaning. I wasn't in pain and surprisingly I wasn't in a panic. I remembered the catacombs and the earthquake and even the image of Ennis desperately reaching out for me, but it all seemed as if it had happened to somebody else.

The first input I sensed was warmth. My face felt warm, and with it, I sensed light. It was then that I realized that my eyes were closed. Was it as simple as that? Had my eyes been closed so tightly I couldn't see anything?

I cautiously opened them and had to squint against the bright light that was shining directly on me. The abrupt change was like a rude slap. I wondered if this was "the light" that so many people reported seeing at the moment of death, but there was nothing ethereal or otherworldly about it. I didn't hear harps or a heavenly chorus of angels. It just felt like a bright light was shining in my eyes and I wanted it to stop.

I realized that I was sitting on a hard floor. That answered one question: I wasn't a spirit who was floating toward the light on the way to heaven. Or wherever spirits go. I turned away and blinked so my eyes could adjust.

"Ennis?" I called out tentatively.

I had fallen into a black hole beneath the stone sarcophagus. Was there another room directly beneath the tomb? Is that where I was? I couldn't remember landing, but I did remember hearing ghostly howls coming from the opening. They had stopped, I was glad to note. Wherever I was, it was quiet. I moved to rub my eyes and realized I was still clutching the golden orb that had fallen from the stone box on top of the sarcophagus. I examined it, rolling it over in my hands. It was beautiful, with intricate carvings. And it was fragile. That much was proved by the bloodstains on my hands from the other ball that had broken.

I rubbed my eyes and turned away from the bright light. What I saw was impossible, but absolutely real. I expected to find myself in the rubble left after the violent earthquake. Instead I found myself sitting on the floor of Grand Central Terminal in New York City. The annoying bright light was streaming in through the wall of glass windows on the west side.

I can't say that everything that had happened since we entered that temple made sense but at least I could logically follow the series of events—until then. I jumped to my feet and spun around, expecting it all to disappear like some fever-fueled hallucination. As impossible as it was for me to be there, what made it that much more bizarre was the fact that the giant station was empty. Completely empty. Grand Central never closed. Even at three in the morning there was somebody around, but it wasn't three in the morning. Bright sun didn't shine in the middle of the night.

There was no train information on the big board. No PA announcements booming through the cavernous space. And no people.

"Ennis!" I called again, with more desperation.

The only response was the echo of my own voice. I may not have panicked when I was floating in black, but that was already ancient history. Panic was now an option. There was no way I could be in Grand Central Terminal, wearing the same clothes I'd been wearing in Greece, holding the same ball I saved in that tomb. All I could think to do was get out of there and get home. Stony Brook was only an hour from the city. I was ready to run outside, grab a cab, and drive to somewhere safe and sane. I started running toward the stairs that would take me up and out of the station, when I heard the first sound that made me realize I wasn't alone after all. It was a mechanical sound that I couldn't place. It wasn't a train, that much I was sure of. I stopped short and looked back to the far side of the station to see a stream of people on bicycles pedaling toward me. They came from everywhere, like water spewing from a sieve. They came from the two parallel entrances on the far side, from under the big clock that led out to Forty-second Street, from the gates that led to the train tracks. I might have welcomed the company, if not for the fact that each and every one of them wore clown masks.

I turned to run up the stairs but another group of masked riders came clattering down the stairs toward me. I backed away toward the center of the terminal and was immediately encircled. There had to be at least a hundred of them. They looked like marauders from across time, all wearing the freakish masks. Some wore military uniforms but from no army I'd ever seen. Others had on police uniforms, worn-out business suits, vintage dresses, and medieval chain mail. A few even wore animal skins that were fitted to their bodies with leather twine.

Nobody said a word as they circled me on their bikes. I wasn't scared. I couldn't wrap my mind around the situation enough to be frightened. The only thing I could come up with was that I was having a surreal nightmare. There was nothing I could do but stand there and wait for it to end.

As if on command, the riders stopped as one, keeping the wheels of their bikes touching, completing the circle and offering no avenue of escape. They stood silently, staring at me through the dark holes of their fright masks. The only thing that kept me from going out of my mind was the conviction that this was all happening in my head. Perhaps, I thought, the red liquid from inside that broken ball was a hallucinogen. That seemed possible. I might have been lying belowground in that catacomb under the influence of the same drug they gave to the pilgrims who visited the Oracle of the Dead in ancient times.

One of the riders moved out of the way, creating an opening for a tall man who entered the circle on foot. He too had on a mask that was framed by a mop of long curly hair. He wore nondescript black clothes that could have come from any era. On his hip was a jet-black sword. He kept one gloved hand above its grip, like a tense gunfighter ready to draw. He strode forward purposefully, but with caution, as if he didn't know what to expect from me. When he got within five feet, he stopped and stood with his feet planted wide. He stared at me for a good long while, appraising me. We must have stood that way, silently, for a full minute.

I couldn't take it anymore.

"I don't know about you," I said, "but this is the wildest dream I've ever had."

The guy didn't react. None of them did.

"Okay," I said. "I know this can't be real so I'll just ride this out until I shake off the effects of the drug."

Again, no response. The guy broke eye contact and looked around, as if taking in the wonder of Grand Central Terminal like a first-time tourist. I looked around too. As odd as it was to be there, I noticed something that made it even stranger.

"This is what Grand Central looked like thirty years ago," I said. "I guess it's official. This is all coming out of my head."

The guy in black focused on me again and finally spoke. "Where is this place?"

I laughed. I actually laughed.

"You're asking *me*?"

"This is your vision," he said calmly. He didn't think it was as funny as I did.

"Sorry," I said, chuckling. "If you want explanations, you've got the wrong girl. And besides, hallucinations aren't allowed to ask questions. This is *my* nightmare."

"It is no nightmare," the guy said, deadly serious. "You have arrived in the Black." He pulled his black sword from its scabbard and added, "And you have come through the Rift."

He held up his sword and started walking toward me, like he was going to attack.

I threw up my hands and backed off.

"Whoa, whoa, I don't know about any rift."

The guy took one more step and stiffened. He stopped and slowly lowered his sword.

"Your hands!" he declared with a gasp.

I was standing with my hands out in front of me. In my right hand was the golden orb from the catacomb.

I finally saw signs of life from the circle of clown riders. There were whispers and gasps but nothing I could understand. Seeing the golden orb had definitely gotten a rise out of them. The big guy raised his hand quickly and they fell silent.

"The marks on your hands," the guy said. "How did you get them?"

I looked at my hands to see the reddish brown stains that had come from the golden ball that shattered in the tomb.

I held out the second golden ball. "From one of these."

I tossed it into the air and caught it casually. It was a simple move, like tossing a tennis ball, but from the way everyone responded you'd think I was handling anthrax. There were frightened shouts and gasps as several made a move forward as if trying to catch the ball before I dropped it.

Whatever this little ball was, it gave me power over these people.

"I won't drop it," I said innocently. "I've got enough stains on my hands."

There were more stunned whispers.

"A crucible was broken?" the guy asked, his voice cracking with tension. "That is what caused the stain?"

"Yeah. There were six of them. For all I know they all broke when the earthquake hit."

The group erupted, screaming in protest. Whatever the golden balls were, they meant a lot to this bunch.

"Look," I said. "I'm going to leave now. Don't try to stop me or I'll break this thing."

"You cannot!" the big guy bellowed, but it was more like a plea than an order.

"Want to bet?" I shot back.

The guy reached up and took off his mask. I was surprised to see that he was a handsome olive-skinned man. Seeing a normal face beneath the clown mask was almost as disturbing as anything else I'd seen. It made the situation seem less like a nightmare, which wasn't comforting. A hallucinogenic nightmare made sense. The idea that this could actually be real, didn't.

"Where did you find it?" he asked calmly, as if speaking to a crazy person.

I wasn't sure what the smart answer was so I told the truth. "In an underground tomb. In Greece."

"Why were you there?" he asked.

"My friend discovered a myth about the tomb and we wanted to see if it was real. Simple as that."

"Do you know who lies in the tomb?" he asked.

I felt like I was being interrogated by a detective who already had all the answers but was testing to see how much I knew.

"An ancient general named Damon," I answered.

I sensed the people around me shift uncomfortably.

I continued, "He was supposedly a sadistic killer from the time of Alexander." I held up the golden orb and said, "These things were meant to keep him in that tomb, from coming back to life, but that can't be true."

"Why is that?" the dark man asked.

"Because there wasn't a body in the tomb. There was—"

"A weapon," the guy said, before I could finish.

"Yes," I said. "A black battle-ax. You already know this, don't you?"

"I should," the man replied. "I sealed the weapon there myself."

I tried to process what he had just said but there was nothing logical or understandable that I could grab on to.

"This must be a horrible dream," I finally whispered.

"This is no dream," he said. "Whether by accident or design, you broke the first crucible that sealed the Rift."

"Rift? What rift? You mean that hole under the sarcophagus? The earthquake uncovered it."

"The disruption of the seals uncovered it," the guy spat at me, angrily. "The blood on your hands is proof of that. The blood of Alexander."

I looked at the brown stains that covered the backs of both of my hands.

"Blood of Alexander?" I repeated, numb. "*The* Alexander? This is the blood of Alexander the Great?"

"Captured in six crucibles upon his death. They alone have sealed the Rift and kept the spirit of Damon at bay. Until now."

"But . . . Damon wasn't in the tomb. There was only the battle-ax."

"The very weapon Damon used to create the Rift. We have guarded it for centuries for fear that this moment might come."

I staggered backward as if his words were physically pummeling me.

"What moment?" I mumbled. "What happened?"

"You have uncovered the Rift," he said. "And with the destruction of a crucible you have loosened our grip on Damon. He will return now. There is no doubt of that. And he will do everything in his power to control the Rift."

"Tell me what the Rift is," I begged.

"It is a portal that Damon will try to use to travel back along the Morpheus Road."

"Morpheus Road?" I asked, delirious. "What is that?"

"The byway between life and death."

"Life and death," I repeated, numb. "I fell into the Rift. Does that mean—"

"You have left the Light and entered the Black. You may have taken an unnatural route, but the result is as you suspect."

"So I'm . . . dead?"

"You have moved into the next life, as we all have."

"Who are you people?" I demanded.

"I am Adeipho. In life I was an ally of Damon's. A friend. But we took different paths and now find ourselves here. We *all* find ourselves here. Our stories may be different but fate has brought us together for a common purpose. We protect the balance between life and death by guarding the Rift. And now that challenge has become even greater, thanks to you."

"But . . . I didn't intend to break anything. Or reveal any rift."

"But you have."

Adeipho lunged out and grabbed my hand, holding it up for me to see.

"You have been marked with the blood of Alexander and have brought a crucible into the Black. The course of your future has been set. When Damon comes to claim the Rift, and he will, you will be here with us to stop him.

"What? No! I'm not stopping anybody!"

"Then Damon of Epirus will be free once again in the Light and the blood you have on your hands will be but a drop compared to the destruction he will bring to the life you have left behind."

21

"I know that picture you took," I said. "Of the temple. It's hanging on Marsh's bedroom wall."

"That means my camera survived, even if I didn't," Ree said wistfully.

She told me her story as we walked through her vision of Grand Central, back to her private train. So much of what she said was incredible, but it answered a lot of questions.

"How did you end up in charge here?" I asked.

She held up her stained hand. "I've been marked. Or blessed. Or cursed. Depends on how you see it. Alexander's blood is sacred to these people so I guess you'd call me a living crucible."

"Yeah, if you were living," I corrected.

"Adeipho is their practical leader but they look to me for spiritual guidance. It's why the Rift is in my vision. And you know what? That's okay. After what happened it's the least I can do."

"So my best friend's mom is responsible for keeping a murderous spirit from ripping open a hole between the worlds of the living and the dead that would let him return to the Light and pick up where he left off centuries ago?"

"Uh, yes, that pretty much sums it up," she said.

"Oh. Just checking." I dropped down into one of the cushy chairs in the subway train and added, "I knew you weren't like the other moms, but geez, I didn't see this one coming."

"But the Rift was already open," she said. "I was just foolish enough to uncover it. I think it's what started the whole myth about the Oracle of the Dead. All those pilgrims who were tricked into thinking they were visiting their dead ancestors didn't realize there was an actual opening to the next life only a few hundred yards away."

"That Damon created," I said.

"Yes. With the poleax. The ancients believed that the essence of a victim's spirit remains with the weapon that took their life. Damon murdered thousands, so do the math. The last time he used it was to defend himself when his own people turned on him."

"Why did that happen?"

"Apparently Damon was a brilliant general but he was more about forming battle strategy than actually doing any fighting himself. He would direct his troops from some-where safe rather than lead them into battle, which is what Alexander and Adeipho did."

"So he was a coward?"

"Maybe, but a successful one. He had many victories, but never received the accolades that Alexander or Adeipho did because he never got blood on his own hands."

"Yeah, except when he was executing prisoners or eat-ing the hearts of generals. Did that really happen?"

Ree shrugged. "So they tell me."

"Man," was all I could say.

"Living in the shadows of Alexander and Adeipho made him resentful and angry. When Alexander died, he tried to take control of the entire army. It led to a showdown between those loyal to Damon and those who sided with Adeipho. In the course of the fight, Damon used the power of the poleax to create the Rift, sending many of Adeipho's men into the Black. But Adeipho had greater numbers and Damon's own men became victims and tumbled through the Rift as well. It finally came down to Damon and Adeipho. Damon was no match for him and Adeipho sent him through the Rift."

"So Adeipho was the last man standing?"

"Yes. He hid the Rift by building the catacombs and a tomb that supposedly held Damon's remains. But there were no remains. The tomb contained the poleax, along with the six crucibles with Alexander's blood."

"And the blood is what kept Damon away?" I asked.

"The ancients had beliefs and customs that we can't begin to understand."

"You get no argument from me. I totally buy it."

Ree said, "The last act of Adeipho's life was to move through the Rift himself."

"Seriously? He chased Damon into the grave?"

Ree nodded. "Adeipho is a noble soldier. He's been in the Black ever since, protecting the Rift, and the poleax, from Damon."

"So all those guys on bikes are Adeipho's original soldiers?"

"Not all. Many spirits have found their way here over the centuries. Some simply pass through, while others chose to stay and become Guardians."

"What's with the clown masks?" I asked.

"Anonymity. Many spirits stumble upon this vision accidently and are encouraged to move on. But not everyone is so innocent. Damon has sent scouts. The Guardians do not want to put their loved ones in danger, either in the Black or the Light, so we wear the masks. So far it hasn't been a problem because none of Damon's scouts have escaped."

"What happened to them?"

"You've seen what the black swords can do," she said soberly.

"They're spirit-killers," I said. "How is that possible?"

"They came through the Rift during the original battle. They are unnatural to the Black, which makes them dangerous. Damon's soldiers have several. As do Adeipho's men. Without them we would not be able to protect the Rift. The standoff has lasted for centuries and would have continued . . . if I hadn't broken that first crucible."

"But why was that such a big deal?" I asked.

"It empowered Damon and put him on the trail of the poleax. Until Ennis and I entered that tomb and broke the crucible, Damon had no idea where it was because the power of the crucibles shielded him from seeing it."

"He still doesn't know where it is," I said. "That's why he's haunting Marsh.

It was Ree's turn to sit down. "Tell me what's been happening," she said.

"Why can't you see for yourself?"

Her eyes began to well up. "I told you, we're in isolation here. My vision acts as a buffer between the Light and the rest of the Black."

"Because of the Rift?" I asked.

"Yes. The very existence of the Rift threatens the natural order of life and death. Imagine if spirits could travel freely between both worlds."

"But we can," I argued.

"Not as physical beings."

"Whoa, you mean if a spirit went through the Rift, they'd become physical beings again?"

"That's the theory. Nobody has tried. The Guardians have seen to that."

I was beginning to understand how Damon planned on getting his life back, and giving me mine.

Ree added, "Spirits can observe the Light and learn from their former lives, but they can't play a physical role."

"Tell that to Damon. He freakin' *killed* me and he's been tormenting Marsh. I don't understand why he thinks Marsh can help him find a weapon buried in Greece."

Ree held up her stained hand. "Because I have been marked and Marsh is my son. The bond between spirits in the Black and those still living is a strong one."

"I know. I've seen."

"Damon can't get to me so he's going after Marsh," she said.

"But that's just stupid!" I cried. "Marsh isn't going to get on a plane and go digging around Greece!"

Ree thought and then said, "From what you tell me, it might not even be in that tomb anymore. If the crucibles were moved, the poleax may have been as well."

"And you can't see into the Light so you wouldn't know."

"Nor would Damon. The remaining crucibles must still be with the poleax, or else Damon would know where it is."

"So that's why he needs Marsh," I said, putting the pieces together in my head.

Ree said, "If Marsh had a crucible, and broke it, that put him square into Damon's sights."

"What about the other guy? What's his name? Ennis?"

Ree shook her head in frustration. "I don't know. Ennis knew about the myth. If he survived the earthquake, he might have been the one who took the crucibles and gave one to Marsh for protection, and kept one for himself."

"And moved the poleax," I added.

"And if he has a crucible, then Damon can't touch him," she said. "But Marsh broke his."

I stood up and paced in the long train car. The whole picture was becoming clear. Damon called Marsh the source. If Marsh had a crucible, it linked him to Ree, and the poleax. Marsh could be Damon's eyes in the Light.

Ree said, "I not only have to protect the Rift, but the crucible I brought with me. Two have already been broken, and from what you've told me, it has given Damon dangerous power in the Light. I can't allow a third to be broken."

"Damon wants me to destroy your crucible," I finally admitted. "That's why I'm here. He said if I didn't, he'd kill Marsh."

She shot me a cold look. I wasn't sure if it was out of fear for her son, or she was calculating whether or not I would actually try to break the crucible. I didn't tell her that Damon had also promised to give me back my life. That would only complicate things.

"And?" she asked suspiciously.

"Do you think I'd break it after all you told me?"

Ree relaxed. "No, of course not. I'm sorry, Coop. But you see what's at stake."

She had accepted my answer, though it wasn't really an answer because I didn't know what I was going to do.

I didn't doubt anything that Ree had told me. It all fit. But it was looking like Damon had changed tactics and Ree's Guardians were the last to know.

"I don't think it's just about guarding the Rift anymore," I announced.

"What do you mean?"

"You haven't seen what's going on in the Light. Damon's gone on the offense. I'm living proof of that. No, I'm *dead* proof of that. He doesn't need the Rift. If he gets the poleax, he can just create another one."

"But even if he finds it, he can't get his hands on it physically," Ree countered. "Not unless he goes through the Rift, and we'll never let that happen."

"What if he gets somebody in the Light to bring it through the Rift for him? Like Marsh? Or that guy Ennis. He could be using Marsh to get to Ennis."

She didn't have a comeback for that.

"The guy's a bully," I said. "I know bullies. The only way to stop one is to out-bully them."

"And how do you suggest we do that?"

"I don't know. Maybe we could go through the Rift and get the poleax ourselves and use it against him!"

"No!" she shouted. "It's wrong and it's a sure sentence to the Blood."

"I thought the Watchers weren't working this neighborhood."

"There are limits."

"Okay. Then, maybe I can get Marsh to find it. I've been in contact with him. If he found it, we could——"

Ree jumped to her feet. "You what?"

Oops.

"It was no big deal," I said, backpedaling. "I just wanted him to know that I was looking out for him."

"But you can't look out for him!" Ree shouted.

"How can you say that? He's your son!"

"Cooper, interfering with the living is exactly what we're trying to prevent Damon from doing."

"But he's causing trouble. We're the good guys!"

"Cooper, imagine if every spirit in the Black started influencing events in the Light. No matter how noble their intentions were, they'd be changing the course of lives. Of mankind. It would lead to chaos."

"Or prevent chaos, and protect some people we care about."

Ree's eyes blazed. "I would do anything to protect Marshall. But the consequences of interfering would be far worse than anything Damon could do to him."

"Even if he kills Marsh?"

Ree hesitated. It was a tough question. When she answered, her voice cracked. "I told you, there are worse things than death."

"I'm sorry, I don't see that," I said. "This guy is trying to cause absolute calamity. Seems to me that anything we did to stop him would be justified."

"We *will* stop him," Ree countered. "But here in the Black."

"Really?" I said. "There were six crucibles, right? Two are gone. One you've got here. That leaves three more in the Light. What happens if they're smashed? Damon's already got some serious abilities. It scares me to think what he'll be able to do if a couple more of those things are broken. How are you going to prevent that?"

Ree didn't have an answer.

"I think there's only one way to stop Damon," I added. "You guys have to go after him."

Ree's eyes lit up. "You're talking about battling evil with evil."

"I don't think it's evil to protect yourself . . . and those you care about."

"And what if we lose the battle?"

"Then, at least you tried. Right now Damon's calling the shots, and I hate to say this but, he's winning."

Ree stepped away from me and went to the door of the subway car. "I trust Adeipho's instincts," she said. "Our mission is to protect the Rift."

"Then, you're fighting the wrong fight."

Ree looked me square in the eye. For a second I thought she might agree with me. Instead, she stepped back from the doorway.

"Leave this vision, Coop," she commanded. "Do not go back to the Light. I know it's tempting, but you'll only make things worse."

"So you're not going to do anything?" I asked.

"We're going to protect the Rift, as always. I know you mean well, Cooper. But stay out of this."

"What if I don't?"

Ree gave me a steely look and offered a simple but straight warning. "You don't want the Guardians as enemies."

Threat received. I walked to the door and stopped in front of her. I didn't want it to end like that. In spite of all that was happening, she was still Marsh's mom.

"Marsh had a rough time after you died," I said. "He really misses you."

Tears came to her eyes again. I didn't mean to make her feel bad, I just wanted her to know how much she was loved.

"He's a good guy," I added.

Ree nodded in thanks. I think if she tried to speak, she would have lost it.

I stepped out of the subway car to find two of Adeipho's soldiers waiting for me. One wore the uniform of a Union soldier from the U.S. Civil War. The other was a woman in green hospital scrubs. Neither had on masks.

"They'll take you to the edge of the vision," Ree said. "From there you can return to your own."

"Will I see you again?" I asked.

Ree smiled. She looked like the Mrs. Seaver I knew. Before.

"I hope so," she said sincerely.

We walked silently up and out of the subway station to

a deserted New York City. The lady in scrubs gestured for me to walk along a cross street. I expected the two of them to wait at the subway entrance, but instead they followed me down the street. I guess they wanted to make sure that I got out of there.

I truly believed what I said to Ree. Damon had to be stopped and that wouldn't happen by sitting back and reacting to whatever nastiness he chose to get up to. He was too smart. He didn't play by the rules, so why should the Guardians?

Why should I?

As I walked through Ree's vision, I wondered what would happen if I actually got my life back. Could I then find the poleax myself? It sounded as though that weapon was like the black swords on steroids. I would have liked the chance to try it out on Damon.

I wasn't a stranger to Trouble Town. I knew that taking the easy way out usually meant you didn't *get* out. It was all coming down to how badly I wanted to protect Marsh. And stop Damon. And being totally honest, how badly I wanted my life back. The real question I had to ask myself was this: Would a full lifetime in the Light be worth risking my eternal soul for?

Thinking of all the possibilities made my head hurt. I crossed a wide avenue and saw two Watchers standing on the far corner, directly in front of the wall of swirling color that represented the far boundary of Ree's vision. I glanced back to see that my two escorts had stopped. I gave them a quick wave. They didn't return it.

"Hey!" I shouted to the Watchers. "Are you going to cut these people some slack or what?"

Their answer was to disappear and go wherever Watchers went when they were confronted by a spirit who challenged them.

I had to leave, but wasn't sure where to go. Should I return to my own vision? What would I do there? Twiddle my thumbs and wait for Marsh to die and show up? I wasn't about to sit back and trust anybody else to make the right choices. I had to do whatever it took to get out of Trouble Town. I wasn't exactly sure how to do that, but I knew a good place to start.

I closed my eyes and stepped through the edge of Ree's vision . . .

. . . to arrive in ancient Greece.

22

I stepped into Damon's vision of the ancient, dusty square.

I looked right to see the warrior statue in the fountain. I looked left . . . and saw a gloved fist headed toward my face.

A second later I was on my back, staring up at Damon and the soldier who had clocked me.

"You are disappointing me," Damon said with disdain. I felt the spray of his saliva hitting my face again, but I was too dazed to do anything about it.

"That was a total sucker punch," I mumbled. "No wonder nobody thinks you were much of a soldier."

Insulting the guy wasn't the brightest thing to do. He nodded to his goon, who reared back and kicked me square in the ribs, knocking the wind out of me. I rolled over, gasping, sucking dirt into my mouth.

Damon chuckled. The guy enjoyed inflicting pain.

"Your arrogance will be your undoing," he said reproachfully, as if to a naughty child. "I would think nothing of ending your existence right here and now."

I turned my head to look up at him and make eye contact. "But you won't," I said defiantly. "You need me."

His eyes flared. He didn't like being outmaneuvered.

"Why didn't you destroy the crucible?" he snarled.

"Maybe I did."

He made a gesture and his thug picked me up by the neck and dragged me toward the fountain. He was too big and I was still too loopy to fight. Before I realized what was happening he forced my head under the water. I knew I couldn't drown, but the idea of gulping in water, even if it was an illusion, was terrifying. I probably could have breathed in, drowned, and then stood up as if nothing had happened, but I couldn't be sure so I held my breath until my lungs felt like they would explode. That's when he pulled my head out.

Damon leaned down and said, "Do not believe for a moment that you are smarter than I am."

"Maybe I should come back later when you're in a better mood," I sputtered.

He nodded and the soldiers dunked me again. I imagined my own vision and tried to go there, but nothing happened. It seemed as though to travel between visions you had to make an actual, physical move and since I was being held in place, I was stuck. All I could do was hold my breath and hope that I wouldn't have to learn that spirits could drown.

I was violently yanked by my hair from under the water until I was once again nose to nose with Damon.

"Will it end here?" he asked, eerily calm.

That was an easy one. I shook my head. The soldier gave me a shove and I landed next to the fountain.

"Now, my friend," Damon said, almost jovially, "let us

reassess." He stood over me with his arms folded and a big smile on his face.

"I didn't have to come here," I said. "I could have gone to my own vision and blocked you."

"But you did not," he said smugly. "Which means you need me as well. We fully understand each other so please, forgo the tiresome games. Did you locate the crucible?"

I nodded.

"Wonderful! Then, why did you not accomplish your task?"

"It was being guarded," I said.

"But you had my sword," he declared. "And now you do not. Did you lose it in battle?"

"Yeah, something like that."

"Did you encounter Adeipho?"

"That's who took the sword."

I sensed him cringe, ever so slightly. "And yet you escaped. I do not understand that. Adeipho is unforgiving."

I didn't know how much Damon knew about Ree and my connection with her so I had to be careful.

"He didn't want to let me go. It was Ree's choice."

"Ah, yes. Marshall's mother. The Guardian of the Rift."

So much for being careful. He knew all the players.

"What do you need me for anyway?" I asked. "You've got more of those spirit-killing swords. Why don't you just fight for the Rift yourself?"

"Nothing would please me more, but the crucible is preventing me from entering that vision. That is why I need it destroyed. Will you make another attempt?"

I didn't answer right away because I didn't know what I wanted to do.

"You have doubts," he said knowingly. "I am not surprised. I can only imagine what Adeipho told you about me."

"Not a lot of good things," I admitted.

"Adeipho is a weak pawn. The true power was held by

Alexander. But he died before he could ensure I would take my rightful place and command his army."

He said this as he looked up at the statue of the warrior in the fountain.

"That's him?" I said. "Alexander the Great?"

Damon snickered. "A title that was bestowed long after his death."

"And you think you were going to take his place?"

"I would have!" Damon snapped. "If not for Adeipho's treachery! What did they tell you? That I was dangerous? That they feared what I would do once I commanded Alexander's army?"

"Pretty much," I said.

"Cowards! I followed Alexander's every campaign, destroying the remains of the opposition, ensuring that his victories were complete."

"Killing prisoners," I said.

"Enemies!" he shot back. "The history of Alexander speaks only of his glorious victories. The triumphant marches. The expansion of an empire. There is no mention of those who destroyed any possibility of counterattack or reprisal."

"So you think by killing unarmed prisoners you were responsible for Alexander's success?"

"My army also fought many a battle," he said defensively.

"Yeah, I heard you were pretty smart about tactics and all."

Damon smiled. He liked that.

I added, "But you never actually led your men into battle yourself. Why was that?"

His smile fell fast. I'd hit a sore spot. He dropped to a knee in front of me and pointed to his face.

"Where do you believe these scars came from? Executing innocent prisoners? I fought valiantly in Alexander's name."

"You said Adeipho's men did that."

That threw Damon. It was like I had caught him in a lie.

"There were many battles," he said, recovering quickly. "This is what my loyalty to Alexander brought me and yet I have been cast as a coward."

"So what? It's done. Nobody cares about what happened two thousand years ago."

"Two thousand years or two minutes," Damon exclaimed. "The spirits of the past still exist. My enemies still exist. I can still take what was rightfully mine."

"What does that mean? You want to get back to the Light so you can keep on killing? Why? To prove you weren't a coward? Maybe you want to eat a couple more hearts while you're at it? You're just . . . sick."

Damon stiffened and stood up.

"And who are you?" he said, sounding all superior. "A privileged boy. A petty thief. You have no right to judge me."

"Absolutely. I'm nobody. But at least I know right from wrong."

"And where did you come by that wisdom? From your difficult life? From the struggle to survive? From the fear of being slaughtered by invading armies?" Damon spat on the ground in disgust. "You are a naive, pampered child."

"I lived in a different time."

"And who taught you the righteous path? Right from wrong? Good from evil? Perhaps your elders? Those you respect?"

"That's pretty much how it works."

Damon smiled. It made the hair stand up on my neck. I never knew where this guy was coming from. One minute he was angry, the next he was giddy, then a second later he was in total control as if he held all the cards.

"Every story has two sides," he said. "Do not make judgments until you learn them both."

"I think I know all I need to know about you," I shot back.

"You see the world as a place ruled by noble goals and high standards. Well, let me educate you. The world is not as noble a place as you believe it to be."

"What's that supposed to mean?" I asked.

Damon leaned down, grabbed my arm, and pulled me to my feet.

He said, "Forgive me for destroying your naive illusions."

I saw the swirling colored lights appear over his shoulder as he yanked me forward, stepped out of the way, and flung me into the fog. I stumbled, tripped, and landed on my knees in another vision. Looking up, I saw the mailbox with the word "Brady" painted on the side. It took me a second to realize that Damon had flung me into Maggie's vision.

I was sitting in front of the house next door to hers. The house that would one day become Gramps's home. There was no mistake that it was her vision and not my grandfather's. The gray sky and barren trees were a dead giveaway.

Why had Damon sent me there? What was he trying to show me?

I stood up, brushed myself off, and was about to look for Maggie when I caught sight of somebody running around the side of her barn. I only caught a quick glimpse but I knew it was the same little girl that had been dodging around the barn when I'd visited there before.

Was this what Damon wanted me to see? I decided it was time for me to find out who this kid was so I took off sprinting for the barn, trying not to make any noise for fear it would warn the kid that I was after her. I circled the barn from the opposite side, thinking I would head her off. When

I reached the back side, I stopped and cautiously peered around the corner to see . . . the kid wasn't there. She'd disappeared again. I noticed a small, ramshackle toolshed that was built right up against the barn. Either the girl had magically disappeared or she was inside that shed. I ran to the structure, grabbed the door handle, and yanked it open.

"Ah!" the girl screamed, and cowered into a corner of the hut.

The girl looked to be around eight years old, so I was twice her size. She wore a short cloth coat over a long white nightgown that was covered with black streaks as if she had been doing some dirty work.

"Come on out," I ordered.

The kid kept her eyes on the ground and shuffled to the door so I backed off to let her out. As soon as she stepped out of the hut, she tried to take off running but didn't get more than half a step before I grabbed her jacket.

"Whoa, I don't think so," I warned.

The girl whipped around and I saw the fear in her eyes.

"Leave me alone!" she yelled. When she focused on me, her fear turned to a look of surprise, as if I wasn't at all what she expected. "You aren't the sheriff."

"I didn't say I was. Who are you?"

"I live next door," she answered defiantly.

I didn't intimidate her, which made me wonder why she was so scared in the first place.

"Well, I'm a friend of Maggie's. Why are you sneaking around her barn?"

She shrugged. Whatever she was up to, she didn't want to fess up.

"Do you know what happened to her parents?" I asked.

"Course I do," she said, keeping her eyes on the ground. "It was just last night."

That threw me, but it made sense. Maggie's vision was

fixed on the day after her father and mother were killed in the fire. Question was, why was this little girl hanging out in Maggie's vision?

"So why are you sneaking around here?" I asked.

There was definitely something on her mind that she didn't want to share.

"Just tell me the truth," I said. "It's okay."

"I'm looking for another way out of the barn," she finally said. "There can't be just one door."

"Why not? It's a barn."

"But there has to be another way out," she insisted. "I just haven't found it. They could have gotten out. They didn't have to die."

"Maybe. But what good would it do to find it now?"

The girl bit her lip and shrugged. I thought we were done, but then she plopped down on the grass and wept as if it were her own parents that had died in the barn. I figured the poor girl was traumatized by what had happened. Having your neighbors killed in a fire was pretty horrible so I sat down next to her to offer whatever help I could.

"It was an accident," I said. "Maggie went back to unlock the lock. She didn't mean to trap her father inside."

The girl's cry turned to a sob as she whispered, "I know . . . but Brady did."

I wasn't sure if I'd heard her right. "What did you say?" I asked.

"But he didn't want them to die. It was an accident."

Blood rushed to my head. It took every bit of willpower I had to stop myself from grabbing the girl and shaking her until she told me what she knew. I forced myself to speak calmly as if what she was saying was no big deal.

"Who's Brady?"

"My brother."

"Isn't Brady your last name?"

"Yeah, but that's what everybody called him."

"Tell me what happened. Exactly."

The girl thought for a second, then started talking. Once she got going, she didn't stop. It was like the story had been bottled up for a very long time and it finally exploded out of her.

"Maggie's father was always yelling at her," she began. "Brady hated it. He was sweet on Maggie, though he never admitted it. Maggie was real nice to him. To both of us. She made us cookies every Friday. Has she made you cookies?"

"No. What happened that night?" I asked, trying to keep her focused.

"Whenever old man Salinger started hollering on Maggie, Brady got upset. That night was the worst. We heard it from all the way back to our house. Brady couldn't stand it. He took off and I knew exactly where he was going."

"Where?"

She pointed to the shed she'd been hiding in. "There's a couple of loose boards in there. Nobody knew about it. We could spy inside the barn and no one was the wiser. I followed Brady and found him inside watching the two of them going at it. Maggie was just as angry as her father and she was giving it back to him real good . . . until he hit her. I never saw anything like that. It was horrible. Maggie ran out and slammed the door in his face."

"And put the lock on," I said.

She nodded and continued, "Brady was fit to be tied. He ran out of the shed and I went with him. If old man Salinger had come out after Maggie, Brady would have jumped him for sure. But the old man stayed inside. The two of us saw Maggie put the lock on the door and go back to her house. But then . . ."

The girl sobbed as if the memory pained her.

"What happened?" I coaxed.

"She changed her mind. She got halfway to her house, then came back and unlocked it."

"So Maggie *did* unlock it?"

The girl nodded. "I guess she didn't want to make him any angrier than he already was. But that didn't stop Brady."

I sat bolt upright. "Wait . . . what? What did he do?"

"As soon as Maggie went inside the house, Brady snuck to the door and locked it himself. I told him not to but he said he didn't want Salinger to bother her anymore."

"So your brother locked the lock? Not Maggie?" I said, trying to hold back my excitement.

"But it wasn't his fault they died!" she exclaimed.

"Of course not. There was no way he could have known there was going to be a fire."

The girl sobbed even harder.

"It's okay," I said feebly. "It wasn't his fault."

"I know!" she cried. "It was mine!"

I sat there with my mouth hanging open.

She went on, "It was me who brought the lantern down to the shed, and left it there when we ran out. After Brady locked the door, I got scared and ran back to the house. I forgot all about the lantern . . . until the fire. I didn't mean for them to die. It was a stupid mistake. I never told nobody. My whole life. I was too scared. Now I'm stuck here in the Black, a little girl again, still not able to make up for what I did."

I was in shock, but managed to say, "Or maybe you just did."

I got up and started for Maggie's house.

"Cooper?" the girl called.

I stopped and turned back to her.

"Try to understand," she said, then got up and ran toward her own house.

What was it she wanted me to understand? That it was hard to admit the truth? I guess that was obvious or she would have done it a long time before. But I wondered why, after all that time, she decided to confess to me.

I turned toward Maggie's house, then stopped short. It had taken a few seconds for her last words to sink in.

"Hey!" I called to the fleeing girl. "How did you know my name?"

Her answer was to run up onto her porch and disappear inside the house. I thought of going after her, but her knowing my name wasn't anywhere near as important as everything else she had told me. Maggie had to know so I ran straight for her house. In seconds I bounded up the porch stairs two at a time and hammered on the screen door.

"Maggie!" I called. "It's me!"

I couldn't wait to tell her the news. She had lived for so long with the crushing guilt of thinking she had killed her parents, but that was about to end. I couldn't help but think the truth would allow her to finally move on from the Black to her next life. I was so thrilled, it was like it was happening to me.

"Maggie!" I called out again.

As I stood there waiting for her, I was hit with another thought: Why had Damon sent me there? Was it to learn the truth about Maggie? Why would he care? He called me naive for believing the world was controlled by those with noble goals and high standards. It sounded like he wanted to reveal some dark truth that would shatter my illusions, but all I found was something that could set a soul free, the soul of somebody I cared about. Why would that matter to Damon?

When Maggie appeared at the door, I forgot all about him.

"Hi, Coop!" she said brightly.

I pulled her out onto the porch.

"You aren't going to believe this," I said excitedly. "I don't know why we got thrown together, Maggie, but it's a good thing we did because I just found out something that's going to change your life. Or your afterlife. Whatever. You know what I mean."

"Uh, no, I don't," she said, totally confused.

"You know the little kids who lived next door? A girl and a boy?"

"Yeah?" she said with a laugh, but I didn't see why it was funny.

"The boy's got a crush on you."

She chuckled. "I know, Coop. I'm surprised he told you, though."

"He didn't. His sister did. She's a spirit in your vision."

Maggie glanced to the house next door and said, "Oh. Right. I don't know if she's in my vision or I'm in hers. I don't see her that often and we never talk."

"Well, you should have. I don't know how to say this so I'll just say it. Those kids used to hear your father yelling at you."

Maggie's expression turned dark but I kept going.

"That night, the night of the fire, they saw you leave the barn and lock the door."

"I don't want to talk about it," she said, and made a move to go back inside but I stopped her.

"Listen. They also saw you go back and unlock it."

"So what? It doesn't matter what they think they saw. I didn't unlock it."

"But you did!" I shouted. "Brady wanted to keep your father away from you so after you left, he relocked it himself. It wasn't you, Maggie. It was Brady. And the lantern that started the fire? His sister brought it into the shed out back and forgot about it. Your parents' death had absolutely nothing to do with you!"

Maggie's eyes went wide and she started breathing faster. I didn't think she knew whether to smile, or cry, or laugh or scream.

"She told you that?" Maggie asked, her excitement growing.

"Yes! Just now. I don't know how long she lived, but

she's here in the Black as a little girl. I think she's here to let the truth be known, and she finally did it."

Maggie started crying. It was like the news was too much for her to accept.

"It really wasn't my fault," she said, as if trying to believe it herself.

"No, it wasn't," I said, and hugged her. "Sometimes things just happen that we can't control."

I suddenly felt Maggie stiffen. Something was wrong. I pulled away and held her at arm's length. Her look had quickly gone from one of disbelief and joy to concern.

"What?" I asked.

"It took your being here to get her to admit the truth," she said thoughtfully.

"Yeah. That's good. Right?"

Maggie looked into my eyes as if searching for something. "My god, you don't know."

"Don't know what?"

Maggie pulled away from me. She went to the rail of the porch and looked to Brady's house.

"Nothing," she said, dismissing it. "Thank you, Cooper. I can't tell you how grateful I am."

I joined her at the porch rail, where she stood staring at the house next door.

"You're supposed to be a lot happier about this," I said.

A tear rolled down her cheek and this time she wasn't crying with joy.

"I *am* happy," she said. "This is great. Thank you, Cooper. Go home, okay? I want to have some time to think about what this means."

She made a move to go back inside but I stopped her.

"Whoa, you are the worst liar. Something's wrong."

"No, it isn't. Things couldn't be better. Let's talk about this more later, okay?"

"No. Tell me what's going on."

She didn't want to answer but I wasn't going anywhere until she did.

Finally she sighed and said, "I'm so sorry, Cooper. I thought you knew."

"Knew what?"

Maggie turned to look next door again, like she was having trouble making eye contact with me.

"All this time," she said, more to herself than to me, "I thought he treated me so badly because of what I'd done."

"What are you talking about?" I asked.

"That family," she began. "The Bradys. They had their own share of tragedy. Their father died in a farm accident when they were babies."

"Wow. I'm sorry to hear that but—"

"Mrs. Brady remarried years later. Just after the fire. He seemed like a nice man, though I never got to know him. They kept their distance. After all, I was a parent-killer."

"So, what's the problem?"

Maggie turned to me and took my hands.

"You are a good person, Cooper," she said. "This doesn't change things. What you said before is true. Sometimes things happen that we can't control. That doesn't make us bad."

"What the hell are you talking about?"

"Coop, we called the kid next door Brady but that was his last name."

"Right. It's on the mailbox. So, what's his first name?"

Maggie took a quavering breath and said, "His real name was Eugene. His sister's name was Collette. The man their mom married was named Foley. Coop, the little boy who lived next door was Eugene Foley. He grew up to become your grandfather."

23

Gramps was alone in his garden, on his knees, weeding around his tomato plants. It was the same place I saw him the last time I visited his vision. Gramps was proud of that garden. He had a green thumb. It was one of the things I loved about him. There wasn't much I *didn't* love about my gramps.

Until then.

I stood on the end of a long row of lush plants hanging with the weight of brilliant red tomatoes. It was like staring at a stranger. I'm not naive enough to think that just because you're an adult you can do no wrong. The older you get the more you realize that the people you idolized as a kid are as human as everybody else. But finding out that the wonderful wizard with all the answers is nothing more than a befuddled man hiding behind a curtain isn't easy to accept. And when that man turns out to be hiding dark, hurtful secrets, it makes you question everything you've always thought to be true.

I watched him for a while, trying to find the right words. I came close to leaving without saying anything, but then I would be almost as guilty as him. Almost.

"You were right," I called out.

Gramps looked up from his work and smiled.

"Coop! Where've you been, kid?"

"I was busy not listening to you. That was a mistake."

Gramps struggled to his feet, wiping his forehead with a grimy bandana as he walked toward me. "That so? What was I right about?"

"You told me that everybody here takes care of themselves. That's the whole point of the Black. You gotta take care of number one. Right?"

Gramps frowned. "What happened, Coop? You haven't been fiddling around in the Light again, have you?"

"Yeah I have . . . Brady."

He didn't react. I think he was trying to figure out how much I actually knew.

"Nobody's called me that for a good long time," he finally said, cautiously. "Guess you've been hanging around with the Salinger girl after all."

"I thought you wanted me to stay away from her for my sake," I said. "Turns out it was really about you."

"I—I don't understand," Gramps said, stuttering, holding out hope that the conversation wasn't going where he feared it might.

"I saw Aunt Collette's vision, Gramps. It's the same as Maggie's . . . the day after the fire. She's a little girl here in the Black."

Gramps deflated. He took a step back and for a second I thought he might pass out. He staggered a few steps until he reached a stone bench that stood on the edge of his garden.

The same stone bench the two of us used to sit on for hours, shucking corn, back when I thought he was the greatest guy in the world.

"So you know," he said flatly.

"Yeah. What I don't know is why you never told the truth—to anybody."

Gramps took off his glasses and wiped his eyes. "I didn't mean to hurt that girl. I cared about her. Did you know she made us cookies every Friday?"

"And you ruined her life. You wonder why you've been stuck here so long? Who are you kidding?"

"I couldn't tell the truth," he said, his voice barely above a whisper. "I was afraid."

"But it was an accident!"

"I was a kid, Cooper! Kids don't think. Our father was killed. Did you know that? I was the man of the family. I had to protect my sister. And my mother. Your great-grandmother."

"So you let an innocent girl take the blame for something you two were responsible for?"

"I wanted to tell. I did. But the longer I stayed quiet, the tougher it got. Collette didn't tell. She was afraid they'd lock us up. Then my mother started seeing Pop Foley. I liked him. We had the chance to have a father again. If I'd told the truth, he'd have left and never looked back."

"So again, you did it for you," I said.

"For my family!" he cried.

"Even if that were true, even if it was right, how do you justify not telling anyone the truth here in the Black?"

Gramps hung his head.

"Why?" I repeated, nearly shouting.

"I was afraid it would land me in the Blood."

It tore my heart out to see my grandfather acting like such a coward. This wasn't the guy I knew. Or maybe it was and I just hadn't realized it.

"At least Aunt Collette finally told the truth," I said.

He shook his head. "I never saw her in the Black. She must have blocked me from her vision."

"This is why you didn't want me to be Maggie's friend," I said, my anger rising. "And this whole time she thought you were giving her a hard time because you thought she'd killed her parents."

He kept his eyes on the ground and said, "I've wanted to tell her. I swear. It's why I didn't block her from my vision. I always thought that one day I'd get up the nerve."

"At least you weren't lying about one thing," I said. "Everybody here is out for themselves. Maybe that's why there are so many people in the Black. They can't see themselves for who they really are."

"It's not that easy, Cooper," he said. "Maybe you're too young to understand."

"Understand what? That it's okay to let somebody take the blame for something you've done? That you can justify ruining somebody's life so long as you come out on top? Is that what I don't get?"

"Things happen," he said, growing more emotional. "And they aren't always good. All you can do is the best you can, and sometimes that's not the most noble way to go. I feel bad for that girl, I really do, but I believe I did the right thing back then for me and for my family. For *your* family. I can't change history, Coop, and even if I could, I'm not so sure I would. I'm sorry if you think less of me for that."

I backed away and said, "I figured there were two ways you could have reacted. Either you'd admit the mistake and want to make things right, or you'd try to justify yourself. Now I know."

"I'm sorry, Coop. Life doesn't always go the way you think it should."

"And that's exactly what Damon wanted me to learn," I said.

"Damon? Is that old spirit still bothering you?"

"He said I was naive. Looks like he was right."

"So, what does that mean?" Gramps asked.

"It means I'm going to take care of number one, just like my gramps taught me."

I turned and walked away. Gramps stood and followed.

"Cooper! What are you going to do?"

"What I think is right, and the hell with everybody else!"

"Coop!" he shouted. "Don't leave. Let's talk and—"

I didn't hear the end of his sentence. I had already left his vision and arrived in the Light. I wanted to see if Marsh was okay. I hoped to find him sleeping at the lake house, safe and sound.

He wasn't.

I found myself in the backseat of a sheriff's cruiser, flying along a dark country road. It was night. We were moving fast. Behind the wheel was a guy I recognized. Sheriff Vrtiak. Sitting next to me in the backseat was Marsh. Separating the front seat from the back was a cage.

Got it. Sort of. What the hell was going on? Was Marsh under arrest?

"Ralph, can you hear me?" I asked.

Marsh didn't react. At least he didn't react to me. He was reacting plenty to the situation. He looked scared.

Sheriff Vrtiak spun the wheel hard and made a fishtailing turn off the road onto another. He gunned the engine and charged into the night.

"Where are you going?" Marsh asked Vrtiak nervously.

"He warned you, didn't he?" the sheriff said. "But you just kept looking. Kept poking around."

This wasn't right. The guy in front looked like Vrtiak but sure didn't sound like him.

"Sheriff, stop the car," Marsh said.

Vrtiak yanked off his sunglasses and threw them onto the seat. The guy was crying, and I soon found out why. Appearing in the passenger seat next to him was a spectral hound. It was huge, with its head nearly touching the ceiling. Rotted fur and flesh hung from a skeletal head. Its tongue hung from its mouth covered with spots of putrid flesh. Dark juices dripped from the blackened tongue as it leaned toward Vrtiak . . . and spoke.

"Faster," it growled.

"I don't want to do this," Vrtiak whimpered as he cowered from the horror.

"Do what?" Marsh screamed. "Sheriff, slow down!"

Marsh couldn't see the dog. He had no idea that Vrtiak was being haunted and manipulated.

The sheriff sped up and took a curve way too fast. The car skidded and nearly flew off the road. But Vrtiak somehow kept control and got back onto the pavement.

There could be only one explanation.

"Damon!" I shouted. "Stop the car!"

The grotesque hound whipped a look at me, stared me down with hollow eyes . . . and smiled.

"Do what he says, all right?" the sheriff said to Marsh, pleading. "If you don't, he'll just keep coming. And the more people who know, the more will be in danger."

"Sheriff!" I screamed. "It's okay. You can stop. This isn't real. It's an illusion."

Vrtiak couldn't hear me either. I had no power over the situation. I could only go along for the insane ride.

I yelled at the dog, "You think this is going to get me to help you? You hurt my friend and I swear you'll wish you never met me."

In response the gruesome dog lifted its muzzle and let out a hellish howl.

Vrtiak whimpered. All I'd done was scare the guy behind the wheel even more, and he had Marsh's life in his hands. The car veered into the opposite lane as headlights appeared in front of us. Vrtiak jerked the car back into our lane.

"Who told you that, Sheriff?" Marsh asked. "Who is he?"

"Give him what he wants," the sheriff whined. "Let him take the road wherever he wants to."

The car was getting closer. I wanted to jump through the bars and grab the wheel but I knew it would be useless.

"What road?" Marsh asked.

"You know," Vrtiak said.

The dog lunged at Vrtiak, snapping his jaws. Vrtiak's response was to steer into the opposite lane—directly in front of the oncoming car. The car blew its horn and Vrtiak snapped us back into the right lane.

"What road?" Marsh demanded.

I knew.

At the same time Vrtiak reached up to the rearview mirror and turned it so Marsh could see his reflection.

Vrtiak had changed. Instead of the face of the frightened sheriff, he had transformed into the ghostly character from Marsh's graphic novel: Gravedigger. Marsh pressed himself back into the seat. This was an illusion he could see. Damon knew exactly how to get into my friend's head.

"The Morpheus Road," Gravedigger said in a low, guttural growl.

Vrtiak, or whatever he was, jerked the wheel and sent us flying directly into the path of the oncoming car. A horn blared but the car kept coming. Vrtiak used both hands to spin the wheel to the right and made a sharp turn away from the oncoming car. The headlights flashed past, missing us by a hair. But we weren't out of danger. Vrtiak had turned so violently that we careened off the road and charged into the woods.

I leaned into Marsh and for whatever good it would do I screamed, "Get down!"

I can't say for sure that he heard me, but he covered his head just as Vrtiak hit the brakes and sent him crashing into the grill between the front and back seats.

Vrtiak screamed as the car flew out of control, bumping over rocks and slashing through bushes. He maintained control long enough to avoid a few trees, but we weren't slowing down. It was then that the hound reappeared in the front seat, but not to intimidate Vrtiak. The dog was looking straight at me.

"You see?" the dog growled. "Bad things happen."

The dog howled again, or was it a laugh? A second later it vanished. I felt a rude bump as if the front left tire had hit something that launched us into the air. The car flipped up onto its side, skidded for a few more yards, and then slammed into something with a jolt before coming to a stop . . . on its side.

I had been thrown out of the car and landed a few yards away, disoriented but generally fine. It's good to be a ghost. I ran back to the wreck to check on Marsh. I was already planning on how I would go to the Thistledown Fire Department and somehow convince somebody to send an ambulance. But first I had to see if Marsh was okay.

I moved through the door of the car and saw that he was dazed but moving.

"Stay put, Ralph!" I shouted. "You might have hurt something."

Yeah. Waste of breath. He seemed okay, though, because he sat up and looked around to get his bearings. The sheriff wasn't so lucky. He was jammed behind the wheel with his eyes open but he wasn't focused and he mumbled something that I could barely hear.

"Are . . . are you okay?" Marsh asked him.

Vrtiak moved his head slightly toward Marsh's voice. He might have been physically okay, but his brain had snapped.

"Sheriff?" Marsh repeated.

"Won't stop," Vrtiak mumbled. "Won't. So many people. So many lives."

"I'll get help," Marsh said.

All I could do was watch as Marsh struggled to stand on the door that was now the floor. He pushed up on the opposite door that was now the ceiling, but didn't have enough leverage to open it. He had to wedge his feet into the cage, lift himself up, and use both hands to twist the handle and push the door up and open. He was out.

"Can you move?" he called down to Vrtiak.

The sheriff answered by drooling.

Marshall dug his cell phone from his pants pocket to make a call, but it was no use. The phone was dead.

"I'll go into town and send help," Marsh told the sheriff. "Don't move, all right?"

Marsh threw his legs over the side of the car and jumped down to the ground. He was a little wobbly, but okay. After a quick look around to survey the accident scene, he took off running back through the woods toward the road. I was about to follow him when I heard a growl come from behind me.

Turning quickly, I saw the ghoulish dog on all fours, hunched down, ready to spring.

"You really think that's going to scare me?" I said.

The shape of the dog transformed and grew until it locked into another image.

Damon's.

"You can end this," he said casually. "Destroy the third crucible."

"And then what?" I asked.

"Then I leave your friend alone."

"Don't you need him to find the poleax?"

Damon gave me a sly smile. "Perhaps not. Once I control the Rift, there are others who can locate my weapon."

"You mean your soldiers that are trapped in the Black," I said. "You'd send them through the Rift into the Light."

"Along with you, my friend. Remember that."

"Me? Why me?"

"That was our agreement," he said innocently. "You still want your life back, do you not?"

Of course I did, but I wasn't going to give him the satisfaction of saying so.

"So, what happens once you get the poleax?" I asked.

"Break the crucible," Damon said, ignoring the question. "Until then I will continue to haunt your friend. I must admit, I am enjoying this game."

"Leave him alone!"

"Excuse me," he said. "I have a phone call to make. Give my regards to your grandfather."

And he disappeared.

"Damon!" I shouted, but he was gone.

I was left alone in the desolate field with a wrecked car and an insane sheriff. Damon was going after Marsh and there was nothing I could do to stop him, except break the crucible.

"What happened?" came a friendly voice.

Maggie rounded the wreck to join me.

"Marsh is lucky to be alive," I answered. "This isn't fair. He didn't do anything wrong."

Maggie gave me a sad smile and said, "Yes, well, who said life was fair?"

If anybody had the right to feel that way, it was Maggie. She may have been coming from another place, but it was the same attitude my grandfather had. Life wasn't fair. Bad things happened and maybe there wasn't always a perfect solution. All you could do was what seemed right . . . and I knew what that was.

"I'm worried about you, Cooper," Maggie said.

"Don't be," I said. "Go back to your vision."

"What are you going to do?"

"The only thing I *can* do." The swirling colors appeared behind me, ready to take me away from the Light and back to the Black. "I'm going to take control."

From the moment I got slammed by that speedboat on Thistledown Lake until Marsh got flipped in the sheriff's car, I'd pretty much been a bystander. Everybody had their own plans and secrets and goals and all I could do was play catch-up and try to understand it all. That had to change. I had to stop worrying about what everybody else might do and start getting people to wonder what *I* might do. That's what I always did in life. Somehow I'd lost sight of that in the Black. I always found my way out of Trouble Town. It might have taken a little longer to figure things out this time, but I finally knew what I had to do.

"What does that mean?" Maggie asked.

"It means I'm going after the third crucible."

24

Ree and her Guardians wanted to protect the crucible. Damon wanted it smashed. If I could snatch it, I would have power over both sides and could start calling the shots myself. I liked that idea. All I had to do was figure out how to get my hands on it.

Yeah. That.

I left the Light and went directly to Ree's vision. My hope was that if I got into trouble with the Guardians, my friendship with Ree would prevent me from getting vaporized on the spot. A couple of seconds might mean the difference between success and oblivion. The one person I needed to avoid was Ree herself. She always knew when I was up to no good.

I landed in her vision in the exact same spot where I left it the time before. I was a few blocks away from Grand Central Terminal, on the edge of the vision that separated the Rift from the rest of the Black. As I stepped out of the wall of color, I saw a Watcher standing on the far street corner.

"Hey!" I called out. "If things start hitting the fan, remember, I'm one of the good guys."

His answer was to disappear. Tool.

I moved quickly across the wide avenues, headed toward the train station. It was eerie to walk through a deserted New York City. It was like being in a sci-fi movie about some deadly outbreak that wiped out humanity. Only this was no movie.

After crossing Lexington Avenue I had to make a decision. How would I enter the train station? When I arrived with Ree, we came up from the subway and there were guards everywhere. I needed to figure out a way to get inside without running across any of those killer clowns. I was prepared to fight, so long as they didn't have black swords. The best thing to do was avoid them for as long as possible. My plan was to go inside and quickly drop down to the lower level. I'd been there before on different trips from Stony Brook. There was a vast space directly below the main concourse that was loaded with restaurants and shops. My thinking was that I could conceal myself down there as I made my way to the stairs that led up to the main floor, and the information booth. It was as good a plan as any so I slipped through the outside door and immediately ran down the stairs.

I hit the lower level without running into any Guardians. Quickly and quietly I made my way along the long corridor that led to the shops. Normally the place was alive with sounds but it was so quiet that every time my foot hit the floor it sounded like an elephant was tromping through. You'd think a ghost would be a little quieter.

When I reached the lower concourse, I was shocked to see that none of the restaurants and shops were there. It was a huge, empty space with only a few old benches. I realized that the shops probably didn't exist back in the seventies. That was bad news because the counters and booths would have given me plenty of cover as I made my way to the stairs. Now I was going to be totally exposed. There was nothing I could do but keep going.

I moved with my back to the wall, trying to be as quiet as possible. It would only be a matter of time before I came upon a Guardian, and I wanted to get as close as possible before jumping him. I was tuned for every sound. I didn't hear anything unusual but didn't believe for a second that the upper concourse, and the crucible, were unguarded. It wasn't a question of whether there would be a fight, but when.

I made it to the bottom of the staircase that led to the upper level of the terminal without a problem. There wasn't a Guardian in sight, which seemed odd. Had something changed? Did they move the crucible? That didn't make sense because Ree's vision was as much about the Rift as it was about the crucible and I didn't think there was any way to move that. I hoped that maybe I'd arrived at the exact right time and they were changing shifts. That would have been a huge stroke of luck.

All I had to do was climb the stairs and I'd be within sight of the crucible. My plan wasn't clever. I was going to sprint across the floor, climb up on top of the information booth, grab the golden ball, and sprint out the far side of the terminal and keep going until I hit the edge of Ree's vision. Your basic snatch and grab. Up until then nobody knew I was there. No alarms had sounded. I'd managed to maintain my biggest advantage—surprise.

I cautiously began climbing to the main floor. There were about thirty stairs, then a landing where I would turn 180 degrees to the bottom of a second flight that would bring me up to the giant hall. Hugging the wall, I made it to the landing and was about to make the turn to the final flight, when I heard something. It was a clicking sound, like something tapping against a hard surface. Multiple things. Whatever it was, there were a lot of them. There was a faint clattering that sounded as if it were coming from the top of the stairs above me. It didn't sound human. My hope was that it was rats, but it didn't seem likely that Ree would have rats in her vision.

The tapping sound stopped. The rats, or whatever they were, had left. I took a relieved breath, turned the corner, and peered up the final staircase to see that the rats hadn't left. They had just arrived. And they weren't rats. The sound I'd heard was the clattering of claws on the floor. Big claws. Standing at the top of the stairs were three of the biggest Rottweiler dogs I'd ever seen. Their ears were up . . . on alert . . . for me. It was a standoff. A frozen moment. They were on top of the stairs looking down. I was at the bottom looking up. My hope was that they were friendly pets.

"Hello, boys," I called out.

They weren't pets. Or friendly. Their response was to charge down the steps, snarling and barking. My hope for surprise was gone, but that was the least of my worries. I turned and ran back down the stairs, taking them three at a time. Spirit or no spirit, getting ripped apart would hurt. I hit the bottom of the stairs and kept running with no idea of where to go. I sprinted across the empty space, scanning for an escape route or a place to use for protection. The doors that led to the lower train tracks were all closed tight. Every other passageway seemed too wide open to offer protection. All I could do was run, though I wouldn't be able to keep ahead of the dogs for long.

I was halfway across when the dogs hit the bottom of the stairs. The floor was hard and smooth, which made it difficult for them to get traction. That slowed them down, but not by much. They howled a warning as if to let me know it was only a matter of time before I'd be lunch. All I could do was keep running until I hit the stairway on the far side of the lower concourse and climb back up to the main floor. The doors to the outside were up there. With luck I'd make it to one. Lots of luck.

I practically flew up the stairs, motivated by the sound of gnashing teeth and sharp claws. I hit the landing and made the turn up to the final flight. All I wanted to do was escape with my limbs intact and hide out somewhere until I figured out a better way to steal the crucible.

When I reached the top of the stairs, and the main concourse, my eyes locked on the brass clock shell that held the prize. My goal was no more than twenty yards away.

Trouble was, there was a pack of wild dogs at my heels . . .

. . . and standing between me and the crucible was a Guardian.

It was Adeipho's daughter. She stood halfway to the information booth with her hands on her hips. She didn't have on her clown mask and had taken off her suit jacket and tie. Her white sleeves were rolled up and her long dark hair was tied back. If she was surprised to see me, she didn't show it.

She held up her hand and let out a sharp whistle.

I stopped.

The dogs did too. They were seconds away from tearing my butt apart in a furious rage, but instantly stopped running and sat down on the top of the stairs, whimpering like puppies. The girl swept her hand out to the side and the three dogs obediently turned and scampered back down the stairs.

"Thanks for that," I said.

She didn't react. Her eyes were locked on mine. This girl

didn't like me. I guess there were a lot of reasons for that. I decided to try and win her over.

"My name's Coop," I said, all friendly. "I didn't catch your name."

"Because I did not throw it at you."

"Right. Well, thanks for calling off the hounds. I guess I'll be going now."

I made a move to leave but—

"Stop," she commanded.

I stopped.

"Yeah," I said, wincing. "Didn't think it would be that easy."

"Why did you come back?"

"To visit Ree," I lied. "She's my best friend's mom. Did you know that? Adeipho's your dad, right? He seems like a pretty cool—"

"Liar," she spat.

So much for charm.

"Whatever. Believe what you want. Obviously I shouldn't have come here, so I'll just take off."

"Come with me," she said. "My father would like to know that you have returned, and this time you will not have Ree to protect you."

I laughed, trying to keep it casual. "No, thanks. I'll pass on that."

"You had the advantage the last time we met," she said. "You had a weapon and I did not."

She walked closer. The last time we'd met she attacked me like a wild animal. Now she was moving with control. And confidence. I expected to have to fight my way to the crucible but didn't think it was going to be with this girl again. There were worse options. The dogs were gone and she didn't have a black sword. If I could take her out, I'd be back in business. Things were looking up . . .

. . . for about three seconds. She took a step closer, getting to within a few feet, then turned her back on me. That threw me. I had no idea what she was doing until I felt her heel driving into my chin. Hard. She had set herself up for a perfect back kick and I wasn't ready for it. My head snapped back and my ears rang. I threw up my arms out of instinct and managed to block the crescent kick to my head she followed with. I was lucky, but not for long. She quickly followed with another crescent kick using her other leg. The blade of her foot caught my head from the side and snapped it the opposite way. The girl knew what she was doing. When she attacked me before she was trying to confuse me and keep me from using the black sword. This time she had no such fear.

I backpedaled a few steps to give myself enough time to get my defenses up but she moved right with me. Now I was the one who started swinging wildly. She knocked away each one of my desperate punches and countered with short, sharp jabs to my chest, my head, my stomach—pretty much anywhere that would hurt. I was in trouble, but getting a beating was the least of my worries. If this girl took me down and brought me to her father, I'd be done and so would Marsh. The thought gave me new energy. Desperation will do that. I launched myself toward her. There was no finesse or technique about it. I had to use the only advantage I had, my size and strength. She landed a few shots to my head but I took them and kept going for her. She realized, too late, that I would not be denied. She turned to run but I wrapped my arms around her and twisted, sending us both crashing to the hard floor. We hit and bounced but I kept her in a bear hug, pinning her arms. If I let go, I knew she'd attack again. It was like wrestling with a shark. If you let it go, it would eat you.

She struggled but I held tight, until I felt a sharp pain

in my neck. I looked up to see Adeipho, her father, standing over me with his foot on my neck and the tip of his black sword inches from my throat.

"Release her," he commanded coldly.

I felt the girl relax. The fight was over. I let her go and she rolled away quickly to stand by her father. I, on the other hand, wasn't so quick to get up.

"I knew you would be back," Adeipho said. "Ree is far too trusting."

"Where is she?" I asked.

"Not here," Adeipho answered. "That will make this easier."

I didn't like the sound of that. I still didn't move, not with that killer sword so close to my neck.

"Damon won't stop," I said. "Sooner or later he's going to get the poleax."

"And he will not have you to help him," Adeipho said.

I liked the sound of that even less.

"I'm not trying to help him," I said. "I'm just trying to protect my friend. Ree's son."

"As I am protecting the Light. Which is why you must be destroyed."

I rolled away and sat up. I had some wild idea of making a fight out of it, but as soon as I looked back at Adeipho, I saw that was impossible. He wasn't alone. There were ten of his Guardians surrounding him.

"Remember," I said feebly. "I could have destroyed your daughter."

"And I allowed you to live. That scale is balanced."

"I'm not with Damon!" I insisted. "I want to stop him as much as you do."

"That is quite noble," Adeipho said. "Then you will understand why your spirit must be destroyed."

"No! That's a mistake."

Adeipho took a step toward me and raised his sword. There was no use running. My luck was finally gone.

"Leave him alone!" came a familiar voice from across the terminal floor.

I hoped it was Ree coming to save my butt a second time.

It wasn't. Everyone turned to see that someone was clinging to the brass clock frame on top of the information booth. She held on to the frame with one hand. In her other hand . . . was the crucible. I was never so happy to find out that somebody didn't do what I'd asked them to do.

"Maggie!" I called out.

"Get away from him or I'll break it," Maggie commanded.

"Give that to me!" Adeipho screamed in horror.

Adeipho pushed his way through the Guardians, headed for Maggie. Maggie's response was to hold the crucible out over the floor.

"I'll drop it," she warned.

Adeipho froze.

I skirted around the group and walked to the information booth. Looking up at Maggie, I said, "I told you not to follow me."

"I'm not a good listener."

"I like that about you."

I helped her down from the booth while she kept her eyes on the Guardians. They were like a pack of angry wolves who were ready to pounce at the first opening.

"You cannot do this," Adeipho pleaded. "You must understand what Damon is capable of."

"I'm thinking you're the one who doesn't know what he's capable of," I said. "While you're all here watching the Rift, he's been wreaking havoc in the Light."

"That cannot be," Adeipho's daughter said. "He has not gone through the Rift."

"But his spirit is getting stronger," I shot back. "If he

gets the poleax, this crucible will be worthless and so will the Rift."

"Tell me what you want," Adeipho cried. "Anything. I will obey."

"Tell Ree that I've got this and I'm not giving it up."

"You will be leaving the Rift unprotected," Adeipho cautioned.

"No, you and your Guardians are here. I think it's time you guys finished what you started and took Damon out. Are you ready for that?"

Adeipho didn't have an answer but he definitely didn't look happy about the idea.

"Don't follow us," I warned.

I took Maggie by the hand and we backed away from the group of Guardians.

"Where are you going?" he asked.

"Tell Ree what I said. She's the only one I'll talk to."

I pulled Maggie toward the exit on the far side of the terminal.

"Are you sure about this?" she whispered.

"No."

We walked slowly until we passed under the giant Kodak display and left the main concourse.

"Let's go," I said, and started running.

We didn't stop until we had left the terminal and reached the edge of Ree's vision.

"Where *are* we going?" Maggie asked.

"Your vision," I answered. "They don't know who you are."

Seconds later we stepped through the swirling cloud of color and found ourselves on Maggie's porch. I immediately noticed that things had changed. It was still her house, but the sky was no longer gray and gloomy. The trees were covered with small green buds that were warmed by a brilliant yellow sun. Maggie's vision had changed for the better. I had to believe her future was going to change as well.

I looked to her and smiled. She knew exactly what I was thinking.

"Thanks to you," she said.

"Why are you still here?" I asked. "I mean, now that the truth is out."

"I don't think the truth matters as much as how I deal with it," she said. "Maybe I haven't done enough to earn my way out."

"Well, you sure helped me. That should count."

"I didn't do it for my sake," she said, then dropped her eyes. "I'm sorry about your grandfather."

"If anybody should be sorry, it's him," I replied. "He owes you."

"No, he doesn't. People do what they have to do."

"That's what he said. Maybe he's right. People have to take care of themselves first and to hell with everybody else."

"I don't believe that," she said. "And neither do you."

"But I do. Isn't that what the Black is all about? Taking care of yourself?"

"Then, why did you look out for me?" she asked.

I shrugged. "It just happened."

"No, it didn't. You were concerned about me and that's why you questioned Collette. And it's why you're looking out for your friend in the Light. I'm sorry that your grandfather disappointed you, but that doesn't change who you are."

"Maybe not," I said. "But it does change how I operate. I'm going to beat this Damon guy, but on my terms. Now that I've got the crucible, I'm in control."

Maggie frowned. "There's a difference between control and arrogance."

"I'm not arrogant. I'm confident."

"No, you're cocky. This isn't a game, Cooper. There's a lot at stake."

"Which is why I'm going to do things my way from now on." I held up the crucible. "Thanks to you."

"So, what do we do now?"

"Not we," I said quickly. "I don't want you following me anymore. You're on the verge of getting out of here. Hanging with me could send you in a completely different direction."

"Or maybe helping you is the last thing I have to do to earn my way out," she said with certainty.

I really liked Maggie. She had been through so much, most of it because of my grandfather. I wasn't about to let anything bad happen to her again. I held her shoulders and she looked up at me with those huge brown eyes.

"I wish we could have met at a different time. Or place. Or vision."

"Or maybe this is exactly what should have happened," she said.

I leaned down and kissed her. She was so fragile. I would do anything to protect her. Keeping her away from me seemed like the best way to do it. The kiss lasted a long time. It had to. It would probably be our last. Finally I pulled away and saw that she was crying.

"Where are you going to go?" she asked.

"I'm not telling. Good-bye, Maggie. Thank you."

As we stood on that porch, I had to wonder if we'd ever see each other again. In any life. It took some willpower, but I let go of her and turned to walk down the porch stairs.

I didn't get far.

Standing at the bottom was Ree.

"Then, tell *me* where you're going, Cooper," she said.

She was clutching a black sword.

25

"I thought you couldn't see outside of your vision?" I asked.

"I said we can't see into the Light. The Black is another matter."

I quickly held out the crucible to let her know I had it. She didn't flinch. She already knew.

"Taking that was a mistake," she said. "Do you understand what would happen if it broke?"

"I know what'll happen if I don't do *anything*," I shot back. "Your Guardians aren't trying to stop Damon and neither are the Watchers. So where does that leave us?"

Ree sighed and put away the sword. "The Watchers are a higher form of life, Cooper. They don't deal in conflict the way we know it. They wait until a spirit has evolved enough to join them, or proves they have no hope of reaching that level before they intervene."

"So they want all us lower life forms to duke it out on our own," I said.

"That's right. We're all guided by our own free will, even Damon. And besides, as long as Damon has the kind of power he's shown, they would never put themselves at risk by forcibly pushing him into the Blood."

"Translation . . . they're afraid of him because of the black swords," I said.

"Of course, and they should be. Destroying a spirit in the Black is tragedy enough. Destroying an evolved life form would be catastrophic. So they don't give him a chance."

"That's not good enough," I said. "He's going to find the poleax, Ree. Maybe now or maybe a hundred years from now. Or a thousand years. He's not going to give up. And when he does, nobody will be safe, including the Watchers. You can't sit back and react to what he does anymore."

"And if you break that third crucible, it'll only get worse," she countered.

"I don't want to break it. I want to use it."

"For what?" she said with surprise.

"To force the Guardians to take him on."

Ree stared at me with disbelief. "You want us to fight Damon?"

"Absolutely!" I replied. "I've seen his soldiers. They're a bunch of drones. Adeipho's guys are way more organized. Heck, even his daughter kicked my ass. The Guardians would wipe them out."

"We aren't executioners," she said with finality.

"Great. Nobody wants a fight . . . you, Adeipho, the Watchers . . . but Damon sure does. So while you're all sitting around hoping he goes away, he's doing everything he can to get more power. If you don't do something to stop him, you won't have to worry about guarding the Rift from inside the Black because he'll be coming at you from the other side."

I saw Ree's jaw muscles working.

"And what will you do, Cooper? You think the threat of breaking the crucible is enough to force us into this battle?"

"I don't know. Maybe. But if breaking this gives him more power, then you'd be crazy to push me there."

"And you're crazy for even thinking about breaking it!" she shouted.

I'd never seen Mrs. Seaver so angry. I didn't like it. Neither did Maggie. She walked up behind me and held my arm.

"Then, do something!" I shouted back. "Have Adeipho rally his soldiers and end this. Adeipho knows how dangerous Damon is. I can't believe he wouldn't be willing to do what's right and finish the job."

Ree shook her head in frustration. "You can't do this, Cooper. You can't be the kid you've always been, jumping in with both feet and worrying about the consequences after. You aren't playing army with Marsh. We're talking about the balance between life and death. Between the physical and the spiritual. The Guardians are the only thing that stands between Damon and chaos. Without us, there would be nothing to stop him from tearing apart the very fabric of existence."

"From what I've seen, that's going to happen anyway," I said.

"And what if we fail?" she screamed. "Do you really want to be the one who brought about the collapse of humanity?"

"Don't put this on me," I shot right back. "Things would have gone on like this forever if you hadn't uncovered the Rift and broken that first crucible. This is on *you*, Ree."

I hated to slam her like that, but I had to get through to her somehow. We stood staring at each other, neither wanting to give in.

A familiar voice broke the tension. "This is marvelous! Who will triumph in this battle of wills?"

All three of us looked toward Gramps's house to see Damon leaning on the fence.

"Such fire!" he bellowed. "Such passion! I apologize if I ever doubted you, Foley. When I selected you, I chose wisely."

Seeing him was a shock, to say the least. He strolled casually toward us with a big smile.

"And you must be Ree," he exclaimed. "You have been hiding for so long I thought we might never meet. I have so enjoyed spending time with your son."

Ree spun toward him and reached for her sword. Damon was faster. He pulled his own black sword from its sheath.

"That would be foolish," he warned. "I do not doubt your bravery, but you would be no match for me in battle."

"Don't bet on that," I said.

Reluctantly Ree took her hand off the sword.

"Now," he said, turning his attention to me, "I am pleased to see you have fulfilled your part of our bargain."

"What bargain?" Ree asked.

"I told you," I answered quickly. "He said he'd leave Marsh alone if I broke the crucible."

"Not only that!" Damon said indignantly. "I promised you your life back." He looked to Ree and added conspiratorially, "He was particularly tempted by that offer."

Ree shot me a look. "Is that true?"

"Well, yeah. But that's not why I took the crucible. I told you I—"

Ree threw her hand up, cutting me off. I felt her disappointment and anger. "You always find a way out of trouble, don't you, Coop?"

"It's not like that!" I insisted. "Yeah, he promised my life back but I didn't even believe it was possible."

"Until you found out about the Rift," she declared.

"Yes! I mean, no! I'm not trying to help this guy."

"Yet you have taken the crucible as I asked," Damon said smugly. "Now please, would you be so kind as to crush it?"

I took a step back from both of them and held the crucible up.

"I'll take off and neither of you will see it again," I warned. "With the crucible gone it'll force this thing to an end."

"Not true," Damon said. "Take the crucible and I will finish your friend." He looked to Ree and added, "Your son."

"He isn't part of this," Ree growled through clenched teeth.

Damon chuckled. "There is no soul, living or dead, who is *not* a part of this."

"Cooper, listen to me," Ree said. "Go. Do what you have to do. But do not break that crucible."

"You could make that choice," Damon declared. "But only if you can stomach watching this."

Behind Damon a cloud of swirling color appeared. I thought, and hoped, that he was going to step through it and leave us alone.

"This will be a treat for you, Ree," Damon said. "Taking the crucible away from the Rift is already paying rewards. Would you like to see your son?"

Ree was near panic. She glanced to me, looking for help but I didn't know what to do.

"I would," she finally said, her voice full of pain, as if she was agreeing to a deal with the devil.

"Of course you would," Damon said with mock sincerity.

He turned to the cloud of color that immediately separated to give us a view into the Light. It was as if a tear had appeared in the thin veil between two worlds, allowing us to see as clearly as if we were actually there.

What we immediately saw . . . was Marsh.

Ree gasped. It was the first time she'd seen her son since she'd left on the fateful trip to Greece. He wasn't a little boy anymore. And he was in trouble.

"Is that your sister?" Maggie whispered to me.

All I could do was nod.

Sydney and Marsh were on a Jet Ski, flying over the surface of Thistledown Lake. It was night and they were moving fast—too fast for safety and it didn't take long to see why. They were being chased down by a monster cigarette boat.

"What's happening?" Ree asked.

"Is it not obvious?" Damon replied. "They are about to die."

Sydney knew how to drive the Jet Ski. We'd raced each other plenty of times on the lake. But there was no way she could outrun or outmaneuver the powerful speedboat.

"You should appreciate the symmetry, Foley." Damon said. "That is the same boat that killed you. A young boy ran you down, and now his father will do the same to your sister . . . and to your son, Ree."

"But . . . why would he do that?" Maggie gasped with confusion.

"Because he is afraid not to," was Damon's answer.

After having seen the dog from hell in Sheriff Vrtiak's car, I had no doubt that Damon was telling the truth. Whatever he was doing to the man behind the wheel of that boat, the poor guy had no power to stop himself.

"No," Ree said, barely above a whisper.

"Oh yes," Damon replied, then turned to me. "If you are going to run off with the crucible, I suggest you do it quickly unless you would like to witness the execution."

"Stop it!" Ree screamed and raised her black sword.

Damon held his ground, flashing his own black sword. Ree backed off.

"Sydney can get out of this," I said, trying more to convince myself than anybody else.

"Do you think?" Damon asked thoughtfully. "Perhaps I should ensure the outcome."

Two more cigarette boats materialized on the lake, headed after the Jet Ski. They were identical to the one being driven by the man, only at the wheel of each of these boats was Gravedigger, Marsh's skeletal character.

Damon looked at me, and winked.

I wanted to smash his pointed teeth.

"What happened?" Maggie screamed. "Where did they come from? How is that possible?"

"They're illusions," I said.

"Tricks of light," Damon said, chuckling. "But they will make it so much more difficult for your sister to find a way to escape."

Sydney started pushing the Jet Ski into tight turns to avoid being run down by the new boats. She had no idea that they couldn't hurt her. No sooner would she slide out of the way of one, than she'd steer directly into the path of another and have to make a quick correction. It would only be a matter of time . . . before she ran out of time.

"Now," Damon said, back to business. "Destroy the crucible and they will live."

I wrapped my fingers around the golden ball.

"Please," Ree begged. "There must be another way."

"There is," Damon declared. "Produce the poleax for me. Here and now."

"I don't know where it is," she sobbed.

"Then there is no other way," Damon said coldly.

I lifted up the golden ball.

"I can find the poleax," I said. "I can go into the Light and get it."

Ree glanced to me, then back to the terrifying scene unfolding on the lake.

"Interesting," Damon said. "Who are you making that promise to? The Guardians? Or me?"

"Leave Marsh alone," I demanded. "He can't help you if he's dead."

"He isn't doing much to help me alive," Damon said with a sneer. "Other than to control you, my friend."

Sydney took another sharp turn and barely missed being sliced by the cigarette boat. The *real* cigarette boat.

Ree sobbed as if she was physically in pain. She lunged at Damon but it was a weak effort and he easily knocked her sword away. Damon wasn't much of a warrior, but he was in control. Though she was hardened by her experiences, Ree was still a civilian mom who was about to witness the violent death of her only son.

"Stop!" I screamed at Ree. "Don't risk it."

"Oh, please do!" Damon taunted.

Ree held the sword in both hands. She was a mess. Even if she had fighting skills, there was no way she could stand up to Damon in that state.

The space behind her seemed to ripple and bend as another cloud of color appeared. Stepping from the swirl was Adeipho, along with several of the Guardians. All were armed, many with black swords. Adeipho stepped up behind Ree and gently took hers.

"It is all right, Ree," he said soothingly. "This is not your battle."

Ree gave up the sword and backed away, but didn't take her eyes off the action that was unfolding in the Light.

"Has it come to this?" Damon said to Adeipho. "Again?"

Before Adeipho could make a move, several of Damon's own soldiers appeared behind him. They too were armed. Each side held the weapons they had fought with thousands of years before and had carried into the Black.

"Is this what you wanted?" Maggie whispered to me.

I didn't know. I thought that the Guardians could handle Damon's soldiers, but now that it was about to happen, I had second thoughts.

"This isn't about them," Ree exclaimed, pointing to the images from the Light. "Leave them alone."

"When my demands are met," Damon said coolly.

Ree looked back to the Light—and screamed. Sydney had turned their Jet Ski directly into the path of an oncoming boat. They were seconds away from a head-on collision.

Damon looked at me with a smile. "I do like your sister. She is quite resourceful."

"No!" Ree sobbed as the Jet Ski hit the oncoming boat . . . and traveled through it as if it weren't there. Because it wasn't. It was one of Damon's illusions. Sydney and Marsh had figured it out.

"And what will happen now?" Damon asked. "They cannot evade the real craft for much longer, and to what end? Whether it be now or a millennium from now, I will find the poleax. I suggest we save ourselves a dozen lifetimes of bother and play this out. Now. Break the crucible, Foley. This battle will happen whether or not they survive, and their sacrifice will have meant nothing."

The illusion boats vanished. It was down to the one real boat and the Jet Ski. Sydney had run out of maneuvering room. The guy driving the boat had them in his sights and was closing fast, seconds from running them down.

I lifted the crucible, not knowing what I would do. Two small armies were facing each other in Maggie's front yard, ready to battle. Adeipho may have been the superior commander, but neither army looked as if they had an advantage. As I looked to the opposing forces I realized that Adeipho wasn't the only general who had gathered forces from every era imaginable. Damon had also recruited warriors from across time. On both sides were modern soldiers next to peasants in rags. Men in tattered business suits beside knights in chain mail. There were Roman centurions, Native Americans, World War I–vintage doughboys, and men and women wearing worn clothing that could have come from any time. Any place. Those in front held the black swords that would be the principal weapons in battle. Everyone else had standard swords, tools, rifles, shields, and knives. Those weapons would not destroy any spirits, but would do some damage.

One side winning would ensure the continued well-being of mankind. Victory by the other side could mean Armageddon.

Looking up at the Light, I saw that Sydney was driving the Jet Ski at full throttle, but the speedboat was closing. Marsh had turned and was holding an orange pistol in his hand that looked like a flare gun. He was aiming it at the oncoming boat. It was their last, desperate chance.

I held up the crucible. My decision was made. I couldn't see how their deaths would change anything that was unfolding in the Black. I had to smash it.

The terror in Ree's eyes as she watched the imminent death of her son hit me like a punch to the gut.

The boat was nearly on top of them.

She looked back to me and screamed, "Don't do it! There are worse things than death!"

Her warning threw me. I didn't expect that. I thought for sure she would want to save her son. It made me hesitate.

Marsh fired the flare gun. The white-hot streak shot toward the boat and veered far to the right. It wasn't going to come close. Their last hope was gone.

To save them, I had to break the crucible. I lifted it higher . . .

. . . and it was suddenly yanked out of my hand. I had

been so focused on the images from the Light that I didn't realize somebody else had arrived.

"Can't let you do this," Gramps said.

My grandfather had taken the crucible and quickly backed away from everybody.

Adeipho made a move for him . . .

. . . too late. Gramps got down on one knee and smashed the golden ball onto a rock. Bits of glass flew everywhere, along with a splash of blood. The blood of Alexander the Great.

Ree let out an anguished cry and collapsed to the ground.

In the vision, the path of the flare suddenly changed direction. It made a sharp, impossible turn and flew directly toward the driver of the boat. The moment it passed the driver's head, it exploded in a brilliant ball of fire, making the man throw his arms up to protect himself as he fell back toward the stern. The speeding craft was out of control and clipped the tail of the Jet Ski, sending it spinning. But Sydney quickly regained control.

The driver of the boat scrambled to his feet, desperate to regain control of the hurtling craft—too late. The boat slammed full-force into a seaplane that was bobbing on the surface of the lake.

The explosion was stupendous. I could swear I felt the heat, though that was impossible. The gas tank of the plane exploded, followed by the grander explosion of the boat's tank. A mushroom cloud of smoke and flame blew into the sky, along with the hull of the doomed boat. Bits and pieces of flaming debris landed in the lake, raining down around Marsh and Sydney, who steered away from the carnage, safe.

Damon had kept his end of the bargain.

And thanks to Gramps, so had I.

The colored cloud enveloped the images from the Light and vanished. There was a moment of stunned silence.

Damon took a step forward to face Adeipho. Adeipho stood up straight. Damon looked to me with a satisfied smile and saluted me with his sword.

"We are so very much alike," he said. "It matters not how the victory is achieved, so long as it is a victory."

"I'm nothing like you," I growled back at him.

"Do not be so sure," he said with a knowing laugh. He gestured to his soldiers and said, "We both want the same thing . . . to return to a life that was left unfulfilled."

He then looked to Adeipho and announced, "And for that, we will fight."

Maggie grabbed my arm. I expected the two armies to charge each other right then and there. Instead, Damon turned his back on Adeipho and marched toward his own soldiers. Another colorful swirling cloud appeared and Damon walked straight into it, disappearing. He was followed by each and every one of his soldiers. They marched together into the cloud and disappeared. A moment later, the cloud was gone.

"What just happened?" I asked, stunned.

Ree was still on the ground. Through her tears she said, "There is only one place for this battle."

I knew exactly what she meant. Breaking the third crucible had opened the door.

Damon's objective was now in sight.

There was going to be a battle for the Rift.

26

Adeipho reached down to take Ree's hand. The poor woman no longer looked like the confidant leader of the Guardians of the Rift. Witnessing the near death of her son had devastated her, among other things. She seemed beaten before the battle could even begin. The tall warrior helped her to her feet with a gentleness I didn't expect from the battle-hardened soldier. Once on her feet, Ree gave him a nod as if to say, "I'm okay." Adeipho backed off to join the Guardians, who stood together, waiting.

"Maybe you're right," Ree said.

It took a second for me to realize she was talking to me because she kept her eyes on the ground.

"This battle was inevitable. But you have to understand, breaking the crucible made it so much more difficult."

I looked to Gramps. The guy was stunned. He had no

idea what was going on. He stared back at me with scared, wide eyes.

"Why?" I asked Ree.

Adeipho answered. "Because now we are vulnerable."

"Go," Ree commanded Adeipho. She was slowly regaining her composure, and her authority.

"Do not delay," Adeipho cautioned.

"I won't," Ree responded.

The swirling clouds of color appeared behind the band of Guardians. Adeipho turned and his people parted to allow him to stride past them and into the mist. The Guardians fell in line behind him and were quickly swallowed up. Just like that, the two armies had retreated to prepare for battle.

Gramps touched me on the shoulder. "I don't know what any of this means," he said tentatively. "But you were going to break that golden ball and I didn't want that on your head." He held up his hands for me to see. Like Ree's hands, they were covered with the blood of Alexander the Great.

"You're right," I said. "I was going to break it."

"Then let the fallout be on me," he declared. He looked to Maggie and added, "I deserve whatever comes my way. I know that saying how sorry I am doesn't mean much, but please know that I am. I've *always* been sorry. I just haven't been strong enough to tell you."

Maggie stared back at him, stone-faced. She was angry and I didn't blame her. She wasn't about to forgive Gramps and I didn't blame her for that either.

"Now you're marked, just like me," Ree said to Gramps, holding up her bloodstained hands.

Gramps looked at his hands, dazed.

"I'm sorry, Ree. Mrs. Seaver," I said. "I did what I thought was right."

She nodded thoughtfully. "For taking care of Marsh, I

thank you. And I understand. But stealing that crucible and taking it away from the Rift was reckless, Cooper. A door is now open that the Guardians have protected for over two thousand years. I'm partly responsible for that, and now you are too."

"Can't you keep him out of your vision?" I asked.

She shook her head. "I don't think so. Not without the crucible."

"So what's going to happen?" Maggie asked.

"Now we hope that the damage we've done doesn't allow Damon to complete his quest."

"And what exactly is that?" Gramps asked.

"It's an old saying that wasn't meant to be taken literally, until now. If the Guardians can't protect the Rift, and Damon succeeds in breaking through, we'll be looking at nothing less than . . . hell on earth."

Nobody said a word as Ree backed away from us.

"Good-bye," she said. "And good luck to us all."

She turned, stepped into her own cloud of color, and disappeared. When the mist vanished, I could see all the way to Maggie's barn. Standing in front were two Watchers.

"You!" I shouted, and took a few steps toward them. I didn't dare go any closer because I didn't want them to disappear. "What is your deal? Do you know what's going to happen? How can you let Damon do this? What is your purpose? Why aren't you taking a stand?"

The two Watchers, a man and a woman, didn't react. I was so frustrated that I ran forward, ready to grab one and shake them into action.

"Cooper, don't!" Maggie shouted.

She didn't have to bother. I only got a few steps before both Watchers disappeared. I stopped short and screamed out in frustration, and it wasn't just about them. I was scared. For myself, and for what I'd done. I'd gotten what I wanted. I'd taken control. But I'd set things in motion that were about as far out of my control as possible. This was no longer about me or Marsh or a ghost who was haunting him. By stealing the crucible I opened up the possibility of a cataclysmic horror. Hell on earth. That's what Ree called it.

Screaming didn't make me feel any better. I stood there, breathing hard, wanting to take some kind of action but not knowing what it could be.

"Cooper?" Maggie called to me.

I looked to the pretty spirit, who was standing next to my grandfather, the guy whose selfishness and fear had given her a lifetime of grief.

"It isn't over," she said.

"Really?" I shouted back. "What makes you say that? Because of all the great and wonderful things that have been happening? Sure! Why not? Let's all live happily ever after. Sounds good to me."

Maggie gave me a sad smile. She then turned to Gramps, held his hand and went up on her toes to give him a kiss on the cheek.

Gramps was wide eyed, not sure what was happening or how to react.

"I forgive you," she said sincerely. "As long as you can forgive yourself."

He stood there for a moment, stunned, then looked down at Maggie's sweet face as tears welled in his eyes.

"Thank you," he whispered. "I'll try. I promise I will."

Maggie touched his cheek gently, then turned to me.

"Maybe some great and wonderful things *have* happened," she said with a shrug.

It was a small gesture. In the scope of all that was going on, it was inconsequential. But for those two people it meant everything. Until then, the defining moment of their lives had been a misguided act that brought nothing but misery and despair to both of them. They had changed that. They had taken control. It was what the Black was all about.

That couldn't end.

I couldn't let it end.

"Stay here," I said to Maggie. "Do not leave this vision." I looked to Gramps and added, "You should go to your own vision too, Gramps. It's where you belong."

"No. I'm just as responsible for what happened as you."

"No, you're not. You're responsible for yourself. You both are."

"What are you going to do, Cooper?" Maggie asked.

I shrugged. "Same thing I always do. I'm gonna look for some trouble."

"Coop, wait," Maggie called.

Too late. I had stepped out of her vision and returned to Ree's vision. Within seconds I was in the main concourse of Grand Central Terminal . . .

. . . and found myself in the middle of an army of Guardians. Each one was armed, many with black swords. They had formed a circle around the information booth, ready to defend the Rift.

I was their first victim. I got whacked on the side of the head by the back of somebody's fist, and kicked in the gut by somebody else. I went down and covered up in the fetal position, ready to get the stomping I deserved. If I hadn't stolen the crucible, they wouldn't have been assembled there to defend the Rift. I actually hoped that they wanted to pound me. I'd rather have taken a beating than get skewered by one of those black swords, which would end any chance I had of redeeming myself.

I covered my head and braced for the pain. Nothing happened. I took a tentative peek over my arm to see that Adeipho was looming over me.

"I should destroy you," he growled.

I didn't say anything. It would only make things worse, if that was even possible.

"Once again you have been spared by Ree," he added. "Get up."

I slowly got to my feet, trying hard not to wince from the pain.

"I really am on your side," I said.

"You have an odd way of showing that," Adeipho replied, and waved for me to walk.

I passed through the sea of assembled Guardians. None said a word as I went by, but all eyes were on me. It was like having a hundred lasers burning into my head. That's the kind of hatred these spirits had for me. I wanted to stop and plead my case, tell them that I did what I thought was best to protect the Light. But the truth was, what I thought should happen was that they should battle Damon and his soldiers. What right did I have to volunteer them to fight? Win or lose, many of these spirits would be destroyed in battle, and that would be because of me. My actions would condemn them to oblivion.

No wonder they hated me.

We were headed toward the east side of the concourse and the giant Kodak photo of the pastoral countryside. A large section of the giant photograph was torn down to reveal stairs that led up to a landing. There was also a long horizontal gash cut through the image of the meadow above our heads. I followed Adeipho up the stairs and to the landing, where Ree was waiting for me. She stood looking out through the jagged gash. The damage now made sense. The hole was there so that the concourse and information booth could be observed from the landing.

"Are you all right?" she asked.

"I'm still here, so I guess I'm fine."

"The Guardians want to destroy you," she said with no emotion.

"I don't blame them."

"Then, why did you come back?"

"I want to help."

"You have done enough already," Adeipho bellowed.

Ree lifted her hand to quiet him. She was definitely back in charge.

"You aren't a warrior, Coop."

"Neither are a lot of those Guardians," I said, gesturing through the gash in the photo to the crowd below.

Ree said, "You're wrong. They're prepared for this. Adeipho has seen to that. They can all use swords and the simple weapons we've gathered. I know you can fight, Coop, but this is different."

"I don't want to defend the Rift with the Guardians," I said.

"So, then, why are you here?" Adeipho asked.

"I want to hunt down the poleax. If I can find it, I can bring it back here and hand it over to you. I still think you guys are going to stop Damon, but unless you destroy him for good, he's going to do everything he can in the Light, as a spirit, to find his weapon. He'll probably go after Marsh again. Maybe even that Ennis guy. The only way we can make sure that Damon never gets it, is to get it first . . . and destroy it."

"That is insanity," Adeipho said to Ree. "No one should be entrusted with that evil weapon, let alone someone who has already betrayed us."

"I didn't betray you!" I snapped at Adeipho. "I was trying to protect my friend."

"You were trying to get your life back," Adeipho said with disdain. "I heard of the bargain you made with Damon."

"The only way to stop him is to destroy him," I said.

"And now you've got the chance. Or maybe you're not up to this fight?"

Adeipho took a step toward me. He wanted to have it out right there. I turned sideways, ready to defend myself, but Ree stepped between the two of us.

"Stop," she commanded.

"Cooper is not our enemy," she said to Adeipho. "But he's headstrong and doesn't always value opinions that aren't his."

I wanted to argue with that, but she was right.

"And how do you intend to find it?" Ree asked me. "You don't have the same abilities in the Light that Damon has, and he hasn't had any luck finding the poleax."

I swallowed hard and took a breath. I knew that what I was going to suggest was going to be a problem, but I had to go for it.

"You're right," I said. "I can't do what Damon can . . . unless I go back to the Light through the Rift."

"No!" Adeipho shouted. "You just want your worthless life back!" He made a move to go for me again but Ree stopped him.

I said, "It's the only way we can find the poleax before Damon. Come with me if you want."

"Neither of you are going," Ree declared. "It goes against every law of nature."

"So what!" I exclaimed. "What would happen? Would the Watchers throw me into the Blood? I'm probably headed there anyway. But what'll they do if Damon wins and marches his army through the Rift? Will the mighty Watchers finally step up and do something about him? By then it would be too late."

Ree looked to Adeipho. He didn't offer an opinion.

I continued, "Wouldn't we be doing humanity a huge favor by destroying the poleax? If I don't find it, we'll be no worse off and the only one who suffers for it will be me. But if I do find it, and it stops Damon for good, don't you think it would be worth it?"

Ree didn't take her eyes off me. I had given her plenty to think about. Even Adeipho couldn't argue with my logic.

I added, "The best thing that could happen is that Damon attacks the Rift and you guys destroy him and every last one of his soldiers. That's what I believe is going to happen. But if it doesn't and Damon walks away from this battle, he's going to find some other way to get the poleax. You can bet on that. I say we get it first."

The quiet of the empty terminal was broken by the sound of something mechanical. Ree heard it first and looked up with curiosity.

"What is that?" Adeipho asked while straining to listen.

The grinding mechanical sound grew louder.

Or closer.

"I don't know," Ree said.

The three of us looked down from the landing to the concourse. The Guardians had heard it too. They glanced around in confusion to see . . . nothing. Yet the sound grew. It was a squealing metallic sound like I had never heard before.

Ree looked to Adeipho with concern and asked, "Is it Damon?"

Adeipho didn't have the answer, but he didn't take any chances. He leaned out of the hole in the photo and bellowed, "Prepare for the attack!"

Hundreds of Guardians scrambled to assigned positions.

"It's coming from the other side of the terminal," I declared.

All eyes went to the landing that was directly across from us. It was a mirror image of the landing we were on, though it wasn't covered by a massive photo. It was wide open and led to a series of doors that opened out onto the street. A shadow loomed from outside that could be seen through the glass doors.

"He's coming," Ree whispered.

Boom! The shadow crashed through the doors, filling the concourse with the sound of grinding wheels and a powerful engine.

"What is it?" Adeipho asked, stunned.

The dark form rolled over the smashed doors, moving closer, revealing itself.

"It's a tank," I said. "An old one. Maybe from World War I."

The mottled brown machine moved forward on treads until it reached the edge of the landing, directly across from us, overlooking the concourse.

The Guardians braced for an attack, though I can't believe they were prepared for anything like this.

The turret on top of the tank began to spin, revealing the long barrel of a cannon. It rotated 180 degrees from pointing back to pointing front.

Directly at us.

The wide barrel locked into position.

The battle for the Rift was about to begin.

27

"Look out!" I screamed, and dove at Ree.

An instant later the thunder from the tank's gun echoed throughout the terminal. I knocked her to the ground as the shell tore into the wall behind us. It exploded, sending a mass of broken glass and splintered wood across the platform and down onto our heads.

I was on top of Ree and got hit with the bulk of the debris but wasn't hurt.

"How is that possible?" I asked, breathless. "This is a vision. It isn't real."

"But it is real," Ree said. "As real as we imagined it would be."

I crawled across the floor to peek out over the concourse. The cannon on the tank was still aimed directly at our platform, over the heads of the Guardians below. There was no way to tell when it would fire again. The tank itself was an antique, but it had plenty of firepower.

"Where did he get that?" I asked.

Adeipho joined me, also keeping low. "Damon has gathered spirits from many different times. As have we."

"Do your spirits have tanks?" I asked.

Adeipho's silence was his answer.

Looking down on the concourse I saw the extent of the Guardians plan to defend the Rift. They had the information booth surrounded, twenty deep. Most of the spirits had swords and rifles but those weapons would only cause temporary damage. The weapons that would ultimately be needed for the defense of the Rift were the black swords. The Guardians with those weapons were the last line of defense. They formed the tightest circle around the information booth.

I couldn't help but think that they were all there because of me. I hoped I was right about Adeipho's Guardians being able to turn back Damon's soldiers. Seeing that the other side had a tank made me a little less confident. Damon might never have led his men into battle, but he was also supposed to be a brilliant tactician. We were about to find out just how good he was.

"Our plan is to repel the attack and send them out of this vision without having to use the spirit-killing weapons," Adeipho explained. "We do not want to destroy spirits if it is not necessary."

"Something tells me Damon's guys aren't as worried about that as you are," I said.

A high-pitched whine started to build, as if a swarm of angry bees was descending on the terminal. From the look on Adeipho's face, he had no idea what it was. Ree joined us and looked out over the concourse.

"I'm afraid that tank isn't the only weapon they've brought," she said.

The whine grew louder and several motorcycles crashed in through the destroyed doors on the opposite landing. The riders blasted over the remains of the doors, rode past the tank, and bounced down the stairs to the floor of the concourse. It was like a macabre X Games stunt, but they weren't riding for show. Strapped to their waists were black swords.

"They're leading with the big guns," I said. "Are your guys good enough to protect themselves?"

Adeipho's answer was to jump up and run for the stairs. He wanted to be in the fight. But as soon as he stood up—BOOM! The cannon fired again. Ree and I jumped out of the way as the spot where we'd been hiding erupted.

"You okay?" I asked.

Ree looked dazed but she wasn't hurt.

"They're trying to pin us down here," she said.

I looked around for Adeipho, but he was gone. I risked looking out of the destroyed picture and saw him charge down onto the concourse floor with his black sword drawn.

The bikers hit the concourse with their own black swords out and swinging. The Guardians were ready for them. Instead of attacking they held back and defended themselves. Many had ancient shields of hammered metal or course wood. As low-tech as they were, they worked. So long as they kept the black swords away from their bodies, those weapons were no more dangerous than an ordinary sword. I counted eight motorcycles that circled the crowd, trying to pick off any Guardians who were unlucky enough to give them a clear shot. The Guardians kept tight, not giving them an opening.

That changed when a bold Guardian rushed out to try and take down one of the bikers. He ran up from behind with his regular metal sword out. It wouldn't have killed the biker, but if he could unseat him, another Guardian could come up and finish him off with a black sword. But the brave spirit wasn't quick enough. The biker lashed back with his black sword, and with one quick swipe the Guardian froze and disappeared in a dark cloud.

Damon's soldiers had drawn first blood, or whatever it's called when a spirit is killed.

"They're testing our defenses," Ree said. "Trying to soften us up."

"But most of those weapons won't do any real damage, right? I mean, a spirit could take a direct shot from that cannon and still be okay."

"True, but the visions hold true to the laws of nature." She picked up a chunk of marble that had been blown apart when the first shell had hit and said, "We perceive this matter as being real, so it is."

"Will everything be repaired when it's over?" I asked.

She gave me a sad smile and a shrug. "I don't know. We've never been through something like this before. Let's just hope we get the chance to find out."

Adeipho launched himself from a counter in front of the ticket booths and tackled one of the bikers. They both fell to the floor as the bike crashed and spun away. Adeipho's sword was out and with one quick thrust, the biker was gone.

So much for trying not to destroy spirits.

The other seven bikers continued to circle the Guardians. It looked to me like Adeipho's plan to keep the black swords on the inside was a mistake because without them in front, the bikers were able to keep the Guardians tight together. They looked like a flock of sheep being herded by a group of aggressive dogs.

The third wave of attackers arrived. They were dressed as old-time soldiers, maybe from World War II. I thought I recognized German uniforms from movies I'd seen, but it was a mix of a lot of different styles. These soldiers ran in through the shattered doors and up to the edge of the landing. Without hesitation they started lobbing what appeared to be small rocks at the Guardians below.

"Uh-oh," I whispered.

I'd seen enough war movies to know what was coming. The stones weren't stones. They were hand grenades. The small weapons hit and exploded on impact, tearing up the floor and spewing smoke and marble everywhere. Several Guardians were hit and knocked down by the concussion, but they weren't killed. Or even injured. The grenades were powerful, but they were still regular old grenades.

"Why are they bothering?" I asked.

"To cause confusion," Ree answered. "And to break us apart. Spirits can still feel pain."

Several more grenades were tossed at the group, sending bodies flying. They even knocked down a few of their own guys on the bikes. No sooner did these bikers hit the ground than they were grabbed and dragged into the sea of Guardians. They were pulled deep within the ranks, where the black swords were waiting.

Damon's soldiers were causing a lot of damage, but it was the Guardians who were knocking off spirits. It made me think that Adeipho's defense might have been pretty smart after all. Things looked even better after a new team of Guardians arrived, running from the large doors to our right that led to the train tracks.

"Archers," Ree explained. "We have some tricks of our own."

The new Guardians fanned out along the wall leading to the tracks, each kneeling and drawing their bow. I didn't think that arrows would do much damage, until they let loose and hit their targets. These weren't ordinary arrows. They were fitted with some kind of explosive tips. Wherever they hit, a small explosion erupted. The arrows blew out huge chunks of marble railing along the landing, driving the soldiers back to the doors. Some were hit dead-on and I saw their bodies explode.

"That won't destroy them," Ree said. "They'll be back."

I had to keep reminding myself that these weren't real people. They were spirits.

"But if you don't destroy them, they'll just keep coming," I pointed out.

And they did. As the World War II soldiers retreated, they were replaced by a dozen more soldiers on horseback, each wielding a black sword. Most were dressed in armor, looking like avenging knights bent on causing as much destruction as possible. They expertly rode their horses down the stairs to the floor of the concourse, and charged into the sea of Guardians.

It was a slaughter. The Guardians on the ground swung at them with their swords and clubs but they did little or no damage. The riders, on the other hand, had the killer swords. They slashed at the Guardians, who tried to fend off the blows, and they did, but not often enough. One by one the Guardians started disappearing. They fought valiantly, and might have done okay if the riders had normal weapons.

"This is horrible," I said. "Adeipho has to get those black swords up front."

Adeipho was too busy to notice. He was the only Guardian doing any real damage to the invaders. He started going after the horseback riders, and succeeded in destroying several of them. But there were too many. The attackers were methodically wiping out row after row of Guardians, driving closer and closer to the information booth. To the Rift. Once they reached the circle of Guardians who were armed with the killer swords, it would be a fair fight, but at what cost? As each Guardian disappeared, I was witnessing the end of a life. Forever.

With horror I realized that I had made the wrong call. The Guardians weren't able to defend the Rift.

Ree looked to me, pained. I knew what she was thinking and was grateful she didn't say it. This was my fault.

"It's all right," she said softly. "Whether the battle happened now or a hundred years from now, the result would be the same."

"It's not over," I said. "We can still win this."

She looked down at the carnage below and said, "I don't see how."

Many Guardians broke away from the tight circle and started battling the riders out in the open, where they had more room to maneuver. It helped. Rather than standing up like rows of corn, ready to be mowed, some were able to run and dodge the black swords. I saw Adeipho's daughter fighting near her father. She was the only Guardian I knew and it killed me to think she might not exist much longer.

It wasn't looking good and Ree knew it.

She said, "There will be more of a fight once our swords are brought into play, but Damon's soldiers will outnumber us by then. When one falls, another will take their place."

"Then we have to go with my plan," I said.

"Your plan was to initiate this battle," Ree said with a raised eyebrow.

"No, I mean my other plan. Let me go through the Rift. Better still, we'll both go. If the Guardians lose, then Damon won't think twice about going through and he'll track down the poleax for sure. We've got to get it before he does."

Ree looked down, sadly, at the battle below. Her Guardians were disappearing quickly, with few casualties on the other side.

"I can't go through the Rift," she said.

"Can't or won't?"

"Won't. It's not right."

"Tell that to Damon."

Ree was torn. She knew the battle was as good as lost. She glanced up at the far landing to see that the tank's cannon was still trained on us. If we stood or showed our faces, I had no doubt that it would unload again. Behind it, several more of Damon's soldiers were gathering. They didn't run down the stairs and attack. They watched the scene below. Waiting. Like vultures.

"That's their bench," I said. "As soon as their guys start going down, their replacements will jump in and pick up the fight. Adeipho can fight, but he miscalculated. The Guardians are going to lose the Rift."

Ree stared out at the horror for a good long while. I wished I could have read her mind. On the floor near our feet was her own black sword. She picked it up and examined it, as if hoping to find inspiration. Or hope.

She then looked to me and with tears in her eyes she declared, "I'll get you to the Rift, but I won't go through with you."

I stole a peek down at the information booth. There was absolutely nothing Rift-like about it.

"Where is it?" I asked.

"You have to enter the booth," she explained. "Once inside, my vision will disappear and you will see the dark hole. It's nothing more dramatic than that. A dark hole."

"And I just walk inside?" I asked.

Ree shrugged. "That's how I got here."

I reached my hand out and said, "Give me the sword. If you're not going through, then I don't want you anywhere near the fight."

She shook her head. "You forget, Coop. My Guardians

think you are as much of an enemy as Damon's soldiers. They haven't been won over by your charm."

"Yeah. Hard to believe," I said.

"I'll bring you to the Rift, Cooper," Ree said. "After that you're on your own."

"What should I do when I find the poleax?" I asked. "How do I destroy it?"

"I don't know," she replied. "You may not want to. That weapon may be the only way to destroy Damon."

I understood. So many thoughts shot through my head, mostly about what would happen once I went through the Rift. Would I actually be a physical being again? Would I get my old body back? That wouldn't be so great. Last time I saw it I was lying at the bottom of Thistledown Lake under a layer of silt. I didn't even want to think about how much damage was done to me by that speedboat. I had to believe that if I got that body back, I'd end up dying again and land right back here in the Black. Or the Blood. There was a good possibility that going through the Rift was an automatic ticket to hell.

Suddenly my smart idea wasn't feeling all that smart. But it was the only thing I could think of.

"Do one thing for me?" Ree asked.

"What is it?"

"Tell Marsh that I love him and that I'm sorry."

That gave me hope. Maybe there really was a chance that I'd get my life back.

"Done," I said.

Ree clutched her sword, took my hand, and said, "Let's get you out of here."

28

As soon as we made a move to run down the stairs, the tank unloaded.

Whoever was in that thing was acting like a sniper, keeping us in his sights, waiting for us to breathe. The shell hit the wall overhead and blasted out a section of ceiling. The concussion nearly knocked me off my feet but I managed to keep going and pull Ree through to the staircase before the bulk of the debris crashed down.

"It'll take a while for him to reload . . . I think," I said.

Ree didn't hesitate. She held on to my hand and led me down the stairs and onto the floor of the main concourse.

It was chaos. Small battles were happening everywhere. Many Guardians were desperately trying to unseat the riders on horseback and most paid the price with their lives. A quick glance to the information booth showed me that the Guardians with the spirit-killing swords had finally entered the war. While many stayed back, maintaining a defensive ring around the Rift, far more jumped into the battle.

Ree led me to the wall with the ticket windows and we made our way along quickly. Keeping our backs covered by the wall was a smart idea, though eventually we would have to fight our way through the war zone if we wanted to get to the Rift.

The Guardians were claiming some victims of their own, but just as one of Damon's soldiers fell, another picked up the sword and took his place. It seemed like they had a limitless number of replacements, where many of the Guardians had been destroyed.

I heard the roar of a motorcycle engine powering up behind us and turned to see one of Damon's soldiers headed our way with his black sword held high.

"Look out!" I screamed at Ree and pulled her close to me.

Ree stood straight, braced herself, and held her own sword up, ready to take the guy on. The rider had gotten to within ten feet of us when a Guardian came running up from the side and selflessly made an open-field tackle and knocked the guy off his bike. The biker never saw him coming. The bike toppled out of control and flew across the floor, barely missing us.

Another Guardian ran up to the fallen rider and nailed him with his black sword. In an instant, the rider was dust. The Guardian who finished him off turned to us with a big smile.

"I told you, Chicken Coop, I see everything."

"Bernie?" I shouted in surprise.

Bernie the mailman winked at me and jumped back into the battle. I looked to Ree with confusion.

She shrugged and said, "I told you, we've collected a lot of spirits. And Damon wasn't the only one sending out scouts."

Between us and the Rift were dozens of spirits in battle. Even if we didn't fight any of them, with so many black swords flying around we could easily be hit by a random swing.

"Father!" came a familiar cry.

Adeipho's daughter was battling two of Damon's soldiers not far from us. One was a United States Civil War rebel and the other looked like a homeless guy from the year one. Both had black swords. They were in an archway that led out of the concourse and directly beneath a heavy, massive clock that had to be twenty feet in diameter.

I made a move to help her but Ree held me back.

"Don't," she warned. "It would be suicide."

As tough as it was to see so many spirits being destroyed, they were all strangers. But I knew Adeipho's daughter, even if it was only to fight her. I couldn't let her die without trying to help. I pulled away from Ree and started for her but I was cut off by Adeipho himself. The girl's father launched himself into the fight before I could get close, taking on both soldiers. She backed off, which was smart. There were too many black blades flying around.

Ree wasn't as interested in the fight as I was. Her attention was on the opposite side of the concourse. The side where the large metal and glass doors that led to the train platforms were shut tight.

"Look," she said.

Damon's soldiers had methodically battled many of the Guardians into a single group in front of the train doors. Most of the Guardians didn't have black swords and those who did were struggling to protect the rest. Damon's soldiers, some on horseback, some on motorcycles, had backed them all up against one of the closed gates.

"What are they doing?" I asked.

I didn't have to wait long for the answer. It came charging

through the wall behind the trapped Guardians. A hurtling locomotive engine smashed through the door, crushing the surprised Guardians under its metal wheels. The train must have been traveling at full speed to have continued off the end of the track with that kind of force. The metal doors were blown out and the entire wall crumbled and cracked around it, crashing down onto the floor, sending bodies flying everywhere. The engine didn't get far into the terminal but the damage was devastating.

Damon's soldiers knew it was coming and had backed off at the last moment. Once the train stopped moving, they quickly leaped forward and attacked the dazed victims, finishing them off one by one.

It was the single most horrifying sight I'd seen yet. It wasn't a battle, it was a slaughter.

Many of Damon's soldiers let out a cheer. Though there was still a tight ring of Guardians around the Rift, they sensed that victory for Damon was near.

So did Damon.

Ree looked up toward the tank that was standing sentry, and gasped.

Damon had arrived. He was on horseback, standing on top of the platform next to the tank, surveying the carnage like a conquering hero.

"Sure," I said, scoffing. "He doesn't show up until the battle is almost over."

Damon carefully made his way down the stairs, on horseback, surrounded by several soldiers with black swords.

Adeipho was still battling the two soldiers beneath the clock. He took one out with a back slash to the head. As the second was about to deliver his own killing blow, Adeipho's daughter rushed in and skewered the would-be killer. Adeipho's only acknowledgment to his daughter that she had saved his life was a quick nod.

"Adeipho of Ehalon!" Damon called.

Adeipho whirled to see Damon approach. He stood up straight. There was hatred in his eyes. Damon pulled his horse to a stop, dismounted, and pulled out his own black sword.

"I have waited centuries for this," Damon hissed.

"Yes, for centuries and until I was battle weary," Adeipho replied, breathing hard. "It is still your way."

"You have lost, Adeipho," Damon announced. "Drop your weapon and I will consider sparing your soul."

Adeipho wheezed a laugh. "And that is why you never earned Alexander's trust, Damon. You are a liar. And a coward. You have no honor and never will."

Damon's eyes flared. "I am and have always been a soldier!"

"A soldier so desperate to prove his worth to Alexander that he scarred his own face to create the illusion that he had actually led his men into battle."

Damon's hand went back to his scarred cheek.

"Yes, we knew of your pathetic treachery, Damon. We laughed at you. The pompous warrior who only raised his sword when the battle was complete."

Damon stood tall and said, "And now I will raise it against you."

Damon charged at Adeipho. It seemed like suicide. He wasn't the battler that Adeipho was. His only chance would be if Adeipho was too tired to fight back.

Adeipho's daughter jumped forward to try and protect her father, but she was instantly smothered by Damon's soldiers and dragged away, her black sword useless.

Damon attacked, hammering at Adeipho with his own black sword. Adeipho easily knocked away every thrust with little or no effort. It didn't matter that Adeipho was exhausted. Damon was no match for him.

Seeing that their leader was in trouble, a few of Damon's soldiers moved in to protect him.

"No!" Damon screamed, motioning for them to move back. "This victory will be mine alone."

Adeipho laughed, which sent Damon into a rage. He charged again, flashing his black sword from every angle. Adeipho parried each attack without bothering to strike back. It looked as though it would only be a matter of time before Damon burned himself out.

"It's coming down to this," I whispered to Ree. "Adeipho's going to destroy him."

Damon continued to attack, but he had a strange style. He would swing, then move to his left. Attack and then take a step forward. Adeipho had no trouble defending himself as the odd dance moved them across the floor . . . with Damon leading.

Most of the fighting across the rest of the concourse had stopped. The ring of Guardians remained around the information booth, but the rest of the Guardians and soldiers had stopped battling one another and drifted closer to witness the fight between Adeipho and Damon. I had to believe they were all thinking the same thing I was . . . what had happened before was prelude. The outcome of this war was going to be determined by this fight, the battle between leaders. One would win, the other would be destroyed. It was as simple as that.

Damon faked an attack to Adeipho's right, which sent Adeipho moving quickly to his left, and between two of Damon's soldiers. Damon had craftily maneuvered him into that spot and the soldiers were ready. They each grabbed one of Adeipho's arms and stripped him of his spirit-killing sword.

"No!" Adeipho's daughter called as she fought to get away. "You fight like a coward!"

Damon ignored her. His confidence was back.

The two soldiers shoved Adeipho back toward Damon, unarmed. Damon took a few swings, trying to end it quickly, but Adeipho dodged out of the way. As strong a warrior as he was, he wouldn't last long with Damon swinging that spirit-killer. Adeipho jumped at one of Damon's soldiers and grabbed the shield from his hands. Damon swung at him, missed Adeipho, and slashed his own soldier, destroying him. Adeipho bought himself a little more time but unless things changed, his death was inevitable.

I knew how to change things.

"This is our chance," Ree said, and made a move for the Rift.

"No," I said, grabbing her arm. "It can't end like this for him."

"There's nothing we can do," she argued.

I reached out and grasped the handle of her black sword. Ree's first instinct was to pull it away from me, but I held firm.

"Without this I may not get you to the Rift," she cautioned.

"Yeah, but my money's on Adeipho," I said with confidence.

With a resigned nod, she released her grip and I took the sword. Pushing past soldiers from both sides, I ran close enough to the fight so that Adeipho would hear me. I had to act fast, before Damon's soldiers could stop me.

"Adeipho!" I yelled as I slid the black sword across the floor toward him.

Adeipho gave me only a glance, but it was enough. Damon hammered down at him, but Adeipho blocked the attack with the shield and dove to the floor. With outstretched arms he scooped up the sword and jumped back to his feet.

Damon tripped back a few steps in surprise, but he wasn't through. As Adeipho raised the sword, Damon attacked with force, moving Adeipho backward. Adeipho went back into defensive mode, warding off the blows, waiting for his chance to strike. All he needed was one good shot and Damon would be done.

Damon swung wildly toward Adeipho's right side, missing him badly. All it did was move Adeipho to his left a few steps. A critical few steps. He tensed up, waiting for Damon's next attack.

But Damon stood still. He lowered his sword and held out his hands as if to say, "I'm finished."

"Is that the end?" Adeipho asked.

"Not quite," Damon answered, and lifted his hand high into the air. It was a signal. *BOOM!* The tank's cannon erupted. I had nearly forgotten about it. I looked up to see that the smoking cannon was trained on a spot above Adeipho's head. The shell hit the giant clock that hung between two columns. The heavy clock exploded and, with a scream of wrenching metal, fell from its perch. Adeipho didn't have time to react. The clock fell directly on top of him.

"Father!" his daughter screamed.

The massive clock fell on its side and crashed to the floor, pinning Adeipho underneath. It didn't kill him. After all, he was a spirit. But it crushed his legs and ripped the sword from his hands. Adeipho was trapped, and helpless.

As the echo of the explosion drifted away, it was replaced by an eerie silence. The fighting had stopped. Each and every warrior stood still, staring at the scene in wonder.

Damon strolled to Adeipho and stood over his fallen enemy.

"My patience has at last been rewarded," he said with satisfaction.

Several Guardians made a move to get to Adeipho but

they were outnumbered and stopped by Damon's soldiers. The ring of Guardians protecting the booth didn't move. Their mission was more important than saving Adeipho.

"I knew this day would eventually come," Damon said. "It is proving to be more satisfying than I imagined."

Adeipho didn't struggle. There was nothing he could do. Instead of acknowledging Damon, he looked to his daughter. The poor girl was held, as helpless as her father. The bold soldier girl had become a terrified child who didn't try to hide her tears.

"I love you, Zoe," Adeipho called to her.

Zoe. Her name was Zoe.

"And I love you," his daughter said.

Damon gave Zoe a sideways look and stood tall, as if her words made him uncomfortable.

Adeipho looked up at him and said, "You still have no honor."

Damon replied, "And you are dirt under my boot."

He lifted his dark sword, its tip pointing straight down, and drove it into Adeipho's chest.

Ree ran up behind me and gasped in anguish.

Adeipho didn't flinch. He kept his eyes on Damon, defiant till the end. It was over in a second. The noble warrior dissolved into smoke, and was gone.

Nobody moved. The stunned silence was broken only by Zoe's sobs.

"I'm going for the Rift," I whispered to Ree.

I didn't wait for her to say anything and took off running for the information booth.

The Guardians surrounding the structure were the last line of defense. They looked to one another with confusion as I headed their way. I was afraid that as soon as I got within sword distance, I'd be smoke, but I kept going.

"Move!" I shouted.

"Let him through!" Ree commanded, running behind me. They were too confused to react.

"Open the door!" Ree shouted. "Now!"

A few finally responded and moved out of the way. I was going to make it. I would get through the Rift. My mind was already on to the next move. I had to find the poleax before Damon did.

My thinking was rudely interrupted by another explosion from the tank's cannon. I thought it was going to try to blow me apart before I made it to the Rift but figured the odds were with me. How could a cannon hit a moving target?

It wasn't trying to. It was locked onto a stationary one. A second after I heard the sound of the cannon, the information booth exploded. There was an eruption of smoke and debris as the bodies of several Guardians were launched into the air. I was hit by the force of the explosion and knocked onto my back. Something smashed down beside me and bounced with a loud clang. It was the brass clock frame that was on top of the information booth. My ears rang and my eyes were filled with smoke and grit but of course I wasn't hurt.

As the smoke gradually drifted away from the impact point, I scanned the concourse. There were bodies everywhere. I assumed that most of them were the Guardians that had surrounded the booth. I made out the wreck of the train. It was surreal to see the huge engine resting in a pile of debris inside the concourse. The Kodak sign was destroyed, along with the entire landing on the east side of the terminal. The platform to the right was scarred, but intact. The ancient tank stood vigil, ready to unleash its fury once again.

It all made sense, unfortunately. I had seen it all unfold. But there was one sight I wasn't prepared for. In the center of the concourse was the destroyed information booth. There wasn't much more left than shattered pieces of its marble base. Inside the circle of destruction there was a wide hole. A black hole. Though there was an entire concourse beneath it, no light shone from below. That was because it wasn't a physical hole in the floor. It was an open wound between two dimensions. An empty, hollow howl moaned from the depths. The sight was impossible, yet made absolute sense.

The Rift had been revealed.

I struggled to get to my feet, thinking I could run the twenty yards and dive through. There was still hope . . . but not for long. Before I could take a step, several of Damon's soldiers circled the Rift. There was no way I would get past those guys.

The battle was over. The Guardians had lost.

And Damon of Epirus, Damon the Butcher, had control of the portal between lives.

29

So many emotions fought for control of my head. Fear. Frustration. Sadness. Guilt. The emotion that trumped them all was anger, and not necessarily at Damon. Before he could seize complete control of the situation, I got to my feet and ran.

"Coop?" Ree called weakly.

My head was spinning from the power of the explosion but I managed to stay on my feet and keep going. A few of Damon's soldiers moved to stop me.

"Let him go!" Damon commanded. "I am done with him."

I almost wanted them to try and stop me, that's how badly I wanted to hit somebody. But the soldiers backed away and I picked up speed. I sprinted toward the destroyed Kodak photo, leaping over piles of debris, headed for the exit to the street. Once I blasted through the doors, I kept running. I was so angry that I had to unload and there was only one target that would do.

After sprinting along the empty street for three blocks, I reached the edge of Ree's vision. Beyond it was nothing. I stopped when I saw a Watcher, alone, standing on a far street corner. He looked to be a guy as old as my dad. There was nothing unusual about him, other than the fact that he held the power to save or condemn every spirit in the Black.

"I don't understand!" I screamed at him. "How could you let this happen? What is your function? Do you even know what just happened? What's *about* to happen? How can you stand there and not do a thing?"

The Watcher disappeared, which was what I'd expected but it still made me crazy.

"Come back!" I shouted. "Face me! I'm watching *you* now!"

Two different Watchers appeared on the opposite corner. A young girl and an elderly man. Like all the Watchers, they were silent and impassive.

"Why are you so special?" I demanded. "What gives you the right to judge us? You're supposed to be evolved spirits? Well, prove it! Why don't you help us poor, backward idiots?"

The two Watchers disappeared and were replaced by a single athletic-looking African-American young woman with a long braid of hair that reached to her waist. It didn't matter to me what she looked like. I knew they all thought the same way.

"Are you afraid? Is that it? Seriously? You don't want to judge Damon because he might send his soldiers after you? Well, that's exactly what's going to happen. There's no stopping them now. Hundreds of brave spirits gave their lives trying to do your job. That makes you no better than him."

More Watchers appeared, joining the woman. They were scattered across the street, some on the sidewalk, others far back on the next cross street.

"Damon's about to go back into the Light. Isn't that

against the rules? And he's not going to pay a friendly visit. If he finds that poleax, he could create more Rifts. What happens then? Are you going to stand around like a bunch of mannequins while the Light is overrun by the dead? The Black could empty out. Then what'll you do? Who are you going to watch then?"

Several more Watchers appeared. I'd never seen more than two or three at any one time so what was happening was definitely different.

"What about all those spirits who've been protecting the Rift? They weren't afraid. They sacrificed themselves to do what was right and now they'll never get the chance to move on to their better life. If anybody earned the right, it was them. Now they're gone. But not Damon. Oh no, Damon is alive and well. At least he will be as soon as he steps through the Rift. And you know whose fault that is? Yours. You're supposed to be rewarding those who deserve it and punishing the hopeless. But you haven't been doing that, have you?"

Still more Watchers appeared. I was drawing a pretty decent crowd.

"You know what I want to know? Who's judging *you*? Who decides if you're doing a good job or not? You better start watching out for yourselves because while you do nothing, worlds are about to collide. If I were judging you, I'd send you all to the Blood and start over. Maybe then some spirits who were truly evolved would step in and do what's right."

Many more Watchers began appearing. The street in front of me was suddenly packed with people, all wearing the same black clothing. No two looked alike. There were young kids and gray-haired grandparents. I saw every race imaginable. Their numbers continued to multiply, with everyone staring directly at me, silently. It was enough to make me finally shut up.

There had to be thousands of them. Multiple thousands.

They filled every inch of the street, stretching off in both directions and disappearing far back . . . and they kept coming. For as many people as were there, it was impossibly silent. I couldn't hear their breathing, the pumping of their hearts, or even their feet shuffling on the pavement. Unlike spirits in the Black, these spirits felt more like true spirits.

I stood there alone, facing them. Behind me the streets were as empty as when I'd arrived. If everything I'd heard about the Black was true, there was no reason for me to be afraid, because I was right. If these spirits had any reasonable sense of right and wrong, of justice and humanity, they *knew* I was right. If they didn't, then we were all in a lot more trouble than even Damon was capable of creating.

"I'm going back to be with the Guardians," I said. "If my spirit is going to die, I want to spend my last few moments with people I respect."

I was about to turn and leave when the mass of Watchers began moving forward. If a signal was given, I didn't hear it but there had to be something that happened because the entire group began walking at the exact same moment. I backed away with my eyes on the crowd. There may have been thousands of individuals, but they moved as one, like cogs in a massive machine. No expressions changed. No sound was made. Multiple thousands of shoes struck pavement but it remained as quiet as if the street were empty.

It wasn't until they had traveled halfway up the block that I realized what had happened: The Watchers had crossed into Ree's vision. I couldn't begin to guess what was happening, but I didn't want to be alone when it did so I turned and sprinted back toward Grand Central. I wanted to be with Ree. And even with Zoe. And with everybody else who was left after having fought so valiantly for the future of mankind.

I didn't stop running until I entered the terminal and

reached the archway beneath the destroyed Kodak sign that led into the main concourse. The place was in ruins. The only thing different from when I left was that the remaining Guardians had been herded together and sat huddled next to the wreck of the train engine. I counted twenty, down from what were probably two hundred when I ran off. What had happened to the others? Had they been executed the way Damon executed prisoners when he was alive?

The only consolation was that I saw Ree and Zoe with them.

A group of Damon's soldiers was guarding them, though it didn't look like they needed to. The Guardians had no fight left. Several more of Damon's soldiers surrounded the Rift, staring into the void and listening to the hollow howl that came from the depths. It seemed impossible that stepping into that opening would shoot anybody back to the Light, and to physical life.

The rest of Damon's army was gathered on the stairs leading up to the landing that held the tank. Sill more were on the landing, lined up along the shattered safety rail. Some had climbed up onto the tank. It was an impossible mix of warriors from many different eras and places. The one thing they had in common was that they had all bought into Damon's plan. Whatever he'd promised them, it looked as if he was going to deliver.

Damon was back on his horse. The proud victor. He rode past the defeated Guardians, looking down on them like they were rats. I could imagine him doing the same kind of thing when he was alive. He had murdered thousands of prisoners. If he decided to kill off Ree and the rest of the Guardians, I think that would have flipped me into insanity. If he so much as pulled out a black sword, I was ready to go after him . . . and die in the process.

"Thank you, Ree," he called down.

Mrs. Seaver kept her eyes on the ground.

"If not for you, none of this would have been possible."

He looked around at the shattered terminal. "Such an impressive vision," Damon continued. "This marvelous structure was created as a place for travelers to pass through on their way to grand adventures. How fitting that it now holds the portal through which I will initiate the greatest adventure of all time."

"It's no adventure," Ree said through clenched teeth. "It's the end of humanity."

Damon scoffed. "Perhaps. But what has humanity ever done for me?"

He looked to his soldiers, who crowded the landing, and he called out, "What has humanity done for any of us, other than to grind us up and throw us aside like spoiled grain?"

His soldiers grumbled in agreement.

"Not anymore. You have been patient. We have *all* been patient. I promised that your time would come, and with this victory it has."

A cheer went up from the soldiers. The Guardians seemed to shrink even more.

Damon rode his horse to the front of his mass of soldiers as he continued his speech.

"We each have different stories. We come from different places and different times. But we share the common bond of oppression. No more will we have to bow to those who unjustifiably consider themselves superior."

The soldiers cheered.

"Gone are the days when we must grovel so that others may thrive."

And cheered again.

"Kingdoms have been built by the sweat from our backs. The blood from our veins. And yes, by our very deaths. History may not remember us in life, but I promise you, they will know of us in death. Such a glorious moment as we march triumphantly back into the Light."

The soldiers went wild.

I slowly made my way along the north wall of the concourse, the wall that held the doors to the train tracks. I wanted to get close to Ree and Zoe.

When the soldiers settled down, Damon continued.

"The gift I give you today is a second chance. We are about to re-enter a world that is very different from what most of us remember. It is a world populated by the weak and the privileged. Their slothfulness was inevitable for they are descended from the same arrogant upper class that tortured us in life. The time has come to even the scales. It is our right—no, it is our duty to push aside the undeserving, the self-entitled, and assume the mantle of power that is rightfully ours."

More huge cheers. They were eating it up because Damon was telling them exactly what they wanted to hear. These soldiers must have been put together by Damon out of the dregs of many generations. They were people who resented those who had more than they did in life and had centuries of built-up animosity. What they didn't realize was that they were being led by a sadistic maniac. It scared me to think what they might do when he let them loose in the Light.

"We shall not inherit the earth!" Damon shouted. "We shall conquer it!"

They went nuts.

Damon motioned to one of his soldiers, who grabbed Ree by the arm and dragged her away from the group. Zoe tried to hold on to her but another soldier wrestled her away. Ree was shoved forward and fell to her knees at the foot of the stairs that held Damon's soldiers.

"There will be no mercy," he shouted to them, "for no mercy was ever shown to us! And to begin, I will personally execute the leader of the dogs who have stood in our way for so long."

Uh-oh. Was Damon the Butcher back to his old tricks? The Guardians sprang to life, jumping to their feet in protest, but were held back by the soldiers. Damon got off his horse and strode toward Ree. Ree wouldn't bow. Though she was on her knees, she kept her chin up and her eyes focused on Damon.

"First the arrogant Adeipho, and now the leader of the Guardians," Damon announced.

He pulled his black sword from its sheath. He was really going to do it. There was only one person in that terminal who had any chance of saving her.

"This is but a beginning!" Damon shouted. "We will become the avengers of the Light. People will fear us, for we have nothing to lose and we hold the ultimate power . . . the ability to execute them in the Light and then destroy their spirits in the Black."

Damon grasped his sword and raised it high over Ree's head.

I took off running.

The Guardians howled in protest. Zoe fought to get away.

Damon's back was to me. All eyes were on him. And his sword. And Ree. Nobody saw me coming.

The soldiers cheered Damon on, screaming for the death of the leader of the Guardians.

Ree didn't flinch.

Damon raised his sword higher . . .

And I hit him square in the back. What followed was a jumble of sound and fury. I wrestled Damon for the sword. It was all about the sword. If I could turn it on him, he'd be done and this whole nightmare could end.

Damon got his wits back quickly and kicked me away as several of his soldiers tried to jump in.

"Stay back!" Damon yelled. "I will execute him myself."

I jumped at the guy, launching myself feetfirst, and knocked him on his butt. He didn't stand a chance because I was out of my mind. I started punching at his head, his arms, his chest. I hit him so many times that he couldn't gather himself to control his sword.

I sensed more than heard the shouting and boos from the soldiers around me. It was like being in a gladiator pit where I was the underdog. Nobody wanted me to win, except for the Guardians and they couldn't help.

I threw more punches at Damon than I could count. He didn't know how to defend himself and paid the price. Destroying his spirit would be quick and painless but that wasn't good enough for me. I wanted him to hurt.

He struggled to get control but I was too fast. Too relentless. He stumbled backward, trying to stay on his feet but I didn't wait for him to fall. I pounced on him, knees first. When his back hit the ground, my knees drove into his chest. I heard him grunt in pain. It felt good.

His head snapped back and hit the floor. With a low cry he dropped the sword. As it clattered to the floor I went for it . . . and felt a burning pain in my lower leg.

I looked back to see that Damon's mouth was clamped on my calf, his pointed teeth tearing into my flesh. Like a shark attacking its prey his eyes rolled back into his head. My stomach turned. The guy was an animal. I coiled my other leg and drove my heel into his face. The pain was horrible as his teeth raked across my skin, but he let go.

And I grabbed the black sword.

His soldiers didn't stay back any longer. They came at me but I jumped at the still reeling Damon, put my foot on his throat, and held the tip of the sword to his chest.

"Stop!" I shouted to his soldiers.

These guys were vicious, but dumb. Nobody knew what to do. But I did. I had to destroy Damon. If I let him go, even if I was able to get Ree and Zoe and the other Guardians out of this vision, he would be back with more vengeance than before. No, it had to end right there.

"Ree!" I shouted. "Go back with the others."

She struggled to her feet. "What are you going to do?"

"Get everybody out of here," I commanded.

"And then what?"

"Yes, Foley," Damon asked. "Then what?"

I looked down to see him licking his lips, as if tasting the blood from having bitten me. But I wasn't bleeding. I was a spirit. He must have been doing it out of habit. Whatever the reason, it disgusted me.

"Do you have the strength to destroy me?" he asked. "That would be unwise, if you wish to regain your life."

"I don't care about my life," I said.

"But you care about Marshall Seaver, don't you? And your family? Destroying me won't end this. I have been grooming loyal followers for centuries. Destroy me and you'll be faced with thousands of angry spirits who would compete for the honor of tearing you apart."

I looked up at the sea of angry faces. I didn't doubt that Damon was right.

"Or we could strike a bargain," he said. "Release me and we both continue. As simple as that. It is wiser to live to fight another day."

All eyes in that terminal were on me. I had the power to finish off this demon forever. But what would happen then? The rest of his soldiers would end me and head for the Rift. I'd win the battle, but lose a very big war. As I stood poised over Damon, I didn't know what to do.

That's when the rumble began.

"What's that?" I asked, looking to Ree.

She had no idea. I looked at Damon. He was as confused as I was. The rumbling grew, like another train was about to barrel through the wall and make an unscheduled stop at the terminal.

"Look!" Zoe cried.

At the far end of the concourse, the end where the destroyed Kodak sign hung, there were two archways that led to smaller corridors and the street beyond. It was the street I had taken to the edge of Ree's vision, where I had encountered the Watchers.

The Watchers. I'd almost forgotten.

A black liquid that looked like oil rolled toward us from each corridor. It was heavy and thick and blacker than night. It stretched from wall to wall and was a few feet deep. It spilled in from the corridors to the main concourse as if it had purpose. The two tides of liquid joined together to form a single wave that kept rolling forward, growing as it moved across the floor.

I was mesmerized, which was a mistake. Damon knocked the sword away and jumped to his feet. I was too dazed to react. In an instant Damon had grabbed another black sword from one of his soldiers. I was afraid he'd go after Ree again, or turn his anger on me, but he was much more concerned about saving his own butt and he went for his horse.

I grabbed Ree by the arm and pulled her over to the other Guardians.

"What is it?" Zoe asked, stunned.

"I'm not sure," I said.

Damon's followers went from confusion to panic. The soldiers on the concourse floor, those closer to the dark oil, reacted first and tried to push their way up the stairs. The soldiers already on top didn't retreat as quickly, which created a confused pileup.

The black entity rolled across the floor toward the center of the concourse. When it hit the Rift, I expected it to pour down into the hole but it traveled over it like it wasn't even there. In seconds the Rift was completely covered by the dark liquid.

Damon pulled himself up onto his horse, but the animal was spooked and Damon had to fight to keep it under control as it bucked up on its hind legs.

"Should we run?" Ree asked calmly.

"To where?" I asked.

The Guardians were all strangely relaxed. They were prepared to accept the inevitable, whatever it was.

The wet, black tide kept coming until the leading edge was directly in front of us. It stopped moving forward, but began to rise up into the air. There was no question, this thing was guided by some form of intelligence. In seconds a slick, dark curtain had been created that was the size of a massive movie screen. Looking into the swirling darkness reminded me of the colorful mist that appeared when we moved through visions in the Black. Only those events were colorful and bright. This dark wall was anything but. As the dense wall grew, I felt as if I was staring at something evil.

Damon's soldiers wanted nothing to do with it. They scrambled over one another to get out of the terminal. Damon himself had finally gotten his horse under control but didn't move from the bottom of the stairs. He was as mesmerized as I was.

Ree said, "It's like a dark doorway between visions."

"It is, but why does it look like—?" I didn't have to finish the question because I knew the answer.

The center of the dark curtain parted to reveal a sight that made me want to scream. What we saw wasn't a glimpse into another vision, but another world. A dark, evil world. I saw winged creatures and hunched demons. There was no horizon. No sky. No life. At least no life as we knew it. I could hear the tortured screams of thousands. Millions. I didn't know if they were calling out for help or twisting in pain. It was a place of shadows and desperation. It was the final stop along the Morpheus Road.

"The Blood," I said with a gasp.

A vile wind blasted from the opening that smelled like rotten meat. The hot stench blew across us, sending dark grit into our eyes. To see I had to squint. I put my arms around Ree and Zoe, though I can't say if I was protecting them, or myself.

The putrid wind was powerful. It swept past us, swirling toward Damon's soldiers. Their confused cries turned to screams of terror as the wind grabbed them and with demonic force pulled them backward.

"Are you all right?" I screamed above the howling wind.

Ree and Zoe both nodded. Looking around I saw that none of the Guardians were being affected. The wind blew past them harmlessly. They weren't the targets. Neither was I.

Damon's soldiers desperately clung to anything to stop from being pulled into the void. They grabbed onto broken railings and twisted brass banisters and even the army tank. They tried to dig their nails into the hard floor, and into one another. It was useless. The first wave of spirits was lifted off their feet and sucked into the abyss, their screams echoing through the terminal.

Damon struggled with his horse to keep from being pulled in as one after another, with horrified cries of terror, his soldiers were dragged closer toward the last stop they would ever know. I saw them desperately grab at the air as they flew by. It was their last act in a place where they'd had the chance to make things right for themselves, but had chosen to embrace the hatred and anger they knew in life.

Some chose the easy way out. I watched in horror as several of Damon's soldiers took their black swords and cut their own throats, turning themselves to smoke rather than be sent into the abyss for all eternity.

Damon was putting up a good fight. Or at least his horse was. I didn't think either of them would last much longer.

Most of the soldiers had been pulled through the dark

curtain, but the wind didn't let up. I thought it was only fitting that Damon would be the last to be taken. Though the event wasn't over, I relaxed.

It was a mistake.

Damon changed tactics. Instead of battling against the relentless pull of the wind, he kicked his horse and charged across the bottom of the stairs, directly at us. We had no choice but to scatter. Ree and I fell one way, and Zoe fell the other. I took my arm from around Zoe's shoulder, and regretted it.

Damon galloped to where we were huddled, reached down, and grabbed Zoe by the throat. The girl was a battler but she was no match for this man who was driven by desperation. He lifted her up . . . and the wind stopped pulling at him. The guy had made a brilliant and ruthless move. He realized that Zoe wasn't being pulled into the Blood and he was using her to save himself. Zoe struggled to get away but Damon wrapped his arm around her and pulled her up onto the horse.

He looked down to me and called, "You did not think I would give up that easily, did you?"

I jumped up and tried to grab at Zoe, but Damon yanked his horse away from me and kicked it into a gallop. The horse, with Damon and Zoe aboard, charged back across the mouth of the abyss with no problem. On the far side, the colorful mist appeared and Damon galloped directly into it, disappearing, along with Adeipho's daughter.

As the last of his soldiers was pulled into the dark opening, the howling wind grew to a crescendo, drowning out the tortured screams of those within. Its mission complete, the black curtain closed, sealing the portal and choking off the last of the howls. The wall then lowered to the ground and slipped out of the concourse the same way it had come in, pulling back and moving over the floor like a liquid snake. It broke in two and disappeared down each of the two corridors that led away from the concourse, leaving no trace that it had ever been there.

The only spirits left in Grand Central were the surviving Guardians. And me. Strewn across the concourse were several black spirit-killing swords. The weapons had not been sucked into the Blood along with Damon's soldiers, which meant the fighters were defenseless against whatever they found in there. I liked that.

Ree looked shell-shocked. All the Guardians did.

"Why?" she asked. "After so many centuries, why were they sent to the Blood now?"

"I think Damon finally went too far," I said.

I didn't tell her about my discussion with the Watchers. Actually, it was more of a tirade. Whatever. It seemed to have gotten through to them. Or maybe it had nothing to do with me and the opening of the Rift was what had sealed Damon's followers' fate. Either way, the result was fine by me.

I glanced across the concourse to see that standing beneath the wreckage of the Kodak photo was a lone figure. A Watcher. It was the same older guy I had first seen when I ran to the edge of Ree's vision. He stood there, alone, expressionless. Maybe I imagined it, but it sure looked as though he gave me a slight nod the moment before he disappeared.

"We have to find Damon," Ree said. "He has Zoe."

"We will," I assured her.

Ree gazed around the terminal and saw something that made her eyes open wide. I wasn't so sure I wanted to have any more surprises, but I turned to look anyway.

"It's gone," she said, breathless.

I followed Ree to the center of the concourse. The other Guardians were right behind us. We walked closer to the destroyed booth to see . . . the Rift wasn't there. The floor of the information booth was just that. A floor. Lying on the spot where the Rift once was, was Zoe.

Ree ran to her and helped her sit up.

"Are you all right?" Ree asked.

Zoe looked around, dazed, trying to focus on her surroundings.

"Yes," she answered tentatively. "When we rode into the mist, everything went dark, and when I opened my eyes, I was lying here."

"Because he didn't need you anymore," I said.

"It was my fault he escaped," Zoe said, dropping her head.

"It wasn't," Ree said quickly. "There was nothing you could have done."

Ree stood on the spot where the Rift once was and stomped her foot. In spite of all the horror we had been through, she smiled.

"Damon created the Rift over two thousand years ago," she announced. "And today it's been closed, thanks to the sacrifice made by Adeipho and the Guardians."

I looked to Zoe and saw pride through her pain.

There was no cheering. No shouts of joy or victory. There were only tears and hugs. Adeipho and the Guardians had done their job. They had protected the Rift. Damon did not get through into the Light, nor did any of his soldiers.

The Guardians' mission was complete.

I wanted to say that the Watchers had also done their job, but there was too much I still didn't know about the Morpheus Road. I could only go as far as to say that the Watchers were every bit the force that the spirits in the Black thought they were. They just worked in mysterious ways.

There was only one issue not resolved, and it was a big one.

Damon was still out there. Somewhere. He may not have gone through the Rift into the Light, but that wouldn't stop him from his quest to find the poleax. We had won the battle, but the war was far from over.

And Marsh was still in Trouble Town.

30

There's a strange thing about being dead. It's really not so bad.

Besides the whole ancient-spirit-bent-on-revenge thing, that is. That part sucks. But if it weren't for that, the transition from the Light into the Black and having a vision of your physical life to help you work on your personal issues is really kind of a cool thing. I think that's why the spirits in the Black aren't all weepy and sad for the most part. They know that being there is as much a part of life as being in the Light.

It isn't all roses, though. Peeking back to your old life is great in theory, but it can also make things harder because it's a reminder of what you can't have anymore. I guess some people handle it better than others and maybe that's part of what it takes to move on to the next, better life. You have to let go of the past before you can accept the future.

But I didn't want to. I liked my life too much. That's why I was tempted by Damon's offer. But I couldn't go back, for all sorts of reasons. I was going to have to accept that and settle for the occasional glimpse into the Light to see what I was missing.

It's all that any of us could ask for.

"Are you okay?" I asked Ree. "You look as white as a ghost. Get it? White as a ghost?"

Ree gave me an impatient glare. "I'm fine."

She didn't look fine. She was tense. Way more tense than when she was facing down an army of ghost soldiers.

"Maybe you should wait awhile," I suggested.

"No," she said quickly. "It's time. It's past time."

"Okay," I said with a shrug, and held out my hand to her.

"You're shaking," I said. "It's going to be fine. Trust me."

She nodded and took my hand, and the two of us stepped through the swirl of colored fog into the Light. It was Ree's first visit there as a spirit, not counting the vision we saw of the mayhem on the lake. We were in the living room of my family's cottage on Thistledown Lake. It was night. The house was quiet. Ree looked around, skittish, as if she didn't belong and didn't want to be there. That is, until her eyes set on something. She let out a small gasp, and the tears were right behind.

What she saw was Marsh, her son, lying on the couch.

She squeezed my hand hard enough to break bones, if I had bones. I put my arm around her shoulder and wrenched my aching hand away from hers.

"Go see him," I said.

She didn't move. I think she was afraid to.

"It's okay," I said. "He won't bite."

Ree walked stiffly toward the couch and knelt down next to her son. It was the first time she had been close to him since she left on the fateful trip to Greece.

Marsh was wide awake, staring up at the ceiling. I couldn't begin to imagine what might be going through his head after all that had happened to him. Knowing Marsh, he was thinking hard, trying to understand. I wished I could help him.

Ree started to push his hair out of his eyes but stopped herself.

"I know he won't feel it," she said. "I just want to pretend like he might."

Seeing Ree watching her son, in tears, was like being on the other side of the looking glass. The departed spirit was broken up over losing a loved one who was still alive. The fearless leader of the Guardians of the Rift had become a mom again.

"It's the hardest part of dying," I said. "Both sides lose."

Ree stared at Marsh and smiled through her tears.

"He's grown up," she said. "I've missed so much."

"Now you can visit him as much as you want. You don't have to miss another thing."

Ree leaned closer toward her son and whispered, "I love you, sweetheart. I miss you."

I felt myself tearing up.

"And I'm sorry," she added.

I didn't want her to go there. This was about visiting Marsh, not dealing with the horrors of Damon and his quest.

"They know about my accident now," I said, wiping away a tear. "The search for my body starts tomorrow."

"How do you know that?" she asked.

"I peeked into the sheriff's office when they were questioning Marsh and Sydney about the accident. I think most everybody realizes I bought it. Everybody but Marsh, that is. He still thinks I'm alive. It's going to be a rough day for him."

"How could he possibly still think you're alive after all that's happened?" she asked.

"I don't know, but he's holding out hope."

She smiled. "Stubborn."

"Yeah," I said. "I wish I could be the one to tell him the truth. Before they drag the lake and pull out, well, me."

"Maybe you can," Ree said. "You've connected with him before."

I laughed. "Listen to you, throwing out the rules."

"You've done a lot worse than that," she said.

"True. But I wouldn't know how to tell him." My eye caught something on the table at the other end of the couch. "Then again . . ."

"What?"

I knelt down next to Ree, very close to Marsh's head.

"What are you doing?" she asked.

I leaned toward Marsh, closed my eyes, and concentrated. If there was ever a chance for spirits to communicate with the living, it was then. I had a strong connection with Marsh, but that was nothing compared to what he had with his mother. Together we couldn't miss.

I heard Ree gasp. I didn't have to look to know the ripple of color had appeared between me and Marsh. I leaned closer to him and blew, pushing his blond hair across his forehead.

"How did you do that?" Ree exclaimed.

Marsh reached up and brushed his hair back.

Ree gasped again.

"He felt that!" she exclaimed, her tears returning.

"C'mon, help me," I said.

I took Ree's hand and led her to the table where I pointed to one of the framed pictures on display. She understood.

"Concentrate," I said. "The stronger the connection between the spirit and the living, the better chance we have of creating the energy."

I knelt down next to the table and focused on the picture.

"I want to move it," I said.

She knelt beside me and held my hand.

Marsh sat up. He sensed our presence, I was sure of it. We had a short window to make it work. The picture was the birthday gift that Ree had given me years before. It was the photo she took of the African tribal elder and his great-grandchild. She called it *Eternity*. I didn't think the message would be lost on Marsh.

Ree and I focused on the picture. I heard a slight squeak. The frame twisted on the glass table, but Marsh didn't hear it. I squeezed Ree's hand, putting all my focus on the picture. The frame shook, tipped, and fell over.

"Incredible," was all Ree could say.

Marsh slid down the couch, reached for the picture, and picked it up. He wasn't even freaked out by the impossible event. He had been through too much. He looked at it with a frown of confusion. Then his expression changed. I saw it. It was so clear. He sat back on the couch and I knew that he had finally accepted the truth, because he started to cry.

"He knows," Ree said sadly.

"Nice, Ralph."

"I'm going back," she said, abruptly standing up.

"You don't have to. You can go see Mr. Seaver too."

"I know. But right now it's just . . . it's breaking my heart."

She backed across the room, all the while staying focused on Marsh, who was staring at the photo.

"Thanks, Coop," she said.

"For what?"

"Closure."

I nodded in understanding, but things were far from closed. Not with Damon still on the loose. Ree left for the Black but I didn't follow. I had other plans. Call it morbid fascination, but I wanted to watch the search for my body.

The searchers assembled throughout the night, but they didn't hit the lake until daybreak. At first it was cool seeing all the rescue vehicles and firefighters and volunteers swarming the lakeshore. Of course most of them were wasting their time. I knew where my body was. Still, knowing that so many people were out looking for me was good for the ego.

The fun didn't last. Seeing how tortured my mom and dad and sister were was tough. I knew what it was all leading to. By the time the rescue boats made their way to Emerald Cove and the divers splashed in, I'd lost my stomach for the adventure. I didn't need to see the last chapter of my physical life play out. Besides, I didn't particularly want to see my body after it had been underwater for a week. I'm a good-looking guy. I preferred to hang on to that image.

I also bailed on the moment when the official news of the discovery was delivered to my family. I didn't want to see that moment of pain. That's an experience no person, or spirit, should have to live through. I'd want to assure them that everything was okay and being in the Black was kind of cool and that I'd see them all again someday, but I knew that was impossible. If I couldn't make it better, I didn't want to be there.

I didn't miss my funeral, though. No way. I wonder how many people show up for their own funeral. Probably close to 100 percent. Why not? How many chances do you get to watch people gathered for the sole purpose of saying nice things about you? That wasn't something I wanted to miss and I'm proud to say that my funeral was packed. SRO. Psyche.

The service was at the old church on the Ave. I was glad to see my entire football team there, wearing their team jackets. Nice touch. Many other kids from Davis Gregory came along with teachers and relatives and friends of my parents. Man, they could have sold tickets. And there wasn't a dry eye in the house. That sounds cold because I know how genuinely upset people were, but I'd be lying if I said it didn't make me feel pretty good to know that so many people cared. There's the ego thing again. Everybody should attend their own funeral, unless they were jerks in life or something. That would be awkward.

The tough part was seeing my family. Mom and Dad were dazed. Sydney looked great, as usual. Leave it to her to find a black dress for a funeral that made it seem like she'd just come from a fashion shoot. I thought it was pretty cool how Marsh and Mr. Seaver sat with my family. I felt like I was part of the Seaver family and having them sit with mine made total sense.

I also didn't like seeing the casket. Having that thing sitting in the center aisle, covered with flowers, knowing my body was inside, was creepy. I could have done without that.

I was proud of Marsh. He's not comfortable speaking in front of people, let alone at a funeral, but he manned up and gave an awesome eulogy. I especially liked the way he ended it when he said: "Cooper taught me how to have fun. He made me laugh at things that most people wouldn't find funny. He taught me to take chances and not be afraid to fail. He taught me not to stress over details but to never accept second best. We visited Trouble Town more times than I can count, and I wouldn't have had it any other way. Does any of this sound familiar?"

Sydney actually smiled. That was a highlight.

Marsh continued, "I'm a better person for having known Cooper Foley, and that's something that won't change when memories fade. I'm going to make sure of it."

He then looked up to the ceiling, as if I was floating up

there, and called out, "And, Coop, wherever you are, I'll bet you're listening to all this and thinking you're something special after hearing all the nice things these people have said about you. Right? I don't blame you. And I want to say one more thing. I owe you."

I'm sure that everybody thought he was doing that for effect, but that wasn't so. He knew I was there.

"No problem, Ralph," I called back. He didn't hear it, but I'll bet he knew I said it.

I didn't want to go to the cemetery. That would have felt a little too final, especially the part about lowering the casket into the ground. Instead, I wanted to speak with somebody who could actually hear me and talk back. Who knows? Maybe that meant I was moving on and accepting my fate.

I left the Ave in the Light and went to Ree's vision in the Black. I wanted to tell her about how awesome Marsh was. I wanted her to know how proud I was of him, and how glad I was to have known him.

Arriving at her vision of Grand Central Terminal was eerie. Nothing had changed since the Watchers had opened up the portal into the Blood except that the black swords were gone. I figured they had been collected by the remaining Guardians and hoped they'd never have to use them. Seeing the terminal in such bad shape made me wonder if Ree's vision would ever return to normal. Could the terminal be repaired? Or would it be this way for as long as Ree was in the Black?

"Hello?" I called out. "Ree?"

No answer. I jogged down the stairs and made my way to the subway platform, thinking she would be in her rolling home. The subway car was there, but Ree wasn't. There were no Guardians around, either. I didn't think much of it. She could have been anywhere. For all I knew she was at the cemetery in the Light, paying her respects at my funeral. I didn't want to hang out until she got back. The place was giving me the creeps.

I left her vision and went to see Gramps. There was a lot we had to talk about and the sooner we got things out in the open, the sooner we could go back to being normal . . . or at least what passed for normal. When I stepped out of the colorful cloud onto his property, I sensed that something was off. The day was darker than usual. The sky was overcast. It was definitely his vision, though, because it was fall and the vegetable garden was still loaded with tomatoes. I ran onto the porch and knocked on the door.

"Gramps? It's me!"

No answer. I pushed the door open and stepped inside.

"Hey! Gramps!"

Nothing. I stepped back out onto the porch to see the trees swaying in a stiff wind. I told myself that nothing was wrong. Gramps could have been at Meade's Pharmacy sucking down one of Donna's famous malteds. That's what I told myself, but I wasn't so sure I believed it. Was it possible that after admitting to the truth, Gramps had ended up moving along the Morpheus Road? It was possible. The question was, which way would he have gone?

I needed to see a familiar face, so I jumped off the porch and ran toward Maggie's house. The colored swirl appeared in front of me and by the time I vaulted the split rail fence between properties, I had left Gramps's vision and arrived in Maggie's.

The day didn't get any brighter. The last time I was there her vision had begun to warm up, along with Maggie's future. Whatever changes had been made, were gone. The chilly wind blew through the barren trees under dark gray skies, banging the barn door open against the outer wall.

"Maggie!" I called out.

I wasn't ready to panic, but I was close. Something was

wrong. Everyone I knew in the Black was missing. Their visions were intact but they'd changed. They felt dead. There's no better word to describe it. The life of the visions was gone, and so were the people I cared about. Had they all moved on to another life? Did visions remain after a spirit moved on? That wasn't likely.

But something had definitely happened, and it wasn't good.

I wished there had been at least one black sword still lying around Grand Central because I would have gone back for it. It would have given me a lot more confidence in doing what I had to do. The calm after the storm was over. I had to find answers and I knew where to get them.

I had to go to Damon's vision.

When I stepped through the colorful fog, I was ready for anything. I leaped out on full alert, expecting a fight. What happened instead was . . . nothing. Literally nothing. I left Maggie's vision and landed in limbo. It was a sea of pure white. There was no up or down, east or west. I wasn't floating, but there was no ground beneath my feet. There was no sound, either. Or smell or sensation of any kind.

I thought I had taken a wrong turn. This wasn't Damon's vision. This was no vision at all. It was wrong and I feared it had something to do with the disappearance of Ree, Maggie, and Gramps.

I was about to leave and step into my own vision when I sensed movement. Turning quickly, I saw that I was no longer alone. Standing ten yards from me was a Watcher. It was the older man who was in Grand Central Terminal at the end of the battle.

After I got over the surprise, an impossible thought hit me.

"I hope this isn't heaven," I said. "Because if it is, I'd just as soon stick with the Black."

Another surprise came . . . when he answered.

"Help."

I thought for sure he said it, though his lips hadn't moved.

"Did you say something?" I asked.

"Help," he repeated. Again, no lip movement.

"Is that you?"

He nodded.

I didn't know if I'd heard him, or if he had somehow jacked directly into my brain, but whatever it was, a Watcher was communicating with me.

My heart started to race.

"Where are we?" I asked.

"His vision is gone," the guy said. Or thought. Or whatever it was he was doing.

"This was Damon's vision?" I asked.

He nodded.

"What happened?"

"It was taken from him," he communicated.

"By who? You? The Watchers?"

He nodded.

"Why haven't you sent him to the Blood?" I asked.

"That would be foolish," the guy answered.

"But . . . why? If anybody deserves it, geez."

"You have encountered his followers here in the Black?" the guy asked.

"Well, yeah."

"After seeing what he accomplished here, imagine what he would do if his spirit was united with the souls of the damned."

I think my mouth fell open. I hadn't even considered that. The army he put together with spirits in the Black would be Little League compared to the force he could assemble in a place that was full of the worst humanity had ever produced. The possibility was too horrible to imagine, which is probably why I hadn't.

"That's why you've kept him in the Black all this time?" I asked, numb. "To keep him away from the spirits of the damned?"

He nodded.

I wanted to cry.

"Where is he?" I asked.

"He seeks the weapon he calls a poleax. He must not be allowed to retrieve it."

"So stop him!" I shouted. "You guys are the bosses, right? You have all the power. Why can't you just destroy him?"

"We do not have that ability," he answered. "The spirits of the living must decide their own destiny. That is why we look to you."

"Me?"

"You and Marshall Seaver and those around you have been placed in this position by circumstance. You have not asked for the responsibility, yet it is yours. Only a spirit of the Black can stop another. If Damon retrieves the poleax, the Morpheus Road will be destroyed, and with it, humanity as it has always existed."

For the first time I understood what Marsh went through when he couldn't handle pressure. I felt nauseous.

"This isn't fair!" I shouted. "All I did was go out for a boat ride at night. It was stupid, but I don't deserve this."

"Agreed."

My mind raced to a thousand different scenarios and possibilities and ways to stay as far away from this particular Trouble Town as possible, but came up empty.

"Where's Maggie? And Ree and my gramps?"

"I do not know."

"How could you not know? You're a Watcher!"

He didn't answer.

I paced, which is weird to say because I was in limbo. There was no sense of direction or space. I had to think.

Where was Damon? What was he doing? What was he thinking? Did he have something to do with the disappearances? And the change in the visions? With his soldiers gone, he had no backup and no vision of his own. He was down, no doubt, but he wouldn't give up. No way. Not as long as he still had hope, and that hope was in the Light. The poleax. He could go after the poleax, and for that, he would go after Marsh.

That was it. That would be his plan.

I needed a plan of my own.

"If I'm gonna help you, I need you to help me," I said. "The poleax is in the Light and Damon is pretty much having his way there. I have to be able to compete with that."

"What are you asking?"

"I need Marsh to see me," I said. "If all I can do is move around some seeds or create a little wind, I don't stand a chance."

The Watcher stared at me for a moment, thinking. He then answered, "Damon's abilities do not come from us. He has developed them over the years."

"C'mon!" I shouted. "Throw me a bone! You must be able to do something!"

He nodded. "We will do what we can, but it will not be anything near what Damon is capable of. We do not interfere with the Light."

"I'll take whatever I can get. And I need something else."

"What is that?"

"Full immunity. If I influence things in the Light, I want to know that you're not going to bounce me into the Blood. Or anybody else who helps me either. I'm not trying to alter the course of history, I'm trying to stop somebody else from doing that."

He hesitated, then nodded.

"All right, good. I'll trust you on that. You're a higher being, right? You don't lie."

I took a deep breath to calm down. The guy standing across from me looked about as normal as could be. But he wasn't. He represented a power that was greater than anything I could imagine, and he was looking to me for help. How scary was that?

"Where's Damon now?" I asked.

"In the Light. With your friend."

"Now?" I screamed. "Right now? Why didn't you tell me?"

"If I told you before, you would not be as prepared as you are now."

I wanted to throttle the guy, even if he was a superior being.

"You better hope Marsh is okay, because if anything happens to him, I'm coming after *you*," I threatened.

"If Damon succeeds, you won't have to bother," the guy replied, and disappeared.

"Damn!" I screamed to nobody but me.

It was on now. It was *really* on. I wished I knew what to do about it. I took a last look around at the void that was once Damon's vision. I was in the wrong place. The wrong reality. The colored fog appeared. When I stepped through it . . .

I arrived in the center of what looked like a massive sea of walking corpses.

31

Had I made a mistake?

Did I leave the Black only to make a wrong turn and end up in the Blood? It sure seemed like it. As far as I could see there were rotten cadavers, standing together in a macabre sea of gruesome humanity . . . a dead man's party in a cemetery full of upturned graves. It was as if a demonic earthquake had awakened the dead.

I didn't want to be anywhere near there and would have taken off if I hadn't heard a familiar voice.

"I don't know where to look," the frightened voice said.

I turned quickly to see Marsh . . . and someone I didn't recognize. It was a tall black-haired guy who had on a short white tunic thing that was edged in gold. He was built like a defensive end with clothes that made him look like a noble warrior from ancient times . . .

. . . and he was stalking Marsh. "The poleax is in the

Light," the guy bellowed with a deep, gravelly voice. "But the answer is in the Black." They moved around a reflecting pool that was built in front of an old mausoleum.

Poleax? Why was this guy looking for the poleax? Who was he? I moved quickly to get a better look at him and got my answer. His face was covered with deep scars. It was the one thing he hadn't changed about himself. He liked those scars. They were his badge of honor . . . that he had awarded to himself.

It was Damon. And this wasn't the Blood. It was a cemetery in the Light. The sea of corpses was another illusion that Damon had created to scare Marsh. He had even changed himself into looking like the kind of warrior he imagined himself to be. He had that kind of power in the Light.

Marsh backed away but couldn't go far because he was trapped by the walking corpses.

"The answer has always been in the Black," Damon muttered.

"What is the Black?" Marsh cried. "What does that mean?"

I was about to jump between them when Damon reached out, grabbed one of the corpses, and ripped off its arm. It was so sudden and violent that it froze me in place. He wrenched off the hand and fingers casually as if it were a wishbone. His work complete, he held the bone like a weapon.

"You will walk the road and enter the Black," he said. "You will find the poleax."

"Tell me what the Black is. Where is it?" Marsh asked nervously. "How do I get there?"

Marsh was losing it and I didn't blame him. I somehow had to tell him that Damon couldn't hurt him. He was a spirit, and like the walking corpses, the bone was an illusion.

"There is only one way to enter the Black," Damon said, smiling.

"Okay, how?"

"You must die," he said as he rounded the pool, getting closer to Marsh.

He was toying with my friend because he couldn't actually kill him. It was all about scaring him into doing what he wanted. Marsh backed away, looking around for an escape route, but there was nothing out there but thousands of corpses. They were illusions, but Marsh didn't know that.

Damon stopped and looked down at him. "This will be painful," he said while tapping the bone into his other hand for effect. "This is your choice. I will allow you to stay in the Light if you bring me the poleax."

He started walking again, stalking my friend. I wanted to tell Marsh not to be scared but I didn't have Damon's abilities.

"Answer me," Damon growled. "Do you live in the Light? Or die in the Black?"

Marsh turned away from Damon. I think he was going to run, but his plans changed. Instead of taking off, he stopped short with a shocked look on his face. He stood there with his mouth open and his eyes wide. As the saying goes, it looked like he had just seen a ghost, which was exactly what had happened.

Marshall Seaver was looking at *me*.

The Watcher had kept his promise. I was in business.

I leaned casually against a marble statue, folded my arms, and with a smug smile looked past Marsh to Damon . . . and gave him the finger.

Damon's eyes flared with anger.

"Is this what you wish?" he called to me. "For him to join you?"

I ignored him and looked to Marsh. "Can you hear me, Ralph?" I asked.

Marsh didn't react. I held my hands up, gesturing for him not to move.

"You can save him," Damon bellowed. "End this now. Make him see."

"Give me a break!" I shouted to Damon. "You can't hurt him. This is all an illusion, just like your new look. Love the dress. Is that what all the cool generals wore back in the day?"

Marsh started moving away, using the opportunity to escape while Damon was focused on me. I didn't want him to do that. Damon's illusions weren't dangerous in themselves, but they made people do things that could hurt, like running somebody over with a speedboat. The safest place for Marsh to be was right where he was, which was the last place he wanted to be.

I held my hands up again and shook my head, trying to get him to stay still but as soon as my hands went up, they flickered. The act of moving took away my ability to be seen. The Watcher was right, whatever power they could give me wasn't much compared to what Damon could do.

Marsh stopped moving, but when he did, Damon charged. With nowhere to go, Marsh cowered to the ground. Damon raised the bone high as if ready to bash him. It was his last desperate attempt to get Marsh to do what he asked.

"I will let you live," he snarled at Marsh. "If you bring me the poleax."

I had to let Marsh know that Damon's threat wasn't real. I took a few steps closer so he could get a good look at me. If he believed that he was really seeing my spirit, he would listen. I lifted both my hands, and as they flickered between ghostly and invisible, I flashed Marsh the double okay sign.

The effort cost me. I disappeared. I could no longer see my hands and from the confused look on Marsh's face, neither could he. I could only hope that I'd gotten my message across.

"What is your answer?" Damon bellowed.

Marsh was my best friend. There were a lot of reasons for that but one was that he trusted me. I'd given him a hard time about not wanting to grow up and face reality, but I was wrong. Marsh had grown up, all right. He was the exact guy he should be.

And he still trusted me.

I watched with pride as he got up off the ground, dusted off his pants, and stared Damon square in the eye.

"I'm not helping you," he said to Damon of Epirus. Damon the Butcher.

Damon the Vanquished.

"Raaaaaa!" Damon screamed so loud I felt the ground shake.

He brought the bone down hard, jamming it into the ground. The bone exploded into a million sharp bits that blew out from the point of impact, spreading impossibly across the cemetery. They flew through Marsh like tiny white phantoms that had no more effect on him than if they were shadows.

The corpses weren't so lucky. As the wave of bone fragments spread, it erased the horrifying zombies. In seconds, every last one was gone, leaving only the destroyed cemetery.

And Damon.

The warrior spirit was down on one knee, his face to the ground. Beaten.

Marsh said, "You have no physical power, do you? Cooper knew that."

"There are worse things than physical pain," Damon said, breathing hard. "I gave you a choice. Now you must live with the consequences. How much are you willing to endure before giving me what I seek?"

Damon looked up to Marsh. Marsh didn't even flinch.

"You will walk the road with me," he said. "And you will suffer."

Damon raised his fist and punched the ground. The impact created a violent earthquake. Marsh stumbled, though I wasn't sure if it was because the ground was actually moving or because he thought it was. Either way, he tripped and fell into the reflecting pool.

The whole world went blurry as if it was being shaken out of focus. As the rumbling lessened, I was able to make out details once again and realized that the cemetery had returned to normal. Grass covered the graves. Tombstones were no longer strewn about. The sun even poked through the cloud cover, turning the haunted day into a beautiful, warm afternoon.

And Damon was nowhere to be seen.

Marsh, on the other hand, was lying in the reflecting pool, soaking wet. I walked toward him and was surprised to see my own legs. I was still semitransparent, but I was no longer invisible. I wished more than anything else that he could hear me. I wanted him to know how proud I was of him. But he also had to know that it wasn't over and that I was going to do everything I could to help him.

But all I could think of saying was, "Man, I thought for sure you were going to take off."

Marsh looked up quickly. He had heard me!

I couldn't help but laugh. "Kinda creepy to be swimming in a cemetery, Ralph."

He spun around and we made eye contact. He could see me too. I had no idea why it was happening, but I didn't question it.

"Close your mouth, you look like a trout," I said.

The effort was too much. I disappeared, but then suddenly found myself looking at Marsh from the other side of the reflecting pool, as if I had been blown there by the wind.

Marsh looked around frantically until he saw me. He stepped out of the pool and walked toward me in a daze.

"I . . . I don't understand . . . Cooper? What's happening?"

"Very cool, Ralph. That took guts," I said.

"Not really. I trusted you."

"I'm trying my best," I said. "It's hard. I don't have much control."

I disappeared again, and reappeared a few feet to my left. It was totally annoying.

"Are you okay?" Marsh asked.

"Well, no. I'm kind of dead, Ralph. But it's cool in the Black. Sort of."

"What is the Black?"

I disappeared again. It was clear that my time and abilities were limited. I had to make the most of it.

"Cooper!" Marsh called out.

I reappeared again on the far side of the memorial garden. "You're in Trouble Town, Ralph."

"Yeah, tell me about it. Who is Damon?" he asked.

I disappeared again and showed up on the other side of the pool.

"A total foul ball," I answered. "But you know that. Don't help him. Whatever happens, whatever you see, don't help him."

"What is the poleax?" he asked.

"I don't know for sure, but he wants it bad. It's why he killed me, Ralph. To get to you, to get the poleax."

Marsh looked about as confused as I'd ever seen him. "But why?" he cried. "I . . . I don't know anything about a poleax."

I disappeared again, and then showed up directly in front of Marsh. He jumped back in surprise. Oops. It wasn't like I had a choice.

"I'm doing what I can to help you," I said. "You know that, right?"

He nodded. "Yeah. Thanks."

"Keep your head on straight. Don't believe the impossible. Damon can do stuff I can't. He's had a lot more practice than me. But remember, it's all an illusion."

"So what happens if he gets the poleax?" Marsh asked, clicking into analytical mode.

"Then it won't be an illusion anymore." There was no better way to say it than that. Marsh had to know what was at stake.

"I got your back," I said, flickering. "Just like always."

"I miss you, Coop."

There were so many things I had to tell him, but it seemed like my time was limited.

"Me too," I said quickly. "Those things I said? I'm sorry. I was mad."

"I know."

"And tell Sydney I think she's cool for what she's doing."

"She really cares about you," he said.

"Of course she does. She's not a total Agnes."

Marsh looked at me with wide eyes. I couldn't imagine how he was processing all of this.

"Don't be sad for me, Marsh. I'm okay. There's a lot going on. Some of it is pretty sweet. Then again . . ."

"Yeah," Marsh said. "Then again."

Marsh reached out for me, but I was fading. I felt the colorful mist rise up around me.

"Be cool," I said. "I'm around."

"Coop?" he called, but it was too late.

I was gone. Completely gone. Not just invisible. I was no longer in the cemetery. I found myself standing in the center of Stony Brook Avenue. The Ave. My vision in the Black.

It was the right place to be. It was my home, or at least what passed for it in the afterlife. I was standing in front of Meade's Pharmacy. I wanted to go inside and talk to Donna the soda jerk and order a malted . . . and find out what a malted was. I wanted to stare at the pictures behind the soda fountain that had been a familiar part of my life since I was little. I wanted to share a booth with Gramps and talk about growing tomatoes, then go to the toy shop next door and claim my teddy bear. I wanted to do all the things that would make me comfortable and convince me that everything was going to be okay.

But I couldn't do any of those things, because Meade's Pharmacy was destroyed. It looked as if a bomb had hit it, or maybe a World War I tank. The doors were blown in, the windows were shattered, and the roof was caved in.

The rest of the Ave looked even worse.

I stood in the center of the empty street, alone. There was no traffic. No pedestrians strolled along the sidewalks. Bernie the mailman wasn't making his rounds. My vision was as dead as Ree's. And Maggie's. And Gramps's. The only difference was that my vision wasn't just deserted, it was destroyed.

It was as if a mechanized army had driven through, firing randomly at the buildings, blowing out huge chunks of the brick walls. I walked up the Ave, in a daze, scanning for signs of life. The building that had housed Santoro's Trophies was gone. All that was left was a rubble-strewn hole as if it had taken a direct hit from a bomb. The street itself was torn up, possibly from the treads of tanks. The church that had held my funeral was desecrated. The entire front wall had been ripped down, revealing the wreckage of the pews and statues within. Across the street was the library. Hundreds of books were scattered across the front lawn of the beautiful building that was beautiful no more. Looking in through the shattered window, I saw nothing but black ash, the result of a fire that hadn't spared a single volume. The pocket park between two buildings was filled with piles of brick and wooden beams from the building next to it that had collapsed. The Garden Poultry deli, home to the greatest fries in the universe, was no more.

As violent as the scene appeared, it was strangely quiet. There was no sound that would have hinted at the destruction that had happened. A slight breeze blew up from Long Island Sound, moaning in anguish as it passed the forlorn remains of what was once my hometown.

No, that was once the vision of my hometown. This wasn't the real Stony Brook. It was my home in the Black, which is why it was destroyed.

Damon had taken his revenge.

The Rift was sealed. His soldiers had been sent to the Blood. The Guardians had stood up to him and triumphed. I stood up to him, and for that, he destroyed my vision.

I didn't believe for a second that Damon was finished after his defeat in Grand Central Terminal, but I never imagined that he still had the power to create such destruction. I thought that protecting Marsh was going to be the final challenge with this monster, but I couldn't have been more wrong.

Seeing my vision was proof of that.

The disappearance of Maggie, Ree, and Gramps was proof of that.

The desperate Watcher was proof of that.

Damon was willing to destroy the Black to finish his quest.

This was no longer about protecting Marsh and getting my life back.

This was about preventing the complete destruction of the Morpheus Road.

Epilogue

If I had told anyone a few short weeks ago that things would work out the way they have, I would have been called delusional. At best. At worst, insane. But I can't deny reality. What seemed far-fetched not that long ago has come to pass. At times I still question it, but the answer I come back to is always the same, as unbelievable as it may be.

Sydney Foley is in love with me.

Believe it. I do. Okay, maybe "love" is a strong word, but we are definitely in serious like. Would it have happened under normal circumstances? Probably not, but so what? People are brought together through shared experiences all the time, and what Sydney and I went through was definitely an experience. I only wish it had been less tragic. And horrifying.

I always thought ghosts were the stuff of fables and urban legends until a vengeful spirit found his way into my head, discovered my most personal fears, and made them real. I would hunt down a dozen poleaxes if I thought it would keep that spirit away from me. But I've been warned against that by my best friend, who happens to be a ghost. And since Cooper has been protecting me from beyond the grave, I have to believe he knows what he's talking about. I trust Coop. Always have.

Now that I know life continues beyond death, I guess I'll trust him forever.

A month has gone by since his funeral. Nothing out of the ordinary has happened since then, other than my relationship with his sister. At first I worried that we were only together because of the haunting and that once it was over we'd realize we had nothing in common. I'm happy to say that I was wrong. To try and get back some form of normal life I helped her study for the SATs. In return she sat through a screening of my entire DVD collection of *The Prisoner*. And she liked it. Who knew Sydney was a closet geek? The irony! After what we had been through I needed a silver lining. Sydney is my silver lining and I hope that I am hers.

It took a few weeks before I could relax enough to get a full night's sleep. It was still summer vacation so I went back to work at Santoro's Trophies and Sydney tutored math at Stony Brook Junior High summer school. At night we hung out together. We never went so far as to pretend like the haunting didn't happen, but after a few weeks of normal I began to allow myself some hope that it was over. For good. That hope grew stronger with the passing of each uneventful day, each time Sydney and I kissed and laughed, and every night that went by without a disturbing dream.

There was a moment. A great moment. One I'll never forget. After weeks of looking over my shoulder and wondering what might be around the next corner, I finally allowed myself to believe that I was no longer going to be tormented by spirits from the afterlife. It happened while I was riding my bike home from Sydney's house. The sun was going down and I wanted to get home before dark, so instead of riding along the street, I took a shortcut that Coop and I always used when we rode to each other's house. It was a well-worn path through a field of dry grass that served as our baseball diamond, army battlefield, and rocket launching zone. When I turned my bike onto the dirt path, I instantly thought of my friend. I couldn't help it. The place held so many great memories.

I hadn't sensed Coop's presence since the cemetery and my day of reckoning with Damon. Riding along that path gave me a feeling of peace. As comforting as it was to look back and remember, I knew it was time to move on to whatever the next adventure would bring. It was a moment I will never forget. I would do anything to recapture it because an instant later it ended . . .

. . . and the next adventure began.

I came over a rise to see a girl standing in the path several yards ahead. The wild grass was tall, making it impossible to ride around her so I stopped.

"Hey, how's it going?" I called out.

She didn't react. I didn't recognize her, which was odd because I thought I knew pretty much everybody around my age in Stony Brook, even if they didn't know me. She had long, curly dark hair and wore a man's business suit, which seemed odd but . . . whatever. Her dark eyes were fixed on me. Staring. Unblinking. Sad.

I got off my bike and walked it toward her.

"Do you live around here? I've never seen you—"

The girl vanished.

I stopped short, my heart in my throat.

"Oh no," I muttered. "No, no, no . . ."

I wheeled the bike around to head back the other way but saw another visitor blocking my way. It was an old man with thick, oversized glasses wearing a plaid flannel shirt. There was nothing threatening about him, except for the fact that he was there. No way he could have snuck up behind me that fast. The guy was looking my way but his gaze traveled straight through me.

It took a second for me to realize that I knew who it was.

"Mr. Foley?" I said, barely whispering.

It was Cooper's grandfather. Cooper's *dead* grandfather.

"What do you want?" I yelled. "What are you doing here?"

He answered me by disappearing.

I fought to control my breathing. "Home. Home," I said to myself, like a mantra. "Gotta get home. Gotta be around people."

I dropped my bike and turned to run for home. For Dad. For sanity. I didn't get more than a step because a third spirit had arrived. I had already seen two ghosts, but I could have seen a hundred and still would not have been prepared for the vision that stood facing me in that deserted field. Standing in the path, as real as the others, was my mother.

I fell to my knees. Whatever sense of well-being and stability I'd managed to put together over the past few weeks was shattered, as wounds that had taken years to heal were ripped wide open.

"Mom . . . no," I cried. "What's going on? Why are you here?"

She looked straight through me the way Coop's grandfather had. There was no recognition, no acknowledgment that she knew who I was or that I was even there. It was the first time I had seen her since the day she had left home . . . to die.

"Say something!" I screamed. "Talk to me!"

She didn't react. It was as if her image was there but her spirit wasn't. Still, it was my mom. I staggered to my feet and stumbled toward her with my arms out to hug her. I reached forward, closed my arms around her, and grabbed only air. The image was gone.

I fell to the ground again, crushed under the weight of grief as if I had just lost her for a second time. I hadn't even reacted like that when she died. It was like my heart had been torn out. I couldn't move. I didn't want to move. I curled up into a ball and hugged my knees. I wanted the visions to end, but I knew they wouldn't.

"I'm sorry that happened, Ralph," came a clear, strong voice.

I dared to peek over my arm to see yet another spirit.

Cooper was back. He walked toward me along the path and knelt down a few feet away. Unlike the other three spirits, he was looking right at me.

"That wasn't right," he said.

"Are you really here?" I asked tentatively.

"Yeah," he assured me. "But not the others."

I didn't dare take my eyes off him for fear he would disappear.

"You look solid," I said.

"Things are changing, Ralph. Fast."

"I don't understand. It's like you're really . . ." I reached out to touch him but my hand traveled through as if he were a projection. I pulled back quickly.

"Easy," he said. "I'm a ghost, remember? Things haven't changed *that* much."

"I don't understand," I mumbled.

"Get up, Ralph." He reached out to help me to my feet, but then scoffed and backed off. "Geez, now you got me doing it."

"But you're here," I said, standing up as I wiped my eyes.

"I've just got more control. That's it. It's not much but at least I won't be winking in and out anymore."

"What's happening, Coop? Why did I see my mother? And your grandfather? And . . . who was that girl?"

"Her name's Zoe. I don't know why you saw them. I'm not even sure where their spirits are. It's like they're just . . . floating. But that's only part of the problem."

"What's the other part?"

Coop thought about his answer, then looked at me with a sad smile.

"What?" I asked.

"We've been through a lot since we were kids," he said. "But this isn't kid stuff anymore."

"We're in Trouble Town, aren't we?" I asked.

Coop laughed. "More than you can imagine—and you've got a hell of an imagination, so that's really saying something."

"Is it that Damon guy?"

Cooper nodded. "Do you have any more of those golden balls? The crucibles?"

"Yeah. I broke one and that started this whole mess. But I've got another. From Ennis Mobley. He promised Mom that he'd give it to me for my protection."

"Seriously?" he asked with surprise. "That's what he told you?"

"What's wrong with that?"

"It's a lie. He never told your mother that."

"How do you know?"

"Your mother told me."

That stopped me short. All I managed to say was, "She did?"

Coop smiled. "We've got a lot to talk about, Ralph. But right now you gotta tell me, do you know where the poleax is?"

"Are you serious? I don't even know *what* it is."

"Well, learn fast because we have to find it."

"We?" I asked.

"We. No more messages in powder. No more moving lights or blowing open windows. From now on it's you and me. Together."

Hearing that gave me confidence. It always did.

"What happens if we don't find it?" I asked.

"Nothing. So long as Damon doesn't either."

"And what if he does?"

Cooper took a deep breath and said, "He'll bulldoze the Morpheus Road, and that illusion you saw in the cemetery with those walking corpses? It won't be an illusion anymore."

"I don't know what that means, Coop."

"It means there would be a war, and not like anything you've seen in the movies or read about in books. If Damon gathers his forces and marches on the Light, there won't be any way to stop them because they'll already be dead. And that's not even the worst part."

"What could be worse than that?" I asked shakily.

"You and I have to stop him."

"Oh."

We stood there for a long moment staring at each other. I swallowed hard, reached down, picked up my bike, and wheeled it up to the spirit of my dead best friend.

"So?" he asked.

I shrugged and said, "So I guess this means we'll be spending the summer together after all."

To be continued . . .

1

Sydney Foley was about to die.

Impending doom rarely telegraphs itself, which meant she was blissfully unaware of the fact that a chain of events had been set in motion that would likely end with her being cast, violently, to the next stop along the Morpheus Road.

Sydney had been working all summer as an algebra tutor at Stony Brook Junior High. It was a job that would normally warrant battle pay for most hapless young tutors, but Sydney had no trouble handling the challenge.

"I'm smarter than you," she would announce at the beginning of each class. "So either pay attention and learn something or zone out and I'll see you back here next summer. Your choice. I get paid either way."

Sydney wasn't subtle. She intimidated the girls and mesmerized the normally hyperkinetic boys who quietly admitted that there were worse ways to spend time than staring at a hot teacher like Sydney . . . even if she was lecturing about exponents and factoring.

When her lesson ended on that particular day, she decided to stay in the classroom and grab a little study time. Her goal was to gain early acceptance to Stanford University, and Sydney never fell short of her goals, even if it meant spending a beautiful summer afternoon in an empty classroom calculating the effect of gravity on linear acceleration. She stared at the open book, glassy eyed, thinking about how she would rather be lying on the beach with her boyfriend.

"Bored," she texted him. "Come visit me at SBJH. I'll be your best friend."

Two months before, the idea that she would be texting Marshall Seaver and calling him her boyfriend was about as likely as her not getting into Stanford. The events of the early summer had changed that. Drastically. The two were thrown together by the tragic death of her brother, Cooper . . . and by the haunting. Sharing sorrow and terror tends to forge a bond between people, and to the surprise of everyone who knew anything about either of them, Marsh and Sydney had become inseparable.

Sydney stared at her phone. There was no reply from Marsh, which was odd. He was usually quick on the draw when it came to returning her texts. With a shrug she reluctantly turned back to her study guide for the twentieth time, and for the twentieth time her mind wandered. She gazed out at a sea of unoccupied desks, suddenly feeling very alone.

Not lonely alone . . . vulnerable alone.

It was too quiet.

Schools were always full of noise and activity, even during lunch. Especially during lunch. Quiet wasn't normal, even during summer school. She thought maybe everyone had gone out to eat, but the entire school couldn't have emptied out so quickly. Something felt off. It raised the small hairs on the back of her neck. That didn't happen often, so when it did, she paid attention. Quickly she gathered her books, phone, and purse and started for the door.

That's when the smell hit her. It was a stagnant, dead smell. The room had grown warm, as if the air-conditioning had failed. Small beads of sweat formed on her upper lip. Her eyes started to burn and tear up.

What the heck?

She stood in front of her desk, trying to understand what was happening when her eye caught movement. She glanced up to the air duct near the ceiling to see tendrils of smoke drifting from the grate.

Fire, was her first thought.

Get the hell out, was her second.

She ran for the door but before pulling it open she flashed on a boring fire safety lecture she'd gotten in third grade. She stopped, cautiously placed her hand on the wooden door . . . and felt heat.

"Oh man," she gasped.

She touched the metal doorknob and quickly recoiled. It was searing hot. There could be only one reason: The building was on fire. She took a quick look through the narrow vertical glass window in the door to see that the corridor was filled with smoke. The fire was close. She didn't panic. Sydney never panicked. Glancing around she saw a red fire-alarm on the wall next to the door. She had always wondered what would happen if she pulled one of those. She was about to find out. Sydney lunged for it and yanked the lever down, breaking the thin glass tube that seemed to have no purpose. She held her breath and waited, expecting the harsh blare of an alarm to break the eerie silence. Seconds passed. No alarm sounded.

"Seriously?" she exclaimed as she fumbled for her purse to grab her cell. "A fire *and* a defective alarm?"

Her fear about being alone was suddenly justified. If the alarm didn't work, she could be the only one who knew about the fire because she just so happened to be in the middle of it. The wispy vapors turned to dark, thick smoke that poured from the air-conditioning vent. Digging for her phone, she hurried toward the only other possible escape route . . . the door at the rear of the classroom. She found the phone, wiped tears from her burning eyes, and punched in 911.

Seconds passed. There was no answer. Sydney shook the phone in frustration.

"How is that possible?" she screamed.

She had full bars and the battery was charged. Why hadn't the call gone through? She stopped worrying about alerting people who weren't there and decided to focus on joining them. She got to the back door, praying that the fire hadn't moved that way. She was about to put her hand on the door to check for heat, and realized she needn't bother. Looking out through the window, she saw flames. The fire was burning right outside the classroom.

Sydney stared at the dancing flames, mesmerized, unbelieving. How could a fire spread so quickly? She leaned in to the window, until her nose nearly touched the glass, to stare into a corridor that had become a furnace. It was almost pretty the way the orange flames twisted and danced . . . as they drew closer, coming to burn her alive. It was hypnotic, but not so much that she forgot how much trouble she was in. The flames would soon be in the classroom. She was trapped and knew if she stayed put the fire would only get worse. She knew what she had to do . . . run through the flames. It was crazy, but better than doing nothing.

While keeping her eyes on the flames through the window, she reached for the doorknob, but stopped when she saw movement outside in the corridor. It was a dark shadow that moved in hazy contrast to the brilliant fire. Her hopes soared. Was it a firefighter battling through the blaze, coming to her rescue? She leaned forward, trying to make out detail of the shadow as it drew closer.

"Hurry up!" she screamed.

The dark silhouette was nearly there. The smoke was getting thick inside the classroom, making Sydney's eyes sting, but she could still make out the vague form of a person. She leaned in closer to the window, hoping to see the face of a heroic, handsome firefighter looking back at her. The shadow floated right up to the glass and snapped into focus, inches from her face.

Sydney screamed.

The face was that of a burning skeletal head with its mouth open in a ghastly howl. Its flesh was on fire, turning black as it burned away from the bone to expose the charred skull beneath. Its hollow eyes were focused directly on Sydney.

Sydney threw herself backward, tripped over a chair, and landed on the floor. If she had hurt herself, she didn't know it. Her mind was spinning too quickly. Who was that? *What* was that? Some poor guy trapped out in the corridor? She scrambled to her feet and ran back for the door to open it and let the tortured victim into the room, though she knew it would be too late. He was a goner. Still, she had to try. She reached for the door and was about to turn the handle . . . as the narrow window in the door smashed in, spewing shattered glass and dark, choking smoke into the room.

Sydney jumped back again, hacking out a cough as a new wave of acrid smoke filled her lungs.

The burning skull pushed through the opening frame where the glass had been and glanced around the room until it spotted Sydney, and offered a ghastly grin.

"Unlock the door, Sydney," the skull commanded in a dry, gravelly voice.

Most people would have snapped. Not Sydney. She had been through too much that summer and had seen things far worse. She now realized the truth: The only victim was her.

"Bite me," she snarled, and turned away, looking for another escape route.

She ran into a large storage closet in the back of the class, hoping it would lead to an adjoining classroom. No luck. Dead end. She quickly realized that if she was going to get out of the building, there was only one way to go. The window.

A low bookcase ran the length of the classroom across from the doors. Above the bookcase were five large sealed windows. Beneath each was a small hinged window that opened in. None were large enough to crawl out of. Sydney yanked them all open, hoping the smoke would be sucked out before she choked to death.

"That's right," the flaming skeleton cackled. "Feed the flames . . . feed the flames."

"Shut up!" Sydney barked. She leaned down to a window and screamed to the outside world.

"Help! Somebody! I'm trapped in here! Help!"

"This is a race you're going to lose," the fiery ghoul taunted as it rattled the door, trying to get in.

The classroom was on the fourth floor. It was a long way down to the parking lot. The empty parking lot. There were no fire trucks or ambulances racing to save the building. Or her. Sydney had to make a choice. Fast. She looked back to the door to see the skull peering through the broken window, only now the wooden door was ablaze. It would soon burn through, allowing the fire to leap inside, along with the ghastly creature.

The decision wasn't a hard one. She grabbed a desk chair, wound up, and heaved it at one of the large windows. The chair hit the glass, bounced off, and clattered back to the floor.

The demon laughed. "Or you could just die gracefully."

Sydney ignored the taunt. She picked up another chair and heaved it at the window. This time the glass splintered as it rejected the chair. Sydney felt the heat at her back. It wouldn't be long before the room was engulfed . . . or she died from smoke inhalation. She coughed, wiped her eyes, and kept fighting. She picked up another chair and whirled it into the glass. A spiderweb of cracks spread across the pane.

Sydney was getting dizzy as the smoke grew so thick, it became hard to see the windows. She grabbed another chair, summoned her strength, and hurled the chair forward. This time the glass shattered and the chair kept going, sailing out into space and falling to the pavement far below. The thick smoke rushed through the jagged opening, creating a swirling storm inside the room. Without stopping to admire her work, she grabbed another chair and used the legs to punch out the remaining glass from the window frame.

She climbed up onto the bookcase and leaned out to see a sheer wall of windows with no ledges or handholds to grab on to. Four stories down was hard pavement.

Sydney couldn't imagine what it would be like to fall so far. How should she land? What possible way could she hit and survive without breaking her legs? Or her back? As the choking smoke rushed past her and out the window, Sydney stood frozen, paralyzed with fear.

There was a wrenching sound, followed by a loud crack of splintering wood as the classroom door blew down. She instantly felt a tremendous rush of heat as the last barrier between her and the flames was removed. Sydney whipped around to see a wave of fire rush into the classroom moving impossibly fast, eating up the desks and the floor, revealing the beams beneath and the classroom below.

"Ready or not!" the voice taunted as the skeletal face appeared through the wall of flame, floating closer.

Sydney focused and made a decision. Burning to death would be worse than falling and being smashed like a china doll. She had to jump. She took a breath, leaned out of the window and pushed off . . .

. . . as strong hands gripped her ankles from behind.

"No!" she screamed, fearing that the skeleton was trying to pull her back into the inferno.

She kicked violently, desperate to get away from its grasp and out into space.

"Stop!" came a voice from behind. "What are you doing?"

The voice cut through her panic. She recognized it. It wasn't the flaming skeleton. But, then, who? Was it a trick to make her think she would be better off giving up and allowing herself to be incinerated? She looked to the ground far below and imagined herself lying in a broken heap. It was too much to bear. She gave in and let the grabbing hands do their work. She was pulled roughly back through the window frame and over the bookcase until she fell rudely to the floor. With the little presence of mind she had left, she twisted from the grasp of her assailant and spun to see . . . Marsh.

"My god, Sydney. What are you doing?" he cried in panic.

Sydney's sense of reality had been wrenched inside out. Seeing Marsh sitting on the floor across from her made even less sense than being grabbed by a flaming skeleton. She stared at him in shock, not sure if he was real or a hallucination that would soon burst into flames. Glancing around quickly, she saw that the smoke had cleared. All of it. Could it have been sucked out of the windows so quickly? A look past Marsh gave her the answer:

The door was still there. The fire . . . wasn't. Nothing had been burned. The floor was intact. People were gathered outside, staring into the room with curiosity, wondering what all the yelling was about.

Sydney looked up to the window she had thrown the chair through. That was no illusion. She had indeed smashed through the window to escape, but from what? There was no flaming ghoul, no smoke, no fire. The only threat was the shattered window that Sydney had nearly jumped through . . . to escape a fate that wasn't real.

"Go away!" Marsh shouted to the people in the corridor. "Close the door!"

They scattered, not sure what they were seeing. To them it looked as though the unflappable Sydney Foley had inexplicably flapped and tossed a chair through the window.

Marsh tentatively crawled closer to her, trying not to scare her any further.

"What happened, Syd?" he asked calmly.

Sydney finally accepted that she was no longer in danger. At least not from Marsh. She relaxed and threw her arms around him, holding him close, grateful to be alive and for his being there for her. But she didn't cry. Sydney never cried.

She did her best to steady her voice and said, "You didn't answer my text."

"Yeah, I did. I was already on my way."

"The fire alarm didn't work."

Marsh didn't have to reply to that. Sydney's focus had returned enough so that she was able to register a blaring horn. The fire alarm was working just fine. She hadn't heard it . . . or had been prevented from hearing it. Another harsh sound intruded. It was the urgent shriek of a siren from a rapidly approaching police car.

Sydney said, "I guess that means my 911 call went through too."

"Did you think the building was on fire?" Marsh said as calmly as if asking for the time of day.

"Isn't it?" she asked tentatively.

Marsh shook his head soberly.

"You didn't see anything?" Sydney asked, though she knew the answer.

Marsh surveyed the room and ended by staring at the smashed window.

"No," he said with a frown. "And I can guess why."

He pulled away from her, reached into his pack, and took out a tennis-ball-size golden sphere that was covered with carved symbols.

Sydney nodded. She understood.

"He's back," she said.

"Damn right he's back," came a bold reply from the other side of the room.

Marsh and Sydney turned quickly to see that someone else had arrived.

"It's about time he showed himself," the new arrival added.

"He tried to kill me," Sydney declared. "Why would he do that?"

"Because he couldn't get to *me*," Marsh said, holding up the golden ball. "This wouldn't let him."

"So it's starting again?" Sydney asked, with a slight crack to her usually strong voice.

"It never ended," the new arrival corrected. "But this time is different."

"How?" Marsh asked.

"This time he's not getting away."

"Bold talk . . . for a dead guy," Sydney said to her brother.

"Hey, it's good to be a ghost," Cooper Foley replied. He walked over to the smashed window and added, "Can't wait to see how you're going to explain this."

Marsh took a deep breath and said, "That'll be the least of our problems."

2

"He was trying to kill me," Sydney bellowed as she paced angrily. "Why else would he create the whole fire illusion? And the flaming skull. That was a particularly gruesome touch, by the way."

"It's not about you, Syd," Marsh said calmly. "If I wasn't protected by the crucible, he would have come after me."

"So you're saying I shouldn't take it personally?" she countered, exasperated. "That doesn't make me feel any better."

Marsh walked to her and took both of her hands. "Take it any way you want," he said softly. "But take the crucible."

Sydney was ready to argue, but when she looked into Marsh's eyes, she softened. He had that kind of effect on her.

She touched his cheek with genuine affection and said, "I can't do that."

"Yeah, you can. I don't want you to be in danger when it's me he's after."

"And that's why you have to keep it," Sydney said. "If he went after me like that, I can't imagine what he'd do to you."

Marsh pulled Sydney toward him and the two kissed.

Marsh then reached into the pocket of his hoodie and pulled out the golden orb that contained the blood of Alexander the Great. He held it out to Sydney and whispered, "Please. Take it."

Sydney shook her head and pushed it away. "I can't. I love you."

"I love you too. That's why you have to."

"Stop!" Cooper shouted, exasperated. "Take it. No, *you* take it. I love you. I love you more. Kissy-kissy. Jeez. If I weren't already dead, I'd have to kill myself just so I could roll over in my grave."

Sydney squinted at her brother. "You'd think death would have made you less obnoxious."

"Sorry," Coop shot back. "And speaking of obnoxious, I don't know what freaks me out more, Damon showing up or you two being all lovey. So strange."

"Said the ghost," Sydney said sarcastically.

Cooper and Sydney may have looked alike, with their dark hair and blue eyes, but their polar opposite styles usually put them at each other's throats. Coop's death did nothing to change that. Though Cooper was a spirit, Marsh looked more like the sore thumb with his blond hair and brown eyes.

The three were in the living room of Marsh's house in the suburban town of Stony Brook, Connecticut. It was a home that had always been so comfortable. So normal. It was a safe haven for Marsh until a malevolent spirit had turned it into a house of horrors.

"This is a no-brainer," Coop declared. "There's one crucible and two of you, so just stay together. You're practically joined at the hip anyway."

"You don't . . . watch us, do you?" Sydney asked with disgust.

"Give me a break," Cooper shot back. "Like I don't have enough to deal with."

"That's not practical," Marsh said, and held out the golden ball to Sydney. "When we're together, we'll be fine. When we're apart, Sydney keeps it."

"But I won't," Sydney argued.

"Give it to me," Cooper ordered, and tried to grab it, but his hand traveled through Marsh's like a solid object passing through a beam of light.

"Damn," he said in frustration. "Can this get any older?"

Marsh and Sydney were the only two beings in the Light who could see Cooper. To them he appeared the same as any other person, though he was anything but.

"Forget the crucible," Sydney exclaimed as she pulled Marsh toward the couch. "It can't protect either of us forever. This is about Damon."

"Agreed," Marsh said.

The two sat close to each other. Sydney kept a firm grip on Marsh's hand out of affection . . . and for security. Her nerves were still frayed.

"I'm way ahead of the curve on this," Coop declared. "I'll handle Damon."

"That gives me exactly zero confidence," Sydney said coldly.

"Let's hear what he has to say," Marsh offered.

Sydney bit her tongue and forced a smile.

"Okay, Mr. Afterlife," she said to Cooper. "How exactly are you going to 'handle' Damon?"

Cooper had already shared with them the entire story of his adventures with Damon in the Black. There were no secrets between them.

"First I have to find him," Cooper began. "I have no idea where he is."

"So much for being ahead of the curve," Sydney said.

Coop ignored her and continued, "I haven't seen him

since his army was sucked into the Blood, but I've seen the damage he's caused since. The guy wants revenge. On me. That much is obvious from the way he busted up my vision in the Black."

"How did he do that if his army was sent to the Blood?" Marsh asked.

"I don't know," Coop admitted. "And I don't know what happened to the spirits who were with me . . . my grandfather, Maggie Salinger, Zoe, and—"

"And my mother," Marsh said.

"Yeah. They're just . . . gone. Damon must be responsible, but as to where they are . . . your guess is as good as mine."

Sydney suggested, "Maybe he took them to his own vision."

"Okay, I lied. Your guess *isn't* as good as mine," Cooper said curtly. "I told you, his vision doesn't exist anymore. The Watchers took it from him. Damon's flying loose somewhere."

"Maybe they all moved on to the next life," Marsh offered hopefully. "You know, the place you go after the Black?"

Coop squinted at him. "Do you *really* think that happened?"

Marsh thought for a moment. "No."

Coop said, "I think Damon knows exactly where they are so he can use them to get what he wants."

"The poleax," Sydney declared.

"Yeah, the poleax," Coop confirmed. "For that he needs *you*, Ralph."

"But I don't know where his sword is!" Marsh declared with frustration.

"Maybe not, but he thinks you can find it."

"That's insane," Marsh grumbled.

Sydney asked, "And what happens if Damon gets it?"

Coop took a tired breath and turned serious. "The guy has something to prove. He feels as though he was never given his due as a general in Alexander's army and wants a second chance."

"To do what?" Sydney asked. "When did he fight for Alexander? Two thousand years ago?"

"Doesn't matter," Coop said quickly. "Time has no meaning in the Black. You can find spirits who lived yesterday or centuries ago. For all I know, Alexander himself is still floating around someplace and Damon wants to show him what a bad little soldier-boy he can really be."

"But why does he need that sword to prove that?" Marsh asked.

"That weapon holds the spiritual power of all those he killed in life. He can use it to tear open another Rift between the Light and the Black. Between the living and the dead. The Black is a very real place, but the spirits are . . . spirits. Not flesh and blood. I think for Damon to prove himself as a warrior, he'll have to do it here in the Light against living soldiers."

"So he wants to tear open a new Rift, come into the Light, and start a war?" Sydney asked. "Won't he be, like, two thousand years out of his league?"

"I don't know, Sydney," Coop said impatiently. "Maybe he'll get his ass kicked but that's not the point. Can you imagine if a doorway was created between two worlds so that spirits could come back to reclaim their lives? There are millions of spirits in the Black. Billions. What would happen if the dam opened up and the Light was overrun by its own history?"

The three fell silent, imagining the possibility.

Marsh finally said, "Armageddon."

"Something like that," Coop agreed. "That's why the Watchers gave me the ability to be seen by you guys. My being here is totally against the way things work, but it seems like it's fallen on us to stop Damon."

Marsh said, "Because I'm the one he's coming after to find the poleax."

"And he killed me to get to you," Coop added. "Let's not forget that."

Sydney asked, "Why don't the Watchers stop him?"

"I think the only thing they can do is send him to the Blood, but that's the last thing they want because it'll put Damon back together with his army. No, they want Damon destroyed, and I don't think they have that ability."

"And we do?" Sydney asked.

"Not 'we.' Me. I'm a spirit. I can move through the Black and use one of those spirit-killing swords on that bastard. That's how this is going to end. It's the only way it *can* end."

"So what are we supposed to do?" Sydney asked.

"Nothing," Cooper answered quickly. "I mean it. Nothing. Stay together and keep the crucible with you. As long as you two have that thing, Damon is powerless over you."

"No," Marsh said flatly.

Cooper shot him a quick, surprised look. "What do you mean 'no'? I told you—"

Marsh stood up to face his friend. "I heard what you said, Coop. I get it. But I'm not going to sit around doing nothing. None of this would have happened if my mother hadn't gone digging around under that temple and destroyed the first crucible."

"So what?" Coop shot back. "This is serious, Ralph. We're not playing army."

"Do you really think I'm playing?"

"No, I don't," Coop said, backing down. "But I mean, c'mon, you're in way over your head."

"I'll be the judge of that," Marsh said quickly.